Bailey Coleman is a woman with a mission.

Bailey's brother, Michael, had seemed optimistic in the days and weeks before his death. He'd hinted at a plan to save Edgewater, the luxury condominiums he had built and managed. Desperate to stall the impending foreclosure, Bailey convinced herself that somewhere in Michael's files lay the answer.

But Stan Muncie and Anthony Walcott had other plans for Edgewater and Bailey.

"So what's up?" Muncie said to Walcott.

"I saw Bailey Coleman and Charlie Eaglequill at the Iron Horse today."

"What the hell is she up to?" Muncie asked. "Did Eaglequill tell her anything? I've had it with her."

"I have an idea," Walcott continued. "If it works, Bailey Coleman won't be a problem anymore."

APRIL CHRISTOFFERSON

A TOM DOHERTY ASSOCIATES, INC. BOOK
NEW YORK

EDGEWATER

A Forge Book
Published by Tom Doherty Associates, Inc.
175 Fifth Avenue
New York, NY 10010

ISBN: 0-812-59045-7

First edition: April 1998

Printed in the United States of America

0 9 8 7 6 5 4 3 2 1

For Kari

ACKNOWLEDGMENT

What a pleasure it is to be able to express my gratitude to the following:

My readers, Lisa Christofferson, Donna Elder, Jeff Barry, Nancy Falconer, Sherry Marsh, Susan Christofferson, Carroll Barry and Suzy Lysen, whose input has been invaluable; Dennis Elder and Tom Holdaas for their generous support and friendship; Matthew O'Brien, Michael Verbillis and Mike Vrable, whose fine legal minds I've tapped from time to time; my editor, Natalia Aponte, for the benefit of her enthusiasm, support and instincts, as well as all the other fine people at Tor/Forge, especially Bob Williams; my friend and agent, Julie Castiglia; Steve Falconer, for inspiration; my parents, Isabel and DuWayne Christofferson, whom I adore; my husband, Steve, my beloved champion and partner in life; Mike, Ashley, and Crystal, my daily reminders of all that is good in this world; and finally, Wayne and Barbara Christofferson and Smokey—guardians of the wild turkeys.

Simply put, for words are always inadequate, *thank you.*

PROLOGUE

THE LOCALS HAVE A saying about the stretch of highway that bisects the panhandle of North Idaho.

I drive 95 and I'm still alive.

Highway 95, mostly two-laned, with enough twists and turns to dizzy the most sober of drivers, leads to majestic mountains, the submarine-depth waters of Lake Pend Oreille, and, hidden amongst the hills and thick pines, remote cabins like the one housing Ozzie Randall. Ozzie's cabin, a long log structure situated on thirty-five wooded acres, approachable only by a narrow dirt road that winds its way along ravines and over ridges that provide sweeping views of the valley north all the way to Canada, does not look like much. It most certainly does not fit most people's idea of a political headquarters. But that's just how Ozzie and the Panhandle Republic want it.

Tonight, there are vehicles lining the last mile of the road to Ozzie's. Mostly battered pickups, several of which bear the same bumper sticker: IF WE CAN'T REFORM IT, WE WILL OVERTHROW IT. Inside, in a large barren room that must once have been intended to serve as a workshop, a meeting is taking place. Several loaded rifles and shotguns lean against one wall. The air is thick with smoke, tension and rhetoric. An argument is brewing between two factions of the thirty or more people, mostly men, gathered in the room.

Standing at a podium constructed of rough-hewn logs and plywood is a silver-haired man short in height but commanding in stature, introduced by Ozzie simply as "the Colonel." It is his words, words that for the last forty-five minutes have espoused racism and violence, that are polarizing the group.

A man in his fifties, bearded and dressed in flannel shirt and jeans, has stood to answer the rhetoric of the Colonel.

"I'm as fed up with the government as any of you. Hell, I lost my job as a logger 'cause the government tells us we can't log. Jim here"—he gestures to a man on his right—"can't turn his cattle out 'cause the government says he can't. Harry there used to make a good living as a miner, but now the mines are shut down and he's living in a house that's owned by the IRS."

Throughout the room, his words are met with nods and clenched fists.

"I'm mad as all hell. And I came here tonight because I'm sick of standing by and watching all this shit happen."

Hearty applause greets these words. When it dies down, he continues.

"But I'm not a racist. Hell, I don't even know a black man. How can I have anything against them? And I'm not a violent man," he says, then pauses briefly. "I've always been a law-abiding citizen, and I plan to remain one. I just hoped that tonight we could come up with some way to change things. To preserve our rights, like the right to own as many goddamn guns as we want. That's why I came. When I saw the flyer, that's what I thought this was all about. But if what this group—this 'Panhandle Republic' or whatever you plan to call it—wants is to bomb buildings and kill innocent people, I don't want any part of it."

Another man, this one grizzled and toothless, rises from the front row.

"I ain't filed no tax return since 1982. And the IRS knows it. But they also know I got half a dozen shotguns and a stockpile of ammunition up there in my cabin. After the Weaver thing, there's no way they're going to bother with my little hellhole of a place. It's all I own and it ain't worth nothing."

A voice from the back row calls out, "So what's the point, Amos?"

There is laughter. But Amos is angry and does not crack a smile.

"The point is, we've got them running scared now. Waco. Ruby Ridge. We're in the driver's seat now. I agree with the Colonel. It's time to unite. Nobody's gonna take no more rights of mine away. And if I have to shoot someone to get my point across, I'll do it."

The response that follows is raucous, and so loud that the Colonel must pound the podium several times with his gavel to be heard.

"That," he says, nodding in Amos's direction, "is exactly our point. We must all unite. That's why you were asked here tonight. Together, as the Panhandle Republic, we must take a stand, prepare—both financially and physically—by intense training for all-out war. That takes guns. That takes money. Our organization offers just that, the foundation needed to win the fight for what all of us believe in. The fight for freedom. Because, deep within your hearts, each and every one of you out there knows that, in the end, that's what it's going to take. War. If blood must be shed, so be it."

At these words, several men, including the logger, have finally had enough. They stand, preparing to leave. While a few particularly ornery-looking attendees shoot them scornful glances, others appear tempted to join them—to get out now, while the getting is good. As the group moves toward the back door, two more individuals, one of the few women in attendance and a thirtyish man, sheepishly join it.

"All I want," says one of the departing men over his

shoulder, before stepping outside into the North Idaho darkness, "is to be left alone."

A voice from the belly of the room calls after him.

"That's all Randy Weaver wanted, too. To be left alone. Look what *that* got him."

On that note, the meeting goes on.

CHAPTER 1

BAILEY COLEMAN SAT STONE still, eyes fixed on the front of the church, marshaling all of her strength—and all of her anger. She knew she would need every ounce of it to keep from breaking down. The service was almost over. She'd made it this far. If she could just stay *angry* with him she could make it through.

Yes, anger was the key.

And if anyone had a right to be angry with Michael, with that brother of hers, it was Bailey. How could he leave her like this? Didn't he know how much she needed him—how much she'd needed him ever since that day fifteen years before when their parents died on a rain-slicked mountain pass? Didn't he know he was her anchor? That just because she was grown now, her need for him was no less than it had been when she was sixteen and he was twenty-three—when, overnight, he'd become not just her big brother but her brother, mother and father, all rolled into one.

What right had he to risk his life like that? She'd pleaded with him to give up his crazy sports. Helicopter skiing in the

Tetons. Mountaineering. White-water kayaking. He was, after all, approaching forty. It was time to settle down. But not even his love and sense of responsibility for Bailey—and now also for his newfound daughter, Clancy—could break Michael's spirit, his need to experience life on the edge. It had once been something she'd admired and envied in him—that ability to throw caution to the wind. To live fully in the moment, without regrets, without worry. But ultimately, it had cost him his life. Ultimately, it had cost her Michael.

When he'd called her in Seattle two weeks earlier, she'd asked him to reconsider this outing. She'd just seen a piece on the evening news about the record-setting spring runoff. Northwest rivers were higher, and wilder, than anyone could remember.

"Don't worry, Sis," he'd said. "I've kayaked the Moyie a dozen times. I know every rock, every hole, on it. Little Jimmy floated it last week and said it was unbelievable. You don't really want me to miss out on something *unbelievable*, do you?"

Michael could bring just about anyone around with his boyish charm, and as his little sister, Bailey had always been especially vulnerable to it.

And so, she'd finally relented, wished him good luck, and reminded him that she was driving over from Seattle the next Sunday. Spring break at the University of Washington Law School was only days away, and she was looking forward to spending it in Coeur d'Alene with Michael and Clancy.

The last thing he said to her, the last words she would ever hear in that rich, melodious voice of his, were so typical of Michael, so full of the love and humor that always radiated from him.

"Just think," he'd said, "a whole week together. I'd better go rent a couple of old movies, stop by the bakery, pick up a good merlot . . . oh, yeah, and a case of Kleenex." He'd always teased her about how readily she cried at movies, especially once she'd had a glass of wine and gotten some chocolate under her belt.

Then he'd grown serious.

"Be real careful on the drive over. Okay?"

He always worried about her driving over Snoqualmie Pass alone.

"And Bailey," he'd said, as he always did before taking off on one of his adventures, "don't forget. I love you."

And just as planned, she'd come to Coeur d'Alene. Just as planned, she'd spent her spring break from her second year of law school at her brother's condominium.

But what she *hadn't* planned—for who can ever plan for a life to be turned upside down in the space of mere minutes?—was the call she'd received two days after her last conversation with Michael. The call in which she'd learned that her beloved big brother had apparently drowned when his kayak overturned in the treacherous rapids of North Idaho's Moyie River. The body had not yet been found, but there was little doubt of Michael's fate. His new kayak, its nose crushed, had washed ashore just one mile past the incomplete Civilian Conservation Corp dam—a dam that drew thrill-seeking kayakers like a magnet. Spanning half the width of the river, even at low water the decades-old structure created treacherous currents and eddies that required equal parts skill and daring to negotiate around it. With record-setting runoffs, only the most experienced boaters would dream of attempting a run that included that segment of the river.

Michael had not only attempted it but had apparently—in contradiction of every principle he'd espoused regarding wilderness safety and, even more significantly, his promise to a friend—attempted it alone.

And so, instead of spending her spring break enjoying Michael's company and getting to know little Clancy, Bailey had spent it in a shocked daze, walking the shores of the Moyie; waiting for word from search parties, which were out in full force both on foot and in helicopters; answering phone calls from grief-stricken friends of Michael's; and finally, making decisions about his memorial service.

She had never planned *this*—to find herself sitting in a strange church in a strange town, trying with all her might to avoid breaking down, *trying to maintain her anger,* while hundreds of people, mostly strangers, looked on.

But most of all, what she hadn't planned, as she sat in the front row of Saint Thomas's Cathedral on this blustery spring day in Idaho, was feeling Clancy's little fingers reaching for hers and curling sweetly, protectively, around Bailey's larger, clenched fist. No, she hadn't planned on *that* at all.

And in that one instant, with that one sweet and loving touch from this frightened little girl who Bailey hardly knew—her brother's only child—Bailey Coleman's carefully constructed wall of anger crumbled.

And, finally, the tears began to fall.

Bailey met with Tony Pappas, Michael's attorney and close friend, three days later. Arriving for her appointment several minutes early, she sat in the corner of the waiting room, staring out the window at the intersection two stories below. When the big Greek emerged from behind the closed door of his office, he enveloped her in an emotional hug.

Bailey had already seen Tony numerous times since Michael's accident. For days, he had walked the shores of the Moyie by her side, refusing to give up hope even after the official search had been called off.

Tony's obstinacy was fueled by grief. And guilt. It was Tony to whom Michael had made the promise not to kayak the Moyie alone. Michael and Tony had been kayaking partners for years. They had planned to kayak the Moyie together, but the evening before the outing, Tony had called Michael and backed out. His wife, Rhonda, was chairing a fund-raiser for their children's school the next day. In a fit of husbandly conscience, Tony—whose freewheeling lifestyle at times put a strain on the marriage—had decided to stay and help out. Michael, characteristically good-natured about it, had told Tony not to worry. He did, however, still want to try out his new kayak, and speculated that he would probably get up first thing in the morning and head out.

"Hey, man," Pappas had said to him, "you know better than to do the Moyie alone. Just hold on. Wait a day or two and I'll be able to go with you."

According to Tony, Michael had responded by promising not to attempt the Moyie. He would instead put in on the upper Spokane River, a tame stretch of water—even this year—just ten miles outside of Coeur d'Alene. Appeased, Tony hadn't given Michael's plans another thought until his phone calls the next evening had gone unanswered. When he still could not reach Michael the following morning, he'd stopped by Edgewater Place, Michael's condominium project, on his way to work. There was no sign of Michael. Or his red pickup.

Before heading to Barker Road, where Michael would have put in had he been kayaking the Spokane, Tony placed a call to the Kootenai and Spokane County sheriffs' offices. The Kootenai County Sheriff, in turn, placed a call to the Bonner County Sheriff.

It was the Bonner County Sheriff who, at four P.M. that afternoon, reported finding Michael's truck on a gravel road outside Bonners Ferry. A road that ran alongside the shores of the Moyie River.

Before nightfall, Michael's kayak had also been spotted, just beyond the dam. It was wedged between the shore and an outcropping of rock, its nose crushed by the force of the raging waters. It was too late to call out the helicopters, but at dawn the next day an aerial search of the Moyie's waters was initiated in conjunction with a ground search conducted by trained search-and-rescue teams and a posse of Michael's friends.

When Bailey arrived, near the end of the first day of the search, Tony Pappas, recounting his last conversation with Michael, had broken down.

"I'm so sorry," he'd said, his big shoulders heavy with

guilt. "This would never have happened if I hadn't backed out."

Bailey had reassured him that it wasn't his fault.

But why would Michael, an experienced outdoorsman—one who consistently, dutifully, took the precautions that minimized the risks of his dangerous sports—have done it? Why would he have kayaked a river like the Moyie alone? Especially after giving Pappas his word that he would not. Bailey could feel no resentment toward Tony for his decision to stay and help Rhonda with her fund-raiser. But as she slipped and climbed along the rocky shoreline of the Moyie, as she witnessed firsthand the awesome power of its frothing white waters, boiling furiously as they tumbled over and crashed against huge boulders and fallen trees (creating logjams under which a body might well be trapped until the spring runoff receded), she did begin to feel a resentment toward her brother for having made such an irresponsible decision. What in the name of God had Michael been thinking?

Finally, when all hope was gone, when the experts had, with considerable delicacy, convinced her that with the upcoming hot, dry weather the waters would recede and the body—"the body"; it was no longer Michael for whom they searched—would inevitably break free from its entanglement and surface, she had agreed to a memorial service. They all needed closure—Clancy, Michael's friends. Bailey. Perhaps a service dedicated to Michael's memory would allow all of them to experience some measure of closure.

With the memorial behind them, Tony had called and asked if she felt ready to deal with Michael's business affairs. Yes, she'd told him. It was time. But as Tony led her into his inner office, Bailey's unsteady legs had her wondering about her response.

Once they were seated, it was Bailey who first breached the silence.

"Now," she asked, "what is it you wanted to see me about?"

From behind his oversized mahogany desk, Tony Pappas

cleared his throat and, in a voice too big for the room, began to speak.

"As you know, Bailey, until just six months ago you were all the family Mike had. Or at least all the family he *thought* he had."

Bailey nodded and remained silent. Tony was referring to the fact that six months earlier Michael had learned that he had a daughter. Clancy.

"I'd always bugged your brother about writing a will, but it wasn't until after he found out about Clancy, after she came to live with him, that he asked me to write this." He held a large, very formal looking envelope in his hand. "Fatherhood—especially *sudden* fatherhood, I would imagine—does that to you, makes you think about this kind of thing."

"Of course," he continued, "it's premature for a reading of the will. But when I explain the situation, I think you'll understand why, as Michael's attorney and a family friend, I am discussing it with you now."

Tony placed the envelope on his desk and pushed it toward Bailey, who did not move to pick it up.

"Basically, Michael's will provides that his assets are to be split between you and Clancy. Clancy's portion is to be put in trust. He appointed you trustee."

Ironically, Bailey's classes this semester included one called Wills, Estates and Trusts. The material had all seemed so remote. So impersonal. Until today.

"I'm not certain why you're telling me this now," Bailey said. She didn't want to be rude, but she found talk of her inheritance not only premature but in extremely poor taste. When Tony called, she had assumed he wanted to talk to her about who would run Michael's project, Edgewater Place, in his absence and who would be responsible for Clancy. She just didn't care that she stood to inherit Michael's wealth. Money had never mattered to her. It certainly didn't matter now.

Tony hesitated.

"The truth is, I struggled with whether or not to tell you

about the will before . . ." His words drifted off. Bailey knew that Tony did not want to say it: *before Michael's body is found.* "But I finally decided that the sooner you knew, the better the chances of salvaging as much as possible."

Bailey's brow furrowed.

"Knew *what*?"

Pappas shook his head slowly from side to side, as if trying to convey to Bailey his disbelief at the situation.

"I'm afraid there just isn't much of an estate to dispense. In fact, at the time of his death, Michael's liabilities may well have exceeded his assets."

"What?" Bailey learned forward. Surely he hadn't just told her Michael had died penniless.

"As you know, four years ago Michael invested everything he had—all of the estate your parents left him and the money he'd made in Seattle in real estate—in the development of Edgewater Place. Well, Michael's will leaves you the condominiums."

There was something in Tony's voice.

"You mean his *condominium*," Bailey corrected, referring to the luxurious penthouse unit that Michael, and now Clancy, resided in.

"No," Tony responded. "I mean *condominiums*. Forty-seven of them, to be exact."

Bailey gasped. "Forty-seven!"

The building only housed eighty units. How could Michael own forty-seven of them? There had to be some mistake.

But before she could voice the myriad questions that had begun racing through her mind, Tony continued.

"The project has been somewhat troubled from the start." Then, seeing the bewildered expression on her face, he grew more candid. "Hell, Bailey, the truth is, the project's been on the brink of disaster since the day ground was broken. It's been one thing after another. Michael never wanted to admit it, but Edgewater Place was a lousy idea. This area just wasn't ready for it. Coeur d'Alene's still a small, unsophisticated town. The concept of condominium living is entirely new to the people who live here. These are folks to whom land means everything. Acreage, trees. *That's* what these people want to own. Not some fancy notion of shared ownership of common areas. Then there was the matter of the prices Michael was asking. Your brother went all out. Insisted on everything being the very best."

Bailey knew that years ago, in Seattle, Michael had established a reputation for the quality of his construction. The best materials, best architect, best interior designer. That was Michael. That was why he'd been so successful in the Seattle condominium market. His projects housed many of the city's movers and shakers, from well-known Sonics and Seahawks to high-profile politicians and TV personalities.

"The only way a builder can afford that kind of quality," Tony continued, "is by pricing the units accordingly. But as a result, Michael was only able to sell to wealthy out-of-towners. The locals can't afford to live in Edgewater Place. So almost two years after the doors opened, only thirty-three units have been sold. That's exactly forty-seven units below the projections Michael used to obtain financing."

Bailey was stunned. At first glance, the tall, willowy beauty's unruly blond tresses and attire of jeans and sweatshirt gave her a youthful appearance. But her face, heavy with grief, now showed each and every one of her thirty-one years.

She sat silently for a long while before finally saying, "Please, go on."

"Well, over the past few months Michael's fallen delinquent on the construction loan. He's been in serious danger of the bank's initiating foreclosure. Now, with him gone, I'm very concerned. The bank had been pretty good about working with us in the hope that to do so would be the most likely way to get this project back on track and help them recover their twenty-two million dollars—"

"Twenty-two million dollars! How much has he paid back?"

"Principal?" Tony asked. "Maybe eight million, tops. Which, practically speaking, is nothing. If payment isn't brought current soon, the bank is sure to give formal notice of default. Then if we fail to cure, their next step would be to foreclose. And without Michael here to steer this thing in the right direction, I'm afraid that's just what they'll do."

He reached for a letter he'd received from the bank's attorney. A letter expressing concern over the delinquencies. It had been faxed to his office the very day that Michael disappeared.

"If you want my opinion . . ." he began.

But Bailey was no longer listening. Instead, she was thinking about the day several years before when Michael had first approached her about his concept, about Edgewater Place. He had been so enthusiastic, so hopeful. Years earlier, while he was still living with her in Seattle, he'd fallen in love with the town of Coeur d'Alene, Idaho, which sits nestled on the north shore of spectacular Lake Coeur d'Alene. While Michael was amassing a small fortune as a developer in the Seattle area, his dream of moving to north Idaho had only intensified. And when he finally made the move, four years earlier, he'd been very happy. He'd never lost his enthusiasm for the town or for his project. She could still hear it in his voice when he described Coeur d'Alene's beauty, his vision for Edgewater Place's future. Had he known how hopeless it was? Sitting there, aware that Tony was still talking to her but no longer hearing what he said, Bailey knew that Michael had never lost hope. He hadn't given up on Edgewater Place, on his dream. It was not in Michael's nature to give up.

"If you want my opinion," Tony repeated, "at this point, foreclosure might just be the best thing that could happen. Even though . . ." His voice trailed off.

"What?" Bailey asked. "Even though *what*?" Something in Tony's tone had recaptured her attention.

"Well, it could be nothing, but recently Michael had been upbeat about things again. He told me he was sure he could save the project now."

"What made him think that?"

"I don't know. He wouldn't tell me. At least, not yet. But

he promised me that he'd explain it all soon." Pappas's dark brow furrowed. "To be honest, he was a little mysterious about the whole thing. Which wasn't like Michael."

Seeing the flicker of hope in Bailey's eyes, he hurried to add. "But I'm afraid he wasn't being realistic. I've been involved with this project with him from day one, and as far as I've been able to determine, there's nothing, absolutely nothing, that can salvage it now. I hate to be so fucking negative—excuse my language—but I'd hate it even more if I were to give you false hope. I'm afraid Michael just got in over his head on this one. Even Michael couldn't turn this situation around."

The room fell silent. Then Bailey, her voice soft but steady, finally spoke.

"Did Michael tell you I'd loaned him money I inherited from our parents' estate? That he invested it in Edgewater Place?"

Tony shook his head and grimaced. "How much?"

"Over two hundred fifty thousand dollars."

He let out a low whistle. "How much of the estate did you keep?"

"None of it. I gave it all to him. He promised to pay my way through law school and then, when Edgewater Place took off, he was going to repay me and cut me in on the profits."

It was Tony's turn to look stunned. "You mean Michael was sending you money?"

"Yes. Each month. And he was paying my tuition. That was our deal." Bailey tilted her head and squinted at Tony out of the corner of her eye. "He still has money in his bank account, doesn't he?"

"Yes," Tony said. "But . . ."

"But *what*?"

Tony took a deep breath.

"But it's certainly not enough to get you through another year of law school."

"That can't be." Bailey protested. "Michael's checks

came regularly, like clockwork. And he'd just assured me that he'd be paying my fall tuition."

The creases in Tony's forehead deepened.

"Michael drew a salary from the Edgewater Place account for the work he was doing as property manager, development, marketing. He must have been paying you from that salary. Most likely, he planned to pay your tuition from it as well."

"And if the bank forecloses, the salary stops."

"Yes. But until there's actually a foreclosure, I see no reason why you couldn't assume his responsibilities and earn that money. Someone has to run Edgewater Place. Since you're Michael's heir, it's only natural that it be you."

"But what about school? This year is almost over, but I've still got one full year before I get my degree."

Tony was silent for a moment.

"Maybe you could transfer to the University of Idaho. Or even Gonzaga University, in Spokane. Both have great law schools. And at this stage of the game, Edgewater Place isn't a full-time job. I don't think you'd have a problem handling both. Hell, Michael was spending as much time on the golf course as he was at work. It's just a matter of being around, overseeing things." He hesitated, then added, "However, there's another problem here."

Bailey's tolerance for problems was wearing thin. How could there possibly be any more?

"When Michael took out the loan," Tony said, "he did something that I strongly advised against his doing. He signed a personal guarantee. Of course, he was so optimistic about Edgewater Place that he felt safe signing it."

"Does that mean the bank can seize Michael's bank account?"

"Yes, once Michael's death becomes official," he said. "That's exactly what it means."

Bailey's mind was swimming. Two weeks earlier she'd been looking forward to a trip to this enchanting little town to spend some much-needed restful time with her brother and to get to know her newfound niece. Now here she sat in this attorney's office, discussing her brother's will, feeling so totally alone, being told that she would soon inherit—how many, forty-seven, wasn't it?—condominium units, a staggering debt, and that she quite possibly had no money to finish law school or to live on. The only other time she'd experienced such a terrifying, sinking feeling was when her parents died.

But *then* she had had Michael. As grief-stricken as she'd been, as dazed and disbelieving as she'd felt back then, she'd at least had Michael. She'd known he would be there for her.

And he always had been.

But now he was gone. Her mind, her heart, still could not process that information. She still half believed this was just some crazy, twisted joke. Michael couldn't be dead. Michael was invincible. Michael would never leave her alone.

Yet here she sat. Alone. Alone and dealing not only with her life, with *her* problems, but, it now appeared, alone and dealing with Michael's problems as well. And, from what Tony was telling her, these weren't just your everyday headaches she'd inherited. This was big. This was *huge*.

And then there was Clancy. What was she to do about Michael's newly discovered daughter? After a conversation with Clancy's mother that left her feeling as though she had no choice, she'd sent her niece home the day after the memorial service. But ever since she'd been filled with misgivings about it. Bailey knew that Clancy's home environment was less than desirable—Michael told her that was one of the reasons he'd asked Clancy to live with him a mere week after receiving the call from her mother. The call in which he'd learned that five and a half years earlier, he'd become a father. Margo Leon, a woman he'd dated twice seven summers before, when she was in training to be a nurse at Seattle's City Hospital, had called six months ago to demand money from Michael. Michael had flown down to Los Angeles and, to everyone's shock, had returned several days later with Clancy. Though he never discussed it,

Bailey suspected that Michael had also given Clancy's mother a considerable sum of money. As he did with everything else in his life. Michael had adapted to fatherhood rapidly and with great enthusiasm.

What would become of Clancy now? Bailey was hardly in a position to keep her niece, but the decision to send Clancy back to her mother had been clawing at her.

The grief had long since settled in, but for the first time since she'd received the call informing her of Michael's disappearance, the reality of its effect on her life was beginning to settle in, too.

She became aware of Tony's voice again. What *was* it he'd been saying?

". . . a meeting with the bank."

"Pardon me?"

Watching her closely, for a dazed expression had taken hold of Bailey's face, Tony repeated himself. "*I said,* I think we should call the bank and set up a meeting. We've got to show them that Edgewater Place is still in good hands to forestall foreclosure. We need to get their cooperation as soon as possible. As difficult as I know this time is for you, we can't just sit back and wait. We have to be proactive."

Tony's words pushed the right buttons. *We can't just sit back and wait.*

What if—just *what if*—Michael were still alive?

Tony was right. She had to do everything in her power to save Edgewater Place. Giving up on Edgewater Place would be the equivalent of giving up on Michael.

"Edgewater Place was Michael's dream. We can't let them take that from him." Bailey said, leaning toward Tony, her hands now grasping the edge of his desk. "And let's face it, foreclosure means I lose everything, too. It could force me to drop out of law school. And leave Clancy with nothing."

For Bailey, the hardest thing about the past couple of weeks had been the helplessness. The waiting. The inability to *do* something that would make a difference. The realization that the situation might actually offer an outlet for her grief—a way to channel, in a constructive manner, the fear, and dread, and anger that had insidiously filled every little nook and cranny of her body—was suddenly empowering—a welcome change from the sense of helplessness that had dominated her every waking moment since getting the call about Michael.

It was, as it turns out, the dawning of a crusade for Bailey Coleman. She must save Edgewater Place.

Bailey and Tony agreed that Tony would call the bank's attorney and set up a meeting as soon as possible.

"I just want to warn you," Tony said before Bailey left. "This banker is a real piece of work. I've dealt with my share of snakes in my day, but this guy . . . I just wish I could spare you from having to deal with him."

"What about their attorney?" Bailey asked.

"Shep Carroll?"

Tony eyed Bailey for a moment.

"You might like him."

Shep Carroll's office was located on the twelfth floor of the Landau Building, Portland's newest and most prestigious office address. After nine years with the law firm of Emerson, Caldwell and Taylor, Shep had recently been named senior partner, and when the firm had moved next door into the newly completed Landau complex, his new status had entitled him to a large corner office with a view of downtown Portland and, just blocks away, the Willamette River. And although the prestige of earning partnership status and a prime office meant next to nothing to him, *that*—the view of the river—meant a hell of a lot. For Shep was a man obsessed with water. He'd already come to believe that being able to look out on that river—dreaming of the day when he would simply climb into his Mackenzie drift boat and float away, never to be seen again—might just be enough to keep him sane.

But right now, Shep was nowhere to be found as his exasperated secretary, Anna, stepped into his office to try to determine just where her elusive boss had disappeared to this time.

On the floor next to his desk lay a rumpled pile that looked suspiciously like the jeans and denim shirt she'd seen him in just two hours earlier, before she'd left for lunch. Anna couldn't help but chuckle softly as she reached for the pile and carefully folded each piece of clothing, hoping to undo the damage that had already been done them by being left in such a heap. After four years, she still got a kick out of her unpredictable boss. While everyone else at Emerson, Caldwell conformed to the unwritten dress code that dictated conservative dark suits, Shep inevitably came in attired in jeans and Nikes. In the closet hung an expensive gray double-breasted suit, which represented his one accommodation to the formality of the legal world and which was pulled out for meetings or court appearances.

With the note containing the urgent message in hand, Anna walked to the window to look for Shep. The clothes on the floor could mean only one thing—that he'd reached the limit of his tolerance a little earlier in the day than usual. As he always did when things started getting to him, Shep must have gone running.

She instinctively looked toward the water. The sidewalks that had been so full just an hour earlier when she'd been returning from lunch were far less crowded now, but there was no sign of Shep. She was about to turn away from the window and give his nearby health club a call when she saw him. From this distance all she could make out was a form running along the river path, just approaching an intersection that would lead back toward the Landau Building. No face was discernible on the runner, but Anna did not need to see a face. There was no mistaking his size and his distinctive, strong gait. With a sigh, Anna realized that she could pick Shep Carroll out anywhere. Even in the midst of a crowd. Just as she'd done last October when she'd viewed the Portland marathon. She and a dozen other people from the office had rented a room at the Marriott Hotel to party, view the event, and cheer on several serious runners from the firm who participated in this annual test of endurance. They'd all been standing out on the balcony of their ninth-floor room when they saw the first surge of runners. There had to have been fifty or sixty of them, heading down the street just below them. To everyone else on that balcony, at that point they were just one big mass of moving humanity, a sea of bobbing heads, but Anna had picked Shep out from the crowd while it was still a good two blocks away. She hadn't even strained to find him. Standing at the window now, she experienced a sense of déjà vu.

She watched as he neared, running with long, strong strides, his near-perfect posture not diminished by the miles he'd already run, his grace as an athlete still evident despite the four knee operations he'd undergone since his days as the University of Oregon's star running back. His dark, thick hair, usually brushed back, fell forward, matted with sweat.

What a specimen you are, Shep Carroll, thought Anna Riley for what must have been the thousandth time, as she watched him approach the building, then disappear into its front door from the sidewalk beneath her. And for the thousandth time, Anna Riley, who had been happily married for six years, silently scolded herself for her thoughts.

By the time Shep emerged from the elevator minutes later and, with the slight limp that was characteristic after his runs, headed down the hall toward her desk, Anna was able to contain her admiration and look appropriately exasperated with him.

"When are you going to start remembering to leave me a note when you disappear like that?" she scolded, reaching out to hand him the message that had prompted her search for him. "Stan Muncie has called three times now. He says it's urgent. Here's the number of his car phone. He should be on the way to the airport right about now. He's on the next plane out here."

"Sorry." Shep muttered distractedly, taking the message and heading right into his office. He waited until he'd closed the door behind him. Then, pulling his sweat-soaked T-shirt off, he sent it flying across the room and let out a resounding "Shit!"

The morning had been bad enough already. News that Stan Muncie was heading west was the clincher.

Maybe Anna had heard Muncie incorrectly. Maybe he was headed somewhere else and he just wanted to get in touch with Shep before he left Chicago. That was the thought that Shep held while he dialed the number Anna had written down—knowing full well that Anna never got anything wrong.

Muncie picked up on the first ring.

"Carroll?" he half asked, half demanded into his cellular.

"Stan, Anna tells me you've been trying to reach me. What's up?"

"I'm catching the next plane to Spokane. I arrive at eight-fifteen. Plan on meeting me in Coeur d'Alene first thing tomorrow morning."

Shep knew better than to press Muncie for an explanation.

"And Shep, clear your calendar for the next couple of days. You may be spending a little time in Idaho." With that, he hung up.

Shep sat still for the next few minutes. What could Muncie be planning now? Muncie was one of Shep's least favorite clients. But Chicago Savings and Loan had been paying Shep's firm big dollars to help it get a handle on its problems with a project in Coeur d'Alene, Idaho. Another loan that should never have been made, with another frantic lender trying to figure out how best to salvage things. Shep felt especially bad about this project because he liked the developer, Michael Coleman, very much. He wanted to see this one succeed. And while he found dealing with Stan Muncie distasteful, he knew that Michael Coleman's chances of success were enhanced by Shep's involvement. Also, as the partners had let it be known at the last meeting, this job was an important one to the firm. Shep's reputation as a skilled handler of distressed properties was starting to bring Emerson, Caldwell big money. But all it took was one unhappy client in the banking world and a carefully built reputation could go right down the tubes. Recognizing Shep's feelings toward Muncie, at the last meeting the firm had cautioned Shep against letting that happen. And the firm paid Shep Carroll's bills.

He looked out the window and beyond, to the river. As it did every afternoon, Portland State University's crew team was out practicing—two five-man sculls gliding smoothly along the water, looking from this distance like a pair of centipedes, arms moving in perfect synchronization. Shep found himself daydreaming about how long it would take him to head home, throw some gear into the Range Rover and hitch the boat up. He'd head to the mountains. Maybe to Wyoming. Do some serious fly-fishing along the way. Find himself a little cabin outside of Jackson and never come back. After all, aside from a job he was losing his enthusiasm for, there really was nothing—and more important, *no one*—to hold him there, in Portland. How long?

But then he remembered. The boat was in the shop. Last weekend, on the Columbia River, it had died on him. He'd drifted a good two miles before someone had come along and given him a tow back to Vancouver.

So much for *that* plan, thought Shep. Maybe next week he'd finally do it. Leave this job, this life, that was no longer providing him with any real sense of satisfaction. Money, yes. Satisfaction, self-worth, no.

Maybe next week.

But for now, all Shep Carroll had to look forward to were a couple of days with his least favorite client.

CHAPTER 2

TWENTY-EIGHT MILES SOUTH of Coeur d'Alene, just off Highway 95, is a small, well-kept wood frame house with a 1987 Jeep Cherokee parked outside. The house is eight miles outside the town of Worley, on the Coeur d'Alene Indian Reservation. The house belongs to Charlie Eaglequill, tribal chief of the Coeur d'Alene.

The Coeur d'Alene Tribe is low-profile. Its members' lives are centered on the reservation, which is nestled between the south end of Lake Coeur d'Alene and the town of Moscow, Idaho, home to the University of Idaho. There are lifelong residents of Coeur d'Alene who are barely aware of the existence of this group of Native Americans. Only thirty miles separate them, yet the two worlds exist on seemingly different planets. Each year, Coeur d'Alene parents delivering their soon-to-be adult children to the U. of I.'s campus for the first time are certain to be taken aback by the Tobacco and Fireworks signs that are the only real reminders that visitors are crossing a reservation.

The idyllic setting—rolling wheat fields, unspoiled shoreline, wooded ridges—can be misleading. It does not hint at the realities of reservation life, which for all too many is a daily struggle. Poverty and unemployment are high. The young either leave and never return, or stay and never get an education. Despite the fact that a tribal timber company and farm—and, most recently, a bingo operation—have reduced unemployment and generated much-needed funds, for many life remains bleak.

But although it is still a tightly kept secret, there may now be reason for hope. And in large part that hope is personified in Charlie Eaglequill.

Charlie Eaglequill is not only a tribal leader, one with a plan, he is also one of a handful of tribal members who have ventured beyond the perimeters of the reservation and integrated themselves into the "outside" world. Charlie grew up watching his father, Charlie Eaglequill Sr., build houses. Ninety percent of the horses on the reservation were built by Charlie Senior, and his father, Windkeeper. Both men were craftsmen who took pride in their work and gained considerable renown for their skills and productivity. Charlie's father was offered a job outside on numerous occasions but chose never to leave the reservation, where he was most needed and most comfortable. But Charlie, who inherited his dad's talent and love of the craft, was different. Charlie wanted to explore outside. Besides, all the houses his father and grandfather had built were still standing and in amazingly good shape. There was not enough work for him on the reservation.

As a young man, Charlie accepted a job as a framer for a small Coeur d'Alene contractor. His hard work and skills paid off. He advanced within the company as it grew, and finally was named vice president of Lake City Construction in 1989. A quiet but well-spoken man, he was elected president of the North Idaho Builders Association in 1994. The significance of this appointment, the fact that he was the first Native American to hold that office in such a powerful state association, went pretty much unacknowledged, for while his name and dark, aquiline looks spoke clearly of his heritage, to non–Native Americans Charlie might just as well have been born next door. He could easily have packed up his family, moved into town and been received with open arms. But Charlie Eaglequill would never leave the reservation. Or his people. He was proud of his heritage and determined to raise his own sons to have equal pride in being born Native American.

That is why, this morning, Charlie's mood is heavy, apprehensive. This morning, as he has done two mornings a week for the past ten years, he will visit his father, Charlie Senior, who lives in a nearby rest home.

Charlie had resisted it, the idea of a rest home. In fact, he'd fought it tooth and nail. But it was what Charlie Senior said he wanted. Several of his lifelong friends were there. And somehow, in that simple but clean brick ranch-style building, they had managed to re-create something of the tribal community of the past that these men so cherished. A past that had been passed down to Charlie in stories told by his father and grandfather to ensure that the stories did not die, that none of it was forgotten. Stories about the world his great-grandfather once lived in, before the white man came, while massive herds of buffalo still darkened entire valleys. Stories about the French Canadian fur trappers who had dubbed the tribe Coeur d'Alene, meaning "heart of awl," for their sharp trading practices, about battles they'd fought against the white man—the ones they'd won—and ultimately, how they had lost.

As a child, Charlie had been told of how his grandfather, a child himself, had been forced to cut off his long black hair, stop speaking his native tongue and attend a school taught by white men. How a law had been passed that punished him—withheld food that had been rationed him by the agency, for by then he and his family were "agency" Indians, living on a reservation—if he was found participating in the sacred spiritual dance that for centuries had been the foundation of his people's beliefs. Charlie remembers seeing tears in his grandfather's eyes when he first told him that story.

Charlie's pride in his heritage was instilled in him at a young age and is there still. His need is to hold on to that past, to pass it along, to preserve it for his children and theirs. It is a constant struggle. Charlie understands the native tongue spoken by his father and his friends when he visits them several times a week at the nursing home, but he can no longer speak it. And his children cannot even understand it. They are patient with their grandfather, Charlie's father, on their frequent visits to see him. They smile and reach for his hand as they implore, "In English, Grandpa. Please, say it in English." And with a sigh, the old man usually complies. But Charlie can see how important it is to him, how with whatever strength he has left in him, his father is determined to hold on to the old life.

But the old life is no more, and Charlie knows the importance of adapting, of accepting the new world. Of becoming part of it. And now, at the age of fifty-two, as the recently reelected chairman of the Coeur d'Alene Tribe, Charlie is determined to change things. Determined to provide more scholarships and better schools. Charlie wants to see their young attend major universities, integrate into the outside world and then return to the reservation to carry on the traditions. He wants to get them, the young people, to stay and develop the tribe's economic base.

But it all takes money. Lots of it. Money there had been little hope of ever generating. Until 1988, when the Indian Gaming Act was passed. Since that time Charlie has watched as the answer to his people's problems lay cruelly just beyond their reach. He has watched as over 170 tribes across the nation have built casinos legitimized by the act. A $6 billion industry had been spawned, bringing sudden prosperity to dozens of tribes, some of whose members, like the Coeur d'Alene, had long been dependent upon welfare to survive.

Charlie hadn't always been a proponent of Indian gaming. At first, Charlie responded to the news that one tribe after another was opening gambling establishments with a sense of sorrow. He once shared the sentiments of his father and the other elders of the tribe, who felt disdain for the entire concept—a proud, honorful people seeking to profit from an activity they deemed sinful, he shared their predictions that gambling would bring crisis upon the tribes.

"As long as we have a roof over our heads and food to eat, we don't need it," were the sentiments voiced by the elders.

Skeptically, Charlie sat back waiting for the crises to come. Waiting for the corruption, the doom, that he, too, felt would accompany this trend. But it had not happened.

What he'd seen instead were Native Americans gainfully employed for the first time in their lives, able to purchase homes, send their children to college. Profits that paved roads, constructed sewer and water systems, and provided health care. After over a hundred years of being the poorest of the poor, many Indian people were becoming self-sufficient. Regaining their self-esteem.

Even the anticipated corruption had not materialized, so responsible and capable were the Native Americans at policing and regulating their own establishments.

And just when Charlie and the other tribal leaders were ready to join in this new phenomenon, just when their hopes were highest, when, after cautious delay and evaluation, they were finally ready to move forward and take the step that could turn reservation life around, the governor of Idaho had stepped in and callously, calculatedly, cut them short.

When the tribe attempted to negotiate a compact with the state, as was mandated by the 1988 act and as was being done successfully in dozens of other states across the country, Idaho's governor called for a special legislative session to propose passage of HJR4—a constitutional amendment prohibiting casino gaming. While the federal government was trying to give Native Americans everywhere a means to improve life on reservations, to build an economic base and end years of dependence on state and federal handouts, the state of Idaho slammed the door on the Coeur d'Alene's hope.

As with so many other things in Native American history, once Charlie's people were given something, someone would inevitably try to take it away.

But the Coeur d'Alene fought back. The tribe filed a U. S. District Court lawsuit. And lost. It appealed the ruling. And lost. Finally, in one last act of desperation, the tribe took its appeal to the highest court in the land—the U. S. Supreme Court. The Supreme Court refused to hear it.

Over the past few years, the Coeur d'Alene had discovered that there was only one thing more cruel than having no hope. And that was having hope dangled before their eyes, watching the difference it made for other tribes, reaching out for it . . . and then having it snatched away.

But all that might now be changing.

Two months earlier, Charlie's telephone had awakened him at six A.M. on a Tuesday.

Charlie recognized the voice right away. It belonged to Jimmy Brown, another tribal leader. Jimmy, an Indian activist, who was also the most politically savvy of the council members. He was calling from Los Angeles, where he was visiting relatives.

"Wake up, brother," Jimmy had said. "The sun is already shining in the City of Angels and Jimmy has something of interest to tell his people back home."

With that morning's Orange County edition of the *Los Angeles Times* in hand, Jimmy proceeded to read the first two paragraphs of a page 2 article to Charlie.

> WASHINGTON—The Supreme Court on Monday asked the Administration for its views in a high-stakes fight about what kinds of casino gambling states must consider permitting on Native American reservations.
>
> The action signals that the court is seriously thinking about stepping into a battle between several tribal groups and the state of California about the boundaries of a federal law that requires states to negotiate tribal-state "compacts" for gambling on Native American land.

"You know what this means, don't you?" Jimmy had asked a now wide-awake Charlie. "The Supreme Court is about to jump into the fray."

"How can you be sure?" Charlie wanted to know. He was a wise man, but he deferred to Jimmy in matters of politics.

"Because, sure as the sun's gonna rise on that ugly mug of yours, the president is going to come out strong in favor of maximizing tribal rights."

Jimmy sounded like he'd already downed half a pot of coffee, but he always sounded like that.

"You're sure about that?"

"Damn sure. For two reasons. First, the people want these casinos. And I don't mean our people. I mean *the people*. White folks, black folks, Asians, Hispanics. A recent poll in California showed that non-natives want to gamble. Period. Same's true in Idaho. And secondly, because this president is a man of conscience. Hell, what other president has even contemplated apologizing for slavery? This is a way for him to help right things for Native Americans. I'll bet this shiny gold watch I just bought down here on a street corner on him. The president will come through."

And, true to Jimmy's word, the president had, indeed, come through, making clear his strong support of the Native Americans, issuing a moving speech declaring, "While we can never completely atone for what our forefathers did to the native people—who wanted nothing more than to live peaceably and honorably, at one with the earth, as they had for generations—we can, through conscientious enforcement of the Indian Gaming Act, finally help right their current situation."

Once the public became aware of the attempts by states to renege on yet another promise made by the government to the Native Americans, there had been a tremendous outpouring of support for tribal gaming. In anticipation of a reversal of the current governor's earlier refusal to negotiate a compact with the state's five tribes, the Coeur d'Alene, led by Charlie, were now moving forward with plans to open a casino.

"If worse comes to worst," Charlie had proclaimed at the last council meeting, "we are prepared to take this matter to the courts again."

Around the table, all the other council members wore the same expression of grim determination as Charlie.

"And next time, we will not lose."

And so Charlie has decided that it is finally time to talk to his father. To tell him of this latest turn of events. But if his heart feels a sense of promise at the venture that lies before them, it is accompanied by the fears that still dwell there, too. And when he arrives for today's visit with his father, Charlie's heart is not just a little heavy with anticipation of Charlie Senior's reaction.

"This is not the right thing," the old man says simply in response to Charlie's news.

"But Father," Charlie answers, "it's the only answer we have right now. Just think of the difference it will make in all of our lives."

"I am thinking of the differences," Charlie Senior says softly. "Nothing will ever be the same if you do this."

They were the words Charlie had most dreaded, coming from the person he most respected.

"Father, you must know the tribal leaders do not come to this decision easily. You know at one time I was against the casinos," Charlie goes on. "I was determined to hold out. Sure that we would find a way to help our people without resorting to gambling."

"And now you have weakened," the old man says. It is an accusation.

"No, Father," Charlie answers. "Now I have changed my mind. I have given this a great deal of thought. I have waited. I have watched what happens with the other tribes. I have watched as our people barely scrape by on government handouts and our children drop out of high school. And finally, after all of that, I have come to the conclusion that this is best for our people. I want you to believe that, too. It's very important to me that you believe that."

Charlie Senior remains silent.

"Father, have I ever let you down? Have I been a good son?" Charlie asks.

"The best son," his father answers gruffly.

"That's because I have had you for a father. I am what I am because of you. I am a Coeur d'Alene. I am a father and a husband. I am a proud son. You must trust me. You must wait and see. I have to have you with me on this. I have never gone against you before and I do not want to now. But I must do this. Our people need this."

Charlie Eaglequill Sr. looks stricken.

"But what about our world? The old world. What about our beliefs? How can gambling do anything but further destroy all of that? Soon there will be nothing left."

The pain in his father's voice stabs at Charlie Junior's heart.

"I won't let that happen," he answers. "We will use the riches from this to ensure that it never happens. We will use it to educate our children, to make them proud of being Coeur d'Alene. We will create jobs on our land so that they will stay. This money will not be tainted money. It will be a gift. This will become part of our history.

"Father, last week the Swinomish dedicated their new casino. The tribe gathered for the blessing. They sang and danced around the totem pole that stands at the entrance. Just as the blessing ended, a bald eagle flew over the casino. He circled the pole."

The old man's eyes brighten for just a second, as his son knew they would.

"This is the truth?" he asks.

"Yes, Father, it is the truth. I give you my word."

The old man grows silent again. The two sit for some time, not speaking. Finally, Charlie Senior clears his throat. His voice is strong.

"Do what you must do," he proclaims to his son.

With those words, some of the heaviness in Charlie's heart lifts.

"Thank you, Father," he says.

* * *

Charlie's wife, Susan, was waiting for him when he returned from the nursing home.

"How did it go?" she asked when he entered the kitchen.

"About like I expected," Charlie answered, dropping his denim jacket on one of the hooks next to the door before walking over to where she stood at the sink and planting a quick kiss on her cheek.

He stood next to her, his back leaning against the counter, and watched as her long brown fingers adeptly snapped the ends off each green bean she extracted from a bowl next to the sink, then rinsed the bean and dropped it into a colander.

She looked at him.

"How upset was he?" she wanted to know.

"Pretty upset," answered Charlie. "But before I left he promised me his support." He was silent for a moment. "God, I hope we're doing the right thing."

She turned the running water off, dried her hands on her apron and stepped in front of him. Then, seeing the anguish and uncertainty in his eyes, she took his face in her cool, smooth hands and said, "It will be all right."

Charlie pulled her to him and held her. She was his rock.

"The kids home?" he asked then, his voice suddenly husky with desire for her.

"Not for another hour," she answered.

In one movement, he picked her off the floor, swirled around, and deposited her rear end on the kitchen counter. Then he stood between her legs and pressed himself into her as they kissed.

"I'm going to make you scream with pleasure," he whispered to her, his hands running under her skirt, between her warm, parted thighs.

A short while later, not one, but two voices cried out. The sounds carried for some distance, but there were no neighbors to hear. Only the animals in the nearby fields, but they did not even look up from their grazing.

They had heard it before.

CHAPTER 3

BAILEY AWOKE TO THE first glimmer of daybreak, misty fingers of light streaming diagonally overhead through the skylight above her bed. She remembered the first time she'd visited Michael in his new home. The day he'd proclaimed the room she now lay in as *her* room. He'd met her in the lobby that afternoon and, though she was visibly exhausted from a final exam earlier that day followed by the five-hour drive from Seattle, he'd asked if she wanted to take a tour of the building.

"Right now?" she'd responded, heavy travel bag in hand, in a tone lacking much enthusiasm.

But then she'd seen the disappointment in his eyes.

"How long have you been waiting down here?"

Michael's sheepish smile gave her her answer.

"A while."

"Of course, I'll see it," she'd said. "I'd *love* to see it."

He'd enveloped her in a bear hug, then proceeded to take her on a floor-by-floor tour of the complex. And though she felt grubby and tired from the long ride, Bailey thoroughly enjoyed the tour. Thoroughly enjoyed seeing the lovely building that her brother had planned and built, watching Michael proudly point out the Olympic-size swimming pool, the impressive art collection hanging in each U-shaped corridor, the central courtyard with its fountains and gardens.

When they'd finished walking the rest of the building, they got on the elevator and punched *P* for the penthouse floor.

When the elevator came to a halt, they stepped off and Bailey let out a gasp.

"Michael!"

The other floors of the building had been done in neutrals, with an understated, European sophistication to them. They hadn't prepared Bailey for what she now saw. For the sheer drama of the penthouse floor.

A highly polished, light oak parquet floor with black inlay along its borders drew Bailey's eyes down a corridor with sixteen-feet-high, sloped ceilings and half a dozen skylights. The walls were white, stark and bare of artwork. None was necessary, for the entry to each of three penthouse units was a masterpiece in and of itself. Framed by white columns, each featured massive carved oak double doors, brass fixtures, and above, a panel of exquisite stained glass salvaged from a turn-of-the-century French cathedral.

Bailey turned to Michael, who had been studying her reaction.

"Not bad, huh, Sis?" he'd asked with a boyish grin on his face.

"It's incredible," she'd answered. "Just incredible."

Then they'd entered Michael's unit. Bailey had walked from one large, airy room to another, loudly exclaiming her delight, while Michael stood in the center of the living room, smiling. No, *beaming* was a far better description of the look on his face, Bailey now decided as she relived that day. Finally, she'd walked into the room in which she now lay. It was huge and bright, with two skylights, a small deck of its own, and a roomy bathroom with a two-person soaking Jacuzzi in the corner framed by windows. No curtains were necessary eleven stories up. Not in Coeur d'Alene, Idaho. Virtually every window in the unit looked out upon the shimmering lake that stretched for miles, the unbelievable blue of its unspoiled waters surrounded by majestic pines and gently sloping mountains. Bailey could still picture Michael standing there in the doorway.

"This one's yours," he'd said casually, nodding toward the room in which she'd stood that day.

"What?"

"I said it's yours. Yours when you come visit. Yours if you want to live in it. *Yours.*"

Michael had always hoped that one day Bailey would move to Coeur d'Alene. He wanted her to join him there when she finished law school.

Bailey had gone to him and wrapped her arms around him. At five feet eight inches, Bailey was a tall woman, but Michael still had four inches on her.

"I love it, Michael. Thank you," she'd said. "Maybe someday I *will* move in with you. But until then, when I visit I will enjoy the *hell* out of this incredible room!" They'd both laughed then.

It seemed like yesterday. If only she could close her eyes again and take back that time. What she wouldn't give to have it to spend over.

What she wouldn't give to be able to spend just one more day, one more hour, with her brother. She felt the now familiar ache rising from her heart to her throat, the sting starting in the back of her eyes.

"No!" she cried out, surprising herself with the sound of her own voice.

No more tears! She'd promised herself she would stop. She could not lay in that bed and drown in her tears another morning. She *would* not. It had been better when Clancy was still with her. Then, her concern for her brother's daughter overrode her own feelings. But Clancy was back in Los Angeles with her mother now. And Bailey missed her. Missed her and worried about her. After leaving half a dozen messages with no response, she'd finally gotten hold of Margo Leon and told her what had happened. If Margo were always as coldhearted and abrupt as she'd sounded that day, Bailey pitied Clancy. "Send her home," she'd ordered Bailey. No "I'm sorry to hear abut Michael," no "How is Clancy taking all of this?" Just "Send her home." After consulting with Tony Pappas, Bailey had felt she had no choice but to comply.

And so, she was alone. The only thing that was keeping her going now was her determination to save Edgewater Place. She was expecting to hear from Tony, hear whether he'd been successful in scheduling a meeting with the bank, any time now.

She got up and wrapped herself in her robe, then went into the kitchen, where she made coffee. When it was ready, she took a steaming mug into the living room and stood at the sliding patio doors looking out over the lake.

The morning's mist hung eerily over the water, but blue sky above promised a beautiful spring day. She saw a lone runner making his way along the lakeshore, heading toward Tubb's Hill, a favorite spot for runners and hikers. For the first time since Michael's death, she suddenly had an urge to exercise. After drinking half her cup of coffee, she changed into sweats and running shoes.

She stepped out into the eleventh-floor corridor. It was quiet, which was to be expected, since she was the sole occupant of the penthouse floor. Bailey wished she had neighbors. But penthouse units started at just under half a million dollars, so they had been impossible to sell.

She started for the elevators, then, eyeing the Exit sign above the stairwell doors, decided to get in the habit of taking the stairs instead. As she reached the landing for the seventh floor, Bailey was startled to have the door open suddenly in front of her. Into the stairwell, arms full with a very fat, very old dachshund, stepped a spry elderly woman whom Bailey had seen around the building on her previous visits.

"Sorry for starling you," said the silver-haired woman when she saw Bailey's expression. "Are you all right?"

Bailey shook her head and smiled. "Yes, I'm fine. I just didn't expect to see anyone here."

Somehow managing to extend her hand without dropping her heavy load, the bright-eyed woman offered, "Well, of *course* you didn't expect to see anyone here. The only ones who use these stairs are Tom, the building's maintenance man, and me. I'm Samantha Cummings," she said with a warm smile. "Sam to my friends."

"Hello, Samantha," answered Bailey, grasping the woman's hand. It was amazingly strong for such a tiny, frail-looking woman.

"Sam," corrected her companion.

Bailey laughed. "Thank you. *Sam.* I'm Bailey Coleman."

"I know," Sam answered. "I've seen you around before, with your brother." Sam's eyes reflected a genuine sorrow as she continued. "I've been wanting to meet you, to tell you what a wonderful man Michael was. I will miss him very much."

Bailey smiled and said simply, "Thank you. And who is *this*?" She nodded toward the dog in Sam's arms.

"This is Gator," answered Sam. "Gator is a dear old fellow. Almost fifteen years old now. My companion and best friend." She looked lovingly at the doe-eyed dog, who appeared to know he was being talked about and returned the look with equal affection.

"Isn't he a little heavy for you?" asked Bailey. Not only was the dog overweight, his long body and short little legs made holding him look quite awkward.

"Nonsense," answered Sam. "Besides, Gator could never make it up and down all these stairs. He has a bad back."

"Why don't you just take him down on the elevator?" asked Bailey.

Sam's expression grew cold.

"I can't do that," was all she said.

Then, after a brief pause, she confessed.

"Actually, Gator isn't supposed to be living in the building.

So I sneak him in and out by using the stairs. He goes out once early in the morning—this place is just full of old fogies, so no one is ever up at this hour—and again after dark. The rest of the time, he uses newspapers I put out for him on the balcony." The animation Bailey had first seen in Sam's soft eyes returned as she giggled. "I'm in charge of the recycling project here in the building, but *those* papers never make it to recycling!"

Bailey chuckled, too, then grew serious. "But that's ridiculous. Why can't you have Gator here? Who made up that rule?"

"The board of managers did. Actually, it was mainly the president's doing. Anthony Walcott. Tries to run this place like the gestapo. Anyway, when I bought my condo I was told that Gator would be no problem, but after I'd moved in I got a notice I had to get rid of him." She paused. "*No one* was going to take my Gator away from me. Your brother, he tried to help me. He was the only one on the board who fought Walcott for me. But as usual, he was just one vote out of five. The only thing I could do was try to sell my unit, but the only offer I got was twenty thousand dollars lower than what I paid for it. I can't afford to lose that kind of money—I'm a widow. I live on my deceased husband's pension. We invested our life savings in this place. So finally, after they'd tacked three notices on my door telling me Gator had to go, I lied. I told them I'd gotten rid of him. And I started doing this—taking him out the stairwell when no one is around. The only one who knew Gator was still here was Michael. He used to come over sometimes late at night and take him for good long walks for me. I sure miss that brother of yours. So does Gator."

Bailey reached out and patted Gator's head. "Well," she said, "your secret's safe with me, Gator. Now, how about letting me carry you the rest of the way?"

Sam resisted, but Bailey would not take no for an answer, and once she had the stout little guy in her arms she was amazed that petite Sam—and Bailey guessed that Sam had to be close to seventy-five years of age—was able to haul him up and down seven flights of stairs twice a day. She made a mental note to remind herself to "run into" Sam in the morning as often as she could.

At the bottom of the stairs, Sam peeked out to be sure the coast was clear, then she took Gator from Bailey's arms, plunked him down on the ground and hurried him out a side door. Gator's little tail wagged happily as the two of them bid good-bye to their new friend.

What she'd just learned troubled Bailey. For several reasons. This Walcott sounded like bad news. How cruel to try to force Sam to get rid of her only companion! Didn't he have more important things to worry about than harassing elderly widows and innocent animals? Just as disturbing was Sam's disclosure that her condominium had actually lost value since she bought it. Bailey added another note to her mental notebook—she should talk to Tony Pappas about the fact that the condominiums might actually have depreciated in value. If that were true, it made her situation with the forty-seven unsold condominiums all the more dire.

As Bailey jogged along the rugged trails of Tubbs Hill, her mind was occupied with the predicament Michael's disappearance had left her in.

First she'd lost her mother and father, and now Michael. Her entire family. Wasn't that bad enough? Did her grief now have to be compounded by the nightmare of inheriting a project on the brink of foreclosure?

Suddenly, she rounded the last bend of the trail and looked up to see the subject of her thoughts, Edgewater Place, silhouetted against a bird's-egg-blue morning sky. It was an unusually impressive building, no denying it. Rising so many stories above all the others around it, its windowed surfaces mirroring the majestic lake and mountains. It looked out of place somehow to Bailey—as if some mischievous giant condor had plucked it from the midst of Southern California and dropped it into the mountains of this unsuspecting, sleepy town.

Yet, at that moment, Bailey understood in full measure Michael's fascination with Edgewater Place. She could not suppress the shiver of pride that seeing his accomplishment in the light of another glorious morning gave rise to.

There it stood. Edgewater Place. Not only the embodiment of Michael's dreams, but now, also, her only chance of recovering the money left her by her parents. Money she would need to finish law school. Money that could make a huge difference in Clancy's life.

Was it her imagination or did it appear less than stable, that tall structure piercing the otherwise empty sky? Was all of it teetering there precariously, ready to topple over and bury her?

If so, was there any way, or anybody, to stop it?

When she got home, the first thing Bailey noticed was the blinking message light on the answering machine. She pressed the playback button, then turned the volume up so that she could listen as she went into the kitchen to make toast.

The first call was from Clancy. It had come in just before eight that morning.

"This is Clancy," a small voice announced. "Can you please call me?" She hesitated then, before adding "I miss you" and hanging up.

Bailey glanced at her watch. Clancy would already be at school. Regretting not having been home for her niece's call, she made a mental note to call Clancy later.

The next voice was that of Tony Pappas. The machine announced that the message had been received at 8:07 A.M.

"Bailey, give me a call first thing this morning, will you? I've agreed to meet with the bank and its attorney this morning at eleven. Let me know right away whether that will work for you."

Bailey picked up the phone and dialed Pappas's number. His secretary informed her that Tony was already with a client.

"Just tell him that I'll be there at eleven."

Glancing at her watch, she decided she had enough time to swim a few laps before heading over to Pappas's office.

These past few years, as an antidote to the endless hours she spent sitting in class and in her apartment reading law books, she'd alternated her morning runs with laps in the gigantic pool on campus. Today, finally beginning to feel some semblance of her old self, she wanted to do both.

Getting exercise, getting out, meeting Samantha Cummings all felt good. She hoped they were precursors to a good meeting that morning with the bank. She would not allow herself to think otherwise. She couldn't afford to.

She stripped quickly out of her clothes, then wiggled into her Speedo bathing suit and tied her hair back into a ponytail.

Standing in front of the full-length bathroom mirror for the first time since getting the news about Michael, she studied her reflection. The time she'd taken off from running and swimming hadn't hurt. She was a bit too thin, which was to be expected since she didn't eat for several days after Michael disappeared, but she still looked fit. Though she had the type of body women spent hours in the gym sweating to achieve, Bailey had never been one to flaunt it. In fact, Michael used to tease her about hiding behind the baggy sweats and jeans that were her trademarks. Still, this morning she couldn't help but take just a little pride in how she looked, feel a little relieved that the emotional ordeal she'd been through had at least not robbed her of her physical self.

Both of the residents she passed in the hall on her way to the swimming pool that morning noticed it. For the first time since she'd arrived at Edgewater Place, some of the old spring had returned to Bailey Coleman's step.

Bailey's good mood did not last long.

When she returned from the pool, she hurried to get dressed, then, glancing at her watch, decided she did not have time to blow-dry her hair.

Minutes later, tucking a loose strand of still-damp hair behind her ear, she was climbing the steps to Tony Pappas's third-floor office. In the corridor as she approached Pappas's suite, she could hear several male voices, but all conversation stopped abruptly when she opened the door.

Standing in the middle of the reception area were three men. Tony Pappas and a short, balding man wearing a double-breasted suit that only served to exaggerate his stout build stood facing Bailey. Tony did not look happy, but upon seeing Bailey he broke into a welcoming smile.

"Here she is now. Gentlemen, let me introduce Bailey Coleman."

At his words, the third man, whose back had been to the door, turned toward Bailey. He was tall and dark. His suit, in stark contrast to that of his companion, accentuated a near-perfect physique. His eyes were a startling blue. Sky blue, Bailey found herself thinking reflexively.

Tony introduced the shorter man as Stan Muncie, vice president of Chicago Savings and Loan. Muncie grunted an almost inaudible greeting and released the hand Bailey had extended before she even had a chance to say anything to him.

"And this," Pappas continued, "is the bank's attorney, Shep Carroll."

"Nice to meet you," Shep Carroll said. His manner was polite but reserved. His handshake was firm. Bailey felt his eyes taking her in and found herself wishing she'd taken the time to blow-dry her hair.

Tony shepherded his three visitors into the conference room that adjoined his office. Carroll and Muncie seated themselves on one side of the table, while Tony pulled out a chair on the other side for Bailey, then seated himself next to her.

It was Shep Carroll who spoke first.

"We'd like to start by offering our condolences," he said, turning to Bailey. "Your brother was an exceptional man. Someone I'd hoped to get to know better."

Muncie nodded but remained silent.

Practice had finely honed Bailey's ability to hide her emotions, but something about Shep's words caught her off guard. She found herself unable to speak. Tony briefly placed his hand on top of hers.

"Thank you," he said for her. "Now, let's get down to the business at hand. We've asked for this meeting because we feel it's in all of our best interests to deal with the situation as quickly as possible."

Muncie spoke up before Tony could continue.

"I agree. Michael Coleman's death was a tragedy. And, as Mr. Carroll just said, Miss Coleman has our sympathy." His voice held not the slightest hint of compassion. "But as I'm sure you can see, his absence dramatically alters everything. We've given serious consideration to foreclosure. However, we've decided that would not be the best course of action at this time."

At this declaration, that the bank had decided not to foreclose yet, Bailey felt Tony's leg nudge hers under the table, but both she and Tony remained stone-faced.

"Once there's a foreclosure you might as well give up on getting any sort of return on those units," Muncie explained dryly. "People will expect to buy them at fire sale prices. So, instead of proceeding with our option to foreclose, we've decided the best thing to do right now is have the bank take over the management and marketing of Edgewater Place. Try to get some units sold ASAP while we evaluate the best course of action for the long term."

Tony looked dumbfounded.

"But the loan documents don't provide for that. This building was under Michael Coleman's sole and exclusive control. As his heir, it will be in Bailey's hands."

"Unless the bank chooses to foreclose." Now it was Shep Carroll speaking. "That's still an option if the loan delinquencies aren't brought current."

"You know as well as I do that you can't foreclose until Michael Coleman is either confirmed dead or declared dead." Tony, concerned about the effect of these words on Bailey, shot her a sideways glance.

"If we have to get him declared dead, that's what we'll

do." Again, it was Muncie who jumped in matter-of-factly, all too ready to bait Tony Pappas.

A look of surprise crossed Shep's face at Muncie's suggestion that the bank would petition for a declaration of Michael Coleman's death.

Bailey was having more success at hiding her outrage than Tony, who, red-faced at Muncie's callousness, clearly wanted to lash out but dared not.

Muncie had them. They could either acquiesce, voluntarily allow the bank to assume control of Edgewater Place, or force the bank to have Michael declared dead, in which case there was nothing to stop the bank from foreclosing. The only thing Tony and Bailey had going for them was the bank's reluctance to foreclose—a reluctance that was well-founded. From a marketing standpoint, forcclosure was a stigma that would be hard to overcome.

"What about joint control?"

All heads turned toward Bailey at the sound of her voice.

"I take it the bank cannot just assume control. That until there's actual foreclosure their involvement would require our consent." She looked to Tony, who nodded confirmation. Then, turning to Muncie, for she found herself avoiding Shep Carroll's gaze, she announced, "Well, I'm not willing to turn everything my brother worked for over to you one day earlier than I absolutely have to. But if it will buy us some more time, I *will* consider shared control."

Shep Carroll and Stan Muncie sat in silence. With foreclosure looming over her head, they'd expected Bailey's unequivocal cooperation in turning control over to them. Her unexpected proposal had ambushed them.

"And there's one more thing," Tony added.

"What's that?" said Shep.

"If we agree to allow you joint control over Edgewater Place, we expect you to release Michael Coleman's estate from the personal guarantee he signed."

At these words, Muncie half stood in protest. "Now wait a damn minute here. We're not about to do any such thing."

Tony would not back down. "You know you would have

given him that loan with or without that guarantee. It was icing on the cake. Besides, without this project's success, Michael's assets won't amount to beans and you know it."

Muncie glared at him. "Icing on the cake," he fumed. "What kind of a goddamn cake might that be? As far as I can see, this thing isn't turning out to be any party for the bank. If Michael Coleman had a dime in his pocket when he died, we're entitled to it."

The volatility in the room becoming palpable, Shep Carroll pushed his chair back from the table.

"Will the two of you please excuse us for a moment?" he asked, his eyes traveling from Pappas to Bailey. Then, turning toward Muncie, he said, "Let's step outside for just a moment and discuss this. Okay?"

When the door closed behind the two men, Tony turned to Bailey.

"Nice work," he said. Then, "You okay?"

Bailey was still steaming from Muncie's comments.

"Did you hear him? The way he talked about Michael?"

"I know. I was ready to deck the son of a bitch. But obviously that would not have been cool. You sure you want to work with him?"

"*Want* to? No. But if that's what it takes to get them to back off on foreclosure, I'll do it. Like I said the other day, I'll do whatever it takes to save Edgewater Place. Even work with that slime."

Within a matter of minutes the door opened and Shep and Stan Muncie reentered. Once they had seated themselves again it was Shep who addressed Bailey and Tony.

"The bank is agreeable to joint control."

Muncie did not look agreeable to anything, but he also did not dispute Shep's statement. Shep looked directly at Bailey then and announced. "Until we decide on a different course of action, I will be dividing my time between Portland and Coeur d'Alene."

Bailey felt herself flush—an almost imperceptible flush, a one on a scale of one to five (which she knew from all those teenage years of racing in horror to the mirror whenever she was embarrassed to see if her fair skin had betrayed her)—at the realization that it would be Shep with whom she would work. Not Muncie. Surely, after Muncie's behavior, this should be welcome news. Why, then, did she suddenly feel an acute sense of embarrassment?

"What about the personal guarantee?" Tony wanted to know.

"We won't void it." Again, it was Shep speaking. "But you have our assurance that we will not act upon it unless or until that time that foreclosure is initiated."

With everyone in agreement and Muncie still too indignant about the way things had turned out to attempt to be civil, the meeting came to an end.

As all four were walking out, Shep manuevered his way to Bailey's side.

"How does your afternoon look?" he asked.

Bailey looked startled. "I'm sorry. I'm afraid I don't understand."

Shep smiled then. Not the same polite smile he'd displayed earlier. This one was warm, with a hint of humor.

"I was wondering whether it would be convenient for you to meet with me this afternoon. To get started. You know, working together."

Bailey flushed again. She didn't need a mirror to tell her that this time it was a five.

"Why, yes. I guess I am free," she said hesitantly. "What time is good for you?"

The lunch crowd had already descended upon Cricket's by the time Stan Muncie and Shep Carroll arrived from their meeting at Tony Pappas's office. As they stood at the Please Wait to be Seated sign and tried to catch the attention of one of the bouncy waitresses hustling about, Muncie's foul mood elevated.

"This is ridiculous. Let's get out of here," he huffed.

"Stan," said Shep Carroll calmly, "it's twelve-fifteen. Everywhere we go we're going to run into the same thing."

"What the hell is *that*?"

Muncie was pointing at the juncture of the wall and ceiling, where a model train track circled the room. A silver model train, its whistle blowing and its lights flashing, was just approaching the area above their heads.

Shep let out a laugh. "Looks like a model train to me. You mean to tell me you never had one as a kid?"

Muncie glared at him. "I'm outta here."

Shep, at whose suggestion they'd tried Cricket's, followed behind his irate client, shaking his head and laughing. "How was I supposed to know they had a toy train running around the ceiling?"

Muncie did not answer. He strode purposefully across the street to the Iron Horse, his favorite eating establishment in Coeur d'Alene, where they were immediately shown to a table. Once seated, he couldn't resist an "I told you so" glare at his attorney.

Shep, who found Muncie's behavior so childish as to be quite amusing, couldn't suppress a smile. "Okay. I was wrong. From now on, we stick with the Iron Horse."

Temporarily satisfied, Muncie turned his attention to the menu. His nose was still buried in it when Shep put down his menu and, while waiting for the waitress to take their orders, idly glanced about the rest of the dining area.

"Isn't that the president of the Edgewater Place Homeowners Association over there?"

Shep nodded toward a table at the back of the room, where three men were just getting up to leave.

Just as Muncie raised his eyes in the direction Shep indicated, the man in question looked their way and saw Shep and Muncie appraising him. He quickly averted his eyes in the direction of one of his companions, and as they walked toward the cashier to take care of their bill, looked to be engrossed in their discussion.

"That's him, isn't it? Anthony Walcott? I wonder why he didn't even acknowledge us. Hard to believe he didn't recognize us." Shep looked around the room, where all the other male diners were clad in far more casual attire—

shirtsleeves, usually tieless, with just an occasional sport coat. "It's not like we don't stick out like sore thumbs."

"I don't know who you're talking about," Muncie replied. "I've never even met the president of the Homeowners Association."

"No kidding?" Shep asked. "I thought you attended that first meeting with me."

"Nope. I can't stand homeowners meetings. Bore me to tears. A bunch of neurotic old people worrying about who left a can of beer in the social room or who's parking their car in someone else's fucking parking space."

"They're not all old."

Muncie looked up from his menu and smiled. It was a lascivious smile, and Shep recognized it as such right away.

"You mean Bailey Coleman?" Muncie said. "No, she's certainly not old, is she? Not hard to look at either. Can't believe I'll be paying you big bucks to spend time with a hot little number like that."

Muncie expected the machismo-type response he usually got from his comrades when his mind decided to descend into the gutter. But instead he got no response at all.

In fact, the two men ate most of their meal in silence. Just before parting outside the restaurant, Muncie to return to the hotel, and Shep to meet with Bailey, Muncie further infuriated his attorney by turning to him and admonishing, "We're not in this thing to be charitable. Don't go getting soft on me. Do you hear? Just 'cause we're dealing with this Coleman girl. This is business. Don't forget it."

Shep shot him a look that conveyed his contempt, but true to his promise to his partners, said nothing more than "Have I ever?"

Muncie grunted and headed down the sidewalk.

Shep looked at his watch, saw he had almost half an hour before his meeting with Bailey, and turned in the direction of the lake. If only he'd been dressed in sweats and running shoes. He had a sudden, overpowering urge to go running. But right now a walk would have to do.

Why had Muncie's comments bothered him so? Had he

ever "gone soft" on a client? The answer was no and he knew it. Perhaps that was it. He'd been through so many foreclosure situations that now, like Muncie, he'd developed an attitude that could easily be characterized as cold. Strictly business. Foreclosing on people's property. Their homes. Not that he felt good about it; he didn't. At first it had bothered him some, but he could always rationalize it. The banks had rights, too, didn't they? They could hardly be expected to tolerate nonpayment of loans. They had salaries to pay, other customers who needed to borrow the money. It was the only way. But usually he was dealing with other attorneys, or shrewd developers, some of whom were in the situations they were in out of sheer greed or stupidity.

It was what he'd gone to law school for, wasn't it? To be the one in control? And he was good at it. No doubt about it. Last year his clients alone had accounted for over one fourth of the firm's income. He'd found a very profitable niche.

So why was he so disturbed by the events of the past twenty-four hours? Of course, his shock at learning of Michael Coleman's death was understandable. He'd liked Michael. Liked him a lot. In fact, the last time he'd been in Coeur d'Alene, he and Michael had talked fishing over a couple of beers. It was after a homeowners meeting. Michael had invited him to a local tavern and they'd ended up closing the place down. The subject of Edgewater Place had never even come up. They'd talked fishing, pure and simple. Some sports, too, for, like Shep, Michael had played college football, at the University of Washington. But they'd mainly talked about fishing holes, and rivers, and technique. Michael had promised that the next time Shep was in town he'd take him just over the border to his favorite river in Montana. Shep had been looking forward to it.

Now that Shep thought about it, he remembered one other topic Michael had talked about that night. Michael's sister, Bailey. That night it hadn't meant much to Shep, but now, now that he'd met her, Michael's words took on new meaning. Michael had talked about Bailey with such pride.

And such concern. He'd told Shep that his little sister had always reminded him of . . . what was it? Some kind of little dog. A bulldog? That ferocious-looking dog that was actually a surprisingly gentle creature. Michael had said that on the surface Bailey always tried to be so independent, so tough. But that their parents' death had left her vulnerable. Shep could tell that night how much Michael worried about her. He told Shep he wanted Bailey to move to Coeur d'Alene when she finished law school so he could keep an eye on her.

Despite her obvious grief at losing her brother, on the surface the woman Shep had seen today appeared quite capable of taking care of herself. One tough little bulldog. Had it not been for Michael's words, Shep might well have taken Bailey's demeanor at face value. Of course, bulldogs didn't blush. Did they?

Is this what was bothering him? The prospect of foreclosing on Bailey Coleman? For despite the bank's decision to hold off for now, Shep knew that foreclosure was virtually unavoidable. And Shep must not let Michael's words—must not let the vulnerability he'd seen today in those lovely, sad eyes—influence him. Despite his loathsome and tactless manner, Muncie was right. This was business. Strictly business. And Shep must not forget that.

When Muncie returned to the hotel, he stopped in the gift shop to buy some Rolaids. As he was passing the registration counter to return to his room and take his midday nap, the young woman working there called out to him.

"Mr. Muncie?"

He walked over to the counter.

"Yes?"

"You had a visitor just now." She smiled the generic smile that all the hotel employees used with guests. "He left you this note." She handed him a folded piece of paper.

Muncie grunted a thanks and walked toward the elevator, unfolding the paper as he did so. The message inside was short and cryptic.

Need to talk to you. If you get this in time, meet me in the city park at 2:00 P.M.

It was signed "Anthony."

Promptly at one-thirty, Shep entered the social room at Edgewater Place to find Bailey Coleman waiting for him. She was dressed in the same clothes she'd worn at their earlier meeting—light blue silk trousers and blouse. She's changed, however, from low heels to gold sandals, and her hair was now tied back loosely. Several strands had escaped the ribbon tied at the nape of her neck and hung on either side of her face, framing it softly. Upon seating himself opposite her, the thought entered Shep's mind that she was quite possibly the most beautiful woman he'd ever seen. And, like a driver who finds himself overcorrecting when he's drifted off the road. Shep's instincts upon having such a thought were to do likewise.

"We've got our work cut out for us," he said, a bit too curtly.

"It appears so," Bailey answered, in a tone that deliberately matched his in its businesslike nature. "Where do we start?"

They spent the next two hours engrossed in an oftentimes uncomfortable conversation in which Shep tried to ascertain just how much Bailey knew about the running and marketing of Edgewater Place. As it became clear to both of them that Bailey knew next to nothing about this project her brother had left her with, Shep could see the panic in Bailey's eyes. He could almost read her thoughts. How could she possibly hope to save Edgewater Place when she knew so little about it? Despite his vowed determination to treat this situation as he'd treated all the others before it, Shep's tone softened.

"This place is important to you, isn't it?"

For the first time that day, Bailey allowed herself to look directly at Shep.

"Yes."

Something happened to Shep then, when he looked into those green eyes. Eyes that spoke so clearly of Bailey's anguish and grief. Something powerful and for a man like Shep, very confusing. For somehow, in that moment, he, too, felt exposed.

"Then we'll just have to give you a crash course," he said quietly.

Bailey's gaze remained locked with his until finally she uttered a quiet, "Thank you." Then, appearing unnerved by what had just transpired between them, she dropped her gaze to her hands, which lay crossed on the table in front of her.

Shep took a deep breath.

"Maybe we should take a walk through the building. To be honest, I've never seen the whole thing."

"That's one thing I do know." Bailey smiled, relieved not only at having the intensity between them pass but also to have stumbled upon the one area in which she was more knowledgeable than Shep.

Shep allowed Bailey to take over, leading him from one floor to another, proudly pointing out the same features that Michael had shown her. Her affection for her brother was evident whenever she spoke of him. They were just leaving the swimming pool when Faith Lammerman, the building's office manager, caught up with them.

"Glad I found you," she said to Bailey. "Clancy has been trying to get a hold of you. She finally called my office. She used to do that when she was looking for Michael, too. I tried to get her to tell me what it was, but she wouldn't. I don't mean to alarm you, but I think something may be wrong."

Bailey's eyes widened. "With Clancy? I'll come right with you."

"No," Faith said. "You should go home. I told her to wait five minutes while I tried to find you, then try calling you there."

Bailey hurried off toward the elevator, then, almost as an

afterthought, turned to look back. She'd left Shep standing in the middle of the hall.

"I'm sorry." *What should she do about Shep?* On impulse she said, "Why don't you come with me?"

"You sure? I don't want to get in the way."

"Yes. Come on."

Shep caught up with her. As they stepped into the elevator he asked. "Who is Clancy?"

"My niece. Michael just found out he had a daughter a few months ago. She'd been living with him until . . ." She didn't finish.

Shep remained silent the rest of the way up to the eleventh floor. They entered Bailey's condo and seated themselves at the kitchen table, where Bailey literally stared at the phone on the counter as if willing it to ring. But five minutes passed, then ten, and still it did not ring.

Finally Shep spoke. "Why don't you try calling her?"

Bailey looked at him, and in her eyes he saw genuine fear. "Because I'm afraid I'll get her mother. Somehow I think this may have to do with her. I'd like to let Clancy call me back instead."

While they were waiting for Clancy to call, Shep decided to check in with his office. He had a cellular phone in his briefcase and said he would use that rather than tie up Bailey's line. In order to give him some privacy, Bailey offered him the use of the living room, which he accepted. Still, his strong voice carried, and as he spoke to someone named Anna—who, Bailey soon surmised, was his secretary—Bailey could not help but pick up snippets of the conversation. Her mind was so preoccupied with Clancy, however, that what she heard failed to register until much later.

She heard Shep ask what messages he'd received. It appeared to be in response to one of these messages that he very matter-of-factly told Anna. "We can't do that. He's had plenty of time. Tell Trish to start drawing up the foreclosure papers."

Shep was silent for a while, apparently listening to Anna's response.

"That's really not the bank's problem," he said. "He either comes up with the payments or he loses the house."

Bailey heard Shep discuss several other clients and cases, then, promising to call in again the next day, he hung up and returned to the kitchen.

"Still no call?"

Bailey shook her head.

Shep nodded at the phone. "Sure you don't want to try her?"

Unable to wait a moment longer, she picked up the phone and dialed the number in Los Angeles. She heaved a sigh of relief when, on the very first ring, Clancy answered the phone.

"Hi, Sweetie!"

"Bailey!" Clancy said.

"How's my favorite niece?"

The silence that greeted Bailey's question was an answer of sorts.

"Clancy?" Bailey pressed, the cheer in her voice giving way to dead seriousness. "How *are* you?"

Bailey heard a small sniffle before Clancy spoke again.

"I'm fine." Nothing more.

"You don't sound so fine. Is something wrong?"

No answer.

"Clancy, please tell me what's wrong. If something's wrong, I want—"

Suddenly the voice on the other end was not Clancy's. The voice that interrupted Bailey in mid-sentence was that of Clancy's mother, Margo Leon. She sounded either very tired or hung over. It didn't take long to figure out which.

"Clancy has a bad cold," Margo explained, her speech slurred slightly. "A sore throat. I don't want her to aggravate it."

No hello, how are you's with Margo, thought Bailey.

"I'd like to talk to her again," she said. "Please. I won't keep her on long."

"I told you, she's not feeling well."

At that moment, Bailey knew without a doubt that Clancy was in some sort of trouble.

"Put her on the phone," she demanded. "I want to talk to my niece. If you don't, I'll be down there on the next flight."

Margo was silent for a moment, then Bailey heard her cover the phone with her hand and speak in a low, threatening tone. When Clancy came back on the line moments later, Bailey was fearful that her insistence on talking to Clancy might have made the situation for her niece even worse.

"Hello," the little voice said.

"Clancy, are you going to school tomorrow morning?"

"Yes."

"I want you to go to the office when you get there and call me collect. Do you understand?"

No response.

"Clancy, do you understand?"

A timid "Yes."

"Now, say something to me like 'I'm fine, I'll write you a letter soon.' Say *anything* to me, and we'll hang up then. Okay?" Bailey was afraid she'd endangered Clancy. She just wanted to get the little girl off the phone without incident. She held her breath, waiting to see whether Clancy could pull this off.

"I'm just fine," the little girl finally said into the phone with forced cheerfulness. "But I have chores to do so I'd better go."

"Thank you, Clancy," Bailey responded with a sigh of relief. "You did great. Now be sure to call me from school tomorrow. First thing. And if you need to talk to me before then, if anything happens that frightens you, call me. If for some reason you can't talk, just dial my number, let it ring once and hang up. I'll find a way to get back to you, to get through."

After waiting for Clancy to hang up, Bailey placed the phone back in its cradle. Her hand was shaking.

"Are you okay?" Shep asked.

"It's not me I'm worried about." She explained the fears she'd had about sending her niece back home, ending with "But I felt I had no choice."

"You probably didn't. Listen," Shep offered, "it doesn't sound like you'll want to be leaving here the rest of the day. Why don't you call me tomorrow and let me know when you want to get started again? This stuff is secondary to your niece's well-being."

Bailey did not respond right away.

"I think I may go mad if I sit here alone all night waiting for the phone to ring," she finally said. "We could continue our meeting here. I mean tonight. If you don't already have plans, that is."

Shep did not hesitate. "That's actually a good idea. I have to return to Portland day after tomorrow, so the more we can get in now, the better. Why don't I pick up dinner for us? I'll head back to the hotel now, then come back around seven. Would that work?"

"Sure," said Bailey. "That would work just fine."

At first, Muncie could not find Anthony Walcott. Then he saw the back of him, his slicked-back head of silver hair too distinctive to allow for confusion with anyone else. He was seated on a bench at the front end of the park. Approaching him from behind, Muncie immediately discovered why Walcott had chosen this particular bench. It overlooked the sandy beach below, where half a dozen bikini-clad girls, undoubtedly students from nearby North Idaho College, lay soaking in the unusually warm spring sun.

"What the hell are you thinking?" Muncie demanded before he'd even seated himself alongside Walcott.

"What do you mean?"

"Leaving me a note, asking for a meeting like this. Out in public."

Walcott finally lifted his eyes from the beach. "Look around," he sneered "See anybody here over twenty?" He snickered. "Besides *us*, that is. This is one place we don't have to worry about being seen."

"Yeah, well Carroll had no trouble picking you out at the restaurant."

"So what?"

"I don't want to push our luck. I just got done telling him I've never met you. We don't need him—or anyone else, for that matter—to see us together."

"You worry too much," Walcott said. Then, as Muncie settled on the bench next to him, he continued. "Listen, things are moving along a little faster than I anticipated. The interest is even stronger than we expected. I'm going to need more money." He stole a glance sideways at Muncie. "I've been thinking. I think the funds should be out here, where I can access them."

At this, Muncie let out a laugh.

"Tell me you're joking! You really think you could get me, or anyone else, to go for that?" He snorted again in amusement, then grew sober. "All expenditures need to be approved. If you need money, you'll get it. But it stays in my bank. You hear?"

Walcott didn't look happy, but he knew better than to push.

"There's something else," he said. "This could be big. It could mean more money." He looked over to see if he'd piqued Muncie's interest. "Maybe twice what we've already made."

Seeing the flicker his words had invoked in Muncie's slit-like eyes, Walcott, pleased with himself, slid closer to his companion.

"I had an interesting visitor today . . ." he started.

For the next forty-five minutes, the two men could be seen deeply engrossed in conversation. A conversation that grew so animated they eventually stopped looking up every few seconds to check out the sunbathers.

Finally, Muncie stood, saying, "I'd better get back to the hotel before Carroll returns from his meeting with Coleman's sister. You let me know when this becomes a sure thing. I'm not going to put any of this into action until then. I've still got a board of directors to report to."

Walcott's eyes were back on the beach.

"Don't worry. It'll happen," he said.

Muncie turned to leave, but first he couldn't resist asking, "Don't you have to get back to work?"

"I'm my own boss. Remember? Think I'll just stay and enjoy the nice day a little while longer."

"Yeah, right," grunted Muncie. "Whatever."

An hour after Shep left, Bailey sat with the newspaper spread out in front of her on the kitchen table. She'd had it turned to the same page for a while, unable to concentrate on anything but the silent phone beside her and the river of unfamiliar emotions running through her. There was still more than an hour to go before Shep was due back. If the past hour was any indication, it would seem like an eternity. She was therefore more than happy to hear a knock on her door and to open it and find Sam Cummings standing in the hallway.

"Am I interrupting anything?" Sam asked cheerfully. She was carrying a bouquet of freshly cut tulips.

"Of course not." Bailey smiled. "Come on in."

"These are for you." Sam said, extending the hand holding the flowers.

"Thank you! They're absolutely gorgeous, but you shouldn't have."

"Nonsense. One thing you must know right from the start, kiddo. When you get my age, you realize that one of life's greatest pleasures is being able to do something nice for someone else. Now don't make a big fuss, just get them into some water. I carried them all the way home from Safeway and I'm not such a fast walker anymore. It's hot out there today and they're starting to wilt."

Bailey hurried to fill a vase with water, then once she'd arranged the tulips on the kitchen table, she invited Sam to stay for a glass of lemonade.

"I'd love to. It's such a beautiful day. Should we take it out on the deck?"

Bailey's smile faded as she explained to Sam her need to stay close to the phone in case Clancy signaled her.

"Why, that's horrible," Sam said. "You actually think she's afraid of her own mother?"

Bailey nodded. "Of course, until I talk to her I can't be sure. But I think what probably happened is that when she came home from school today she was alone. That's when she tried to call me. My guess is that Margo showed up then, and that's why she didn't call me back when Faith told her to. When I got hold of her it was obvious she didn't feel she could talk in front of her mother. I hope we'll know what's going on for sure tomorrow."

Suddenly Bailey had a terrifying thought—what if Clancy didn't call her in the morning?

Sam's face scrunched into a scowl that surprised Bailey in its ferocity. "I'd like to get my hands on that woman if that's true. That little girl is such a darling. She used to come visit me with your brother. She just loves Gator. Just the thought that someone—her own mother, of all people—would mistreat her . . . well, I'd just like to get my hands on that miserable . . ."

Bailey had to fight back a smile. She was growing very fond of her elderly friend, who had a heart of gold but was also amazingly feisty. Bailey wouldn't want to be the one to tangle with Sam Cummings.

"Well, I hope I'm wrong about all of it," Bailey said. "But I'm not taking any chances."

They visited for a while longer, then Sam offered to bring Bailey dinner.

"Thanks, but that won't be necessary. I'll be working here with the bank's attorney tonight." She explained to Sam the agreement she'd reached with the bank, and finished with "He offered to bring dinner with him when he comes back in a while."

Sam arched her eyebrows in surprise and mouthed a silent O.

"You mean that good-looking young man who was at the last homeowners' meeting?"

For some reason, Sam's reference to Shep Carroll's good looks rubbed Bailey the wrong way. Was it because she, herself, was all too aware of Shep's appeal? Because she was trying to deny her attraction to him? No, she decided instantly. It couldn't be. Looks had never been important to Bailey. In fact, if a man who showed an interest in her was too good-looking, she'd always automatically rejected his advances. She remembered the one time she and Michael had even argued about it. One of his best-looking friends, Scott Williams, had wanted to date Bailey. Michael was all for it. When Bailey refused to even entertain the possibility, even though she'd been complaining about being dateless, Michael had accused her of being afraid to go out with such a good-looking man.

"Afraid?" she'd cried, indignant.

"Yes, afraid," Michael had answered.

"I'm not the least bit afraid," she'd said. "It's just that looks don't happen to be a priority for me."

"Good," he'd shot back. "They shouldn't be. But they also shouldn't be the basis for turning guys down when they ask you out. Besides being good-looking, Scott's a great guy."

Michael was being absurd. Of course she wasn't afraid to date a good-looking guy like Scott. What was there to be afraid of? The discussion was too silly to continue, so instead of arguing, she'd responded with, "I already have one good-looking man in my life. My brother. What do I need with another one?" And sensing her discomfort with the subject, Michael had finally given it up.

Why was it that Sam's comment had reminded her of that conversation with Michael? There really was no connection at all.

"I wasn't at the last homeowners' meeting," Bailey finally said to Sam, "but I suspect that's him." When Sam's face continued to wear a coy grin, Bailey found herself getting impatient. "Now, don't you go getting any ideas. The only reason he's coming here is because of this situation with Clancy. Otherwise, we'd be meeting in the social room."

"All I can say is if I were twenty years younger, I'd jump at the chance to have dinner with him, too."

Bailey refrained from pointing out the fact that even if Sam *were* twenty years younger, she would still have a good fifteen or twenty years on Shep Carroll.

"Believe me, *I'm* not jumping at the chance to have dinner with him," she said instead. Without knowing she was doing so, she then echoed the very thought that Shep had had earlier that day. "This is strictly business."

Sam didn't respond. But she knew better than to believe Bailey.

Bailey's doorbell rang at just after seven. When she looked out the peephole, there was no one there. Slowly, she opened the door and saw why. Shep was bent over the floor, which was strewn with containers of varying size and shape. When he heard the door open, he looked up. His face was beet-red.

"I dropped it," he said.

There were several white cardboard to-go boxes, one of which lay on its side, a semiclear, thick liquid slowly oozing from the top. Shep grabbed it and with his bare hand tried to wipe away the sauce that had leaked onto the floor.

A plastic bag sitting next to the leaking box held several Styrofoam containers, most of which looked to be upright. And a flat, skinny box that obviously contained pizza lay with its top sprung open and a piece of pepperoni pizza six inches away, one long, skinny string of cheese still connecting it to the contents remaining in the box.

All of which Shep was frantically trying to reassemble and clean up while Bailey stood watching, one hand clamped over her mouth, fighting, without success, to stifle the laughter that shook her shoulders and chest.

"It was the pizza box," Shep said. "I put it all on top of the pizza box so that I could ring the bell. And the damn thing . . ."

He looked up again at Bailey, who still had her hand over her mouth, and then he too, began to laugh, which was just enough to throw him off balance. He fell back and ended up sitting on the floor, all pretense of dignity gone. Utterly destroyed.

"I'm so sorry," Bailey finally gasped between chortles. "Don't move. I'll be right back."

Shep was still sitting in the hall surrounded by food, a goofy smile on his face, when she returned with a wet sponge and a roll of paper towels.

Together they got down on their hands and knees and reassembled all of the containers, stacking them neatly in two piles, and wiped the parquet floor clean.

"Pretty smooth, huh?" an embarrassed Shep asked as they were finishing.

Bailey looked up from her position on all fours. A strand of hair dangled in front of her eyes, which were, at that moment, wonderfully alive and joyful. She flashed Shep a smile that went from ear to ear.

"Pretty smooth," she said.

They carried the food into the kitchen, where Shep started opening containers while Bailey went to the cupboard for plates.

"I've never seen so much food in my life," she said when she returned, plates and forks in hand.

"I forgot to ask you what you like." Shep wiped one last bead of perspiration from his brow. "So I thought I'd bring a little of everything. Let's see, there's pizza"—he smiled sheepishly, pointing to the box—"*obviously*. And over here, courtesy of Mad Mary's, we have a couple of Thai dishes—Thai noodles and Pod Thai. And these two containers have Mexican—beef enchiladas in one and chicken fajitas in the other." He looked across the table at Bailey. "How'd I do?"

She smiled, and once again Shep was struck by the way the laughter in her eyes literally lit up her face. "You did great."

They dished up in the kitchen, then, after Bailey had opened the shutters that separated the kitchen from the dining room, so that the phone could be easily reached if it rang, they took their meals into the dining room.

Shep's disaster with the food turned out to be an effective icebreaker, one that completely and thoroughly undermined both Bailey's and Shep's earlier resolve that their meeting would be "strictly business." It also helped lighten the sense of dread Bailey had felt since talking to Clancy that afternoon.

Another factor that contributed to the relaxed atmosphere of the evening was Bailey's ability to put Shep at ease—something he'd rarely experienced with other women. It was Shep's nature to be reserved, but often, with women, he was downright ill at ease, to the point of appearing stiff. *He* knew why that was, knew that it was his way of protecting himself from intimacy with a woman. Not physical intimacy. He'd had his share of that. But, understandably, all the women he dated wanted more than that. Eventually, they all wanted the same thing—to get inside his head, his heart. He understood their feelings. Respected them. And hated, more than any of them ever seemed to realize, to disappoint or hurt them. Shep, too, would have liked the comfort of a close relationship. But he simply could not change the fact that he'd long ago locked certain parts of himself away, making them inaccessible to anyone. And so, as a defense mechanism, over the years he'd developed a demeanor that created an ongoing dilemma for him: his reserve didn't drive women away—in fact, at times he thought that, for some crazy reason, it actually seemed to attract them to him—but also, by keeping his innermost self locked away, well protected by walls it had taken years for him to erect, he didn't allow relationships to develop and flourish either. Tired of going through the inevitable process of beginning a relationship only to have it fail, lately he'd all but given up on dating, concentrating instead on his career and, when he was not working, fishing.

But there was no trace of unease as he sat across from Bailey, talking freely. It all seemed so natural, so right, that at first he didn't even realize what was happening. Until

Bailey asked him a simple question. A playful question, really. But when he answered, when he found himself sharing something with her that he'd never before shared with another human being, he knew. Something was happening. Something quite new to Shep. And quite nice.

They'd begun asking each other get-to-know-you-better questions like: What's your favorite movie? Color? Food? Bailey had just confessed her affinity for wine and chocolate, a combination that brought a grimace of distaste to Shep's face.

"Okay, my turn." She laughed. "Heroes. If I asked you to name just one, who would it be?"

Shep's expression grew solemn, his voice immediately softer.

"My father," he said without hesitation.

Bailey studied him in the fading light. When they'd sat down to dinner, the setting sun had provided more than enough light to eat by, but now it was half gone, disappearing into the mountains behind the lake, and they sat in semidarkness.

"Is he sill alive?"

Shep shook his head. "No, he died right after I got out of college."

"What was he like?"

Shep grew thoughtful. No one had ever asked him that question before. He'd never allowed anyone to get close enough to ask it.

"He was a simple man," he said quietly, deliberately. "Hardworking. Kind. Very family oriented." He broke into a wistful smile. "He loved to fish. He used to tell me I'd never catch anything till I learned to keep my mouth shut. I was a real talker back then. Never shut up. I tried, but I could never do it for very long. He'd be working some nice big old trout, real patiently—he had the patience of a saint—then all of a sudden I'd open my big mouth and let out a holler and that'd be the end of it. That fish would disappear and all his work would go right down the drain."

Bailey listened attentively.

"Did he get angry with you?"

"No. He never got mad. I *told* you"—this time Shep's smile was slow—"he had the patience of a saint."

She waited for him to say more, but he did not, for it was then that it hit him. The significance of the moment. Never had he discussed his father, his childhood, with another soul.

The shrill ring of the phone brought the moment to an abrupt halt. While they'd sat talking, they had all but forgotten the reason they were having dinner together in the first place.

Clancy.

Bailey's face, which had been animated throughout dinner, instantaneously drained of all expression. She jumped up, answering on the second ring. Shep could actually hear her release her breath in a sigh of relief when the voice on the other end turned out to belong to Tony Pappas, not Clancy. He was calling to see how her meeting with Shep that afternoon had gone.

"Well, actually," Bailey reported, "Shep's here right now."

Shep could not hear Pappas's response, but he sensed from Bailey's expression that it had been one of surprise.

"We decided to keep working, and I couldn't leave my place," Bailey tried to explain, somehow managing to sound as though she'd been caught doing something wrong, "so Shep agreed to come here. I'll call you in the morning and tell you all about it. Okay?"

The conversation was short, no more than a minute, but by the time Bailey hung up the evening's magical air was gone. Both Shep and Bailey were experiencing the same thought. They should not be enjoying themselves this much. And at that thought, both suddenly felt awkward. Bailey returned to her seat at the dining room table, but for the first time that night there was silence.

Shep cleared his throat.

"Guess we'd better get these dishes washed and get to

work," he said, the businesslike tone of the afternoon returning to his voice.

But the truth was that neither of them had the heart to start talking business. Or maybe they simply wanted to end the night with their thoughts unsullied by talk of loan payments, and foreclosure, and homeowners' issues. Maybe they wanted to make the magic last just a little while longer.

And so that's just what they did. After rinsing the dishes and loading them into the dishwasher, side by side and in silence, they called it a night and agreed to meet again in the morning, after Bailey had heard from Clancy.

Later, when Bailey finally slid into bed, she lay looking up at the starlit sky. When Michael was still alive, concerned about the danger during an earthquake, he'd forbidden her to place her bed under the skylight. But she'd recently heard a lifelong resident of Coeur d'Alene state that she had never experienced so much as a discernible rumble or tremor, which immediately prompted Bailey to shove her bed directly underneath the oversized skylight—giving her a view that rivaled that from her deck in Seattle. "Sorry, Michael," she'd whispered skyward that first night.

The events of the day whirred through her mind. The meeting with the bank. Clancy's alarming call. Dinner with Shep.

Shep. Her thoughts kept returning there. How had she managed to enjoy the evening so much when the circumstances—the looming foreclosure, her financial straits, and most important of all right now, Clancy's well-being—were so incredibly troublesome?

How was that possible? she asked herself. But then, as quickly as the thought came to her, she pushed it from her mind. For instinctively she knew that she did not really want to know the answer.

For the answer to that question was almost as frightening as the rest of her problems.

* * *

When Shep returned from Bailey's condominium, he was surprised to find a message from Stan Muncie directing him to meet Muncie for an early breakfast the next morning. Apparently, the banker had decided to fly back to Chicago later that morning.

Muncie was already sitting at a window table in the hotel's restaurant when Shep arrived.

"So where were you last night?" he wanted to know.

Shep settled into the booth, opposite Muncie. "Meeting with Bailey Coleman." He didn't offer the fact that the meeting had taken place at her condo. Nor that it had included dinner.

"At night?"

Shep looked him straight in the eye and answered, "Yes. At night. I've got to get back to Portland soon. We need all the time we can get before I leave."

Muncie squinted at him over the steaming coffee cup that he held to his lips. "Don't invest too much of your time, or my money, in this thing."

Shep's face drew into a scowl.

"What is *that* supposed to mean? We just agreed yesterday that I should assume as much control over Edgewater Place as I possibly could."

Clearly that had been their consensus just yesterday, that the only way to maximize the bank's investment—or, worst case, minimize its loss—would be for Shep to take a very active role in the sales and marketing of the remaining units. If that didn't work, they had decided, foreclosure would follow. Just what was Muncie up to now? Shep sensed a hidden agenda in Muncie's admonition not to spend too much time on Edgewater Place, but Muncie was not about to explain.

"It doesn't mean anything. I'm just giving you a hard time," Muncie sneered, "about spending too much time with the Coleman broad. Can't you tell? Lighten up."

While it wouldn't be the least bit out of character for Muncie to be doing just that, Shep's instincts were that he was lying. But there would be nothing gained by pushing

Muncie. He was leaving town, which meant Shep didn't have to spend any more time in his miserable company. At least not this trip.

After breakfast, Shep returned to his room. He picked up the phone to check the voice mail at his apartment in Portland, and when he hung up he noticed that the message light on his phone was blinking. Bailey had called, saying she'd heard from Clancy. She would be waiting for him in the social room.

When he arrived, she was sitting in the same spot she'd been in the day before. She was dressed in jeans, a plain white shirt and a Navajo vest. While the women Shep worked with seemed inclined to overload themselves with jewelry, and to a person sported long, perfectly manicured nails, Shep noticed that Bailey wore absolutely no jewelry. Her nails were short and bare.

"Have you been waiting long?" he asked.

"Just a few minutes."

She looked tired. When Shep inquired about Clancy, she told him her niece had done precisely as Bailey had instructed her—once she'd gotten to school that morning, she'd called. Bailey hadn't been able to get much information out of her, but the little girl had admitted she was unhappy living with her mother and told Bailey she wanted to come back to live with her at Edgewater Place. Bailey had reassured her, then asked to speak to the principal, a Mr. Osborn. She'd explained what was going on, and Mr. Osborn had promised to look into the situation and call Bailey back the next day.

"So you're still very worried," Shep observed.

"Yes. I am."

"If there's anything I can do—"

"Thanks," Bailey cut him off, then smiled. "I'll let you know if there is. Till then, it's probably a good thing I have this to take my mind off Clancy."

For both of them there was an initial awkwardness that stemmed from the intimacy of the night before. Shep worked with attractive women on a daily basis. In addition to female secretaries, receptionists and paralegals, Emerson, Caldwell had a higher percentage of young women attorneys than most other large Northwest law firms. And, of course, he'd had more than a few female clients, many of them high-powered bankers and corporate executives, many of them sophisticated and sure of themselves. And many who had made it perfectly clear they were attracted to Shep. Still, never had Shep been faced with the dilemma now confronting him. Never had he been so aware of the physical presence of a woman with whom he was working. Never during meetings or court proceedings had he had to struggle so to keep his mind from straying, from hungering for more knowledge, more insight into the person seated opposite him.

The more time he spent with Bailey, the more intrigued he grew. The more he wanted to know everything about her. What, besides the sight of a clumsy lawyer mopping their dinner off the floor, made her smile? Why at one moment did she seem so approachable, only to turn reserved and distant the next?

For the first time in his career, the line between business and personal had become blurred. And Shep didn't quite know what to do about it. He sensed that Bailey felt it, too; that she was as confused by it as he.

And so the morning had started with both of them a bit ill at ease due to the wonderfully unbusinesslike evening they had shared. But in what would prove to be a pattern of their emerging relationship, their discomfort didn't last long.

Shep had asked Bailey to bring Michael's financial files on Edgewater Place with her. They spent the better part of the morning poring over the logistics of running the building. With responsibility for forty-seven unsold units, Michael's finances were anything but simple, but Bailey was a fast learner. She also happened to have strong math skills, frequently running an equation through her mind and coming up with the answer simultaneously with Shep, who had the benefit of a calculator.

When Faith Lammerman stuck her head in the door and

asked if she could bring sandwiches back for them, Shep suggested that they go out to eat instead. Without hesitation, Bailey accepted.

"Ever been to Cricket's?" he asked.

Bailey laughed upon seeing the train running around the ceiling. She loved the restaurant's funky atmosphere, the old jalopy suspended over the entry, the weathered street signs adorning the walls. All the things Stan Muncie had hated.

What *Shep* loved was to watch her. One moment she was a poised businesswoman, the next she was taking in her surroundings with the wide-eyed wonder and enthusiasm of a child.

And this woman could eat. At Bailey's suggestion, they started with an appetizer of fried zucchini. For the main course, Bailey ordered the house specialty—a juicy double burger with bacon and cheese, curly fries and a salad—all of which she finished.

"How about dessert?" Shep asked when she'd downed the last bite.

"Will you lose all respect for me?"

"On the contrary, I'd be most impressed," he said with a grin.

Walking back to Edgewater Place after lunch, Bailey found herself uncharacteristically chatty. She told Shep about the first time she'd visited Coeur d'Alene, before construction had even begun on the condominiums. She and Michael had decided to spend Christmas there. The holidays, she'd explained, were always the hardest time for them. It had been Michael's idea to get away.

"It must be beautiful here in the winter," Shep commented.

"That doesn't even begin to describe it," Bailey answered. "It was magical. Just magical. They have this ceremony. We didn't know anything about it; we just happened to arrive that afternoon. But there was this crowd downtown, all around the hotel, so before going in to register we stopped to see what was going on. Suddenly that clock"—she pointed toward a giant clock tower that sits at the mouth of the drive leading to the hotel—"strikes six, and just as the last chime sounds the entire city lights up. It was like Disneyland, only better. All these wonderful white lights, strung everywhere. Thousands of them. No, *millions*."

Shep laughed.

"And big flakes of snow falling, covering everything with this soft blanket."

She paused, thinking of that day. Remembering the look on Michael's face. It had been after that trip that he came up with his idea for Edgewater Place.

"It was just the most amazing sight," she said. "Turns out it's an annual event, kicks off the holiday season, I haven't missed it since."

At Shep's silence, she glanced his way and saw that he'd been watching her. Self-conscious, she looked away.

They walked the rest of the way in silence. It was actually a nice silence, thought Bailey. A comfortable silence. And then, as they neared Edgewater Place, it was shattered by the ear-grating clamor of a jackhammer coming from just around the corner, the backside of the building.

"What the heck is that?" Shep asked.

"They've been doing work around here ever since I came," Bailey answered. "Something to do with the building's foundation."

"I've never heard anything about that," Shep said. "We'd better take a look."

They cut across the grass in the direction of the noise, which had now stopped.

Rounding the corner, they saw a sweat-soaked workman, his back turned to them. He was short and squat. His shoulders and arms, well exposed by a deeply scooped tank top bearing the words ARNIE'S CONCRETE SERVICES, were those of a bodybuilder. As they approached, he fidgeted with the jackhammer, then, in frustration, lifted it into the air as if it were a toy, shaking it angrily. The thick headphones he wore over his ears made him completely oblivious to Bailey and Shep as he yelled. "Turn over, you piece of shit machine."

Shep stepped up and tapped him on the shoulder.

The man turned, then lowered the headphones to his neck.

"Damn thing keeps cutting out on me," he explained, eyeing Bailey.

His gaze shifted back to Shep.

"What's going on?" Shep asked, nodding toward a foot-wide chasm, apparently just created by the muscleman, where the building's wall met the foundation. Sitting several yards away was a cement mixer and an assortment of shovels, buckets and other tools.

"Foundation repair," he answered. "Just got some cracks we're covering. More cosmetic than anything else. This building's riddled with them."

"With cracks?" Shep appeared concerned. "Why would that be?"

"Sounds worse than it is," the man said. "Any building this size is gonna have 'em. The ground shifts a little, you get cracks. It's nothing to be concerned about. But let's just say it makes people nervous to see them. I'm just cleaning a few of them out, covering the rest of them up."

"They were working in the garage when I first got here," Bailey offered to Shep. "They'd just resurfaced it."

"Don't remind me," the man groaned in response. "After I was through with the garage, some yokels walked right across part of it, like they didn't even see the signs telling them to stay off." He took a swipe at his brow with his forearm. " 'Course, if it were me I wouldn't have bothered touching it up. Who gives a shit about a few footprints? But it's not up to me."

"Who do you report to?" Shep asked. "Who gives you orders?"

"Used to be Michael Coleman. Now it's Walcott. Guess he's president of the Homeowners Association or something. I can tell you, I'd much rather be working for Coleman. At least he knew what he was doing."

"What do you mean?"

"He knew construction. And he was a good guy. This Walcott, some of his decisions are downright off the wall. Like being so frantic about me covering up those footprints in the garage. If you ask me, the guy's a head case."

Bailey looked at Shep again, who now appeared far more amused than concerned.

They thanked the man for his information and headed back toward the building's entrance.

"There's a guy who calls it like he sees it," Shep said once they were out of earshot. "The thing I want to know is how did he know we weren't related to Walcott or something?"

"Maybe the fact that Walcott's short, white-haired and ugly as sin, while you're tall, dark and . . ." Bailey hesitated, then finished, "handsome."

Shep stopped and turned to her.

"Thank you," he said simply.

It was true. He was incredibly good-looking. Better looking than Scott Williams had ever been. And the truth was that Bailey *did* find Shep's looks intimidating.

She could feel her chest tightening. Her "You're welcome" came out way too breathy, but she couldn't help it.

The rest of the afternoon was strictly work oriented. By five o'clock they were ready to call it quits. They agreed to strategize more the next time Shep came to town, and finally, before Shep took off for Portland, their talk turned to the upcoming meeting of the board of managers.

"It's scheduled for a week from Monday," Shep told Bailey. "And it's sure to be an important one. I'll fly in for it."

"What makes it so important?" Bailey asked.

"Well, to start with, they'll fill Michael's seat on the board. Needless to say, we want you to be a director. That's critical. We need to be able to make decisions and implement policies that fit with our marketing plans. And I can tell you right now, those plans are frequently at odds with what the rest of the homeowners will want. You may not win many popularity contests around here."

"But if I represent forty-seven units, can't I sway any vote?"

"Yes, when something comes before the association as a whole. But a lot of issues never even go to the general association. The board has a lot of power. They don't run to the homeowners for most matters. In fact, filling Michacl's position on the board doesn't even go to the general association for a vote. When a board member vacates his seat bcfore his term is up, the rest of the directors select his successor. That could end up being someone with an entirely different agenda than you, as an owner of forty-seven units, might have. That's why this meeting is so important."

"Well, then, I hope you *can* be here," Bailey responded eagerly. "Sounds like I may need you."

The truth was, meeting or no meeting, she liked the idca of Shep's coming back as soon as possible. She enjoyed his company. He was unfailingly polite. Attentive. And when he relaxed, when he let down that tiresome suit of legal armor, he could be real, and sweet, and funny.

At times it was so very easy to forget what he was there for. So easy to forget what he did for a living. And for whom he worked.

So much so that when they finally parted and she was climbing the steps to her penthouse unit, Bailey experienced a distinctively let-down feeling.

Maybe it's all this worry about Clancy, she told herself.

Or maybe it was the fact that Shep Carroll was leaving Coeur d'Alene. Heading back to Portland.

Whatever the reason, Bailey had never felt so alone.

CHAPTER 4

BACK IN PORTLAND, SHEP Carroll spent most of the following week in depositions. He was representing a consortium of lenders in their $7 million fraud suit against Pacific Rim Investment Properties, a California developer whose eighteen-month-old shopping mall sat half empty, resulting in Pacific's falling delinquent on loan payments. After the lenders had come to Shep for help, he'd discovered that many of the leases initially presented by Pacific to obtain financing were shams. The lenders sued.

Trial was set for July 1. In the usual last-minute rush to meet discovery cutoffs, both parties had set depositions for the same week. Today Pacific's attorneys were taking the deposition of Shep's client, Tom Pelt, vice president of the lead lender. Shep sat in close proximity to his client, but at the moment his mind was somewhere off in the distance—in Idaho, to be exact. He was grateful that his role today was simply to listen and safeguard his client as best he could, which by the new rules of civil procedure allowed little room for his interference. Grateful that he was not conducting *his* depositions of Pacific officials today. Those were set for later in the week. Maybe by then he'd feel more focused. Maybe by then he'd be able to get Bailey Coleman and Edgewater Place off his mind.

As Pacific's attorneys ran his client through some preliminary questions, Shep allowed himself a moment of self-examination. What had gotten into him? Since he'd first laid eyes on Bailey Coleman in Tony Pappas's office, she'd been on his mind. Last night, on the plane, he'd actually caught himself smiling at thoughts of their evening together—an evening that had been supposed to be all business, but that had felt more like a date. Only thing was, Shep had never had a date that enjoyable.

So why did he feel so troubled? Why not just appreciate the fact that his work had resulted in the rare opportunity to spend time with someone he actually enjoyed?

Perhaps because he knew what lay ahead. Knew that in the very near future his role could switch from one that allowed him to work side by side with Bailey to one in which he would become her worst enemy. He would be the bad guy. The attorney for the bank foreclosing on her brother's project.

Sitting there now, engulfed in yet another ugly legal quagmire, he had to remind himself of why he became an attorney in the first place. Certainly it hadn't been so he could foreclose on people like Bailey Coleman.

No, he became a lawyer for other reasons.

Mostly, it was because of what had happened when he was a teenager. To his father. It was then that Shep vowed he would never allow himself to be victimized so, never again allow those he loved to be helpless. Back then, becoming a lawyer seemed the best way to accomplish that.

He was born in Los Angeles, where his father worked for a paint company and his mother was a stay-at-home mom. When Shep was two and his brother was just four months old, his parents moved them to the little town of Somers, Montana, to get their sons out of the smog and growing craziness that already was L.A.

Life in Somers had been good. The little town of three hundred inhabitants sat nestled on hills overlooking Flathead Lake. Kalispell, a big city to the other inhabitants of Somers, was a mere eight miles away and was always a special outing for the boys when they were young. It was also where they would both attend high school, becoming stars on the Kalispell Braves football team, which would ultimately lead to Shep's scholarship to the University of Oregon.

Their home in Somers was a wood frame two-story that—in the minds of these two young boys anyway—sat on one acre of the nicest land God ever created. It had everything: a big hill with a huge climbing rock on the very top from which Shep and Hank could view Flathead Lake to the south and the Flathead Valley to the north, and from which they could plot their next trick on Lester Blake, the mean-spirited drunk who lived in the run-down house next door; a large flat grassy area for their scrimmages (which became increasingly physical as the years passed); and a big front porch with a swing. To Shep, the swing might have been the most special. It was there that Shep and Hank's mom and dad sat each summer evening, holding hands and watching, with undisguised love and pride, their boys grow.

The reason for Somers's existence was the Burlington Northern tie plant, a big barracks-type building that sat on twenty acres owned by the railroad and surrounded by hill after hill of neatly stacked railroad ties. Shep's dad worked at the plant. After several years as a laborer, he'd become a treatment supervisor, which meant that he oversaw the chemical applications that went into the preparation of the ties. He loved his work and took great pride in it. He worked the night shift, and every evening, five nights a week, he'd take off for the plant on foot, lunch box in hand, waving to Shep and Hank as they stood watching through their upstairs bedroom window.

Shep didn't mind that his dad worked nights, because Somers felt safe. And it meant that Dad could take them fishing during the day. It was only a ten-minute walk to the lake. Shep could still close his eyes and visualize every step of that walk—down two blocks to Main Street, past Sal's, the local bar (which for a small town boasted an impressive number of patrons—never fewer than half a dozen cars out front at any one time), take a right, pass through the rest of town (another seven or eight houses), then another right down the unnamed gravel road. His favorite part was the gravel road, coming around its final bend and suddenly seeing the magnificent Flathead laid out in front of him. While the rest of the walk was nonstop talk for the three of them, they all grew silent when they first saw it. Flathead Lake.

They'd stowed a three-man metal canoe behind some brush along the lake when they'd first discovered their little beach. While the boys would run to pull the canoe to the shoreline and give it a good wiping out, their dad would busy himself with their tackle and poles. Finally they'd climb in and Shep, being the oldest son, had the privilege of pushing it out from shore, running along on the fine sandy bottom until his pants were wet to the knees before jumping into the rear of the canoe. It took great agility and grace, that final jump, to avoid capsizing and throwing them all into the frigid waters. But that had happened only once. Years later, when he was running a play on the football field, leaping over a downed opponent, Shep would sometimes flash on this maneuver and, he believed, jump just a little higher and lighter.

The idyllic quality of their life came to an abrupt end when Shep was sixteen.

There had been rumors that the tie plant would be closing down. In an area where unemployment was already high and good-paying jobs like the ones at the tie plant were few and far between, such talk had a profound effect on morale, which was uniquely capable of being quantified by the increase in business at Sal's tavern. Men in Montana work hard and drink hard. In the good times, Sal's was a fun place to be—still plenty raucous, as is any Montana bar worth its salt, but serious fights were a rarity. In the bad times, Sal's was sometimes a downright dangerous place to be.

Shep's dad didn't frequent Sal's. Not that he wasn't fond of beer or good company. But his family came first. And his job kept him away from them at night enough without his prolonging his absences by parking his behind on a stool at Sal's every night. Besides, as a supervisor at the plant, he felt it more appropriate to avoid throwing back drinks with his employees. There was nothing arrogant or superior in his attitude; he was, in fact, especially well liked and respected by all the men on his night shift. Which is why two of his men showed up at his door one morning at two A.M.

It was a Tuesday. His dad didn't work Tuesdays and Fridays. Shep still remembered being awakened by the insistent pounding and loud voices of the two men.

"There's a problem down at Sal's," he heard them telling his dad. "Stanley Knobbin's gettin' the shit kicked out of him by Lester."

Shep knew that Stanley was on his dad's crew. He'd met him many times on his visits to the plant. Lester was undoubtedly their neighbor, Lester Blake. He was always getting into trouble.

As the men departed, Shep thought he heard one of them tell his father, "Lester's got a gun."

"Did you hear that?" Shep had whispered to a sleepy Hank. "Did he just say Lester's got a gun?"

"Lester's always got a gun," moaned Hank, who, as the wilder of the two boys, had just climbed into the window an hour earlier after a midnight rendezvous with his new girlfriend and was simply too tired to be concerned. "Go back to sleep."

But Shep couldn't sleep.

And that is why he heard it with such clarity. The gun going off. Shep was running down the street, barefoot, ignoring his mother's shouts for him to come back, within seconds.

The scene he saw when he arrived at Sal's would never

leave him. He saw it still each night in his sleep. And all too often when he closed his eyes during the day. In fact, for some reason, the only time he could be certain he would not see it was when he was running. Which was why he could not give up running, bad knees or not. Sometimes running was his only way to escape what had happened.

His dad was conscious, but in shock. His legs would not move. The bullet had severed his spine.

"Get him out of here," were the only words Isaac Carroll could manage to say when he saw his beloved boy push through the crowd of men encircling him.

And they tried to do it. To get Shep out of there. But he was sixteen, and big and strong. And nobody, not even a half dozen husky Montana mountain men, could keep him from his dad.

He fought them like a wildcat, pushed them all aside, and fell to his knees beside his dad. He enveloped him in his arms and held him like that, cradling his head protectively against his chest, until the ambulance arrived. No one dared interfere.

The next day they learned that his dad would never walk again.

Shep's life, and that of his family, would never again be the same. The sad truth was that *Shep* would never be the same again.

The town of Somers and all of the tie plant employees mobilized in support of Isaac Carroll and his family. By the time Isaac was released from Seattle's Harborview Medical Center, the Northwest's premier critical care facility, their house had been renovated by friends and co-workers to accommodate Isaac's new life in a wheelchair. Hefty contributions from Burlington Northern and Sal's, supplemented by numerous car washes, bake sales and other fund-raisers, enabled a group calling themselves Friends of Isaac to purchase a wheelchair-adapted van, which was delivered to the family in Seattle toward the end of their two-month stay there while Isaac was hospitalized.

Lester Blake was convicted of assault and battery and

sent to Deer Lodge to serve his ten-year sentence. No one in Somers would ever hear of him again.

The day they brought Isaac home from the hospital, a beautiful late-summer Montana day, a gathering of no less than two hundred friends—bearing banners, flowers, and enough food to feed half the town—greeted the van's arrival. Shep drove, with his brother in the front seat beside him and his mother seated in back next to Isaac. Though he had been wheeling his dad around Harborview's corridors for weeks, Shep had a little difficulty negotiating the short sidewalk leading to the newly installed ramp to the front door. But sometimes tears will do that.

Shep became his father's watchdog. It was the start of his junior year. Though his parents urged him to go out for football again, he refused. Each day he'd hurry right home from school to be by Isaac's side. If the weather permitted, they took walks.

One day in late autumn, Shep grabbed their fishing gear and, wheeling his dad in his wheelchair, headed down to their old beach. Isaac, who by this time was deeply depressed, almost refused to go, but something in Shep's manner that day told him it was important to his son that he cooperate. He did not want to sit and watch his son fish, which had to be what Shep had in mind. There was no way Isaac could fish from a wheelchair on the shore. It would only intensify the pain he already felt to have now become a spectator of the one pastime he'd truly cherished. But he knew how hard a time Shep was having, and if fishing would give him some pleasure, he was willing to go along.

Just before they got to the bend in the road, Shep stopped.

"Close your eyes," he ordered.

"What?" Isaac said, confused.

"Close your eyes," Shep repeated.

Isaac did as he was told.

They stopped again a few minutes later and Shep said, "Okay."

Isaac opened his eyes. They were on the water's edge.

Directly in front of them was a newly built dock. It extended eighteen feet over the water.

"Let's go fishing," was all that Shep said. Then he wheeled his father out to the end of the dock that he'd spent the previous six weeks building, oftentimes instead of attending school.

They each caught their limit that day, something that rarely happened. And over the next couple of years, their time spent fishing from that dock would be a source of great pleasure to all three of the Carroll men. For they were all men now. Even Hank, who was only fourteen.

During Shep's senior year, his parents were successful in convincing him to play football again. By then, finances were already becoming a concern for the Carrolls. Shep's prowess on the football field offered his only chance of getting a college education. Shep didn't care about college. In fact, he did not plan to go to college—he would not leave his father. But when he saw how important it was to both his parents, he turned up for the first practice. It was soon apparent that sitting out his junior year hadn't diminished his abilities, and he found that the playing field was one place he could release some of his feelings, some of the incredible hurt and anger he'd kept bottled up inside. That fall his name made the headlines in the *Kalispell Times* sports page no fewer than a dozen times, which is exactly the number of games the Braves played and won. During the last game of the season, six college scouts and coaches braved a bitterly cold November night in Montana to watch Shep Carroll carry the ball.

After weighing all the scholarship offers that poured in, Shep went along with his parents' selection of the University of Oregon.

Leaving his father was the hardest thing he'd ever done. It was only Isaac Carroll's absolute insistence that got Shep to actually leave the Flathead Valley for Eugene, Oregon. Shep hated college. Away from his family, almost overcome with worry about them, he withdrew. The once good-natured, easygoing Shep was now sullen and uncommunicative.

He did not date. He did not socialize. His life consisted of class, football and what little sleep he could manage to get. Twice he packed up and went home, only to be ordered back by Isaac Carroll. The second time he drove up to a For Sale sign.

Initially, his father's insurance had covered almost all of his medical expenses, but then his parents starting receiving notices denying coverage for this or that bill. It wasn't long before the bills the insurance company refused to pay had eaten up all the family savings. The Carrolls were forced to sell their only remaining asset—their house. Besides, his parents explained unconvincingly to Shep, Hank would be going off to college the next year, also on a scholarship, and they would be more comfortable in a small apartment in Kalispell.

His dad went downhill after the move. The doctors could explain the deterioration with legitimate medical conditions—poor circulation, a given with his condition, was causing his kidneys to fail—but Shep knew the real explanation. His father, deprived first of his legs and now of his home, no longer wanted to live.

Shep moved back to Kalispell upon graduating with what he considered to be a useless degree in sociology, got an apartment in the same complex as his parents, worked days at a construction job and spent his evenings and days off with his dad. He treasured those last days with his father.

In seven months, Isaac Carroll was dead.

Shep stayed in Kalispell for three more years to be near his mother. The first year he barely had time to grieve, concern for her dominating his every waking moment. But by the second year she was growing stronger. And then, the next year, she met someone she would marry six months later. Shep was happy for her. He felt tremendously relieved. She'd recovered and would go on.

He wasn't so sure he'd ever do the same.

Eventually his mother and her new husband retired and moved to Phoenix. Shep, whose life consisted solely of work and fishing, had managed to save a considerable amount of money, but with both parents gone and his brother now settled in San Diego with a new wife, he felt lost. The Flathead area might still be his home, but every day there only served to remind him of what had once been.

One day he picked up the paper and read about a trial that was taking place in Kalispell. A former worker at the tie plant, one who had lost both legs in an automobile accident, was suing the insurance company through which the plant provided coverage. No longer able to work and having incurred horrendous medical expenses since his accident, the man was suing the insurance carrier to force it to pay his medical bills. The paper quoted him as saying that if he lost, he would have to sell his home to pay the hospital bills.

The next day on a break from work, Shep slipped into the Flathead County Courthouse and observed final arguments. The plantiff's lawyer argued convincingly that in failing to pay bills for which his policy provided coverage the insurance company had defrauded his client. Shep listened and observed with intensity. It had never occurred to the Carrolls to sue the insurance company, to force it to pay the many bills it had denied responsibility for. Perhaps if they had, they would not have lost their home. Maybe then his father would still be alive. Maybe.

It was a jury trial. Shep could not make it back to court the next day to hear the jury deliver its findings, but the first thing he did when he got off work was buy a newspaper. The headlines trumpeted the verdict: INSURANCE COMPANY FORCED TO PAY ALL MEDICAL EXPENSES. LARGE DAMAGE AWARD.

At that very moment, it came to him—what to do with his life. A way to avoid ever having to sit by helplessly again and watch his loved ones be victimized. Perhaps a way to make a difference in others' lives. The next week, he applied to law school at the University of Oregon.

Law school agreed with Shep. It was good for him to get away from Montana. He felt some sense of purpose again, which was something he'd lost when his mother remarried and no longer needed him. He started dating a little, but nothing ever came of it—he could tell the women he went out with found him stiff, even boring. But he didn't much care. There was really nothing he could do about it. He could not open up. There was simply too much pain locked inside. And that's where Shep intended to keep it. Forever.

He graduated cum laude and was offered jobs by some of the better firms in the Northwest. He never gave serious consideration to returning to Montana. Too many painful memories there. Instead, he decided on Emerson, Caldwell in Portland. Oregon was starting to feel like home by that time, and Emerson, Caldwell was the right size and had a good reputation.

As often happens, he was sidetracked from his original plan—which was to do plaintiff's work against insurance companies—when the first case he was called in on at Emerson, Caldwell turned out to be a workout of a distressed property. He worked under a senior partner on the case, but he did so well that the next such client, a local lender with a troubled commercial property, was given to Shep to handle solo. Again he did an exceptional job, and from then on he became known as Emerson, Caldwell's distressed property specialist. Although he'd made his preference to handle plaintiff's work known time and time again, his reputation as a skilled handler of problem projects grew quickly, bringing the firm big-money clients and pretty much sealing his fate.

He wasn't entirely displeased. At first he'd found this type of law challenging. He was establishing quite the name for himself, enough so that lenders from all over the country were turning to him for help.

Over the years, though, his satisfaction had begun to diminish. And any vestige of it vanished altogether at the prospect of foreclosing on Bailey Coleman.

He looked across the table at the hotshot lawyers Pacific had flown in from Beverly Hills for the day's deposition. Two young men, probably in their mid-thirties. Both good-looking, impeccably groomed and dressed. Well-manicured hands. What were they pulling down a year? Two hundred thousand? Three hundred? They both had a certain edge about them, an aggressiveness that seemed to—was most certainly intended to—intimidate Tom Pelt. Shep had seen it many times before, in other lawyers' eyes. He found himself wondering whether they were married, whether they had children. And if they did, whether they had any time to spend with them. Whether they ever thought of taking them fishing.

He was, in effect, sitting in judgment on these two men. An unflattering judgment, at that.

What makes me think I'm any different?

Finally, with no small amount of effort, Shep Carroll pushed such thoughts out of his mind and turned his full attention to the proceedings at hand. Pacific's questions had escalated from basic background information to more pointed questions about early loan negotiations, and Shep could see that Tom Pelt was beginning to squirm.

They did it every time, thought Shep. Whether they had anything to hide or not, they always started squirming when their depositions were taken.

Shep requested a short break. It was time to reassure Tom, to let him calm down a bit.

Time to take care of his client. Bailey Coleman and Edgewater Place would just have to wait for now.

But Shep knew better than to think that he could keep them out of his mind for long.

On Monday night, as Bailey buckled her little niece into her seat belt for the drive back to Coeur d'Alene from the Spokane airport, she finally felt some degree of calm descend upon her.

"How was your flight?" she asked her waiflike niece. Watching her walk off the plane, Bailey thought the little girl looked bone thin. But the smile and the hug Clancy gave Bailey upon seeing her were exuberant.

"Good. The man next to me read me stories," Clancy reported. "He has a little girl, too, but she lives in New York with her mom, so he said he was happy to have me to talk to."

Bailey felt a sense of gratitude to Clancy's seatmate. Clancy needed all the kindness and attention she could get. Bailey had been beside herself with worry and anger ever since Clancy's principal, Mr. Osborn, had called her the day after they'd first spoken. He reported that he'd visited Clancy's home the evening before. Her mother was not home. The house was a nightmare—dirty clothes and dishes everywhere, no food in the refrigerator or the cupboards. When asked, Clancy confessed that the only thing she'd eaten that day had been the free school lunch. In fact, it appeared that was basically all Clancy had eaten for several days. The lock on the front door was broken—when he'd arrived at the house, Mr. Osborn had heard Clancy pushing a chair away from the door to let him in after he'd identified himself. When her mother still had not returned by midnight, Mr. Osborn had called the appropriate child welfare authorities and taken Clancy home with him. She'd spent the previous two nights with the Osborn family while Bailey scrambled to make arrangements to have her flown back to Coeur d'Alene.

Getting Clancy's mother to consent to Clancy's returning to Coeur d'Alene had not been a problem. The only problem had been finding her. Once she finally showed up and realized she stood to have charges filed against her for the neglect of her child, Margo Leon quickly accepted Bailey's invitation to have Clancy live with her.

And so it was that Bailey Coleman and her little niece were reunited.

Bailey knew it would not be easy. But easy no longer mattered. What mattered was making a life with Clancy. A good life. She would try to give Clancy the life Michael had intended to give her.

As they crossed the Washington/Idaho border on Interstate 90 and were greeted by the giant Welcome to Idaho sign, Bailey looked over at her niece and saw a flicker of relief cross her worried little features.

We'll make it, Clancy, she silently promised the little girl as she reached for her hand in the dark.

We have to make it.

On Friday afternoon the Pacific depositions were finally over. It had been more than a week since Shep last saw Bailey Coleman; a long, miserable week spent in close quarters with attorneys, court reporters, nervous witnesses.

An unhappy Shep sat in his office, looking out at the Willamette, absentmindedly massaging his swollen and aching right knee.

Anna, who was just leaving for the day, stood in the doorway.

"Shep?"

He turned and looked at his secretary.

"Really bothering you today, huh?" she asked, nodding toward the knee.

Shep immediately withdrew his hand.

"It's fine," he said. He did not like talking about his aches and pains.

Anna sensed that there was something more than his knee bothering Shep. He did not have the TGIF look on his face that everyone else was wearing. Of course, he never did. But Shep had been even quieter than usual recently. Something was troubling him.

Maybe it was something personal. Of course, if *that* were the case, she'd never find out what was going on. Shep Carroll was tight-lipped about his personal life. Every single female in the firm had at one time or another approached her to try to get the lowdown on Shep, but all Anna could tell them was that he wasn't married, liked to run, like to fish . . . and liked his time alone. With most of them, that had only served to heighten their interest.

Anna would be the first to admit that Shep Carroll was an interesting man. But at the moment he was clearly also a troubled man.

"Anything wrong?" Anna asked.

"Nope, everything's fine," answered Shep. "You taking off now?"

"Yes. We're going up to Seattle for the weekend. Visiting my husband's brother on Vashon. How about you? Any plans?"

"No."

"Not even some fishing?"

"Too much work. Remember I'm flying to Coeur d'Alene Monday morning. I've got that board meeting that night."

Anna looked dubious. Shep always had work to do, but rarely did he let it interfere with his weekend fishing. She took steps closer and leaned into his desk.

"Shep," she started. "I don't mean to be a mother hen, but you've seemed upset the past few days. If there's anything . . ."

Shep smiled tiredly and dismissed her concerns with a nonchalant wave of his hand.

"It's nothing. Really, Anna. Thank you for your concern, but everything is fine. Just fine."

"Then why aren't you going fishing this weekend? Or camping? It's supposed to be a glorious weekend. I can't stand the thought of you working here in this office all weekend long."

Shep laughed. "Okay, maybe I *will* go camping. Tomorrow night, after I finish this affidavit I'm working on. Does that make you feel better? Now, you go ahead and meet your husband. And have a great time. Okay?"

Anna hesitated, then, realizing there was just so much "talking" that Shep would tolerate, she gave his shoulder a little squeeze and left.

When she'd gone, Shep turned back to the Willamette. The afternoon sun was dancing on its waters. The path that ran along it was filling up with people already starting their weekend. A spring weekend of sun and warm weather created an almost carnivallike atmosphere in Portland. Couples walked hand in hand, their sweaters tied around their shoulders or their waists. A group of three runners made their way through the thickening crowd. Rollerbladers whizzed by the slower strollers. The park was alive with dogs.

The sight—one most people would find irresistibly inviting—served only to remind Shep of what was bothering him. And what was bothering him was his life. The thought of sitting in the office and looking out at other people enjoying themselves, enjoying their *lives*, all weekend suddenly seemed unbearable.

Anna was right. He had to get out of there. Out of Portland. Had to go away. At least for the weekend. But where could he go? Where could he go to escape his life, the feelings of emptiness that had recently settled over him? His thoughts of Bailey Coleman.

Bailey Coleman.

His mind stopped there.

Bailey Coleman.

That's it, thought Shep. He had to be in Coeur d'Alene Monday anyway to work with Bailey Coleman, then attend the board meeting. Why not go for the weekend? If he hurried, he could catch a plane and be in Coeur d'Alene that night. He'd take his fly rod, rent a car, and try to find that stream Michael Coleman had told him about. Yep, that's just what he needed—some fresh air, a mountain stream and some soul-enriching fly-fishing. He could definitely handle that.

And the knowledge that he was some five hundred miles closer to Bailey Coleman might prove medicinal, too.

Whenever they made the trip to Coeur d'Alene together, at Stan Muncie's dictum, the two men stayed in a high-priced waterfront hotel. Though the accommodations were luxurious and the views were spectacular, Shep did not want to stay there this time. He did not want to be reminded of past business trips. *This* badly needed trip was strictly for pleasure. This time he would stay where *he* chose, which turned out to be at the no-frills Treetop Inn, about half a mile down the highway from the lake.

First thing Saturday morning, Shep rolled out of bed,

brushed his teeth, took a look in the mirror at his disheveled head of hair and morning stubble, and opting for a ball cap instead of a shower, quickly dressed and hopped into his rented Toyota 4-Runner to head for Fins and Feathers. Every single time he'd visited Coeur d'Alene for the past two years, always accompanied by his stuffy banker client and always dressed in those obligatory suits he hated so, he'd passed the local fishing shop, and every single time he'd eyed the plaid- and denim-clad locals wandering in and out of the shop's door with envy. This morning was a dream come true for Shep Carroll; he pulled up in front of the shop just as the Open sign appeared, promptly at six A.M. Shep was Fins and Feather's first customer of the day.

"Howdy," said the strapping kid behind the counter. He, like Shep, was dressed in faded blue jeans, boots, a T-shirt and a baseball cap. A shock of red curls flowed from under the back of the cap. "How 'bout some coffee?" he offered, nodding toward a big pot perched on the countertop.

"Thanks, don't mind if I do," said Shep, feeling immediately at home.

After pouring himself a steaming cup of the strong, dark brew, he wandered slowly around the shop admiring the clutter of fishing gear, elaborately tied flies, guidebooks and other paraphernalia that filled table after table and hung from hooks and shelves with no sense of order whatsoever. He felt like the proverbial kid in the candy shop. For years he'd frequented the outdoor outfitter–type shops in Portland—all with the latest in equipment and outerwear, all beautifully arranged and displayed—always feeling impressed by the inventory but at the same time slightly disappointed by the upscale, Eddie Bauer–type feeling they conveyed. This was supposed to be about fishing, not fashion. Fins and Feathers looked like one of those shops after a small hand grenade had been thrown into it. Shep loved it.

"This your store?" he asked the burly redhead.

"Nope," the lad answered, removing the cap to rub a tangle of matted hair. "My uncle's. I just run it for him while he sits back and counts the money." His smile revealed a mouthful of even, white teeth.

"Business is good, huh?"

"Yep. Better than ever. Coeur d'Alene's been discovered, didn't you know? Used to be we'd see half a dozen locals on any one day and call it a good one. Now, with all the tourists coming in and out of town, we stay busy all day long."

Something in his tone told Shep his newfound friend had mixed feelings about this development. Shep knew enough about the locals to know that many of them resented the growing population and increasing influx of tourists each summer.

"You grow up around here?" Shep asked.

The kid nodded. "Just down the street. On Fernan Lake. Used to be able to fish twenty feet out from my front door. One year during spring runoff the yard flooded and me and my brother actually caught a trout from our bedroom window." He chuckled at the memory, holding up his hands, palms facing each other, about fifteen inches apart. "A rainbow. About this big."

"Damn!" Shep laughed, shaking his head in wonderment. "A rainbow trout, right out your window!"

The reservations the kid usually had about out-of-towners dissolved instantly when he saw the look of absolute delight on Shep's face upon hearing this story.

"My name's Randy." He smiled, extending his right hand to Shep. "Randy Tawney."

"Shep Carroll," said Shep, whose unusually strong grasp further enhanced Randy's appreciation of his newest customer.

Three cups of coffee, a dozen hand-tied flies, a map and a pair of hip waders later, Shep strode out the door of Fins and Feathers. He'd so impressed Randy Tawney with his easy manner and enthusiasm for the sport that Randy had done something he'd never done before—he'd shared with Shep a well-guarded secret, one known by only a handful of select locals: the location of the hottest fishing hole within a hundred miles.

By seven-thirty A.M. Shep Carroll was headed east along I-90 with a fresh mug of coffee, a tackle box at his side, a good country music station on the radio and a rare look of contentment on his face.

As the freeway pulled away from the shores of Lake Coeur d'Alene and headed for Montana, Shep took one final look across its blue waters and was suddenly struck by the thought that Bailey Coleman might just be looking out at those same waters that very moment. The thought, along with the entire experience of this perfect morning, gave him immense pleasure.

"This must be Heaven," wailed a twangy male voice on the radio.

Yep, thought a contented Shep Carroll. *This must be Heaven.*

CHAPTER 5

When Charlie Eaglequill was first elected tribal leader, he moved the monthly council meetings, which for as long as anyone could remember had taken place on Friday nights, to Saturday mornings. "Clearer heads" had been the explanation he gave all who grumbled. But with time, the complaints had diminished. And now the council members arrived, sometimes still sleepy, but almost universally good-natured and eager to partake of the pastries and camaraderie that awaited them.

As several members settled around the long conference table in the headquarters building for this month's meeting of the Coeur d'Alene Tribal Council, Charlie, eager to get started, ushered those still gathered at the refreshment table to their seats.

The council consisted of six members (four men and two women) and Charlie, its chairman. The youngest member, Georgann Jones, was in her early thirties. The oldest, Floyd Rainwater, was approaching seventy. Floyd was a lifelong friend of Charlie Eaglequill Sr.

They were a diverse group and they took their responsibilities to the tribe seriously. To a person, they also took great pride in their heritage. They were not, however, united in their vision for the tribe's future. And no issue had ever polarized them to the degree that the proposal to bring casino gambling to the reservation had.

But the vote had already been taken. In the end, only Floyd Rainwater voted against the plans to pursue, to whatever extent necessary, casino-style gambling on the reservation, though two others, not surprisingly the next eldest members of the council, had expressed serious concerns. Still, when Jimmy Brown, whose job it was to negotiate a compact with the governor, got up to make his status report, no one was disinterested.

Jimmy, medium in height and sturdy, with pitch-black hair that was short and graying on top but worn longer in the back, flashed his usual gold-capped, toothy smile.

"Not much to report," he said. "But that's not necessarily bad news. There are signs the old guv is weakening. With the president's recent statement and the latest Supreme Court ruling, I'm pretty confident he'll back down from his earlier refusal to negotiate with us." Jimmy lifted a Styrofoam coffee cup to his lips and took a sip. As usual, he was heavily laden with jewelry—the large gold watch he'd bought in L.A. and on each hand, two oversized silver-and-turquoise rings. "Don't hold me to this, but I just don't think it's going to take another lawsuit. And as far as I'm concerned, as long as we keep the other things moving along, like the financing and building plans, his delay in making a decision can only work to our advantage. 'Cause this whole thing—the public interest in this—is just gaining momentum by the day."

Heads nodded. It was true. The California cases had brought the issue to the forefront. The papers were reporting demonstrations. Petitions were circulating throughout the states of Idaho and California.

"If you ask me," Georgann Jones said, "that PBS special on the West touched a nerve in white people. I honestly don't think half of them really knew our history till they watched it. I've talked to people I've known all my life who are suddenly apologizing to me, breaking down in tears. I'm not kidding. That's happened to me at work." Georgann worked at the university library. "Twice now."

"It's suddenly very chic to be pro–Native American," Jeff Zarate offered.

Zarate's comment elicited several sardonic smiles and murmurs of agreement at the irony—from outcasts to chic.

"That may be true," Georgann said, "and this may sound naive, but I truly believe this feeling—of people wanting to make up for the past—is genuine."

"That does sound naive," Zarate responded. "What people want is someplace to gamble without having to fly to Vegas. That's what they want."

When Floyd Rainwater cleared his throat, a sure sign that he had something to say, all conversation ceased. As their elder, Floyd was afforded great respect.

"Every man must be judged separately."

Succinct as ever, that was all Floyd had to say on the matter.

As Jimmy seated himself, Charlie took over again.

"I've got good news about financing. I met with Anthony Walcott of Idaho Fidelity the other day. He was very enthused about our plans and is optimistic about our chances of getting funding for the casino. In fact, he suggested that we look into establishing a golf course as well. Make this whole thing kind of a destination resort. He can put me in contact with a guy from back east who does that type of thing—develops golf courses. Apparently he's working on a similar project with one of the western Washington tribes."

"Why would we want a golf course?" Zarate asked.

Charlie opened the file that had been sitting on the table in front of him.

"Maybe this will help answer your question," he said as he withdrew a newspaper article and passed it to Georgann, who was seated to his left. "This is an article from the

Seattle Times. If you look at the chart, you'll see that the Washington tribes all have something besides casino gambling to offer. They're trying to offer vacation getaways, some way to distinguish each casino from the others. For us, it could be golf."

As the article was passed around the table, each member studied it carefully. A chart showed ten Washington gambling casinos that offered other attractions ranging from marinas and outlet malls to art galleries. There was even a horse track planned at one.

"We don't know anything about golf courses," Ann Holt, seated to Charlie's right, said.

"That's true, but according to Walcott, we don't need to. They would do it all—develop the course, fund it, run it. We would basically be silent partners. Split everything, including the loan payments, fifty-fifty. We'd promote the course with the casino, offer gambling-golfing packages. That kind of thing."

"Sounds too good to be true," said Zarate.

"It's a great idea," Jimmy Brown chimed in. "A classy idea. With several reservation casinos in eastern Washington, we need to do something different. To make it worth their while for people from Spokane to drive over here. Besides, it doesn't sound like there's much to lose. It's certainly worth pursuing, along with everything else."

"That's how I saw it," Charlie said. "There's only one hitch."

"What's that?" asked Zarate.

"Walcott asked me to keep all of this—the plans for the casino and, if we go ahead with it, the golf course—quiet until we've actually negotiated a compact with the state."

"Why would he ask that?"

"I guess he thinks once word gets out we'll have banks approaching *us* to provide funding. In exchange for an agreement to fund both the casino and the golf course, which he's willing to give us now, subject, of course, to our being able to negotiate with the state, he wants us to keep all this quiet."

It was Floyd Rainwater who spoke next.

"Something is not right."

"With all due respect, Floyd, it makes sense to me," Jimmy said. "So long as their rates are competitive, I don't have a problem with keeping this quiet. It would be premature to make an announcement before we get a compact anyway. The more things we have resolved ahead of time, the faster and smoother it's gonna go when we do get the go-ahead. By the way, Charlie, how are the plans coming along?"

"Good. Michael Coleman was a big help to me. We'd already worked a lot of things out. With what I have now, I should be able to get final architectural drawings within a week or two. But rather than incur the expense now, I'm waiting for the green light first." Charlie's tone grew somber. "By the way, I got a thank-you note from his sister for the flowers we sent. And for those of us who helped in the search. I'll pass it around before we leave today."

"Such a tragedy," said Ann Holt.

"Yes." Charlie's eyes reflected his sorrow. "Michael was a good man. A good friend."

At the mention of Michael, the earlier upbeat mood of the meeting had been dampened. Although Charlie was the only council member who had any kind of personal relationship with Michael—both of them belonged to the North Idaho Builders Association—several other members knew him and liked him. As many as half a dozen tribal members had participated in the search of the Moyie.

Eager to proceed with the business at hand, Charlie made a motion to approve the agreement with Idaho Fidelity. Several voices offered seconds. An oral vote was taken, with everyone but Floyd casting an aye.

By this time, everyone had decided that Floyd Rainwater was just not ready to step into the future. Which is why those members who heard his last utterance—another "Something is not right"—before leaving chose to ignore it.

* * *

While Shep Carroll was headed west on I-90 to fish, Bailey's nose was buried deep in a book. A mystery by Earl Emerson, her favorite writer, who just happened to be from Seattle, too. She'd awakened early and immediately, as was happening all too often these days, her thoughts had turned to Shep. To cut them short, she'd reached for the stack of books she kept next to the bed. But not even that strategy was foolproof. Ironically, the title of Emerson's latest work served as another reminder. *The Portland Laugher.* And was it her imagination or did Thomas Black, Emerson's lead character, remind her of Shep? Once she'd made that connection it was hopeless. Disgusted with herself for her inability to keep him off her mind, she put the book back down, got up and went to the kitchen. Maybe she'd make something special for Clancy's breakfast.

While the little girl still slept, she looked through Michael's cupboards for a recipe book. She found what she was looking for in the top drawer, next to the oven. But it was not just any recipe book she found. She recognized its worn, bright red cover instantly. *Betty Crocker's Cookbook.* It had been their mother's. She picked it up gingerly, overcome by the rush of memories the mere sight of the once so familiar book unleashed. She took it to the table and sat, slowly flipping through its pages, many of which were smudged and spattered, more than likely by her own frequent attempts to "help" her mother in the kitchen. On page 75 she found it. The recipe for cinnamon rolls. The one her mother had used for special occasions, like Bailey's birthday.

Bailey was pleased to discover that Michael had all the necessary ingredients, and when Clancy finally awakened to the sweet smell of the baking pastry, Bailey was witness to the wisdom of Betty's cheery introduction to this particular recipe, written so many years before but still, apparently, valid: "Watch early morning moodiness dissolve into a sunny smile." Just as Bailey had done when she was a child, Clancy enthusiastically helped frost the rolls while they were still warm.

Both Bailey and Clancy were delighted when Sam showed up a short while later.

"What a nice surprise!" said Bailey, giving Sam a little hug. "I wish I could offer you a cinnamon roll, but I'm afraid Clancy and I just managed to eat a whole batch all by ourselves."

"Don't worry about the rolls. The kitchen sure smells wonderful, but I've already had my morning muffin."

Was it Bailey's imagination or was Sam more reserved than usual?

Bailey offered Sam a cup of coffee. While Bailey busied herself brewing it, Sam visited with Clancy. Bailey listened as Clancy told Sam about the boys in her class, all of whom Clancy found "gross." Sam chuckled several times, but Bailey could not shake the feeling that something was bothering her friend. When Clancy finished talking, she rushed off to watch her Saturday morning cartoons on TV.

Bailey finally found out what it was that had been distracting Sam.

"Bailey, is it true you're moving back to Seattle?" Sam asked.

"What would make you ask that?"

"I overheard something this morning, and I think you should know about it."

"What?" Bailey, wide-eyed, wanted to know. "What did you hear?"

Sam proceeded to explain the unusual situation she'd found herself in earlier that morning. She'd slept a little later than usual, which meant she'd had to sneak Gator down for his morning walk later than usual. On her way back into the building, with Gator in tow, she'd heard voices approaching the other side of the door and instinctively she'd ducked behind some bushes to keep from being seen with Gator. As she cowered on the ground, hoping that Gator would cooperate by remaining silent, Anthony Walcott and Tom Ryan had emerged and stood talking to each other for several minutes.

"Tom Ryan," interrupted Bailey. "Isn't he on the board?"

"Yes. He's the miserable-looking little man who's always lurking around the lobby. Don't turn your back on that one," Sam warned.

"Go ahead, Sam," urged Bailey. "What did you hear?"

"Well, according to Walcott, you'll be moving back to Seattle soon."

"Why on earth would be say such a thing?"

Intent on finishing her story, Sam ignored the question. "That's not all he said. He said the bank will be starting foreclosure soon."

Bailey was stunned. "How could he know that? Especially since it's not true. I told you about my meeting with the bank and Shep Carroll. There's not a grain of truth to that. But why would Walcott say such a thing? And where is he getting his information?"

Sam shrugged her shoulders. "I have no idea. But I know what I heard. He also told Ryan not to breathe a word about it to anyone."

"It doesn't make any sense. None at all," Bailey muttered.

"Well, then, let's not worry ourselves about it," Sam suggested, looking markedly more cheerful now that Bailey had assured her there was no truth to Walcott's statement that she was moving away.

Throughout the day, Bailey's thoughts returned to what Sam had overheard. Why would Anthony Walcott think there was going to be a foreclosure? Who had given him that misinformation?

And why?

Late that afternoon, Bailey looked at her watch and realized that Clancy had been entertaining herself for hours while Bailey paid the bills that had piled up since Michael's death. She found Clancy parked in front of the TV and suggested they take the new bicycle Bailey had bought her niece earlier in the week out for a ride.

While Bailey ran alongside, Clancy pedaled furiously,

talking the whole while. Bailey enjoyed her nonstop chatter immensely. They took the side roads down to Fernan Lake and were just turning back toward town when Clancy's bike made a loud clunking noise and Clancy exclaimed, "Uh oh!"

The chain had slipped off and now hung loose from the brackets.

"No problem," said Bailey cheerfully. "I can fix it."

But it was a problem. Without any tools, Bailey found she couldn't get the chain back onto the sprockets. Half an hour and two black, greasy hands later, she finally conceded defeat.

"Well," she said, turning to her niece. "Guess we'll just have to walk it back."

"Walk it that far?" asked a horrified Clancy. They were a good three miles from the building, which didn't faze Bailey a bit but seemed quite formidable to Clancy.

"You can do it," Bailey reassured her.

"I don't know," answered Clancy, shaking her head in doubt.

They'd gone about a mile. It was considerably tougher going than even Bailey had anticipated as the chain kept catching on the bike, making it jerk along as Bailey pushed.

"Maybe I'll give it one more try," she finally said, turning it upside-down and dropping to her knees to tackle the chain one more time. Clancy plopped down on the grass next to the road, grateful for the reprieve.

Bailey was lost in her task, oblivious to the sound of a slowing vehicle, when a male voice called out, "Need some help?"

Standing and wiping a strand of hair from her face, which left a streak of black grease across her nose and forehead, she turned. A tall, well-built man was climbing out of the four-wheel-drive vehicle he'd pulled over onto the shoulder. Something about him made Bailey's pulse quicken. His baseball cap hid his face but could not hide the fact that he was ruggedly good-looking.

As he approached Bailey and Clancy, he and Bailey simultaneously caught their breath.

It was Shep Carroll.

"Bailey!" he said awkwardly. "Is there anything I can help you with?"

Bailey felt easily as awkward. "Thank you, but no. We'll be fine. My niece's bike is just giving us a little trouble, but I've almost got it fixed."

Shep didn't know whether to insist on helping or to leave. He could tell Bailey was embarrassed by the situation. But he couldn't leave her there, stranded by the side of the road. Nor did he want to pass up the chance to be with her. He was grateful when Clancy spoke up.

"Aunt Bailey, you've tried to fix it two times now. I don't know if I can walk all the way home from here," she said plaintively.

Shep's formal manner melted with his smile. "So you must be Clancy," he said. "I'm Shep Carroll. It's nice to meet you."

Clancy, suddenly shy, nodded and smiled.

Shep looked at Bailey then. She stood there with grease smeared across her face, clearly not knowing what to do. Finally, she laughed weakly.

"The truth is, I can't fix the damned thing. I think all I've done is make it worse."

Shep examined the bike and tried to get the stubborn chain back in place, but without a wrench, he, too, was unsuccessful. He got up and went to his vehicle to see if there were any tools in the glove compartment, but came back empty-handed.

"Let me give you a ride back to your building. I can put the bike in the back of the truck."

When Bailey hesitated, Clancy piped up. "*Please,* Aunt Bailey."

"That would be very nice of you," Bailey finally answered, her heart racing. Part of her felt like jumping for joy at this turn of events. Shep was back. She'd spent so much time thinking of him since his last trip to Coeur d'Alene, had been so looking forward to seeing him again. But for those very same reasons, another part of her felt like turning the other way and running for dear life, so afraid was she of her own reaction to this man's presence.

And there was another thing. Here she was, the proverbial damsel in distress with Shep coming to her and Clancy's rescue. Not unlike their recent meetings concerning Edgewater Place, in which Bailey's inexperience was so evident, Shep was here again to "fix" things for her. Though she knew he didn't intend for it to, his offer of assistance seemed to her an affront to her own capabilities, her own strengths and resourcefulness. She didn't want Shep or anyone else thinking she needed help.

Still, there was Clancy to think of. The little girl was tired of walking.

What was the big deal? He was just stopping to help with Clancy's bike. Nothing more. Nothing less.

Clancy and Bailey climbed into the 4-Runner while Shep loaded the bike into the back. They'd driven several blocks when Clancy, seated in the backseat next to Shep's tackle box and the leather case for his fly rod, spoke up.

"Were you fishing today?" she asked.

"Yep."

The little girl looked around for evidence of fish.

"Catch anything?"

"Nope."

"How long were you fishing?"

"Oh, I'd say about five hours."

"And you didn't catch *anything*?"

"Clancy, that's enough," Bailey interjected. She snuck a sideways glance at Shep to see whether Clancy had embarrassed him with her undisguised amazement that anyone could spend that much time fishing and come up empty-handed. But Shep wore an amused grin.

"Nope. Not a thing."

They rode the rest of the way in silence. At the front entrance of Edgewater Place, Shep jumped out and opened the door for Bailey and Clancy. Then, as they stood waiting, he lifted the bike from the back of the 4-Runner. With his back to them, Bailey allowed herself the luxury of an appreciative glance at his long, muscled arms. As she thanked him for his help, she did not look into his eyes.

She and Clancy were halfway through the front door of the building when she heard him call out after them.

"How about if I come by tomorrow morning with some tools and fix that?" he said.

Bailey stood silent. Dumb. Not knowing what to say.

Clancy had no such problem. "That'd be great! Wouldn't it, Aunt Bailey?" she answered.

"Sure," said Bailey finally. "That'd be great." She sounded less than enthusiastic.

When she got back to their unit and caught sight of her grease-stained face in the hallway mirror, Bailey could not help but let out a laugh.

"What's so funny?" a cheerful Clancy asked. She was in an especially good mood. She had liked the nice man who stopped to help. And tomorrow he would be back to fix her bike.

"Life," answered Bailey.

Finding a hardware store open on a Saturday night proved to be a challenge for Shep. After driving around with the Yellow Pages opened on the seat beside him and locating three stores that were already closed for the night, he began to feel a slight panic. But then he passed the huge Shopko next to the freeway, pulled in, and soon was relieved to find that the bicycle section included a selection of tool kits.

He made just one more stop, at the grocery store across from Shopko, where he picked up a sandwich and some fruit salad from the deli, then, on impulse, a bottle of wine. Then Shep headed back to his motel room, turned on the television, and waited for the morning to arrive.

* * *

Alice Walcott was the first to roll over and answer the demanding phone.

"Who the hell would call this early on a Sunday morning?" grumbled her husband, just rousing from a deep sleep.

"It's for you," she said, handing him the receiver. "Stan Muncie."

"I should have known it'd be you at this hour. Don't you realize it's only seven o'clock here?" grumbled Walcott into the phone.

"Yeah, well, it's nine here," answered Muncie. "And I've got a tee time in twenty minutes. What have you found out?"

"Nothing yet. I told you, Charlie Eaglequill was supposed to get back to me. They were supposed to be having some kind of a tribal meeting this weekend. My guess is I'll hear something Monday."

"Let's hope so," Muncie said. "I wish you would have let me know about this sooner."

"Hey," Walcott answered testily. Muncie always seemed to be on the attack. "I told you the same day he first came to my office. What's the big fucking hurry all of a sudden?"

Muncie was silent for a moment. "I don't know," he muttered. "I just got done arranging for Shep Carroll to take things over, work with Coleman's sister to try to turn things around. Then you tell me about this Indian thing. Just bad timing, I guess."

"I wouldn't worry about Carroll." Walcott laughed. "He's a lawyer, isn't he? As long as you're paying his bill, he's gonna do whatever the fuck you want him to do."

"Yeah, you're probably right." Muncie laughed then, too. "After all, he *is* a lawyer."

Shep was up by six A.M. He could tell it would be a bad knee day for him, but he'd long since refused to let that stop him. By eleven o'clock he'd already run five miles, read the Sunday sports page and taken a drive along the lake. He'd started toward Edgewater Place about an hour earlier, then decided ten A.M. on a Sunday morning might be too early to arrive at Bailey and Clancy's doorstep. Didn't want to appear too eager.

He arrived at eleven-fifteen with two lattes and a hot chocolate in hand. The espresso craze had reached north Idaho. Starbucks and other espresso shops had long been a dime a dozen in Portland, but Shep had been surprised, and a little disappointed, to see them in Coeur d'Alene.

They settled in the breakfast nook. Shep had been nervous about this visit, but so far he hadn't had to worry much about conversation as Clancy talked a mile a minute.

"Want to see my room?" she asked Shep excitedly after winding down a five-minute explanation on why she liked living in Edgewater Place. Shep had asked the question expecting to hear Clancy say she liked it because of the swimming pool, beautiful views, nice neighbors. It hadn't occurred to him that for a six-year-old, the real fun would be racing the elevators via the stairwell, dropping water balloons down the trash chute, rollerblading in the hallways. He was grateful for the little girl's enthusiastic chatter, as Bailey seemed especially restrained today.

Shep and Clancy disappeared down the hall. When they returned several minutes later, Bailey was standing and staring out the floor-to-ceiling windows that overlooked the lake. Shep had never seen a sight so lovely. Standing there, in a cropped sweater and jeans, with her hair hanging loose over her shoulders, framed by the morning sun dancing off the waters of the lake, she looked downright celestial. Like some kind of angel. He approached her but then couldn't think of a single word to say. Their eyes met briefly before Bailey turned away.

"Well," Shep said, turning back to Clancy, "maybe we better get started on your bike."

"Great," Clancy answered. "I'll go get it. It's in the garage."

"We might as well work on it outside. It's nice out there today," suggested Shep.

He turned to Bailey again.

"Coming?" he asked, trying for nonchalance.

She hesitated a moment, then looked into the kitchen at the morning's dishes stacked next to the sink. Shep was sure she'd use them as an excuse not to join Clancy and him.

"Coming," answered Bailey Coleman.

While Clancy and Bailey went to the garage to get the bike, Shep excused himself to get "his tools" from the car. When they met moments later in the building's parking lot, Shep had a tool kit in hand. A plastic bag peeked out from his back pocket, and while he labored over the bike's sprockets and chain, at one point, unbeknownst to him, the bag fell out of his pocket onto the ground. Bailey picked it up and, seeing that it was empty, walked over to a garbage can to throw it away. Before tossing it, she looked inside one more time and saw a Shopko receipt for $19.99.

Bailey looked at it in disbelief. Shep had actually gone out and bought a tool kit just so that he could fix Clancy's bike. It was one of the sweetest things she'd ever known a man to do.

Perhaps that was why she did it. Asked Shep to come back to dinner that night. It seemed natural enough at the time. They'd had such a nice time together. Clancy was enjoying Shep's company immensely. She simply did not want this day to end yet.

While Bailey and Clancy went to the market to buy pasta and vegetables, Shep went back to his motel.

At seven that night he returned, a bottle of Duckhorn merlot in hand. He'd also bought a decadently rich chocolate cake.

"Wine and chocolate," Bailey observed.

"Your favorites!" Clancy added.

Bailey laughed. *This man is too good to be true.*

The evening had turned cool, but it still held the promise of fast approaching summer nights, so after a vote of three to zero, they all put on sweatshirts and ate their Linguine

Alfredo and Caesar salad outside, on the deck. At eight-thirty, Bailey sent Clancy to bed.

She debated about asking Shep to stay, but did not.

They bid each other good-night at her front door.

"See you tomorrow," Shep said.

Was she imagining it, or did he seem reluctant to leave?

"Yes," Bailey answered, "see you tomorrow."

The next day, which Bailey and Shep spent working together, was a full one. It was time to develop a marketing plan. Shep was in favor of arranging for an on-site realtor, one person devoted exclusively to selling units at Edgewater Place.

Bailey agreed that it was a good idea.

"What about a model unit?" she suggested. "I know Michael had one in the beginning, but that unit was one of the first to sell. The furniture's been in storage in one of the empty units. Why not finish an unsold unit and use it as a model?"

"That makes a lot of sense." Shep could tell that Bailey was enthused about their plans, which pleased him. "Especially if we have someone on-site. Not too many people have the imagination to see beyond drywall and cement. A model might make a big difference. I'll have to get Muncie's approval for the expenditure, but I'm sure that won't be a problem. Why don't you take charge of decorating it?"

After meeting with three different realtors that afternoon and agreeing on the selection of a vivacious southern transplant, who had previous experience in condominium sales, to head the marketing effort, Shep was actually feeling some degree of optimism. Maybe they could do it after all. Save Edgewater Place from foreclosure.

But there was another hurdle ahead. That night's board meeting. Again, Shep warned Bailey not to expect a warm reception. The board would undoubtedly prefer to fill Michael's seat with someone else, he explained, someone whose agenda more closely fit the agenda of the rest of the homeowners.

He promised her that he would be at the meeting with her, be there if she needed him, then wondered whether Bailey derived the same sense of well-being he experienced from that promise.

The way he felt was so new to him, so foreign. It reminded him of his young self. Of Shep Carroll from Somers, Montana. Before his dad's accident. It reminded him of a young boy who still felt safe, still believed that good things can happen.

And it felt good.

Shep was so pressed for time that he didn't return to his hotel room before the meeting. He and Bailey met right up until six P.M., then, when she went home to feed Clancy, he ate a quick dinner out. He therefore never got the urgent message that Stan Muncie had left for him that afternoon.

He would not become aware of it until the next morning.

And then it was too late.

Walcott picked up his phone just as he was leaving for the meeting. It was Muncie.

"Did you talk to Carroll?" Walcott asked immediately.

"No. I tried to reach him all afternoon. Ever since you called about your meeting with Chief Whats-his-name. Never could get a hold of him," Muncie answered. He clearly was not happy. "So as far as he knows, our plan to save Edgewater Place is still in effect. He's sure to push Bailey for that seat on the board tonight. You've got to call that meeting off. Reschedule it."

"It's too late for that. The meeting starts in five minutes." Walcott, too, sounded annoyed. "Listen," he said, "I'll do what I can, and I think I can count on Tom Ryan to go along with me. But even if she somehow manages to keep Michael's seat, we won't have to deal with her for long."

Muncie was silent for a few seconds. "Yeah, I guess you're right. She'll be out of the picture soon. Still, the less involved she becomes, the better. This thing is starting to look so sweet, I just don't want anybody messing with it. You know?"

"Yeah, I do know. It's gonna be sweet, all right."

Before hanging up, Walcott added some final words of reassurance.

"Don't worry too much about Bailey Coleman," he said. "I can handle her."

At seven P.M. sharp, Bailey, accompanied by Shep Carroll, entered the social room on the second floor of Edgewater Place. A good-sized group had already assembled—though this was formally a meeting of the board of managers, such meetings were open to all homeowners, and most chose to attend. Most of those present looked to be in their mid to late fifties or sixties. Males outnumbered females by a considerable proportion. Most were dressed casually.

The noise level was high. Almost a dozen people milled around the table at the front of the room, where five chairs represented the seating arrangement for the board of managers. Bailey's and Shep's arrival caused a sudden, noticeable hush to fall over the group. Several of the board members exchanged concerned looks upon seeing Shep. The bank's presence always gave rise to a certain level of discomfort.

Anthony Walcott approached Bailey and Shep.

"Welcome," he said without enthusiasm. Then, looking at Bailey, he said, "I'm a little surprised to see you out and about so soon. . . ."

Bailey was caught off guard at the reference to Michael's death, the clear inference that it might be inappropriate for her to be there.

Shep jumped right in.

"Certainly you didn't expect Ms. Coleman to miss a meeting of the board of managers," he stated.

Walcott glared at Carroll. Muncie was going to have to get rid of this guy. "As a homeowner, Miss Coleman is more than welcome here," he said stiffly.

With that, he turned abruptly, headed back to the table, and called for the meeting to begin. Most of those gathered in the front of the room headed for the rows of folding chairs, while four men settled around the table. With Shep at her elbow, guiding her, Bailey Coleman also took a seat at the table. Walcott jumped up immediately in protest.

"Now see here!" He scowled, addressing himself more to Carroll than to Bailey. "Just what is she doing up here with the board?"

Shep opened his mouth to respond, but Bailey beat him to it.

"As my brother's heir, I'm assuming his position on the board," she said with a calm that totally belied the knot in her stomach.

Walcott was so flustered that for a moment he remained silent. He looked to another board member, whom Bailey recognized to be Tom Ryan, for support. Ryan simply shook his head and raised his hands in an "I don't know" kind of gesture.

Finally, Walcott found his voice. "Miss Coleman. The board does not wish to be disrespectful to you, especially at this sensitive time, but you have no right to be seated up here. I'm not a lawyer, but your brother's body hasn't even been found. How can you have inherited his place on the board?"

"That's a good point," Shep Carroll said from the first row. "Isn't your attempt to replace Michael Coleman a little premature? What's the hurry?"

Walcott looked flustered. "The hurry is that this board has important business to take care of on an ongoing basis. We can't put the operations of this building on hold because Michael Coleman is missing. The board is within its rights to replace Coleman." He turned back to Bailey. "So we would appreciate it if you would seat yourself with the rest of the homeowners."

Bailey looked to Shep, who signaled to her to stay put.

When Bailey made no move to comply, Walcott looked

around the table for support, but the other men on the board all seemed to be avoiding his eyes.

"Tom?" Again he singled out Ryan.

Ryan looked uncomfortable. "I don't know, Anthony," he answered. "Maybe we should adjourn and speak to the board's attorney about the matter before proceeding."

This suggestion brought murmurs of agreement from the other members.

"May I ask a question?" Bailey Coleman, the cause of all this commotion, spoke up.

Walcott nodded.

"When was my brother's term up?"

Walcott looked only too happy to answer. "In August, at the annual meeting. His two-year term is almost up."

"Please forgive my ignorance, this has all happened so quickly. I'm not familiar with all the rules yet," Bailey continued innocently, "but at the annual meeting, don't all the homeowners get to vote to elect the board members? By then I'll have inherited Michael's forty-seven units. That means I'd have forty-seven votes to cast, wouldn't it?"

Slowly, the men sitting around the table realized the drift of Bailey's questions. Come August, she would be able to vote herself into Michael's scat and there was no way they could stop her.

A man at the end of the table, one who looked considerably more friendly than the rest of them, finally spoke up. "That's right, Miss Coleman. You do have forty-seven votes to exercise. That being the case"—he looked around the table for the others' reactions—"I certainly don't see what's to be gained by contesting Miss Coleman's right to sit on this board. If that's what she wants to do, soon she'll be able to do just that. I don't see any reason to go spending a lot of money on that expensive lawyer of ours just to fight something that's inevitable anyway. Do you?"

The others at the table were speaking quietly among themselves. Bailey looked over at Shep. He gave her a thumbs-up sign. Her gaze then scanned the room. So many unfamiliar faces turned to her. Most were neutral in their expressions. One or two smiled at her faintly. A few looked somewhat hostile.

What on earth was she getting herself into?

The consensus of all the board members except Walcott seemed to be that Bailey should be allowed to assume her brother's seat. Walcott, protesting ferociously, forced a vote on the issue and lost. Three to one. She'd won.

Bailey Coleman was officially a member of the board of managers of Edgewater Place.

Walcott was furious. Immediately after announcing the results of the vote, he called for adjournment despite the protests of several homeowners who counted on these monthly meetings for an evening's entertainment.

"The purpose of this meeting was to select a new board member. We've done that. Meeting adjourned!"

No one on the board seemed inclined to push their president any further, so with that, people started getting up from their chairs and filing out of the room.

"Shortest meeting we've ever had," Bailey heard someone grumble in disappointment.

Shep grabbed Bailey by the elbow and, wanting to spare her any more aggravation, steered her quickly out of the room and into the privacy of the stairwell that exited into the corridor just outside the social room.

"Good job," he said, turning to face her as the door closed behind them.

Bailey leaned back against the cement block wall and beamed. "Thanks. Couldn't have done it without you."

Shep's eyes narrowed with his grin, and Bailey had the sudden urge to reach out and run her fingers along the deep creases that framed either side of his mouth when he smiled. For some time now she had longed to touch him. Right then, in her celebratory mood, the desire to do so was overwhelming.

"Not true," he said. "You were sensational in there. You didn't need me at all."

Bailey wanted to correct him, to tell him that he was wrong. She *did* need him.

They stood like that, smiling at each other, reveling in their evening's success. Then, reluctantly, Shep started to say good-night.

"Why don't you come up to my place?" Bailey suggested. "We could toast our victory. Open that wine you brought with you last night."

"What about Clancy? I don't want to keep her up."

"She's spending the night at Sam's," Bailey answered. "When I couldn't find a sitter for the meeting tonight, Sam offered. Clancy should be in seventh heaven right about now. There's nothing she'd rather do than spend time with Sam and Gator."

"And there's nothing I'd rather do than take you up on that offer."

They took their wine into the living room, where, relaxing on opposite ends of the taupe-and-white-striped canvas couch, they talked quietly. As in their first evening together, it was comfortable, effortless talk about everything—their pasts, his job, Portland, Seattle, Bailey's classes.

Everything except Edgewater Place. For there was no pretense now that their being together was business. At this point, they were a man and a woman thoroughly enjoying each other's company. That was their only reality. Edgewater Place was another reality, one that, right now, they refused to let in.

Right now all that either of them wanted was for this evening to last. To hear the other's voice. And finally, after the bottle of wine had run dry, to feel the other's touch.

They'd fallen into silence. Both were keenly aware of the fact that the distance between them—once the whole length of the long couch—had now shrunk to such a degree that when Bailey leaned forward to place her empty wineglass on the coffee table, her hand brushed Shep's knee.

It was then, at her touch, that Shep lifted his eyes to hers, and in those eyes, those incredible blue eyes, that Bailey saw a longing, a tenderness, that simply drew her, like some irresistible magnetic force, into his arms.

Nothing could have stopped them at that moment. Nothing. No wisdom. No fear. No question of ethics, or logic, or common sense. Nothing.

And when they made love, when they at last held each other and whispered each other's names, when they became one, *nothing* could have been more right.

CHAPTER 6

THE LAST THING SHEP wanted to do the next morning was return Stan Muncie's phone call from the day before. But—as he told himself as he dialed the Chicago number—even Muncie couldn't spoil the mood he was in today. No, it would take more than his disdain for the banker to bring him down this morning.

For what he felt this morning was nothing short of miraculous. He hadn't realized it was possible to feel this good, this happy. This full of anticipation. Could one person, one night, really have had this effect on him? Could the mere fact that the night before he'd made love with Bailey really have changed *everything*—his life, his outlook, the blue of the lake waters dancing in the distance—so dramatically?

Maybe today he'd even like Stan Muncie, he told himself as he waited on hold. It was possible. He could feel it. Yes, even Muncie had his good points.

Or at least, so Shep thought.

"Carroll?" Muncie's voice finally came on the line. "Why

the hell were you so hard to track down yesterday? I needed to talk to you. Where the hell is the Treetop Inn?"

"It's just down the street from the hotel," Shep answered, still cheerful despite Muncie's immediate attempt to put him on the defensive. "Sorry about that. I didn't think to let you know I was staying somewhere else. I'm glad you were able to get hold of Anna and get my number. What's up?"

"There's been a little change of plans," Muncie said. "I'm coming back out there. Tomorrow."

Shep's heart sank with these words. His grasp on the phone tightened as a sense of foreboding suddenly enveloped him.

"What kind of change of plans?"

"I've decided to go ahead with the foreclosure. I've set up a meeting with Pappas for tomorrow afternoon."

"You *what*?"

"You heard me. We're foreclosing on Edgewater Place. It was gonna happen sooner or later, we both knew that."

A rush of conflicting words and images and feelings raced simultaneously through Shep's mind, muddling his thoughts. *Hold on,* he told himself, fighting an anger that, if expressed, could have but one outcome. *Stay calm. Think.*

"You can't do that," was what finally came out of his mouth.

"What the fuck do you mean I can't do that?" Muncie shouted into the phone. "Who do you think you are, telling me what I can and can't do."

"I'm your lawyer," Shep said, a false calm now sounding in his voice. "And we just agreed to work with Bailey Coleman. We gave her our word."

Muncie's laughter cut him short.

"Our *word*." He snorted. "Our word. That's priceless. Fucking priceless. My lawyer's telling me we can't protect our twenty-two million, can't assert the rights our loan documents give us because of our word."

"Whether it's legally binding or not, when I give my word it means something," Shep answered sharply. "And let's not forget the reason we agreed to work with Ms.

Coleman in the first place. Before we even went into that meeting, we'd decided that foreclosure at this time would do nothing but slash the value of those units in half. What about that? Even if integrity has no meaning to you, what about the effect foreclosure will have on selling prices?"

He was trying to reason with Muncie. Trying to stay calm.

"Yeah, well, I've rethought all that. We're foreclosing. That's all there is to it. End of discussion. Either you're on-board on this or you're not. That's your call. I can always find another lawyer. You guys are a dime a dozen and you know it."

Shep knew he was being baited. And while his anger was so intense, so ugly and overpowering, that he wanted nothing more than to take Muncie up on his threat to find a new attorney, something instinctively cautioned him against it.

Still, by the time he'd hung up, after agreeing to meet Muncie in the morning, he'd already made up his mind.

He'd have no part of this foreclosure. There was simply no way that he could do that now.

"Aunt Bailey," Clancy called as she opened the front door at half past eight o'clock.

Bailey sat bolt upright and looked at the clock. She'd overslept! She'd planned on picking Clancy up from Sam's at seven-thirty to get her ready for school, which started at nine.

"I'm in here," she called from her bedroom.

Seconds later, the door flew open and in a whirl Clancy ran through it, jumping onto Bailey's bed to give her a big hug.

"Morning," the little girl said, smiling.

Bailey hugged her back, grinning widely. "Good morning to you. How was your night at Sam's? Did you sleep?"

"Yep," Clancy said, wiggling out of Bailey's arms. "I slept good. With Gator. Sam let him sleep on my bed."

"She *did*? Wow," Bailey responded enthusiastically.

"Yes, I did," a third voice said from the doorway. It belonged to Sam. "Hope you don't mind. Sorry to wake you, kiddo."

Bailey, still half groggy with sleep, looked up at Sam. "*I'm* sorry," she said emphatically. "I'd planned on getting Clancy well before now. Don't know what got into me, sleeping this late."

"Heavens, it's not a problem. We've had so much fun. Clancy's already had breakfast. Pancakes and sausage. All she needs now is to get into her school clothes."

Sam soon departed, leaving Bailey and Clancy sitting on the bed.

"How was your meeting last night?" Clancy asked.

"Good. I'm officially a member of the Edgewater Place Board of Managers," Bailey announced.

"Neat," Clancy responded. Then, "What does that mean?"

Bailey giggled.

"I'm not sure. But it sounds good, doesn't it?" They both giggled. Clancy liked seeing her aunt so happy.

"Now," suggested Bailey, "how about getting dressed for school?"

Obediently, Clancy skipped happily out of the room, leaving Bailey to bask in her feelings of utter contentment. She laid back against the pillow. *Just one minute more,* she told herself. Her eyes closed and suddenly she was back in Shep's arms. She could feel his breath against her neck, her bare breasts. Could hear his sighs, and finally, his anguished, exquisite cry for her.

Maybe if she just stayed there, never again got out of that bed, she could make it last. Forever. The memories from last night. She would have given anything to accomplish just that.

But when she opened her eyes again and saw the hands of the clock fast approaching 8:45 she had no choice. With the wondrous realization that the day might just have the makings of more precious memories in store for her, she got up, eagerly slipped into jeans, and after inspecting the somewhat mismatched clothes Clancy had chosen, decided to respect the little girl's creative sense of style. They hurried down the stairs to the garage where Bailey kept her Jeep Wrangler.

"Can we take the top down?" Clancy pleaded. "Sam said it's gonna be hot today."

"Why not?" Bailey quickly unzipped the tan canvas that constituted a roof and folded it into its pouch in the back of the vehicle. Then, donning a Mariners hat that she kept in the glove box for just such days, she climbed back in and, with Mariah Carey's "Dream Lover" emanating from the speakers, manuevered the little car out of the parking garage and into the morning's already bright light.

"What a day!" Bailey proclaimed as she turned onto the street and, to Clancy's delight, gunned the motor.

Little did she know how prophetic her words would be.

There was only one outlet for Shep's anguish, and even that was woefully inadequate today. He'd already run six miles, all the way down to Fernan Lake and back into town, then down toward North Idaho College. As he jogged along the beach road, he did not even notice the glorious sunshine reflecting off Lake Coeur d'Alene's waters. Was not even aware of the severe pain in his right knee. Did not even see the other runners that morning who nodded in acknowledgment as their paths crossed.

The only awareness he had was that of Stan Muncie's words. He was coming to Idaho to foreclose. Never mind the fact that less than two weeks ago the two of them had decided that foreclosure was a bad option. Never mind the fact that Muncie had not even discussed this decision with his own attorney and was not willing to explain its basis.

Never mind the fact that the woman who had touched Shep's heart in a manner he'd never before known, a manner that, in two short weeks, had changed him forever, was to be the victim of that foreclosure.

The real irony of it all, thought Shep as he ran past a couple of fortyish female power walkers, was that he'd all but given up on ever finding true love. He had come to believe that the woman who could break through the walls he'd long ago constructed around his damaged heart simply did not exist.

And then he'd met Bailey. And in just a matter of the few days they'd spent together a whole new world had opened up to him. A world he'd dared not even dream of before. One that made his previous world, the life he'd created for himself, pale in comparison. For while on the surface it might appear that nothing had really changed much—after all, he was still living in the same apartment in Portland, still working for Emerson, Caldwell—in reality, since meeting Bailey, nothing was the same.

And now he was faced with becoming this woman's antagonist. Her worst enemy.

What typical Shep Carroll luck. What bullshit.

He would not do it, Shep vowed, his long strides becoming more and more lopsided as his knee signaled to him its warning. He could not go back on his word to her. Make a mockery of the time they'd spent together. He could not do a single thing that would hurt her.

Regardless of the price he would pay.

When Shep knocked on Bailey's door it was almost ten o'clock. He'd waited in the social room for half an hour, thinking maybe she was just running a little late. They had, after all, been up until well after three A.M. the night before. But when ten A.M. rolled around and she still did not appear in their designated meeting place, he'd gone looking for her.

There was no response to the first knock. He waited, then tried again.

Finally, the door opened.

It was Bailey who answered. But not the Bailey Shep had come to know. This Bailey had no warmth in her eyes, no ready smile. This Bailey did not even stand aside to invite him in.

"Why are you here?"

Shep was so taken aback by her demeanor that at first he could not find words.

"I have some news. Something I have to tell you," he finally said.

Bailey's mouth turned up in what might have been mistaken for a smile; however, Shep did not make that mistake.

"Let me guess," she said icily. "The bank has decided to foreclose."

Of course. She already knew. Muncie had said he'd already set up a meeting with Pappas.

"Did Pappas call you?"

"Yes. He told me Muncie called him yesterday and told him about the foreclosure."

The emphasis on the word *yesterday* did not escape Shep. It helped explain her near arctic demeanor.

Shep moved toward her. But Bailey immediately took two steps backward. Her message was clear.

"How could you?" she practically hissed at him. And then she said it again, this time her voice smaller. "How could you?"

"Bailey," he said, reaching for her. Again, she shrugged him off. "Please. Let me explain."

"*Explain? Explain?* What do you mean? Explain why you made love to me knowing that this was going to happen? Explain how you can do this, how you can make a living forcing people from their homes? Go ahead. I'd like to hear that. Your explanation for it."

Shep took a deep breath.

"May I come in? *Bailey, please.*"

Bailey stood aside to let him pass. But once the door had closed behind them, she stood her ground, remaining in the foyer.

"I did not know about the foreclosure last night," Shep said emphatically. He was trying to get her to look at him, but she would not. "You have to believe that. I simply would not do that."

Bailey failed to respond.

"And I want you to know something. I've decided not to do it. I won't be part of this foreclosure. I can't. Not after what happened last night." He was trying to tell her how important last night had been to him, how much he cared for her, but it did not seem to matter to Bailey. "Tomorrow when I meet with him, I'm planning to tell Muncie to find another attorney."

Finally Bailey raised her eyes to his. They'd assumed an impassive quality now, one her voice also reflected.

"I wouldn't do that," she said.

"What do you mean?"

"I mean, if you think you have to give up your client because of us, don't do it. Last night was nice, but that's all it was. One night."

Shep was stunned to hear her nonchalance.

"You mean . . ." he asked, letting his words trail off.

"I mean last night should never have happened. I just got carried away. You know. The board meeting. A little too much wine. It didn't mean anything."

Before Shep could say anything else, Bailey was reaching for the door, opening it again.

"Please," she said. "Leave. Now."

He should have stayed, talked to her, convinced her that what they had was too precious to simply throw away. He should have made her take back those words. Surely she hadn't meant them, had she?

But this was all too new for him, this matter of opening his heart to a woman. What was that song—the one about the cowboy who could never say what he was really feeling? That was Shep.

He'd tried, really he had. After all these years, he'd finally tried. And what had happened? It had backfired on him.

And so, with a sadness that was all too reminiscent of another time in his life, a time heavy with loss, Shep Carroll turned and walked away from the woman he loved.

* * *

Bailey leaned against the door she'd just closed in Shep's face and finally allowed the tears she'd been fighting to fall.

Had she done the right thing? Despite what she'd believed after getting Tony Pappas's call, Shep had apparently *not* known about the foreclosure when they were together last night after all. And he'd said he would quit, that he wouldn't be part of it.

Why then had she turned him away, told him that last night meant nothing to her, when, in fact, it now defined her very being? Why had she done it?

You know why, a silent voice answered.

Because if she did not, if she allowed this relationship to go any further, she would never be able to survive when it ended. It would be hard enough now, but if she let herself fall any more deeply in love with this man, it would be next to impossible. And as sure as she was standing there, as sure as the morning's mist over the lake each day gave way to the late morning sun, it would eventually end. Sure, Shep seemed to care for her. He'd truly looked wounded today. That had been the hardest part—seeing the hurt in his eyes. She'd wanted to reach out for him, pull him to her. Soothe him.

But she mustn't forget who Shep really was. He was a man who made a living coldly, calculatedly pursuing the rights of big businesses and banks, steamrolling over anyone who got in their way. She'd heard him on the phone that first day they worked together, casually instructing his secretary to begin a foreclosure on someone's house. Someone's *house*.

He might have developed feelings for Bailey that would prevent him from taking part in this foreclosure, from forcing her and Clancy from their home, but that didn't mean she could trust him. He'd been at this too long, was too good at it. And anyone who could make a living that way, blithely wreaking havoc on people's lives, was fully capable of breaking a heart.

And so, reaching down and turning the lock on the doorknob—the one she'd never before bothered to use—

she finally, sadly, concluded, she *had* done the right thing. As much as it hurt, as much as it would continue to hurt, at least she had the peace of mind of knowing *that*.

She had definitely done the right thing.

Sorting through his muddled thoughts that day had not been easy. Since he would be meeting with Muncie in the morning, it made no sense to return to Portland. And with his work with Bailey suddenly cancelled, Shep was left with an unexpected and rare day off. Rarer still was the introspective mood he found himself in.

It was the perfect day to spend fishing from the weather-beaten, partially submerged dock that enabled the Treetop Inn to add "Lake Access" at the bottom of the long list of amenities its highway sign boasted in an attempt to lure guests.

Shep was pleased to find the dock empty. Right then he was incapable of polite conversation with strangers, even if they might turn out to be die-hard anglers.

For a man well practiced in the exercise of control and sound reasoning, Shep was having a very difficult time putting the events of the past few hours in perspective. When you've become as successful in mastering the ability to walk through life without being hampered by emotion as Shep had, there's really not much that can throw you off. But suddenly there was a chink in that armor of Shep's, one just big enough to have unleashed a flood of unfamiliar, unpleasant emotional tremors. Tremors causing self-examination and doubt.

How could Bailey react as she had? Could last night really have meant so little to her? He'd finally dared to open his heart to someone, finally learned the meaning of *making love* to a woman. And her response was that it should never have happened.

Though a part of him did not believe her, refused to believe her, her words had pierced him.

And on top of that she had been so quick to judge him. She'd all but called him a legal shark. What was it she'd said, that he made a living forcing people from their homes? Those words had also hit their mark. Was she right? Was that what he had become? Hadn't his own motivation once echoed what she'd told him just the night before as they sat sipping wine—that the reason she'd decided to go to law school was to help others. What had happened to *him*? Just who was he helping? Banks. Big businesses. In his attempt to immunize himself from ever being the victim, ever being at the mercy of the system as his father had, what had he done? Was he now everything he'd learned—in those tragic years before his father died—to abhor?

He wanted to go back and explain some things to her. Tell her she had opened his eyes. For the first time in his career, a victim of the legal expertise he'd worked so long and hard to hone had a face. *Bailey*'s face. Clancy's face. He could no longer overlook the fact that in every foreclosure situation there might well be a Bailey or a Clancy on the other end. He wanted to tell her that, thanks to her, it would be next to impossible for him to continue doing this kind of work.

But most important, he wanted to tell her that the only life that now seemed worth living to him was a life with her in it.

Several times that day he'd come close to doing just that, going back to her condominium and demanding that she hear him out. How ironic—this man who'd spent a lifetime hiding his innermost thoughts and feelings from others suddenly having such a need to share them.

But then something had occurred to him. When he'd finally turned his thoughts away from Bailey's painful words, when he'd finally achieved some state of clear-headedness and had started to analyze Muncie's actions—and had decided that they made no sense—he realized that something was very wrong. What could have made Muncie change his mind so abruptly? Suddenly, intuitively, Shep suspected a hidden agenda on Muncie's part. He couldn't quite put his finger on it, but it was there nonetheless. He'd always had an underlying distrust of Muncie, but now alarm bells were clanging in his head, loud and clear.

As Muncie's attorney, Shep needed to know what was *really* going on. What was behind Muncie's recent and abrupt change of heart. It would be irresponsible to quit before he had some answers. Irresponsible to the bank. Irresponsible to Shep's firm. And—*this* was the realization that really hit him—irresponsible to Bailey. For if Muncie were up to something, who would protect Bailey?

Shep realized that if he quit this case Bailey would be at Muncie's mercy. And he would not allow that to happen.

As much as he wanted to share what he was feeling—what he'd decided today and why—with Bailey, he could not. If he was to continue representing the bank, he still had an ethical obligation to his client. One that prevented him from going to Bailey now.

His actions, Shep knew, would be a huge gamble. In continuing to represent the bank after having become involved with Bailey, he could well be putting everything that mattered to him at risk.

But if he walked away now, he had no doubt whatsoever that Bailey and Clancy would be forced to leave Edgewater Place.

And so the choice was not so difficult after all.

Later that afternoon, by the time another motel guest—a heavyset, older fellow whose clothes and fishing gear spoke of authenticity—sauntered down the dock, Shep had finally achieved enough peace of mind about the course he'd set upon to appreciate a distraction from his predicament.

Glancing up at the approaching stranger, he nodded an acknowledgment.

"Mind havin' a little company?" the man asked with an easy smile, exposing a toothpick that jutted out from between his front teeth.

"Not in the least," Shep answered. "You're just in time. They're starting to rise. There's been a mayfly hatch."

From under the felt hat that shaded his eyes, the stranger's grin grew considerably wider.

"No kiddin'?" he said. "I've got just the thing then."

Shep watched as he pulled a fly that closely resembled the

mayflies dotting the surface of the lake out of one of the many pockets on his fishing vest, tied it to the end of his line, then gracefully whipped it back and forth in the air in several near-perfect arcs before landing it precisely where he'd intended, in the midst of the insects on the water's surface.

"Nicely done," Shep commented.

"They don't all look that pretty." His companion laughed. "Maybe this will be my lucky day."

They stood in silence, Shep facing east and his new fishing partner west, until Shep heard a grunt of excitement.

"Got one," his companion cried.

As the man stripped the line in, slowly, surely, working what was certain to be a good-sized fish to within a few feet of the dock, Shep dropped to his knees and, with a net in hand, reached out over the water.

"A nice rainbow," Shep announced, scooping the fish up and out of the water.

"Goddamn! That's sucker's got to be fifteen inches."

"At least." Shep smiled, handing the catch over.

Gingerly, the man worked the fly's hook out of the fish's mouth. Then, his aged, roughened hands holding the fish ever so gently just below the water's surface, he gave Shep a chance to examine him.

"Look at that color," Shep said, shaking his head in awe. There was nothing like it.

The two men continued to stare in admiration for a few more seconds, then the hands opened, and after a moment's hesitation the fish darted off. Free again. No worse for the wear, after having given two human beings a few minutes of incomparable pleasure and satisfaction.

"So long, big fella," Shep's nameless companion said.

Lying in bed later that night, Shep thought back to that moment and wondered if perhaps, like the fleeting pleasure given him by the sight of that magnificent trout, that was all he was meant to have of Bailey as well. One transforming, soul-piercing moment that would stay with him always.

Somehow it was an analogy that brought him little comfort.

* * *

The meeting was already in progress when Bailey finally arrived at Tony Pappas's office the next afternoon at two. She had no way of knowing whether Shep would be there. Yesterday he'd said he would quit this case. Had her harsh words talked him out of doing so? If so, the possibility of sitting in the same room with Shep, after all that had happened, was so distressing that at the last minute she'd thought of calling Tony to say she could not attend. She'd vascillated long enough to make herself late, then, in a burst of defiance, she'd set out on foot for Tony's office. At first her strides were determined. Angry. But as she neared Tony's building, they slowed, and as she climbed the steps to the third floor, she wondered if her legs would give out. By the time she opened the door to the conference room, she was a nervous wreck. Would Shep be there?

One quick glance and she had her answer. Yes, there he was, sitting across from Tony. She instantly regretted having come. But it was too late.

Tony, who stopped mid-sentence at her entrance, stood and gave her a perfunctory smile. She could not bring herself to look at Shep as she lowered herself into the seat Tony pulled out for her. She could barely hear Shep's and Muncie's brief greetings over the thundering of her heart.

Bailey sensed she'd interrupted a heated discussion.

Tony was the first to address her.

"As you know, the purpose of this meeting is for the bank to give formal notice of its intent to foreclose on Edgewater Place. I've attempted to reason with Mr. Muncie and Mr. Carroll, have reminded them of the decision reached in our last meeting, but apparently their word means next to nothing. Mr. Muncie has also informed me that they are now preparing a petition to have Michael declared legally dead, a process that, I'm afraid to say, can be accomplished with a single hearing." Tony's scorn was as evident in his words as in the expression he wore as he glared at Stan Muncie, who seemed to be the focus of his anger.

"Now you wait just a minute," Muncie said. He looked to

Shep, as if he expected him to jump in and defend their good name, but Shep remained silent. "We have every right to take this action and you know it. In fact, it's my duty to protect the bank's interest in Edgewater Place and that's just what I intend to do. There wasn't a snowball's chance in hell that Miss Coleman here could turn this thing around and we all knew it. There's no point in prolonging the inevitable."

Three sets of eyes were focused on Muncie, but no one offered a single word in response—as a result, he just kept rambling on.

"From what Mr. Carroll has told me, the only idea Miss Coleman has been able to come up with so far is spending more money to furnish a model. Well, we've already tried that and it didn't make a damn bit of difference. If that's the only solution she can come up with, there's just no sense in delaying this thing any longer."

Bailey did not see Shep cringe at Muncie's words. She was too busy being humiliated at his having made a mockery of her ideas—ideas for which he had professed enthusiasm—to Muncie. How dare he? How dare he even be there today? It no longer mattered that she had been the one to tell him not to bother extricating himself from Muncie and Edgewater Place.

Her anger did it. Turned the tide. She was not about to accept this, to hand things over to these two.

"But Michael was on the verge of something—" she blurted out, then hesitated as, all eyes on her, she sought to come up with something more. "He was about to come to you with . . . with . . . a *proposal*."

Tony Pappas looked as surprised as anyone by this announcement. But he recovered quickly and nodded knowingly, as if he'd just been waiting for her to make this disclosure.

"What *kind* of proposal?" asked Muncie. When no answer was forthcoming from Bailey, he again looked to his attorney, as if to say, Okay, what now? *Fix* this.

Shep wore a strange expression.

"Just what was this proposal you think Michael was about to make?" he asked.

Bailey maintained her poise. A plan had begun to materialize in her mind. She'd come to the meeting with an awful acceptance of the foreclosure. But just sitting there, knowing that Shep had decided to continue working with the bank, listening to Stan Muncie tell his lies—looking at the wretched little man for whom all of this was little more than a game—she found that she simply could not accept it. She had to put aside her feelings about Shep Carroll and focus on the situation.

Her plan, for now, was simple. She had to buy some time.

"I'm not ready to disclose it to you. Not quite yet," she answered calmly. "It's something Michael had been working on, something that will turn things at Edgewater Place around. But he died before he could finish the proposal. I need the time to do that, to finish it, before I can present it to you."

Finally she allowed her eyes to wash quickly over Shep. It would have been natural at this point for him to speak up, to ask why she hadn't brought this so-called plan of Michael's up when they were working together. But he remained silent.

Everyone present, Tony Pappas included, looked bewildered. This meeting was to have been a mere formality, a means of providing notice of the bank's intent to begin foreclosure.

Tony jumped in.

"It's a reasonable request, gentlemen," he stated. "Just a little time. Time that could save all of us a lot of trouble. And, needless to say, a lot of money."

Muncie looked furious. "We've given you time enough already. We came here to begin foreclosure and that's what we're going to do."

Shep Carroll, seemingly deaf to his client's words, his client's unequivocal wishes, turned to Bailey.

"How *much* time?" he asked.

Bailey looked at him then, directly into those eyes that had so recently feasted on her nakedness.

"Thirty days," she said.

"Impossible!" exploded Muncie.

"Two weeks," countered Shep Carroll calmly, continuing to ignore Muncie, his eyes still locked with Bailey's.

"Two weeks," answered Bailey in acceptance, quickly looking away.

Muncie, muttering under his breath, motioned Shep outside, into the hall. As they had during the last meeting, the two men disappeared for a private conference.

Tony shut the door behind them, then turned to Bailey.

"What the fuck are you talking about?" he asked. In his exasperation he omitted his customary "excuse my language." "What's this about a *proposal*? Michael never told me anything about a proposal."

"That's because there isn't one," answered Bailey softly. "But there *will* be."

Tony only had time to shake his head in dismay as Muncie and Shep reappeared.

"We'll give you exactly two weeks," announced Shep in his attorney voice. "No longer. Two weeks from today we will meet you here and we will listen to your proposal. We're willing to do this as a courtesy, a show of respect for you and your brother. But the very next day, there will be only one way for you to avoid our beginning foreclosure proceedings."

"And what is that?" asked Bailey in her naïveté.

"By paying us the delinquencies on Michael's construction loan."

His next words finally brought a smile to Stan Muncie's face.

"By paying us one point three million dollars."

Everyone in the room knew the likelihood of Bailey's being able to do that.

Out in the building's corridor, Muncie lit into Shep.

"What the hell kind of a job did you do in there?" he growled.

"What do you mean?"

"It's bad enough that you agreed to give her two weeks, but you didn't do one damn thing to defend our position. You made me look like a goddamned fool."

Shep stopped walking and turned to face Muncie. He was almost a full head taller, and that, coupled with a distinctly new attitude toward his client, made him appear downright menacing.

"You did that all by yourself," was all he said.

They parted ways at the lobby of Pappas's building. Unbeknownst to Shep, Muncie had scheduled a rendezvous with Anthony Walcott. Muttering something about needing to make some phone calls, the banker said he was going back to his room and headed off on foot in the direction of the resort, where he was staying. They would meet again that night for dinner, then head back to their respective cities in the morning.

Shep just started walking, aimlessly at first, but before he knew it he was headed in the direction of Edgewater Place. Bailey had practically run out of the conference room when the meeting ended. He knew he should stay away from her. Now that the bank had declared its intention to foreclose, now that the plan no longer involved his working with her, he would be violating professional ethics to go to her condominium. But if he just happened to run into her . . .

As he approached Edgewater Place from the street behind it, he stopped dead in his tracks. Just ahead of him, disappearing into a side door, one that they had never before used on any of their many trips, was Stan Muncie. Following closely behind him was Anthony Walcott.

Shep stood, staring, long after the men disappeared. What was Muncie up to? Why would he be with Walcott? At lunch two weeks earlier, Muncie had professed not to even know Walcott.

He was still frozen to the spot, lost in thought, when a small voice greeted him.

"Hi, Shep!"

It was Clancy. She was helmeted and riding the bike he'd fixed.

"Hi there," Shep said, breaking into a smile for the first time that day. "How's the bike doing?" He stooped to the little girl's eye level.

"Great! Are you coming to see us?"

"No." Her question zapped Shep back into cruel reality. "I was just taking a little walk."

"Can I ride along with you?" Clancy's eyes pleaded with him.

"I'm not sure that's such a good idea," he said. "Your aunt might not like it."

"She went to the store," Clancy reported. "She said I could ride around for half an hour. But I have to be home by three-thirty. Please. Just for a few blocks?"

Shep weighed the situation for a moment. It was hard to say no to her. In fact, there was nothing he wanted more than to escape the adult world that was at that moment tearing him apart and walk alongside a chattering Clancy. And so, promising her he'd escort her back, they took off toward the lake. But Shep's pleasure in the moment was short-lived—they'd only gone a block when a white Jeep pulled up abruptly to the curb.

A furious Bailey Coleman jumped out to confront him.

"Just what are you doing with my niece?" she practically shouted. She looked at Clancy and said sternly, "I told you to stay on the sidewalk in front of the building, where Faith could see you. I want you to go home. Right now."

"But, Aunt Bailey," Clancy tried to explain. "It was my idea. I asked Shep if I could ride along with him."

Bailey, her red-rimmed eyes filled with contempt, seemed not to hear. She turned again on Shep.

"Leave us alone," she said. Her usually lovely face was distorted with anger. "Haven't you done enough already?"

In agreeing to give her more time, Shep had actually just done her a big favor—one that jeopardized his standing with his client. But he refrained from pointing that out.

By this time, Clancy was in tears.

"Please, Aunt Bailey," the child whimpered. "Please don't be mad at him. It was my fault."

"No," Shep Carroll said, correcting Clancy. As he did so, he reached out and wiped a tear from her cheek. "It was my fault."

He looked directly at Bailey and repeated himself—for after all, that was exactly what he was feeling.

"It was all my fault."

Then he turned and walked slowly away. He could hear Clancy sobbing behind him. He turned back just once and saw Bailey kneeling in front of the little girl, hugging her. She was crying, too, telling her niece, "It's okay, honey. I'm sorry I yelled at you. It's okay."

It was all he could do to stay dry-eyed himself.

Shep was in an ugly mood that night when he joined Muncie in the hotel dining room. The sight of Bailey and Clancy holding each other and crying that afternoon had damn near killed him.

The two barely spoke before they ordered. Muncie was still angry about Shep's conduct at the meeting, and Shep's distaste for Muncie made being in his presence hard to take. But Shep wanted some answers.

"Get your phone calls made this afternoon?" he started off casually, testing Muncie to see whether he would admit to his afternoon visit to Edgewater Place.

"Yep," answered Muncie. "Then I took a little nap before dinner."

"I was thinking we might want to stop by Edgewater Place in the morning before we leave for the airport."

"Why would we do that?" Muncie asked.

"Might be a good idea to give the president of the homeowners association a little visit. Explain what's going on. It's important to work with the association during a foreclosure. Can create a lot of hard feelings if they're left out." Shep watched Muncie closely for his reaction. "You know who I mean, don't you? The guy we saw at the Iron Horse last time we were here."

"How would I remember someone I've never even met?" growled Muncie. "I'm not worried about the fucking homeowners association. We're going to foreclose and they don't have a thing to say about it."

You lying son of a bitch, thought Shep as he lapsed back into silence, absorbing this newfound knowledge. His suspicions about Muncie had been confirmed. Muncie was deliberately hiding the fact that he'd visited Edgewater Place that afternoon, denying any familiarity with Anthony Walcott. What was he up to?

"Besides," Muncie went on, "I'm sick and tired of you worrying about everyone else. I'm the only one you need to worry about. You hear that? And if you can't manage that, then maybe it's time somebody else steps in. Somebody who will do what I fucking tell him to do. And stand up for me when I'm being attacked."

Shep was about to blow. There was nothing he wanted more than to step aside. Walk away from this case, this client. Shep would be off the hook, but where would that leave Bailey?

His next words to Muncie were spoken with absolute calm, absolute clarity.

"It is my job to represent you, to pursue your legal rights and remedies. And unless you fire me, I intend to continue doing just that. To the best of my abilities—and let me assure you, I am the best." Locking eyes with Muncie, Shep leaned forward to be sure that every single word hit its mark. "But it is not, and has never been, my job to defend you as a person. I will fight for and defend your legally enforceable rights, but my job ends there. Is that clear?"

Muncie answered by grunting and shoving a forkful of bloody New York steak into his already half-full mouth.

The two men ate the rest of their meal in silence, tipped the waitress generously, and then, without so much as an attempt at civility, gladly parted company.

CHAPTER 7

TWO WEEKS. FOURTEEN DAYS.

Bailey sat hunched over Michael's daily planner. On the floor, beside the chair in which she sat, lay a stack of files a foot high.

Bailey Coleman was a woman with a mission. The first day she'd met with Tony Pappas, he'd told her that Michael had seemed optimistic in the days and weeks before his death. That he'd hinted at a plan to save Edgewater Place. She was now pinning all her hopes on Tony's words. Desperate to forestall foreclosure and to force her mind to focus on something other than Shep Carroll, she had now convinced herself that somewhere in the appointment book, somewhere in those files, lay the answer. Michael's plan. The reason he'd begun to feel hopeful again.

She'd started with his daily planner, hoping that something in it would give her a clue, maybe a note he'd made, an appointment. But after going through his entries for the month of January, she realized she had her work cut out for her. Michael had been a very busy man. He had appointments scheduled for almost every day, sometimes two or three. Problem was, most of the names meant absolutely nothing to Bailey. This was not, she realized, something she could do alone. She needed Tony Pappas's help. He might recognize the names. She reached for the phone and dialed his office.

"Tony's in trial," his receptionist responded to Bailey's request to speak to him. "Will be most of the week."

Bailey left a message for Tony to call her that evening.

Maybe I should be starting with these instead, thought Bailey, eyeing the dozen or so files at her feet, the ones she'd been avoiding. She was just reaching for the one on top when her doorbell rang.

She opened the door to see Sam Cummings's smiling face.

"Good morning, kiddo," Sam greeted her. "Hope I'm not intruding. When I got home from the market, I found the note you left on my door this morning and just thought I'd drop by to say hello." Then, seeing the strain on Bailey's face, she asked, "Is everything all right?"

Bailey ushered Sam in. She was happy for the interruption.

When Bailey explained her task and her frustration at not being able to identify any of the entries in Michael's planner, Sam jumped in enthusiastically.

"Maybe I can help."

Bailey smiled. It was sweet of Sam to want to help, but Bailey had a big job ahead of her and couldn't imagine Sam's doing anything but slowing her down. Still, she didn't have the heart to say no. Instead, she reached for the black leather book and motioned Sam to sit beside her on the sofa.

Half an hour later, two pages of Bailey's notepad were chock-full of Bailey's frantic scribbling. To Bailey's astonishment, Sam Cummings knew everybody in the town of Coeur d'Alene. No, make that North Idaho. She and her husband had moved to Coeur d'Alene nearly thirty years before. And although the town had grown since then from less than ten thousand to the more than twenty-five thousand who currently made it their home, Sam seemed to have a line on all twenty-five thousand of them. Bailey could hardly write fast enough to keep up with Sam's commentary.

Sam Cummings was not only able to identify ninety percent of the names logged in Michael's planner, she was a veritable fountain of information on each of them.

"March twentieth," read Sam as she turned yet another page. "Let's see, on March twentieth your brother had a meeting with Charlie Eaglequill. He's the president of the North Idaho Builders' Association. You may have met him right after . . . during the search. He and several other people from the reservation—it's just south of here, about half an hour down the west side of the lake—helped. Such a nice man. An interesting man. He's tribal chief of the Coeur d'Alene."

Bailey laughed and threw her arm around Sam. "You're something, you know that?" she said. "How on earth do you know all these people?"

"Oh, I don't know all of them personally. A lot of them, but not all. Especially the newcomers. Some of them I just know from reading the local paper. Your brother moved in pretty prestigious circles here. A lot of these names are people I've read about for years, people active in local politics, bankers, successful builders. People like that. A lot of the other long-term residents resent all the people who've moved here over the years, especially the Californians, but I think the more the merrier. Makes life interesting. Used to be I picked up the paper and all there was to read about was the local bake off or someone's prizewinning cow. I'm not kidding. Back in my early days here, they considered that news. Today, there are *exciting* things going on—educational reform, environmental issues. Those horrible Aryans. By the way, did you see that article in last night's paper? They arrested three men for stealing five hundred pounds of explosives from a mine in Kellogg. Turns out they're part of one of those militia groups. Who knows what they were planning to do with those explosives? Did you see where almost one hundred pounds are still missing?" Suddenly Sam looked embarrassed. "Oh my! I'm wandering, aren't I? I have a tendency to do that."

"Please, don't stop," said Bailey with a laugh. She was thoroughly charmed by this woman. And Sam had given her a lot of valuable information. The notes Bailey had taken would be enough to keep her busy for days.

With that realization, and the realization that Sam was starting to look a little weary, Bailey made them both a cup of herbal tea. They chatted for another fifteen minutes, then Sam announced that Gator would be looking for his dinner. Before she disappeared into the hallway, she gave Bailey a jaunty little rodeo queen–type wave and promised to return the next morning to take up where they'd left off.

Stan Muncie hated being put on hold. It was his practice to hang up if no one came back on the line within thirty seconds. But this call was important. They'd been playing telephone tag for two days now.

It was a good two minutes before he heard a voice on the other end of the line.

"Walcott here."

"It's me," huffed Muncie.

"Finally! I thought you were meeting with Coleman's sister and her attorney the day before yesterday."

"We did meet with them."

"Then why haven't I heard anything about the foreclosure?"

In a town like Coeur d'Alene and in a building the size of Edgewater Place, word traveled fast. Especially a word like *foreclosure*. Walcott had been holding his breath in gleeful anticipation of hearing that the bank had lowered the boom on Bailey Coleman at the meeting between Coleman and Muncie that had taken place two days earlier in Tony Pappas's office. But so far he'd heard absolutely nothing. The banking community wasn't aware of it yet, nor, apparently, were the homeowners at Edgewater Place—for the last two days Walcott had been hanging around the lobby a little longer than usual after the mail was delivered (mail delivery brought just about everyone in the building together on a daily basis and was always a good source of gossip), just to get wind of the news. But each day he'd been sorely disappointed. If a foreclosure was about to take place, no one seemed to know about it. Eager for a firsthand account of the meeting between Muncie and Bailey Coleman, he'd left several messages for Muncie. The lack of news had been frustrating him.

"You haven't heard anything because we agreed to *delay* foreclosure," announced Muncie dryly.

"You *what*?" Walcott could hardly believe his ears. "What the hell do you mean, you agreed to delay foreclosure? What about our plan—that was the whole point of your coming to town again. To start the foreclosure. What the hell happened?"

"Bailey Coleman. *That's* what happened," a clearly chagrined Muncie answered. "According to her, when Michael Coleman died he was on the verge of making some kind of a proposal that would rescue his beloved project. His sister asked for a month to present Coleman's proposal to us."

"And you *gave* it to her?"

"We gave her two weeks."

"May I ask why you did that?"

"I couldn't avoid it. I had Mr. Goody Two-Shoes with me, telling me what a reasonable request it is. You know how he is. Always encouraging us to work with Coleman, telling us in the long run it's to both parties' benefit. I wanted to tell him to go fuck himself and just start the damn foreclosure, but I didn't dare. I have the feeling he's beginning to wonder about how I've been handling things and I didn't want to give him reason to think I had any ulterior motives. *That's* why."

"What do you mean, he's starting to wonder?"

"I don't know. It's nothing I can put my finger on. It's just a feeling I get whenever we discuss our options."

"Then get rid of the son of a bitch."

"I'd *love* to. But if I fired him it would just raise a red flag with my board of directors. They think he's doing a great job. I have no reason to get rid of him—at least none that I can give *them*."

"What's this about a proposal?" Walcott asked.

"That's what *I* want to know," answered Muncie. "Michael's sister says that before he died, Michael was working on a proposal that would save Edgewater Place. I had hoped you'd be able to tell me something about it."

"I don't know what the fuck she's talking about."

"Well, you better find out. Do some digging. She has two weeks to come up with something. Frankly, I think she's blowing smoke. But if she does have something, or if somehow she's learned something, I want to know about it right away. Do you hear?"

"I doubt she knows anything, but I can ask around a little. Nothing stays a secret in this town. If Coleman was on to something, *someone* knows. And I'll find out about it."

"And if I'm right, and his sister is lying through her teeth—which, by the way, would make her a hell of a lot more clever than I thought she'd be—you won't find anything," predicted Muncie.

"Then what?" asked Walcott.

"Then, two weeks from now, we begin foreclosure."

"And we're back on track?"

"Yep, we're back on track," answered Muncie with a note of undisguised satisfaction.

The morning was not unlike every other morning for Charlie Eaglequill. After feeding the dogs and the two ponies he kept for his boys, he sat down with a cup of coffee to visit with Susan, his wife of twenty years, before leaving for work.

"Did you check the messages I saved for you last night?" Susan asked as she settled into the chair next to Charlie.

"Not yet," Charlie said. "Didn't get home from the builders meeting last night till ten-thirty. It was too late to return calls. Anything important?"

He knew that Susan always listened to his messages before saving them for his review.

"Not really," she answered as she reached over to dab a crumb of her home-baked bread off Charlie's chin. Then she remembered. One message had stayed with her. "There *was* one message from a woman. She seemed anxious to talk to you."

Pure reflex caused Susan to study her husband's reaction—Charlie Eaglequill had never given his wife reason to worry, but it *was* unusual to hear a woman's voice on the answering machine. And there had been an urgency in her voice.

Her focus on him was not lost on Charlie, who laughed.

"Jealous?" he teased.

"Of course not," Susan scoffed.

Still, Charlie knew it would be in his best interest to return *this* phone call in his wife's presence. Four years earlier, Charlie's brother, Tom, had been shot in the stomach by his wife when he came home one night with lipstick on his shirt. Tom had survived, but barely. Remarkably, he and his wife were still together, and Tom now walked the straight and narrow. Susan had never been anything but trusting of him, but Charlie saw no reason to toy with the emotions of a devoted wife.

He got up and went to the phone to play back his messages, then jotted down the number left yesterday afternoon by a Bailey Coleman. He looked at his watch. It was only eight-thirty A.M.

"It's pretty early to be calling anyone," he said. But one look at Susan and he said, "But I'll give her a try."

The phone rang just once before Bailey came on the line.

A short time later, Samantha Cummings answered her door to find an unusually animated Bailey standing outside, dressed in running gear.

"Hello there! What do I owe this nice surprise to?"

"I have good news," Bailey blurted out excitedly as Sam ushered her inside. "Or at least I think I do. I just got off the phone with Charlie Eaglequill. Remember, he was one of the appointments in Michael's book? Well, when I struck out with everything else, I decided to go back even farther in his appointment book. I started calling people he'd scheduled appointments with all the way back in March. I'd left a message with this guy—he's the Native American you told me about, the builder, isn't he?—and this morning he called me back. I think he knows something, Sam. I think he may know what Michael's plan was. We're meeting for lunch today."

"That's wonderful. Charlie's a good man. You'll like him."

"I could tell. He was a little bit hesitant. But when I explained how important it was, he said he'd meet me."

"Did he tell you he knew what Michael was up to?"

"Not exactly, but I'm sure he knows something," answered Bailey. "I can just tell he does."

Upon hearing just how scanty Bailey's conversation with Charlie had actually been, Sam's enthusiasm dimmed. What if Bailey's excitement were nothing more than wishful thinking? It was a worrisome thought. She didn't want to see Bailey disappointed again.

They talked for a while longer, then Bailey excused herself to get a run in before lunch.

"Be sure to let me know what you find out," Sam called after Bailey. She wanted to tell Bailey not to get her hopes up, but decided there was little point.

And maybe Bailey was right. Maybe, just maybe, Charlie Eaglequill did know something.

Maybe, thought Sam as she watched her young friend disappear into the stairwell. But somehow she doubted it.

Susan Eaglequill knew her husband. Knew that the look in his eyes as he hung up the phone after talking with Bailey Coleman meant he was troubled.

"Who is she?" Susan asked.

"Michael Coleman's sister," said Charlie.

"Oh," said Susan, the significance settling in.

"She wondered if I could tell her what Michael was involved in that might have given him reason to believe he could turn things around at Edgewater Place. She found my name in his appointment book from that meeting I had with him back in March."

Susan looked at her husband and waited for him to go on.

"She wanted to meet with me. She says that if she doesn't come up with Michael's plan, the bank will foreclose. She sounded pretty desperate." He paused. "We're having lunch today," he said, more than a little disturbed by the prospect.

They both sat silently for several minutes, then Charlie got up to go to work.

"You're not going to tell her anything, are you?" she asked as he reached for the door.

Charlie looked at her then, that same forthright look—a look that could hide absolutely nothing—that she'd loved since they were children.

"I can't," he stated flatly. Then he left.

At the end of her run, Bailey decided to detour and go by Clancy's school. If she remembered correctly, Clancy had recess about now. Though she'd just said good-bye to her niece a few hours earlier, the prospect of seeing her again, especially the prospect of paying her a surprise visit, appealed immensely to Bailey.

The call from Charlie Eaglequill had lifted her spirits. In just two hours she was meeting him for lunch, and she knew, she just knew, that he would be able to tell her what Michael had been up to before he died. She had the feeling this was just the break she needed. The one that would enable her and Clancy to stay at Edgewater Place.

As she approached the elementary school, Bailey could hear the children playing outside well before she actually saw them. She picked up her pace, and by the time she arrived, her lungs burned. As she stood behind the chain-link fence and scanned the playground for her niece, she felt a wave of nostalgia. A sense of peace. The children looked so happy. So safe. It took her back to her own childhood.

Her own playgrounds. Standing there observing, she felt a comfort in knowing that some things still seemed as they should be.

Clancy spotted her first.

"Aunt Bailey!" she shouted, running to the fence and lacing her fingers through the chain links to make contact with Bailey's similarly laced fingers. "What are you doing here?"

This surprise visit clearly delighted her.

"I thought it would be fun to come by and say hi on my run," answered Bailey.

"Want to see me do a pullover on the bars?" Clancy asked excitedly.

"What's a pullover?" asked Bailey.

"Watch!" answered Clancy, taking off for the jungle gym.

Bailey watched as Clancy jumped up to grasp the five-foot-high metal bar, hung there for a moment, then kicked out her legs and, with the momentum she gained, flung her body backward, feet first, over the bar. Before her feet hit the ground again, her eyes were already searching for Bailey's approval.

Bailey cheered and clapped from behind the fence just as the bell signaling the end of recess sounded.

All the children immediately fell into neatly ordered lines, but Clancy broke rank and raced over to Bailey, smiling ear to ear, puckered her lips, and they kissed through the fence.

"Thanks for coming," she said sweetly. She raced to catch up with her class and with one last wave disappeared into the building.

You're welcome, mouthed Bailey. Then, once Clancy was out of sight, she reached up and rubbed away the dampness from the corner of each eye.

When Sam went to get her mail in the early afternoon, she ran into them in the lobby. Tom Ryan and Anthony Walcott. As soon as she came around the corner from the elevator, they stopped talking to each other and greeted her civilly. She knew right away that they didn't want her to hear their conversation, so just to goad them, she dawdled a bit, standing there going through her mail instead of taking it back to her condo first as she usually did. She always took advantage of any opportunity to get under Walcott's skin.

Finally, she wished them a good day and retraced her steps toward the elevator. As she stood waiting for it, they remained silent, and she realized they were waiting for her to get on the elevator before continuing their conversation. When the bell signaling the elevator's arrival sounded and the doors opened, Sam stepped inside, pressed the button for the seventh floor, then quietly stepped back into the vestibule outside the elevator, just off the lobby. The elevator took off without her.

Only then did Walcott and Ryan resume their conversation. Actually, it soon became apparent to Sam, whose sense of hearing at seventy-five was every bit as sharp as it had been when she was twenty, that the conversation was more argument than discussion.

"I don't see why you're so set against hiring that engineer to inspect the building," Ryan was saying.

Though he spoke in somewhat of a hush, Walcott's voice still managed to have an intimidating quality to it. "I've told you, we're not hiring an engineer. It's a waste of the homeowners' money. There's nothing wrong with this building. Nothing."

"I hope that's true," Ryan said. "But what's wrong with finding out for sure? According to our insurance agent, State Farm may reduce our premium if the report comes back clean. It could actually save us some money."

"All an inspection is going to do is cost a small fortune and create mass hysteria. Chances are our premiums would go *up*. I know about these things. No respectable engineer is going to walk through here and not come up with a laundry list of problems. Problems that he can fix for us—for a price, of course. You know how neurotic the people in this building are. Every defect an engineer finds—and with his fancy language, even a minor defect will be made to sound ominous—will send the homeowners into a near cardiac. I know. I've dealt with these things before. This building was built by the best, with the best." Sam could hardly believe her ears, Walcott heaping such lavish praise on Michael Coleman. "There's nothing wrong with it and no reason to create problems where none exist."

Ryan was silent for a moment.

"But the board hasn't even voted on the matter. In light of that anonymous note we received suggesting an inspection, it seems that at the very least we should put it to a vote," Ryan said.

"There will be no vote," said Walcott. "It will be a sad day when this board starts taking actions based on anonymous notes."

Sensing that the conversation was winding down and deciding that the better part of wisdom would be to get out of there before she was seen, Sam did not wait to hear more. She tiptoed to the stairwell door and slipped through it. Not having her usual armful, Gator, to contend with, she climbed the seven flights of stairs with relative ease. Still, she paused to catch her breath at each landing.

Approaching her unit, she noticed a note tacked to the front door.

"Please call," was all it said. It was signed "Bailey."

Oh dear, Sam thought as she hurried on up to the eleventh floor. *I hope this isn't bad news.*

Actually, though she was genuinely concerned for Bailey, Sam was in quite a cheery mood. The truth was, she loved a little excitement, and she had the feeling there would be plenty of it in the near future. One of the things that had attracted her to Edgewater Place in the first place had been the chance to be part of the mini-community that condominium living inevitably spawned. There was always someone coming, someone going, someone getting married or having a baby, while someone else was having an affair and getting divorced—and the daily encounters with neighbors that took place in the lobby, elevators, or garage ensured a general awareness of it all. It was almost like living on the set of a soap opera. But this was real. And Sam sensed that what was developing now—what with Bailey's mission to save her brother's interest in Edgewater Place and the intriguing conversation she'd just overheard—promised to exceed even her wildest expectations. With any luck, she might end up right in the middle of it.

When she arrived at Bailey's unit, the door was half open. Sam walked in to find Bailey on her hands and knees, furiously scrubbing a kitchen floor that already looked spotless.

"That bad, was it?" asked Sam.

Bailey looked up. Her face was mottled. It looked as if she'd been crying.

She was slow to answer.

"He knows something, Sam. But I can't get it out of him." She wiped hair from her eyes with a suds-covered hand and stood to face her visitor.

"It's not like Charlie to be anything less than forthright," Sam said, clearly puzzled. She trusted Bailey's assessment that Charlie Eaglequill was holding something back, but it was not consistent with the Charlie she knew.

"He seemed like a good guy," Bailey said. "And I got the feeling he really liked Michael and felt really badly about what's happening with Edgewater Place. I think he wanted to help."

"What did he tell you?"

"He just said that the reason he and Michael met back in March was that they were discussing a project they were going to work on together."

"Did you try to get more information out of him than that?" Sam asked.

"Yes. I told him how much was at stake. He seemed genuinely concerned. But all I could get out of him was that he and Michael were talking about this other project. Nothing more. Nothing that will help. Nothing at all."

On her way up the stairs, Sam had debated briefly about telling Bailey about the conversation she'd overheard between Tom Ryan and Anthony Walcott, but seeing how upset Bailey already was, she didn't have the heart to add to her worries. Instead she said, "Listen, kiddo, we still have some time, don't we? We can't give up yet."

Bailey's shoulders slumped. She looked on the verge of tears.

"What *is* it?" Sam wanted to know. There was something else bothering Bailey. Something in addition to her meeting that day. "Why are you so upset?"

Fighting to maintain control, Bailey answered, "I really don't want to talk about it. I'm sorry. It's just been kind of a bad week. Ya know?"

Charlie Eaglequill's call had not only given her hope about saving Edgewater Place, it had enabled her to get her mind off Shep for a short while. Somehow her disappointment at how things had gone at lunch with Charlie weakened *all* her defenses, including her ability to be stoic about Shep. She'd come home from the restaurant overwhelmed by a sense of hopelessness. But, of course, the last thing she wanted to do was tell Sam about Shep. Tell her that she'd gone to bed with him. That she'd fallen in love with him.

No. She really didn't want to get into that right now.

"So what's up?" Stan Muncie wanted to know. Walcott rarely called him at home, especially at this hour.

"You won't believe this one."

"Try me."

"Guess who I saw having lunch together at the Iron Horse today."

"You just woke me up from a sound sleep and you want me to play fucking guessing games? Are you nuts?"

"Okay," Walcott said. "I'll tell you. Charlie Eaglequill. And Bailey Coleman. That's who."

There was a long silence before Muncie responded.

"What the hell is she up to?" Then, after another pause, "Do you suppose she knows?"

"No, I don't think so. I made a point of running into her tonight. She always helps that old lady down the hall from me sneak her mutt out at night, thinks I don't know about it. Anyway, I wanted to see how she would react to me after her lunch with Eaglequill. Figured I could tell if she knew anything."

"And?"

"And nothing. She's either a damn good actress or he didn't tell her anything.

"But that doesn't mean he won't tell her some other time. Or that someone else won't. There has to be a reason she was with him," Walcott said, "and knowing her, she won't give up till she gets what she's after. If she keeps nosing around, she's eventually going to come up with something."

"That's what I'm thinking."

Both men grew silent.

"I've had it with the meddling bitch. If I have to come out there myself to handle this, I will."

"That won't be necessary," said Walcott. "I have an idea. If it works, Bailey Coleman won't be a problem anymore."

CHAPTER 8

WHEN HE GOT BACK to Portland, Shep placed a call to an old friend of his from law school. Johnny Barletto had flunked out in their second year, but as roommates for the first year, they'd forged a bond that survived Johnny's subsequent move to Southern California, where he became a private investigator. He now worked for several big Los Angeles law firms. Shep and Johnny kept in touch, always talking at least once each year, usually over the holidays.

"Shep, my man," exclaimed Johnny in the Brooklyn accent he'd struggled so to lose since coming west. He was delighted to hear his old crony's voice. "How 'bout them Ducks? What a year they had! Almost as good as your last year."

Like Shep, Johnny had attended the University of Oregon as an undergraduate. He was an avid football fan, so when they met at the start of law school, Johnny already knew Shep from four years of watching him play. It was Johnny's idea for Shep to move into the funky house that Johnny shared with his brother.

"The truth is they're better. I ran into Coach the other day. He's predicting Rose Bowl next season," said Shep. "We never made it to any of the major bowls."

"Whatcha' mean, you never made it to the big ones? What about the Aloha Bowl, 1982?" Johnny corrected him. "Best college game I ever saw. That pass you threw Butler for the winning TD was so goddamned beautiful. Haven't seen one like it since."

Shep laughed. He'd always enjoyed Johnny's enthusiasm. Johnny knew how to have a good time—too good to make it through law school. But when they lived together, which was shortly after the death of Shep's father, Johnny's zest was just the antidote Shep needed.

"Aloha Bowl's no Rose Bowl, but it was still one of the biggest thrills of my life," Shep, always modest, answered.

"Kind of unusual to hear from you this time of year," Johnny observed. "You coming down this way or something? It'd be great to see you."

"No, that's not why I called. I need you to do something for me. Need a favor."

Shep Carroll had never asked anything of him before. Johnny was more than happy to help his old friend. And more than a little curious.

"Anything. Just shoot."

"I need you to see what you can find out for me about a couple of guys. A Robert Muncie and an Anthony Walcott. Muncie's vice president at Chicago Savings and Loan. I don't know what Walcott does, but he lives in Coeur d'Alene, Idaho. He's the president of the Edgewater Place Homeowners Association there. That's about all I know about him."

"What about Muncie?" asked Johnny. "Know much about him?"

"Yeah," answered Shep dryly. "He's my client."

Johnny whistled.

"And you're thinking the guy's not all he makes out to be, huh?"

"Something like that."

"I'll get back to you within twenty-four hours," promised Johnny.

The Board of Directors at Chicago Savings and Loan did not respond quite as Muncie had expected.

"Please explain to the board one more time just what grounds you have for changing attorneys at this stage of the game," Dennis Jackson, a dignified-looking, fair-haired man in his early forties, was saying from his seat at the head of a long mahogany table.

Sitting at the opposite end of the table, Muncie cleared his throat, then responded to the five men and three women in front of him. The board consisted of seven members. Their attorney, Amy DiCasio, a petite, stern-looking woman, also was in attendance.

"I think the bank would be better served at this time by a fresh perspective," Muncie offered. His second explanation was no less vague than the first, offered just minutes ago, had been.

"Are you unhappy with the manner in which Mr. Carroll has handled this project?" asked DiCasio.

Muncie hesitated. He couldn't very well state that Shep had been doing a lousy job all along or they'd want to know why he'd waited so long to bring it to the board's attention.

Finally he answered, "Yes and no. For the most part, Mr. Carroll has done an adequate job of representing us. He seems to know the ins and outs of projects like this one in Idaho, but he's entirely too passive."

"How so?" Again, it was the attorney voicing questions.

"He's dragging his heels on this foreclosure. Earlier this week we went out there specifically to serve notice of default on Michael Coleman's sister, who inherited Michael Coleman's interest in Edgewater Place. Instead of serving notice, he agreed to give her two weeks to come up with some silly proposal she thought her brother was working on at the time of his death."

"These things fall under your domain," Jackson said to

Muncie. "We've always given you free reign. However, I don't see the need to rush this thing into foreclosure."

"Nobody is rushing this thing," Muncie answered defensively. "We worked with Michael Coleman, gave him time, our cooperation, had an open-door policy with him. But now it's time to take action. It's obvious this sister of Michael Coleman's cannot turn things around. There is nothing to be gained in delaying the inevitable."

The way that Amy DiCasio was looking at him made him most uncomfortable.

"When I last spoke to Mr. Carroll," she said, "he told me you and he had agreed to delay foreclosure and work together with Ms. Coleman to try to get some sales. What I don't understand is what's happened between now and then to warrant a change in plans."

At these words, all heads at the table turned Muncie's way.

Muncie's chubby cheeks and large protruding ears were fast turning a crimson red. He'd had no idea Carroll and Amy DiCasio had been in contact.

"We had no reason to believe that additional time would make a difference. There hadn't been a sale in months, and over the winter tours of the building had dwindled. There was no point in giving her more time."

"And that was Mr. Carroll's position as well?" Now it was Dennis Jackson speaking again.

"Well," stammered Muncie. Then he looked at the attorney, whose eyes were bearing down on him, and continued, "Not exactly. As I said, Carroll was in favor of giving her two more weeks."

Dennis Jackson now addressed DiCasio. "Amy," he said, "what is your impression of Mr. Carroll and the job he's done on the Idaho project?"

"I've found him to be quite impressive, actually," she answered. "He knows his stuff. And he's a reasonable person. I have a little trouble believing he's acted in any manner that falls short of being highly professional. I think granting Ms. Coleman's request for two more weeks was a reasonable thing to do."

Muncie was sweating now.

"Frankly, I don't like to think we've been too ruthless with Michael Coleman. Or his sister, for that matter," Jackson said to the entire group. "But I suspect Stan is correct in doubting the ability of Michael Coleman's sister to make this thing work when her brother, who was a successful developer, was unable to. And we've embarked on a path now that we should probably remain committed to. If she fails to come up with anything during this two-week time, I'm going to defer to Stan's judgment on this foreclosure. However"—now he turned to address Muncie—"I haven't heard a single thing that would warrant changing attorneys. I trust Amy's assessment of this Mr. Carroll." This was a direct insult to Muncie, whose assessment he clearly did not trust. "At this point, to change attorneys would be very costly. From the records I reviewed just before coming to this meeting, it appears we've already paid Mr. Carroll's firm in excess of fifty thousand dollars for the work they've done for us. Starting from scratch with a new firm—or, for that matter, even another attorney from the Emerson, Caldwell firm—would only needlessly duplicate legal fees. We already stand to lose enough money on this project without throwing money down the drain."

Muncie was silent. There was little he could say.

"Shep Carroll stays," Jackson proclaimed finally. "And I want to be kept abreast of all developments on this project. Now, let's move on to the next order of business. . . ."

Muncie waited for all faces to turn away from him, then he slipped silently out of the room. He was not a happy man. He headed to his office, picked up the phone and dialed Anthony Walcott's personal number.

"We've got to watch ourselves," he moaned into the phone. "I just came from my board meeting. They refused to let me fire Carroll. For a moment there I thought they were going to tell me to stop the foreclosure."

He listened to Walcott's response, then said, "Calm

down. That's not going to happen. I'm still in charge and the foreclosure's going ahead as planned. In fact, I'm going to rush that son of a bitch through in record time to avoid anything else screwing us up. You just make sure that Indian doesn't start talking. Do you hear? We can't afford any more problems."

After a few more cursory words, he hung up the phone. Then, with an ache in his gut that he hoped was his ulcer and not something premonitory, he reached into the top drawer of his desk and extracted a pack of Rolaids.

Johnny Barletto's call came early the next morning.

"Did you know Walcott's a banker, too?" he asked Shep.

"No kidding?"

"Nope. He's currently president of Idaho Fidelity. And he and Muncie have a history together. They both worked at a Bay Area S and L in the late '70s, early '80s."

"Damn," exclaimed Shep. At dinner the other night, Muncie had even denied knowing Walcott's name.

"What's the name of the S and L?" asked Shep.

"Was. It was San Francisco Capital Savings and Loan. It was one of the first in the state to go under."

"Were Muncie and Walcott fired? Anything on their records?"

"Nope. Apparently, they lost their jobs when the feds closed the doors. Nothing bad on their records from the bank. Of course, that doesn't always mean much. But your man Muncie had some other interesting dealings in the fine state of California before he relocated to Chicago."

"Such as?"

"Your man a golfer?" asked Johnny.

"Big-time," answered Shep. "Every chance he gets. He's not bad, either. I've played with him twice. Lost to him both times."

"Well, apparently his interest in golf isn't limited to playing it. He's been involved in the development of at least two Bay Area courses, both of which are in big trouble. Had two suits filed against him, but both settled. In the first one, apparently Muncie managed to get forty-five investors to each pay fifteen thousand bucks for memberships in this supposedly phenomenal course he was planning in Marin County. Over half a million dollars, all of which he told them would go into an account to build the clubhouse. But according to court documents, your pal raided the account, then sold his interest in the development to another developer. Made about three point one million dollars on the sale, without counting the half million that disappeared from the clubhouse account. Oh yeah, here's the real clincher. Apparently, Muncie never secured water rights for the property. A championship golf course with no water. How do you like that? Of course—no pun intended—no one knew any of this until after he'd sold out."

"Holy shit," was all Shep could think of to say.

"Holy shit is right. They sued him for fraud and overreaching, but their case was weak—they got their golf course, after all. And the promises about the clubhouse were never put in writing. He settled with them for peanuts. This guy must be some charmer to get people to part with that much money on a handshake."

"I wouldn't exactly call him charming," said Shep. "What about the other course?"

"That one was another interesting story. Apparently, Muncie bought the option on four hundred and fifty acres just outside Pleasanton, but he needed partners to provide the financing to develop it. He ended up getting two Japanese companies to back him. Together they invested almost five million. You know how golf-crazy the Japanese are. These guys jumped at the chance to get involved in American real estate, especially a golf course. Problem is, Muncie never assigned title to the property to the corporation. Then, of course, he sells his interest in the course, for millions more than he paid for it, cutting his investors out of the deal altogether, and his Japanese friends sue him."

"And?"

"This time he doesn't have it so easy. He claims he had no intent to defraud his investors, that he sold the property as president of the investors corporation, had every intention of sharing the proceeds with them. They had him—it had already been eight months since he sold it and the only way they even found out about it was by visiting the property and seeing the new developer's name plastered all over the signs. Looks like Muncie was planning to just disappear with the money. And he almost made it. The investment group could have bled him dry, but he gave them their share of the money and they went away. Didn't press charges. Suit was dismissed. This guy is a real sweetheart. Slippery as all hell. Not exactly the kind of guy I pictured you representing."

"Me neither," said Shep. "But I'm stuck with him. At least for now."

"Well, you'd better have eyes in the back of your head," said Johnny. "Guys like this, they can get real dangerous. They get away with it a couple of times, they think they're invincible, that nobody's as smart as them, nobody can figure them out. And for all practical purposes, this guy's gotten away with it. These lawsuits have been no more than slaps on the hand. Who knows how many other of these deals he's put together. How many other people he's screwed without ending up in court. This guy's trouble, Shep."

"I've suspected as much for a while now. Still, I didn't know he was this bad. I'm surprised Chicago Savings and Loan would hire a guy like this," said Shep thoughtfully.

"Hey, aside from these lawsuits, the guy's got a clean slate. And the first of these suits wasn't filed until 1986. That's a year after he went to work for Chicago Savings and Loan. They'd have had no way to know about all this," answered Johnny.

"Listen, Johnny," said Shep, "you've been a huge help. I owe you one."

"Hey, you kidding? You don't owe me a thing," his friend said. "Just promise me that you'll keep in touch and that you'll call me if you need anything else. I could make life a little miserable for this asshole. And enjoy doing it."

"You'll be the first person I call if I need anything," Shep promised.

"Looks like you got a coupla real winners there."

Shep laughed then, too.

"Yeah. That's a good word for them. Winners."

But neither one of them really saw any humor in the situation. Shep hung up the phone with the sudden realization that the suspicions he'd had about Muncie might well be mild in comparison to the reality of what his client was up to.

The turnout for the night's meeting of the newly formed Panhandle Republic was disappointing. Of the thirty-three who'd attended the first meeting, only twelve had returned. And they were a pathetic-looking assortment. Based on the feedback he'd been getting over the past few weeks, the Colonel had expected a much larger group. But he knew better than to show disappointment. No, as their leader, it was his job to bolster morale. This, after all, was just the start. As word spread, more would come. They were out there, he knew they were. Just waiting for the word.

At least the ex-marine had come. The Colonel had spent some time going over his personal profile. Special operations during Desert Storm, then a dishonorable discharge for an attack on a black recruit. Broke the fucker's back. This was someone to keep an eye on. The perfect man for a special assignment. After the meeting, he would pull him aside. Tell him he had a mission for him. A way of proving himself to the hierarchy.

The Colonel had no doubt the marine would jump at any chance to rise within the organization. No doubt at all. He knew his type—knew, in fact, just what he'd see in those intense dark eyes when he detailed the assignment for him. If this one proved himself, he would be a natural as an instructor at their soon-to-be-established paramilitary training site.

Before the meeting officially began, as he waited, hoping for more to come, the Colonel passed out several catalogs containing such items as a $10 "Sniper Training Video," a book titled *Blueprint for Survival* for $20, an assortment of knives, flags, camouflage clothing, and traps of all sorts.

"All proceeds go right back to the organization," the Colonel explained. "So it's money well spent."

He could see the glimmer of excitement in their eyes as they quickly perused the thin booklet's pages. The marine leaned forward, straining to see over the shoulder of the man in front of him.

"Yes," the Colonel said, already doing that which he did so well—stoking their enthusiasm, feeding their paranoia—"it's money well spent, indeed.

"Money that could help buy all of us back our freedom."

CHAPTER 9

HELLO. THIS IS BAILEY Coleman. I'd like to speak to Dean McCloud."

Bailey had had enough. She might have struck out so far in trying to come up with Michael's plan to save Edgewater Place, but she still had a career as a lawyer ahead of her. No one—not Stan Muncie, and certainly not Shep Carroll—could take that away from her. Of course, once the foreclosure commenced, she would be cut off from the salary Michael had been receiving and would no longer have the money to pay for school. She would have to get a job and take out student loans. But she would not be the first to do it—to work, go to school, and now, with Clancy living with her, raise a child on her own. There were plenty of other women out there who did it. Women who raised entire families on their own and accomplished great things. Bailey had never imagined herself in that situation, but if that's what it was going to take, so be it. But before she started looking for work she had something else to worry about. Finals. She certainly couldn't afford to let the past semester go down the drain.

She'd missed the last three weeks of class. Finals were starting this week. She hoped her professors would still allow her to take them, despite her prolonged absence. She was fortunate to have good relationships with most of her instructors. There were two professors with whom she had already taken courses her first year. She was confident they would cooperate. But the other two classes—Federal Tax Law and Maritime Law—were large lectures where she had very little personal contact with the instructors. She decided that the best strategy would be to call Dean McCloud, the head of the law school, and ask for his cooperation.

There would be no more self-pity. Whatever happened, she would handle it. She'd moped about long enough. She was not about to give up on Edgewater Place. But she had made up her mind that even if the worst happened, even if she and Clancy were to lose the home Michael had intended for them to keep, they would be okay. She would finish law school, then get a job to support both her and Clancy. She would take Clancy to Seattle when she took her finals, to give her an opportunity to decide whether she'd rather live there or in Coeur d'Alene. The decision had to be one that they were both happy with, both she and Clancy. From now on that's how it would be.

When Dean McCloud came on the line, Bailey explained her circumstances to him. First expressing condolences, he followed by assuring her that he would talk to her professors and urge their cooperation in allowing Bailey to take her finals late.

Bailey thanked him, hung up the phone, then immediately dialed another number. This call was local. Very local.

She'd decided another thing while lying in bed the previous night. She would not sit by idly any longer while Sam Cummings carried old Gator up and down the stairs at odd hours of the day and night.

Bailey Coleman might be on her way out, but she was not about to go quietly.

"May I please speak to Mr. Walcott?" she asked politely when a woman's voice answered the phone. "This is Bailey Coleman."

When she was informed that Walcott was unavailable and that he could not be reached at work either, she decided to leave a message.

"Please ask him to give me a call," she said. "I would like to request a special meeting of the homeowners association."

According to the association's CC&Rs—Covenants, Conditions and Restrictions—which Bailey had fallen asleep reading the night before, any member of the association could call a special meeting by simply requesting it of a board member. The CC&Rs also provided that any regulation, including the no-pets provision, could be amended by a majority vote at such a meeting. Until the foreclosure went through, Bailey could exercise Michael's forty-seven votes—enough to pass any amendment she damn well pleased.

Before she left Edgewater Place, if indeed she was forced to leave, Bailey Coleman would at least have the satisfaction of knowing that Sam and Gator would be riding the elevators with the rest of the building's esteemed residents.

For the next few days, Bailey stayed behind closed doors, studying frantically for her finals. True to the dean's promise, her instructors had been most cooperative. Two even offered to mail her the exams. They would arrive via Federal Express by ten A.M., one in four days and the other in six. She would have approximately five hours to answer the essay questions. Fed Ex would be instructed to pick up the completed exams after two P.M. on the same say they arrived.

While the other instructors didn't offer Bailey the option of taking their exams in Coeur d'Alene, they did agree to delay them until she finished the first two. She was to call them the next week to schedule the exams.

Sam saved the day by practically taking over where

Clancy was concerned. Though Bailey protested when Sam first insisted on helping, she later wondered how she'd ever have managed without the kindness of her newfound friend. Each morning Sam arrived by seven-thirty A.M. and whisked Clancy away to feed her breakfast and get her ready for school—her last week before summer vacation. Bailey would take a short break from studying each afternoon when Sam and Clancy stopped in at about a quarter past three, on their way home from the bus stop. Then it was back to the books. Clancy returned home each evening before dinner, and after putting her down for the night, Bailey would study until well past midnight.

On the day before her first final was due to arrive, Bailey walked down to the lobby just after lunch to get the mail. She needed a breather. She was studying for her Uniform Commercial Code class. The code language was so infuriatingly complex and confusing that she'd found herself reading some of its sections over and over and still not comprehending them. She would either go blind or go batty if she didn't get away from them for a while.

After waving to Faith Lammerman, who was on the telephone, she opened her box to find several bills, still addressed to Michael, and one handwritten envelope addressed to her. With sunshine beckoning outside, she decided to take a short walk. Maybe that would clear up the fog in her head. As she strolled slowly around the courtyard, she slid the bills into the pocket of the light summer sweater she wore, then, her hands freed, tore the end off the envelope addressed to her. She blew into the envelope to open it and could see what looked to be a newspaper clipping inside. Extracting it, she saw that it was an article from the *Idaho Gazette*. On one side was a portion of a Safeway ad. She turned it over. On the other side was an article that had meticulously been cut out from the previous day's paper. It was headlined FAMILY HARASSED IN SOUTHERN IDAHO.

Bailey lowered herself onto a wrought iron bench located next to the fountain and read.

RIGBY—A family of five has been methodically harassed over the past month. Carl and Juanita Jimenez, recent transplants from Southern California, have put their house up for sale after a series of incidents in which they and their three children, ages 6 through 13, have been targeted by what appears to be a militia-style hate group. The first incident occurred when the Jimenez family was attending services at St. Anthony's Cathedral. They returned home to find their two-car garage in flames and a red swastika painted on the structure's side. Two days later, their nine-year-old son, Juan, had red paint thrown at him from a passing pickup truck as he walked home from school. According to the boy's statement to the police, the vehicle's occupants were adult males, dressed in camouflage clothing.

On Saturday night, as they slept, the Jimenez car was broken into. Hate literature and dozens of spent bullets were left inside. The words "Spics go home" had been scrawled in red paint on the roof.

"We came here to get our kids out of L.A.," said Carl Jimenez. "We wanted them to be safe, to be able to play outside, ride their bikes wherever they wanted, without fear. But now they are afraid to leave the house. Now L.A. looks awfully good to them. Now it looks good to all of us."

The sheriff's department reports few leads, but concedes that the area is home to several offshoots of the white supremacist movement. Sheriff Archer has vowed to find and prosecute the perpetrators, to send a strong signal that such unlawful activities will not be tolerated. Meanwhile, the Jimenez family has left their home in the hands of a local realtor and returned to Southern California.

Bailey continued to stare at the article long after she'd finished reading it.

Why would anyone have sent it to her? Was it because

Clancy was Hispanic? The mere possibility—that this had something to do with Clancy—sent a shiver of dread throughout her entire being.

It had to be. What other relevance could this article possibly have to Bailey?

Was someone trying to warn her?

Or—and it was this thought that suddenly gripped her like some giant vise squeezing the air out of her every cell—to threaten her?

She knew that these groups existed. Knew that there were some in North Idaho. But she'd never seen any sign of them, never before read of anything like this actually happening. Who would have sent this to her?

She looked again at the envelope. There was no return address. No marking at all other than the postmark, which read "Coeur d'Alene, Idaho." It had been mailed just the previous day. Right there in town.

Surely, Bailey rationalized after many minutes of struggling to maintain her calm, her ability to reason, this had been sent by some well-meaning person, someone who knew Clancy. Maybe the parent of a classmate.

Someone who knew Clancy had read the article and decided it warranted being brought to Bailey's attention. They probably knew they were overreacting, were even somewhat embarrassed about it—which would explain why they had not included a letter or a return address—but they just wanted to play it safe. Make sure Bailey was aware. Yes, that's undoubtedly what this was. A well-intended warning.

Surely there was no chance that anyone would actually harm, or even intentionally frighten, Clancy. That sweet, dear little niece of hers who considered every human being an ally, every stranger a potential friend. The very thought was . . . Well, it just couldn't be. Those hate groups were full of sick, twisted individuals. But surely not that sick. Not that twisted.

Even though she'd convinced herself that the sender of the article had meant well, had only intended to warn her,

Bailey wished whoever it was had just kept their fears to themselves. Fear, she well knew, could be incapacitating. Almost as destructive as the thing feared. She would not succumb to it, she'd finally concluded, crumpling the article into a ball and tossing it into the wastebasket in the lobby before heading back to her apartment to try to resume her studies.

Still, when Sam and Clancy came through the door that afternoon after school, Bailey was right there, greeting them, enveloping Clancy in an unusually long, heartfelt hug.

"Aunt Bailey," Clancy said from within Bailey's grasp.

"Yes?"

"You're holding me so tight I can't breathe."

Bailey laughed and loosened her grip.

"Sorry 'bout that," she said.

And during that night, as Clancy slept peacefully, Bailey—still vowing not to give the newspaper article another moment's thought—tiptoed silently into the little girl's room not just once but a total of three times, before she finally climbed into her own bed and fell into an exhausted sleep herself, just before dawn.

The morning after she had finished her second final, Bailey awoke at six A.M. In light of how much class she'd missed and how little time she'd had to study, she felt she'd done well on both the exams she'd taken. Just two more to go, in Seattle. This morning she and Clancy were driving over. She had two days before her Tax and Maritime Law finals. There was plenty to do—still some studying, and she knew she'd arrive home to a mess. When she'd received the news about Michael, she'd left so suddenly, literally walked out of her apartment without making any provisions for her absence except the call she'd made to her neighbor in the upstairs apartment, Ann, to ask her to pick up the mail and the newspaper. She was excited about getting back to the city, back to familiar territory. Even back to school, to take her exams.

Mostly, she was excited about taking Clancy with her, getting her out of Coeur d'Alene, especially after having received that newspaper article. It had weighed on her mind, causing her to be reluctant to allow Clancy to leave the apartment without her, even though she was always accompanied by Sam.

Bailey had shared the article with Sam. It was Sam's opinion that it had been sent with good intentions.

"I've lived here forever, dear," she'd said, sensing Bailey's deepfelt concern. "The media, especially those big-city papers, make a big deal of these groups, but in reality, you'd be hard-pressed to find one longtime resident who'd ever so much as sighted one of those kooks. If it weren't for the papers, we wouldn't even know they were up here.

"I'm sure that this was sent by one of Clancy's schoolmates. Or maybe even someone here, in the building. Someone new to the area who still has that big-city mentality." She'd reached out and taken Bailey's hand then. "Don't you worry. And I promise I will keep an especially close eye on her. Okay?"

Bailey had felt better after that. After hearing that Sam also believed the article had been sent by some well-meaning but misguided individual. But still, she was looking forward to getting away. To showing Clancy around Seattle. She'd promised her a grand tour of the city—the Woodland Park Zoo, the Pike Street Market, the aquarium, a ferry ride. The whole works.

After securing the lock on the front door, she left a still-sleeping Clancy and went down to the pool to swim laps. Afterward, she climbed into the Jacuzzi and allowed herself a few minutes of some much-needed relaxation. The pool area was completely empty and, aside from the rhythmic gurgle of the Jacuzzi's air jets, silent. She sat facing the wall of windows that flanked the pool and Jacuzzi and watched as the sun came up, its soft light first skimming the treetops and distant mountains, then permeating downward. For once, she was not haunted by thoughts of Shep. Even with her recent intense focus on her studies and her concerns about Clancy, he'd never been far from her mind. Maybe her exhausted brain knew its limits.

It was one of those moments that would stay with her. The physical pleasure of the hot, bubbling water; the solitude; outside, the beauty of the morning. Though she was looking forward to getting back to Seattle, in so many ways this town, this building, already felt like home to her. She did not want to lose it.

Clancy had already awakened by the time Bailey got back to their condo. She, too, was anxious to get going.

They were on the road by seven-thirty. Bailey had never much liked it before, the three-hundred-mile drive between Coeur d'Alene and Seattle. But she'd never before had Clancy's company on it, either. Forty-five minutes into the trip, they pulled off in Spokane to drive through McDonald's for breakfast.

For almost two hundred miles after Spokane, the scenery remained virtually the same: treeless, rolling hills. Bailey still remembered the first time she'd traveled that route as a child. The desolate feeling the barren land had left her with that wintry day. But as an adult, she'd grown to appreciate its special beauty. This was wheat country, and at this time of year, the golden fields rippled in the wind and shimmered in the morning sun. Mile after mile, they rolled and spread in front of the Jeep, the highway one long black ribbon that dipped and twisted between the fields, extending as far as they could see.

"It looks like it goes on forever," Clancy commented without much enthusiasm. And then, when they saw a lone farmhouse, she asked, "Do you think any kids live there?" To Clancy such a life was unfathomable, living way out there in the middle of nowhere. She had, after all, grown up in Los Angeles. Bailey tried to tell her that it might be kind of fun to grow up on one of the farms they passed—all the animals, the farm machinery, the clean air—but Clancy wouldn't buy it.

"Where are the sidewalks?" she wanted to know, thinking of the rollerblades she'd thrown in Bailey's trunk just an hour earlier. "What about the stores? Where do you rent videos? And how do you order pizza?"

They drove past Martha's, a restaurant located alongside the interstate in George, Washington. Having just learned about the first president of the United States, Clancy was ever so tickled to think that adults—founders of a town and restaurant owners, no less—had shown such ingenuity, such playfulness, in their choice of names.

Then, just a few miles later, they came over the crest of the hills towering over the vast waters of the mighty Columbia River—a powerful sight that often still gave Bailey's flesh goose bumps—and Clancy let out her first real yelp of enthusiasm.

"Cool!" she cried. "What lake is that?"

"It's not a lake. That's the Columbia River," answered Bailey.

"But it's too big to be a river."

"That's the same thing I said when I was little," said Bailey, smiling.

"You did?" asked Clancy, somehow impressed. And then, "Maybe we're a lot alike." And then, after another pause, "Maybe that's 'cuz we're related."

"I think you're right," Bailey responded in a husky voice.

"I know something you'll really like," Bailey announced a few minutes later. All the times she'd driven over to visit Michael, she'd sailed right on past, but today she and Clancy would take the time to explore.

"Look up there," she said, pointing to the highest bluff. Silhouetted against the morning sky was a herd of wild horses, the lead stallion rearing magnificently on its hind legs. Half a dozen other mustangs followed behind in perfect formation, all frozen in motion.

"Wow!" Clancy cried. Then, "Hey, wait a minute. They're not moving."

Bailey pulled over at the next exit. Wild Horse Monument. They parked the car and climbed the dusty trail that led to the life-size metal sculptures. Bailey helped Clancy climb onto the second horse's back.

"Michael told me you had horses when you were little."

"Yes, we did," Bailey said, touched by the thought that Michael had shared that with Clancy, with his daughter. What must it have been like for him? Trying to make up for all those years when he didn't even know she existed? The two of them getting to know each other, hungry to learn about the other's past. What was that like?

And then the answer came to her. It was just like this. And she realized that she and Clancy were now embarking on a very similar adventure.

The rest of the drive passed too quickly. Clancy's earlier reservations about this new country had evaporated. Just outside Cle Elum, as they began to climb, the majestic Cascades towering ahead and several picturesque ranches, their horses dotting the fields, nestled in the valley below, Clancy turned to Bailey and said, "This is nice."

"It *is* nice, isn't it?" Bailey answered.

Johnny's information had been helpful, but Shep needed more. Two days after their talk, it occurred to Shep that, with any luck, he might already have just what he needed at his fingertips.

On the far corner of Shep's large desk sat a mostly unused computer. Shep was not much of a typist, which was one of the reasons he'd never warmed up to computers. To Anna's chagrin, he still wrote everything out in longhand. Some of the younger attorneys in the firm were so computer literate that they were practically self-sufficient. They did their own pleadings and relied on interoffice e-mail for almost all of their communications, drastically reducing the need for support staff. With Shep, either Anna or Trish, his paralegal, typed and prepared documents. And Anna routinely checked his e-mail, printing out any messages she deemed important and leaving a stack of them on his desk each day.

When Shep was in law school, and in his first years with Emerson, Caldwell, research was done by going to the library and physically locating the applicable casebook or law journal. Finding the latest case on a point of law could take hours. It required patience and thoroughness.

Today a computer could do in minutes what had taken hours back then. Shep's practice was such that he rarely needed research anymore. But luckily for him, just a few weeks earlier, when he was preparing a last-minute brief—one that didn't afford him the time to do it the old way—he'd called Trish into his office and she'd talked him through the process.

With her recent instruction still somewhat fresh in his mind, he sat down at his computer and, after fumbling around a little to get into Windows, he clicked on the Westlaw logo, entered his seven-digit, four-letter ID and watched as the screen presented him with a directory of databases. He chose the ALL CASES option, then, in response to the screen's next query, he typed in the phrase SAVINGS AND LOAN FAILURES.

After almost a minute, a list of a hundred and eight cases appeared on the screen. Shep scrolled quickly down to the *S*'s. There it was: SAN FRANCISCO CAPITAL. Shep's hunch had been right. There *had* been litigation surrounding the savings and loan where Walcott and Muncie both worked.

He double-clicked on the bank's name and the case magically appeared. It was a twenty-three page decision, a civil racketeering suit filed by the government against five of the S&L's officers, claiming they had looted San Francisco Capital of more than $50 million. Neither Muncie nor Walcott was listed as a defendant, but before long Shep knew why. Muncie had been given immunity from prosecution in exchange for testifying against his fellow officers, who were found guilty of booking up to $500 million in loans without "any reasonable basis for concluding the loans were collectible." All of the officers, including, it appeared, Muncie, had received bonuses in excess of a million dollars apiece for booking these loans, in addition to their considerable salaries. All were now serving sentences ranging from two to fifteen years. All, that is, except Stan Muncie, who'd walked free.

Shep read the case with more than a little interest. What had happened at San Francisco Capital was not new to him. The bulk of his practice for the past few years had, in fact, focused on working through real estate loans that had gone bad. New deregulatory laws passed in 1980 and 1982 allowed S&L's to make new, far riskier investments than had previously been allowed. Construction loans to commercial real estate developers were there for the asking. Loans were made that should never have been made. The mentality was almost that the borrowers were doing the lenders a favor. By the time regulators finally caught up with what was happening at San Francisco Capital and declared its loans in default, its net worth was pegged at minus $200 million. From the judge's ruling, Shep had to conclude that Muncie was the only one to come out of it unscathed. There was no indication that he'd had to repay any of the bonuses he'd earned for booking loans, and long before the case went to trial he'd already secured another job.

When Shep had heard about Muncie's dabbling in golf course development, his first reaction had been to wonder where the banker could have gotten his hands on that kind of money. Now he knew. Million-dollar bonuses for the loans he'd booked. Shep was beginning to get a picture of Muncie as a wheeler-dealer cloaked in the respectability of a bank vice president's title—cunning and living on luck, always just one jump ahead of due process.

One thing was certain. Whether or not Muncie had himself been guilty of wrongdoing at San Francisco Capital, clearly he'd had the opportunity to observe what was going on. Surely, if he was of such a mind, he could have taken what he'd learned at San Francisco Capital and put it into practice in his new position as vice president of real estate development at Chicago S&L. It was possible, even quite likely, that he could have accomplished it without the awareness of Chicago S&L—the institution was, after all, a highly reputable one. If there was something going on, Shep's instincts were that it didn't go beyond Muncie. From what Shep had seen, Muncie had complete autonomy within his department. He approved the loans. He called the shots when they went bad. It all fit. An out-of-state loan to an out-of-state developer. It was typical of the all-too-risky investments made by San Francisco Capital and other S&Ls during that period. Muncie might even have paid himself a handsome bonus for obtaining Michael Coleman's business.

Yes, the picture of what was happening with the Edgewater Place loan could well fit what had happened at San Francisco Capital.

But there was one element that did not make sense: Muncie's eagerness to foreclose. Why was he suddenly in such a hurry? If anything, Muncie should be going out of his way to avoid declaring it a bad loan, avoid drawing attention to it. That part didn't make sense.

And there were other nagging questions as well. Where did Walcott figure into all of this? And what to make of the golf course scams Johnny had uncovered? Were they relevant? Shep could not see how they could be.

On the whole, the information he'd obtained so far probably raised more questions than it answered. Still, at least Shep now had something solid. Someplace to start in trying to sort things out.

But the clock was ticking. He didn't have a lot of time. Unless Bailey came up with something almost immediately, which he doubted, he expected to get a call from Stan Muncie any day now telling him to deliver official notice that her thirty-day cure period had commenced. He had to find out what Muncie was up to before Edgewater Place actually went into foreclosure. Before Bailey and Clancy lost their home.

It was time for him to head back to Coeur d'Alene.

CHAPTER 10

JUNE IN SEATTLE OFTEN behaves more like late March or early April in other parts of the country. The day after Bailey and Clancy arrived, the cool rains started. While Bailey finished up her studying, Clancy entertained herself by watching videos and playing with the neighbor's cat, who especially liked its perch on the deck railing outside Bailey's apartment.

Bailey lived in a three-story frame house on Capitol Hill. Long ago the residence, which once must have housed a family of considerable affluence, had been converted to an apartment house. Bailey's two-bedroom apartment occupied half of the second floor.

In addition to watching videos and playing with the cat, Clancy also spent a great deal of time sitting at one of several oversized, wood-framed windows that brightened the kitchen and dining room area even on these dark Seattle days. The house was on a corner, just two blocks from Broadway, the heavily congested main drag of Capitol Hill. Clancy was fascinated by the foot traffic just below the window. Even life in Los Angeles had not prepared her for the daily procession of the local inhabitants.

"Six," Bailey heard her niece say to herself as she kneeled in front of the window, her elbows resting on its sill.

"Six what?" Bailey asked, raising her head from the casebook in which she'd been engrossed all morning.

"Six green hairs so far today," Clancy answered. "Yesterday I counted nine."

Seattle was the capitol of grunge, and Capitol Hill was its mecca. For lunch the day before, Bailey had walked Clancy up to Broadway for pizza. It wasn't until she saw the wide-eyed amazement on Clancy's face that she realized that what had long since become commonplace to her would hardly be so to a six-year-old. Anything went on Broadway—anything, that is, except the conventional. Hair of every color and configuration was the norm. Green was the most popular, but purple and a dark metallic red were right up there. Earrings were seen piercing any spot of flesh capable of exposure. Men clad in tight, frayed cutoffs that exposed a significant amount of their buttocks walked hand in hand with other men. Upon seeing Clancy's reaction, Bailey wondered how good an idea it had been to take her there.

"Does that bother you?" she asked Clancy as the little girl diverted her eyes from a gay couple walking arm in arm toward them.

"I don't know," Clancy answered.

"I guess I'd forgotten that it took me a while to get used to it when I first moved here," Bailey said.

"It did?"

"Yes," answered Bailey. "It's not that I thought there was something wrong with it. I don't feel that way at all. It's just that I wasn't accustomed to seeing men together and women together."

"And now you're used to it?" Clancy asked.

"Yes. Now I'm used to it," Bailey answered. "But if you're not comfortable with it, that's okay. We can go have lunch somewhere else if you want. Or even go back to my apartment and order pizza in."

Clancy thought for a moment as she and Bailey continued walking hand in hand.

"No," she finally said. "It's fun here."

Bailey knew what she meant. Broadway *was* fun. Day and night, the street teemed with life, the sidewalks, shops and cafés swarming with people. Still, over lunch, she realized that what she wanted for Clancy was something very different from the life that she herself had led the past few years. Capitol Hill, thought Bailey, is not where I want Clancy to grow up. It was not where Michael would have wanted her to grow up.

She knew where Michael would have wanted Clancy to grow up. She knew where Clancy would be happiest. And more and more she knew where she, too, wanted to be.

The morning of Bailey's last final exam—another cool, blustery, wet day—her neighbor, Ann, came down to stay with Clancy.

Driving over to the UW campus, Bailey felt myriad emotions. Nervousness prevailed. This would be her hardest final. Federal Tax Law was the class she'd enjoyed the least this semester, the one she felt the least comfortable with. She would be vastly relieved to get this final over with—her last final of the year. A strong sense of nostalgia swept over her at the realization that, if she didn't finish law school in Seattle, it *could* be her last final at UW. After all the classes she'd attended, the study groups she'd participated in, the exams she'd dreaded and then somehow miraculously passed, this could be it.

It seemed somehow appropriate that this trip to school was made in driving rain; that she had trouble finding a parking spot at one of the meters in front of the law school and ended up two blocks away; that when she finally settled into her desk with the exam in front of her, her clothes and hair were uncomfortably damp. After all, how many classes had she sat through in that condition—wet from the mad dash in the rain?

She was given exactly three hours for the exam, which consisted of five essay questions. Bailey had just started the fifth when her professor walked in to announce that time would be up in ten minutes. She spent the rest of the time scribbling her jumbled thoughts down frantically, hoping to at least touch upon some of the issues she knew the question raised. When he returned again and collected her papers, she was far from satisfied with her last answer. But she felt she'd done a decent job on at least three of the first four questions. She might not have passed with flying colors, but she had passed it. She knew she'd passed it.

As she stepped outside, she turned her face up to the sky and let the rain wash over her. She'd done it! She had completed another year of law school.

Back in her car, the reality of it was slowly starting to set in. Another reality, one that she was trying to disallow into her consciousness, was also lurking there—the reality that neither Michael nor her parents were there to share in her joy, her relief. But she would not invite that reality in. Not today.

She hurried back to her apartment and burst into the kitchen, where Clancy and Ann were microwaving two cups of Top Ramen.

"Let's celebrate!" she cried, sweeping Clancy up in a hug and twirling her around.

"Did you pass?" Clancy asked excitedly, her arms and legs wrapped tightly around Bailey's torso.

"You bet I did," Bailey said.

Ann lifted her right arm in a high-five gesture, which both Bailey and Clancy slapped gaily.

"Way to go!"

"Thanks, Ann." Bailey smiled. Then, eyeing the Top Ramen, she proclaimed, "No way. We're not eating anything that comes in Styrofoam today. Grab your umbrellas, ladies, we are going out on the town."

They headed for Palisades, a popular waterfront restaurant situated in the heart of the Magnolia marina, on the north shore of Elliott Bay. They hadn't made reservations, but when Ann told the hostess, a tall and lovely redhead, the cause of their celebration, she set off in a flurry of activity—corralling two already frazzled-looking busboys, then hurriedly helping them clear and set a just-vacated table on the much-coveted upper floor. Soon she was back, ushering them to a window table that afforded them a view, through the marina's forest of bobbing sailing masts, of the bay and, in the distance, the Seattle skyline.

Clancy read the menu out loud, asking Bailey to describe each entree, then finally settled on steak. Bailey and Ann chose the house speciality of the day, fresh Copper River salmon. Bailey ordered a bottle of champagne, which was uncorked with a dramatic flourish by a handsome waiter while they waited for their food.

They took their time, enjoying the sight of huge tankers streaming by and, at regular intervals, the ferries. There was a light fog over the water that served to heighten the effect of the big vessels moving silently across the steel-gray water.

"You mean you drive your car onto those?" Clancy asked the two women as her eyes followed the *Spokane*, a ferry that shuttled passengers back and forth between downtown Seattle and the quaint Bainbridge Island town of Winslow.

"Yep," Ann answered. "Then you get out and walk around the ferry. You can stand on one of the decks or get something to eat. They even have video games inside."

Clancy was impressed.

"Want to ride it? Take the ferry over to Bainbridge Island?" Bailey asked impulsively. After all, today anything went.

"Can we?"

"You bet. Only first Ann and I are going to finish this champagne—which means that I'm leaving my car here. We'll call a cab to take us to the terminal," Bailey replied. "We can walk on."

"You can do that?" Clancy asked. "Awesome!"

They lingered for another forty minutes. Bailey and Ann had a lot of catching up to do. They hadn't really talked since Bailey left for Michael's funeral, and Bailey was eager to share her new life with her friend and neighbor.

Though they gave it a good try, they couldn't quite finish the whole bottle of champagne. Both women, however, had had enough to feel its effects. Ann, whose modest student/waitress budget precluded any luxuries of this magnitude, was almost giddy with the experience. And her joy at Bailey's accomplishment was genuine—and considerable. They'd lived next door to each other for three years and had grown fond of each other. Their mood was celebratory, silly. It had the one quality that had been in short supply in Bailey's life recently—lightheartedness.

A taxi deposited them at the ferry terminal just before the big vessel took off. They hurried on, stopping at the cafeteria for lattes before settling into a roomy booth at the rear of the vessel, where they could watch the Seattle skyline fade as they pulled away. Bailey pointed out the sights to Clancy—Smith Tower, the Pike Place Market, the Kingdome. Clancy was especially delighted by the seagulls that hovered around the ferry, drifting here and there, riding the air currents created by the big vessel. When one flew alongside them, keeping abreast with their window for a full minute or more, she stood with her face pressed to the glass, giggling and calling to it.

"Maybe that was Jonathan Livingston Seagull," she said as her feathered friend finally fell behind. Bailey had read her Richard Bach's novel the first time they'd met, on one of Bailey's visits to Michael.

"Maybe." Bailey smiled.

It turned out to be a perfect day. A perfect way for Bailey to celebrate her accomplishment. For Clancy to experience the essence of Seattle. For two friends to reconnect.

A perfect way for Bailey to say good-bye to Seattle.

For they would head back to Coeur d'Alene the next day, and though Bailey knew that she would return to Seattle often, she also realized this day that her future was three hundred miles away. In a quiet little city on the shores of a lake. A new life awaited her and Clancy. And this day, in her heart, she said good-bye to the old life.

That night in bed, she realized just how much the past few weeks had changed her. She thought she'd come back to Seattle with an open mind. Maybe, just maybe, she and Clancy would decide to live there. She'd finish school, take the Washington bar, get a job with one of the city's big firms and enroll Clancy in school. They'd spend their weekends exploring the city, going to games at the Coliseum or Kingdome, riding the ferries.

But for some reason, despite the fact that she'd enjoyed their day out immensely, it'd had just the opposite effect on her. It had caused her to realize, with absolute certainty, that her future held something entirely different.

When she returned to Coeur d'Alene she would check into transferring to the University of Idaho or, better still, Gonzaga University in Spokane, which was only a forty-five-minute commute.

Whatever lay ahead, whether or not she could hold on to Edgewater Place, at least she had Clancy. And Sam. She would have a full life.

If she just worked hard enough, focused on that, on creating a future for Clancy and her, eventually this ache in her heart would go away. She would never, of course, stop missing Michael. But certainly, eventually, she would stop thinking about Shep Carroll.

Wouldn't she?

When he took off for Coeur d'Alene after work, Shep did not really have a plan of action in mind. All he knew was that he had to find out more about what Muncie and Walcott were up to. The precise way to do that was still unclear to him, but he knew that staying in Portland would get him nowhere. And when the trial that had been set for the next week suddenly settled, he did not waste a minute in informing the firm that he would be taking the week he had scheduled for the trial for a much-needed vacation.

It was the first time he'd made the trip by car. The seven-hour drive gave him time to think, an opportunity to ponder just what he was getting himself into. He was going to Coeur d'Alene to investigate, to find out more about what Muncie, *his client,* was up to. Somehow his professional ethics courses in law school had never covered this situation. Was he willing to compromise his professional integrity, violate the code of ethics he'd long ago sworn to uphold, for Bailey Coleman? Or were his actions justified? As the bank's attorney, he was obligated to inform someone there if the activities of one of the bank's employees would have an adverse legal affect on the bank—certainly, if Shep's suspicions about Muncie were based in fact, the bank would be exposing itself to serious legal problems and Shep's actions in investigating Muncie would be in line with his professional responsibilities.

Which was it?

Questions. That's all he seemed to be coming up with these days. Questions without answers. Shep only hoped that in the days ahead at least some of the answers would be forthcoming.

He hadn't thought to make reservations before leaving Portland. Upon arriving in Coeur d'Alene, he headed straight for the Treetop Inn and was acutely disappointed to see a No Vacancy sign flashing above its entrance. He proceeded on down Sherman, the main drag. Half a dozen new motels had sprung up in the past couple of years to house the overflow from the increasingly popular lakefront resort. But tourist season had already started, and each parking lot he passed was already full. After driving by several more No Vacancy signs and pulling into two motels that did not display signs, only to be told there were no rooms available, Shep began to regret not having thrown his tent into the Range Rover before leaving home. He remembered then that on his last visit to the area a Motor Inn Express had still been under construction just a mile or so farther down the road, at the Sherman Avenue exit on I-90. As he approached the location, the huge Now Open sign and a parking lot that was only half full were welcome sights.

The young woman at the front desk, a pert, bouncy type with big hair and a big smile, announced that yesterday had been their first day of operation and that, yes, they did indeed have a vacancy.

"How long will you be staying?" she asked Shep, her eyes wandering to his hands in search of a wedding band as he filled out the registration form.

"A week," he answered.

"Tell you what," she said then, "if you're going to be here that long, you'll want something nice. I'm going to put you in 107. That's one of our suites, even has a kitchenette. And I'll just charge you for a single."

Shep returned her smile, a reflection of his genuine gratitude at having found a room, much less a suite.

"See you tomorrow night," she called out cheerfully as he headed back out to move his car closer to the side entrance he would be using to access his room. "Don't forget there's a pool and Jacuzzi right there," she added, pointing to a door marked POOL just off the lobby.

It was almost two A.M. by the time Shep settled into his room. He fell asleep within minutes of climbing into the king-size bed, too tired to pay attention to his surroundings. But in the morning he saw that the night clerk had, indeed, done him a favor. The room was large and almost apartmentlike, with a separate sitting area under the oversized, paned window and a fully equipped kitchenette just off the bath area. Early morning sunshine, the first Shep had seen in over a week, flooded through the eastern exposure windows.

Shep went to the window and looked out to get his bearings. Across the street was a large, brick warehouselike building marked COVE BOWL. The motel sat at the eastern edge of the downtown area. Shep knew that farther down the road, no more than a mile away, was Fernan Lake. He remembered the story told him by Randy Tawney, the amiable kid who worked at Fins and Feathers, about catching a trout from the bedroom window of his house on the lake, and promised himself that he would get up early the next morning and try his luck there. He knew that the big lake, Lake Coeur d'Alene, was also no more than half a mile away, to the south. The business at hand might not be pleasant, but Shep had to admit that he could not complain about his surroundings.

A sign in one of the Cove Bowl's windows indicated that the building also housed a restaurant. After showering and shaving, Shep walked across the street and settled into one of the few unoccupied plastic-upholstered booths. There was nothing fancy about the Cove Bowl's café, but judging from the business it was already doing, Shep concluded that he'd come to the right place for breakfast. He picked up a *Coeur d'Alene Press* that someone had left on the seat. A no-nonsense, heavyset waitress poured coffee for him as he scanned the front page. While there was brief coverage of national interest, the paper had a decidedly local flavor to it. A big picture on the front page bore the caption "Come Rain or Shine" and featured a bikini-clad North Idaho College coed shivering on the city beach. The sports page focused on local softball leagues and golf events, making no mention at all of a rumored Cliff Robinson trade that had filled a quarter page of the *Portland Gazette* the day before. There were two separate columns devoted entirely to fishing.

He was flipping through the rest of the paper when a picture on the fifth page caught his eye. It had been taken Thursday evening at a Planning and Zoning Commission hearing. It accompanied an article about a hearing to approve a rezone of land from agricultural to commercial. The applicant, a developer by the name of Bayshore Inc., was seeking to have four hundred acres of land located twenty miles down the west side of the lake rezoned to allow the development of an eighteen-hole golf course. The caption on the photo identified the man at the podium, who was addressing the Planning and Zoning Commission, as a local attorney who represented the applicant. Ordinarily, none of it would have been of interest to Shep, but something in the picture caught his eye. He looked closer. There it was. In the audience at the hearing. It was a little difficult to make out, but sitting at the back of the room, just barely visible over the shoulder of the attorney, was Anthony Walcott. No mistake about it.

Shep reread the article twice. It was brief. Nowhere was there mention of Walcott. Chances were Walcott had been at the hearing on unrelated business. Shep was familiar with the workings of most planning and zoning commissions—typically a hearing addressed more than one application. Walcott's purpose for attending Thursday night's hearing probably had nothing whatsoever to do with the proposed golf course that was the subject of the article. Still, in the light of Johnny Barletto's recent discoveries—that Muncie and Walcott had worked together in San Francisco and that Muncie had been involved in several golf course development scams—could Walcott's attendance at a hearing related to a new golf course be pure coincidence? And even if it were not a mere coincidence—even if Walcott and Muncie were involved somehow with this new golf course—how could there be any connection between that and Muncie's involvement at Edgewater Place? For a moment Shep felt almost foolish about the way his mind was working. Was he getting paranoid? On a rational level, he did not see how there could be any relationship between the two, yet on an instinctive level, he could not just dismiss the ominous feeling he had gotten from seeing Anthony Walcott in the audience of the hearing.

On Monday, when the municipal building opened, he would try to find out more about the hearing, but until then there was little he could do—he might as well enjoy the plate stacked high with pancakes, hash browns and a western omelette that the waitress had just deposited in front of him. When he left the Cove Bowl half an hour later, he knew he'd be back again during his stay.

Later that day Shep stopped by Edgewater Place. He'd hoped to find a way inside and do some snooping around, but the front door was locked. The only way to gain entry was by intercomming one of the residents from the vestibule and having that person buzz him inside. He would have to come back during the week, when Faith Lammerman, the property manager, whose office was just inside the lobby and who served the dual purpose of daytime security, would be there. Faith had impressed Shep on earlier visits as one of the few people associated with Edgewater Place who had the intelligence to realize that he and the bank—to most they were indistinguishable entities—were not necessarily the bad guys.

He bought groceries, stocked them in the mini-refrigerator and ate dinner in his room that night, rigging up his fishing pole before climbing into bed. The alarm went off at five A.M. on Sunday. By five-thirty he'd already settled on a rock outcropping on the north shore of Fernan Lake, a thermos of coffee and the *Sunday Spokesman Review* by his side. During a span of three hours he caught and released two nice-size rainbow trout and a lake-bottom scavenger. It had been years since Shep had done anything but catch and release. Fishing was food for his soul, not his body.

When the Coeur d'Alene City offices opened at nine A.M. Monday, Shep was there. A male clerk who seemed none to happy to be starting a new workweek directed him to the resource room, where he quickly found the three-ring binder he was looking for: *Minutes of Planning and Zoning Commission meetings*. Thursday's hearing was at the top.

Three matters had been heard that evening. He flipped quickly to the application for a zone change but soon found that nothing in the minutes regarding the proposed rezone for a golf course was helpful. It was the first in what looked destined to be a number of appearances in front of the commission for the applicant, a corporation by the name of Bayshore, Inc. The commission had ruled that Bayshore would have to provide a traffic impact study, as well as an environmental impact statement, before further consideration would be given the recent application for rezone. Only the corporation's attorney, a Jake Whitecomb, who must have been the man in the photo, spoke on behalf of the proposed change in zoning. There was nothing in the minutes to indicate who the principals in Bayshore, Inc. were.

Nowhere was there anything to indicate why Walcott had been at the meeting. Maybe his presence had nothing to do with the golf course. Perhaps he'd been there because of one of the other items on the agenda. A second, more thorough reading of the minutes gave Shep no indication whether that might be the case.

After poring over the minutes for almost an hour, Shep left the municipal building and, leaving his car in the city parking lot, walked toward Edgewater Place. On the way, he stopped at the Doughnut Shop and bought a couple of cinnamon rolls and two cups of coffee.

Faith Lammerman was standing in the middle of the lobby talking to a satellite TV repairman when he walked in. She gave Shep a friendly smile and told him she'd be with him in a minute. Shep stood there listening as she described the problem residents were having getting certain channels and as the two discussed whether it would be best for the repairman to visit each unit that was experiencing the problem or to start by taking a look at the satellite dish on the building's roof. They decided the latter course might prove to be the most efficient, which meant that Faith would have to escort the repairman up to unlock the door to the roof.

"I'm sorry, Shep." Faith smiled apologetically. "I'll be back in two minutes. If you'd like to wait for me in my office, please feel free." She locked the front door of the building—in her absence, visitors would have to use the intercom for entry—and hustled off efficiently, the cableman walking behind, no doubt admiring the body of a thirty-year-old on this woman whom Shep guessed to be at least fifty.

Shep stepped into Faith's office. It was no more than a ten-by-twelve cubicle, windowless, but with an old, well-worn oak desk that overflowed with papers, photographs, two small vases (one blue and one red) of flowers, and a box of chocolates. There were also a couple of chairs with equally worn plaid cushions, and the whole space had a welcoming, easy feeling to it. Faith's desk faced the door, affording her a view that enabled her to monitor all the comings and goings of residents, visitors, and miscellaneous service people.

Shep settled into one of the chairs facing the desk and tried to read the little placard—one of those ready-made decorations on a plastic stick that florists always put in the middle of flower arrangements—in the red vase.

"Thanks for all you do," the card said. It was signed "Alice Walcott."

A security report sat on top of a pile of papers in the center of the desk. Shep scooted his chair up closer to the desk and tried to read the report upside down. Luckily it was written in a bold, meticulously formed script. The report appeared to one of a series of reports done on a nightly basis. This was the most recent one, from Sunday night. It reported that a patrol of the entire building and grounds had taken place at ten P.M., one A.M., and most recently, at five A.M. It had apparently been a quiet night. Aside from the guard's reporting two burned-out lightbulbs in the corridors of the fourth and seventh floors, the only event worthy of note had been the fact that one of the residents had lost his keys and needed to have security let him into the buildings and then, with the master key, into his apartment.

Not wanting Faith to catch him snooping around, Shep was about to push his chair back to where it had been when he'd first seated himself when something else on the desk caught his eye. It was a Federal Express package. It appeared to have been just delivered. It took him several seconds to realize why his pulse had involuntarily quickened upon seeing it. It was the airbill. Again he was reading upside down, and the letters were smaller and less distinct than those on the security report, but even upside down he could read it. The recipient's name. It was Bayshore Inc. The address was simply that for Edgewater Place. There was no unit number given.

He'd barely leaned back in his chair when Faith breezed through the door.

"Now," she said, "what can I do for you?"

Shep lifted the cardboard carry-tray with the coffee and the bag containing the cinnamon rolls in offering. Faith accepted graciously.

"I was in town on business and just thought I'd drop by to say hi," Shep answered. Faith, who was a real people person and who had always found Shep likable—far more so than the banker, Stan Muncie—was more than happy to sit and visit with him over coffee.

They talked a little about the weather, two new restaurants that had opened in the past few months, local politics. It almost seemed to Shep that Faith was avoiding talking about the situation at Edgewater Place. Here he sat, the bank's attorney, and the only thing they hadn't discussed thus far was Edgewater Place. But then, out of the blue, she asked, "So, is it true about the foreclosure?"

"Yes," he answered matter-of-factly, "it is." What else could he say?

"It's a shame," Faith said, no trace of blame in her voice. "Michael worked so hard to make this building a success. And now there's Bailey and her niece, Clancy. It doesn't seem fair to them. I'm just crazy about that little girl. She comes down here every afternoon to visit with me."

"I understand how you feel," was all Shep could say. He wanted to say more. He wanted to tell her that he shared the same feelings. That he was there to try to do something about it. He wanted to ask her to help him. But, of course, he could not.

Instead he motioned to the flowers.

"A special occasion?" he asked.

"No," Faith answered. "Just thoughtful gifts from some of the homeowners. They spoil me, really they do. I got these"—she pointed to the blue vase—"from Mr. Liebowitz last week. These," she said, bending over and sniffing the flowers with the thank-you note sticking out, "are from Alice Walcott. They arrived this morning. Notice I said Alice and not *Anthony* Walcott. She's the thoughtful one. It would never occur to him to do something like this. I don't know how she puts up with that man. Anyway, the Walcotts have been out of town for a week, and I'm watching their unit. And keeping their mail for them." With that she nodded toward the Federal Express package and, as if demonstrating the task she'd accepted, picked it up and slipped it on top of a pile of neatly stacked mail that had earlier been bound together with a fat rubber band.

Shep hoped that his expression did not register the surprise he felt. Then Faith said something else that jolted him.

"They were planning to be gone longer but they'll have to be back for the special meeting that Bailey Coleman called."

"Special meeting?" Shep repeated.

"Didn't you see the notice on the lobby door?"

He hadn't. He looked out into the lobby. It was visible to him now, but because it was affixed to the back of the door, it was only in evidence when the door was shut.

"It's being held this Thursday," Faith offered.

Shep departed minutes later, making a mental note of the time of the special meeting as he read the notice upon leaving. He walked directly to his car, got in and then simply sat in the parking lot thinking. His visit to Faith Lammerman had paid off. She had put the Fed Ex package addressed to Bayshore, Inc. in the pile of mail she was holding for the Walcotts. Just as Shep had suspected, Walcott had to have been at the hearing on Thursday because of the proposed rezone for a golf course. And if Walcott was involved, there was little doubt in Shep's mind that Muncie was, too. Another piece of the puzzle had fallen into place. But at this stage it was no more than that—one more piece in a giant puzzle.

And now another mystery had arisen. This special meeting that had been called by Bailey Coleman.

Shep was beginning to feel more like a private investigator than a lawyer.

Starting his car, he decided that he'd had enough P.I. work for the time being. A warm, sunny day was beckoning. He was not going to waste it. He headed toward Fins and Feathers, where he was soon engrossed in fishing talk with

Randy Tawney. There wasn't much that could have taken Shep's mind off the situation with Stan Muncie and Bailey Coleman right then, but the discovery that Fins and Feathers was in the midst of its annual Fishing Derby came close. According to Randy, the winning fish inevitably was hooked out at Beauty Bay, on Lake Coeur d'Alene. Last year's beauty, a twenty-six-pound, forty-four-inch chinook salmon, was mounted on the shop's wall with a plaque bearing the winner's name.

Sometimes the most effective way to deal with a problem is to not deal with it for a while. The fishing contest was just what Shep needed. He spent the rest of the day arranging to rent a sixteen-foot, 100-horsepower boat and trailer and acquiring the equipment necessary to troll the waters of Lake Coeur d'Alene.

By sunset, a glorious, sky-aflame affair that night on Beauty Bay, Shep and his boat were positioned in the middle of what looked to be a formidable armada of boats of varying size and degree of sophistication—only if they looked closely would passersby on the highway that night just barely be able to make out, in the fast-fading daylight, the shadowy silhouettes not of weaponry but of fishing poles, gracefully extending from the rear of each boat, and of the boats' occupants, huddled beneath sweatshirts and blankets, oblivious to the night chill, dreaming of the derby-winning fish.

Shep Carroll was happy to be one of them.

Bailey and Clancy returned home from Seattle on Wednesday, in time for the next night's special meeting. It was almost midnight when they pulled into the parking garage.

Clancy had fallen asleep halfway through the drive. Leaving their bags in the car, Bailey quietly gathered Clancy in her arms and carried her into the elevator and up to the apartment.

At the door, not wanting to wake Clancy by putting her down, Bailey struggled to find the right key. Blindly choosing one that felt about the right size and shape, she tried to slip it into the keyhole, but the moment she pressed it against the knob the door creaked open on its own.

Had she actually forgotten to close and lock it when she'd left for Seattle?

She started into the darkened apartment and immediately, instinctively, knew that something was wrong. She distinctly remembered having turned on the entry light before she left. Could it have burned out? She had, after all, been gone four days.

As she backed slowly out into the corridor, Clancy began to stir.

"Shhh," Bailey whispered.

Once out in corridor, she hurried to the elevator, casting a frequent eye in the direction of her unit.

"Where are we going?" Clancy wanted to know.

"I'm going to take you to Sam's," Bailey answered. "That way I can go back to the car and get all our things."

"I'll go with you," Clancy muttered.

"No," said Bailey, stepping onto the elevator. "I want you to go back to sleep."

They rang Sam's bell several times before she finally answered.

Bailey apologized for disturbing her and asked if it would be okay for Clancy to lie down on Sam's couch while she retrieved their bags from the car.

Sam, slightly disoriented from the abrupt awakening but good-natured as ever, welcomed them in. But as Bailey left, she looked concerned.

"Is everything okay?"

Bailey, not wanting to alarm either Sam or Clancy, quickly answered, "Of course."

Bailey headed to the elevator, then changed her mind. She did not want it to announce her arrival. As she climbed the stairs to the eleventh floor, she debated about the wisdom of returning to her apartment alone. But the alternative meant stirring things up, making Clancy aware of her fears. And since the likelihood that something was actually wrong was so slim—surely she had, indeed, just forgotten to lock the door, and the light had, after four days of continuous use, burned out—she just didn't want to do that to Clancy.

In a way, she did not want to do it to herself, either. If she reacted to this situation by calling for help, it would be an acknowledgment of her fear. A fear that she knew was silly and unfounded.

Still, as she silently approached her front door again, she could feel her wildly pulsing heartbeat, the hairs on the back of her neck and arms bristling against her shirt collar and sleeves.

She stood at the half-open door and listened. Nothing. Then she reached for the light switch. It was still in the on position. She flipped it down, then back up. Nothing happened. It must have, indeed, burned out.

Relieved, she gave the door a slight nudge, but the moment she stepped inside, she could almost smell it, smell the fact that something was wrong.

Irrationally choosing to go forward into the darkness, to confront whatever it was that awaited her rather than run, she moved along the hallway, feeling for another lightswitch. Finally, she reached the switch that operated the light outside the dining room. She flipped it on and let out a gasp.

There was furniture everywhere. Turned on its side, upside down. Glass. The dining room table's glass top had been shattered.

Her hand held to her mouth, Bailey moved on down the hall, flipping on lights as she went.

Michael's office had papers strewn everywhere. Lamps crushed from being thrown against the wall. A family picture, its ceramic frame stomped into pieces, in the middle of the floor. She picked it up and felt a wetness roll down her arm from the frame. Then she recognized the odor. Urine. Sickened, she dropped it.

Clancy's bedroom was the same. Bedding ripped off the bed. Drawers open.

Her room, too.

Bailey rushed, disbelieving, from one room to the next.

It was in her bathroom, however, that she made the most horrifying discovery. Across her mirror something had been written using her lipstick. It took her a moment to decipher it.

"Not a good idea to leave her alone," it read.

"P.S. You look great in a bathing suit."

They had seen her at the swimming pool the other morning. And they had known she'd left Clancy alone, sleeping.

Shaking uncontrollably, she reached for the telephone and dialed 911.

"Please send someone over to Edgewater Place," she said. "Unit 11A. And please don't use sirens. I'll meet you at the front door."

The police officers had been most professional and thorough. They'd spent hours going through the apartment, taking photographs and making notes. She'd told them about the article she received anonymously. While their many questions about its contents and the envelope in which it had arrived indicated their genuine interest, they seemed reluctant to declare a connection between the two events.

"It's not out of the question," a young blond officer, the man apparently in charge, had told her. "But if this is the work of some hate group, it will be a first. These groups are mostly rhetoric. Sending you threatening letters, or copies of articles from the paper, that's their style. But actually breaking into an apartment, especially one in a secured building like this, that's way out of line with their behavior up till now. And the truth is, we have quite a few Hispanic families in this area. I've never heard of any of them experiencing harassment. It just doesn't add up.

"Still," he'd concluded, "we'll want to keep a close eye on things. We'll have extra patrols around the building.

And," he'd added, needlessly, "I wouldn't leave your niece alone in this apartment again."

Bailey had returned to Sam's and explained the situation. Clancy, sound asleep again, would stay with Sam for the rest of the night while Bailey cleaned up the apartment. There was no chance she'd get any sleep anyway.

By the time Clancy and Sam arrived the next morning, with the exception of the dining room table and the picture frame, things were back to normal.

But, as Bailey's life seemed determined to establish, normal was now a state in which everything that could go wrong did. The phone soon rang with news from Tony Pappas.

"I'm afraid I have bad news," he'd said, unaware of the poor timing of his call. "I just got off the phone with Shep Carroll. The two weeks are up today. If you have a proposal to make, he's more than willing to meet with us tomorrow to discuss it. If not, he'll deliver us a written notice of default that your thirty-day cure period has begun. It's your call."

"Then what?"

"Then we have exactly thirty days to cure the default by coming up with the one point three million dollars we're now delinquent. At the end of that thirty days, they foreclose."

Bailey wanted to scream. She wanted to cry.

Instead, she told Tony, "There's no reason for a meeting. Tell him to go ahead. To do what he has to do."

She was simply too tired, too numb, to tell Tony what had just happened, what she had come home to. She'd wait until next time she saw him.

Maybe then she'd feel better. Maybe then she'd feel more like talking about it.

CHAPTER 11

JUST BEFORE THE MEETING Bailey noticed a folded piece of paper peeking out from under her front door.

She was angry and tired. As she reached for the piece of paper, she felt ready to explode. If she ever found the sicko who was trying to intimidate her, she'd go for his jugular.

But when she opened the paper, it turned out to be something else entirely.

"You have enough votes to approve a building inspection at tonight's meeting," was written in a cramped scrawl. There was no signature.

What was this? Just what about her made people want to send her anonymous notes and clippings?

She refolded the note and stuck it in the pocket of her jeans. She tried to call Sam before leaving, hoping her friend might be able to shed some light on the meaning of the note—maybe, knowing Sam, she would even have some idea as to its author. But then she remembered Sam's telling her that she was attending a day-long seminar put on by the environmental group Save Our Planet that was being held at nearby North Idaho College, followed by dinner. She would be coming to the meeting straight from that dinner.

Bailey had made arrangements for Doris Peacock's visiting teenaged granddaughter, Cynthia, to sit with Clancy. Doris was a widower who lived on the eighth floor. An easy-going, friendly woman, she was one of the few residents who chose not to attend meetings. "Too much conflict," she'd explained to Bailey. In her current mood, Bailey had selected a baby-sitter based on two factors: having Clancy watched somewhere other than Bailey's apartment and having her watched by as many eyes as possible. With Doris and Cynthia both home for the evening, Bailey felt comfortable leaving Clancy.

After dropping her off, she headed for the social room for her second official meeting of the Edgewater Place Homeowners Association. She had been nervous about the first meeting, but this one was different. Little things like homeowner meetings no longer had the power to get to her.

Once again, the room was full. Once again, the reception she got from Anthony Walcott and the rest of the board was cool.

When the board had settled itself at the table, Walcott called the meeting to order. A flash of green at the back of the room caught Bailey's eye. It was Sam, just arriving. She was dressed in a blindingly bright green, oversized T-shirt that read "It's Time to Mother Mother Earth," blue jeans and white sneakers. She gave Bailey her little rodeo queen salute as she lowered herself into a chair. Bailey couldn't help but chuckle, which caused both Anthony Walcott and Tom Ryan to turn and glare at her.

"This special meeting is being held in response to Miss Bailey Coleman's request," Walcott said. "The purpose of the meeting, as stated in the notice all of the homeowners received, is to vote on amending the CC&Rs to allow pets in the building. As you know, pets have never been allowed in this building. There are good, sound reasons for this, which I'm sure all of you appreciate. I don't think I need to go into them at this time. However, the CC&Rs provide that any provision can be amended by a majority vote of the home-owners association. Now, we all know that at the moment"—he placed special emphasis on "at the moment"—"Miss Coleman can exercise forty-seven votes. Since there are only eighty units, it doesn't take a genius to realize that Miss Coleman alone has the power to pass this amendment. For that reason, there is no need to waste all of our valuable time in prolonged discussion or debate that will, for all practical purposes, be moot.

"But before we vote, I for one want to go on the record as having expressed my disappointment in Miss Coleman's actions. I find this eleventh-hour attempt of hers to stir things up in our building unconscionable. But I believe in living by the rules, and as the president of the homeowners association, I feel we have no choice but to allow her to manipulate the provisions of the CC&Rs in this manner. Now, Mr. Secretary," he said, turning to the man on his right, "will you please conduct the vote."

"Wait just a minute," came a frail voice from the middle of the chairs in the belly of the room. A petite, well-dressed woman in her late sixties was rising from her chair. "I'm Estelle Rouchon, from Unit 414. Discussion is never moot, Mr. President. I don't care how many votes Miss Coleman has. I have something to say on this matter and I would like to hear what Miss Coleman has to say as well. And I might point out that you've managed to get *your* say in. So please don't be so eager to cut the rest of us off. But first, I want to know what you mean by her 'eleventh hour' attempt."

Walcott looked like he wanted to bite the old lady's head off. Not only was she thwarting his plans to keep this meeting lightning quick, she'd also managed to make him look like an idiot. But even he knew the perils of going head to head with her in front of the rest of the homeowners.

"I'm afraid I can't answer that question," he said with feigned consideration. "Out of deference to Miss Coleman. I wouldn't want to say anything that could cause her embarrassment."

With that, Bailey pushed her chair back from the table and stood.

"I'd be happy to explain what Mr. Walcott meant to Mrs. Rouchon. As of today, Chicago Savings and Loan declared me in default on the loan my brother took to build Edgewater Place. That means I have thirty days to come up with one point three million dollars. If I'm unsuccessful in doing that, all forty-seven of my brother's units will go into foreclosure." Her words brought a response that ranged from gasps of "Oh my!" to shocked whispers from the rest of the homeowners. "That is what Mr. Walcott was referring to when he called this an eleventh-hour attempt on my part. And the truth is, he's right. I *am* attempting to take advantage of my voting power before I lose it, before I am forced out of Edgewater Place. But I am not trying to stir things up, as Mr. Walcott claims. What I'm trying to do is correct a situation I believe is wrong. One that has created a hardship on at least one of you." She looked at Sam, who was sitting calmly with her hands clasped in her lap, for a moment, then scanned the room. "When she bought a unit here, Samantha Cummings was told that her pet dog, a now-fifteen-year-old dachshund named Gator, could live here. Then, after she moved in, the board told her she had to get rid of Gator. As most of you must know, Sam lives alone. She loves that dog. He's her companion—as she told me, her 'best friend.' I think the board's actions were wrong, quite possibly illegal, and simply put, downright cruel. I want to right that tonight. At the very least, I want to pass an amendment allowing Sam to keep Gator here, in Edgewater Place. And in thinking about Sam's situation, it occurred to me that there might be others here who would like to be able to have pets." Bailey noticed Mrs. Rouchon—who in her eagerness was sitting so close to the edge of her seat that Bailey feared she'd end up on the floor if she weren't soon given a chance to say what was on her mind—nodding her head in agreement. "Mrs. Rouchon, would you like to say something now?"

"Thank you, dear," she said with relief, standing again. "I

am a widow, too. When I moved in, I had to give my daughter my two cats because of this ridiculous no-pets policy. Those two cats never caused anyone a moment's grief. They are clean and quiet, and most importantly, like Sam's Gator, they are my best friends. They keep me company. Or at least, they did. I've been thinking of selling my place here and buying a small house just so that I can have them back again. I think you should be commended, Miss Coleman, for what you want to do for Sam. But I would like to ask you to use your votes to enable all of us who live here to keep our animals. It's not fair to force us to choose between our pets and living here. It's not fair, and it's not right."

Her words were met with several nodding heads and murmurs of agreement. But scattered about the room there were also a number of scowls. The owner of the nastiest one was on his feet before Mrs. Rouchon had finished her speech.

"I for one did not buy an expensive condominium just to have to put up with the mess, stench and chaos that will come with allowing pets into this building. I was on the budget committee. I know what kind of money we have invested in the furnishings and carpets in this building. This place will look like hell within one year if we allow the pet policy to be amended."

Bailey waited for him to stop, then she spoke again.

"You're right. This is a beautiful building. Everyone here tonight paid top dollar to live here. And because of the price range of these units, we've ended up with a building full of very successful, very responsible people. I don't believe any of them who would choose to have a pet would be so irresponsible or inconsiderate as to permit any damage or disruption in this building. And there are ways to ensure that won't happen. I propose that the amendment we vote upon tonight also provide for the formation of a committee to regulate the keeping of pets in the building. Owners will have to adhere to the committee's rules. If they don't, they'll get a warning. If they fail to heed the warning, they'll lose the right to keep their pet. How does that sound?"

The man who had just spoken continued to look less than happy, but in general, there were nods of agreement.

A very bald, very rotund man sitting in the front row raised his hand to speak. "Sounds fair to me," he said. "But what I'm more concerned about right now is this foreclosure thing. Just what will happen if there's a foreclosure on all of those units?"

Bailey did not have an answer. But Walcott, who'd been doing a slow burn at his perception that Bailey had taken over the meeting, couldn't resist responding.

"They'll auction those units off," he said authoritatively. Then, seeing the quizzical look on Bailey's face, he quickly added, "At least, that's one scenario."

Discussion of the pet amendment died down as concern over the impending foreclosure mounted, but Walcott was quick to head it off.

"It's entirely improper for us to use this forum to speculate about what the bank will do. Besides, it's quite insensitive of us to subject Miss Coleman to this. Let's have the vote. Do I have a motion?"

Bailey made the motion. It was seconded by Mrs. Rouchon and at least two other homeowners whose names Bailey did not know. The secretary called for a secret written ballot. After a five-minute recess, the tally was announced. Of the sixty-nine units represented at the meeting, there were sixty-two votes favoring the amendment and seven opposing. Sam Cummings let out a little cheer at the announcement.

"There being no other business on the agenda tonight . . ." Walcott said, attempting to adjourn the meeting. But he was cut short by Bailey.

"I know it isn't on the agenda, but I do have another item for discussion," she said.

"What is it now?" Walcott asked impatiently.

"I would like to propose a vote to approve the hiring of a construction engineer to conduct a building inspection."

The room fell silent.

Walcott, after an initial moment of paralysis, jumped to his feet and in a raised voice thundered. "This is preposterous. This is not the time or place to bring that up. That would clearly be a management issue, and all management decisions are made by the board of managers."

"Then I'd like to call a meeting of the board of managers," Bailey said, not willing to be bullied into backing down.

Walcott's only response to Bailey was a glare.

"This meeting is adjourned," he said angrily, grabbing the papers he'd spread out in front of him and shoving them into his briefcase.

As the homeowners started filtering out of the social room, Sam and Mrs. Rouchon hurried over to Bailey.

"Thank you!" the two cried out simultaneously. Sam gave her a hug, and Mrs. Rouchon reached for Bailey's hand and clasped it appreciatively. The three women walked to the elevator together. Several homeowners smiled at Bailey as they were leaving, and she heard more than one call out, "Good luck!" to her.

In the elevator, Mrs. Rouchon said, "I'm going to call my daughter tonight and arrange to pick up my cats. How about you, Sam? When will you get Gator back?"

Sam and Bailey looked at each other, then both broke into laughter.

"The truth is, Estelle," Sam said, "I've had Gator with me all long. Only now, thanks to Bailey, we'll be able to come out of hiding."

Estelle looked both shocked and delighted at Sam's confession. Her joy at the prospect of being reunited with her own pets was obvious. Before she got off the elevator, she turned to Bailey and said, "I do hope you can work things out with the bank. We could use someone like you on the board—someone who cares about the people who live in this building more than the building itself."

Sam exited at the seventh floor, promising to stop by at Bailey's in the morning. She was anxious to talk to Bailey, to find out why she'd suggested a building inspection, but there was another homeowner in the elevator with them. It would have to wait.

Mrs. Rouchon's words stayed with Bailey that night. The truth was that up until then, with the exception of her feelings for Sam Cummings, Bailey *had* cared more about the building than its residents. Her sole interest had been saving Michael's project, keeping a home there for Clancy and her. But at the meeting, the homeowners had suddenly become real people to her. Some had managed to endear themselves to her. And for the first time she'd seen that the foreclosure was a threat not just to Clancy and her but to many others as well. It had undoubtedly been one of them who had written her that note that very day. If the units were auctioned off, there's no telling what would happen to Edgewater Place. Tony Pappas had said it was the worst-case scenario, something the bank would do only as a last resort. Why was it, then, that Walcott had suggested it would be the most likely course of action? And how would he have any idea what the bank's plans were? And what about this building inspection? There was no doubt that Walcott was furious at her for having brought it up at the meeting.

She was just starting to doze off, her mind drifting from one troubling thought to another, when her bedroom door opened. She looked up to see Clancy's tiny form framed by the light from the bathroom down the hall, which she always left on in case the little girl got up during the night.

"Everything okay?"

"Can I sleep with you?" Clancy asked sheepishly.

"Sure you can," Bailey answered, lifting the covers.

The little girl climbed in and instantly molded her shape to the curvature of Bailey's. "Did your meeting go okay?" she asked.

"Yes. It did," answered Bailey sleepily. "From now on, Gator gets to ride the elevators like the rest of us."

"Awesome!" Clancy said. "Maybe now Sam will let me walk him sometimes."

"I bet she will. Now, let's go to sleep. Okay?"

"Okay."

Bailey had just dozed off again when Clancy said softly, "I saw Shep tonight."

"You *what*?"

"I saw Shep. When Cynthia and Mrs. Peacock took me down to the rec room."

Bailey was now wide awake and sitting bolt upright.

"Where was he?" she asked.

"He was standing outside the social room," Clancy offered weakly, knowing her words would upset her aunt but having a need to confess the knowledge that had been weighing heavily on her mind all evening.

Bailey took a deep breath.

"Did you talk to him?"

"No."

"Are you sure it was him?"

"Yes."

There was silence. Then Bailey slipped back under the covers next to Clancy and put an arm around her. "Thanks for telling me that, sweetheart. Now, you go to sleep. Okay?"

"Are you mad at him?" Clancy asked.

"Yes, I am," Bailey answered.

Clancy was silent long enough that Bailey thought she'd finally fallen asleep. But she hadn't.

"Is everything going to be okay?" the little girl wanted to know before finally giving in to her exhaustion.

"Everything will be fine," Bailey answered.

For some reason, Shep slept in on Friday morning. He'd planned on being out in the boat on Beauty Bay before dawn, but he'd slept right through the five A.M. wake-up call he'd requested. When the phone rang again he was shocked to see that it was already almost eight-thirty. The bigger shock, however, was the identity of the caller.

"What room are you in?" a familiar voice demanded to know.

"What?" Shep was still half asleep.

"What room are you in?" the voice repeated. It was Bailey.

"One-oh-seven," Shep replied without thinking to ask why.

"I'm on my way."

"Holy shit," Shep said, jumping up to slip on a pair of jeans. He'd barely pulled a T-shirt from his still-packed suitcase when he heard her at the door. She'd apparently called from the lobby. He started toward the bathroom to at least slap some water on his face, but her knock was growing louder and more impatient so he went directly to the door instead.

"May I come in?" Bailey asked.

"Of course," Shep responded, stepping aside to allow her in.

Bailey looked as though she hadn't slept the entire night before, which was, in fact, quite close to the truth. She also looked incredibly angry.

As soon as he'd shut the door behind her, she turned to confront him. Her face bore the same anger and hurt he'd last seen on it.

"I want to know why you were lurking around the social room last night during the homeowners meeting," she said.

"I was not lurking," Shep answered. "I was debating whether to attend."

This answer seemed to only further infuriate Bailey.

"You had no right to be there. How did you even get into the building?"

Shep would not retreat. "I have every right to be there. The bank or its representative has the authority to attend every meeting of the general homeowners association. And I was let into the building by the security guard. The same one who has let me in for every homeowners meeting I've attended."

"How did you even know about it?" Bailey hammered. "And if you had the right to be there, why didn't you just come in?"

"The bank automatically receives notice of all meetings.

That's how I knew about it," Shep lied. He did not want to say he'd learned about the meeting from Faith Lammerman on Monday. Then Bailey would know he'd been in Coeur d'Alene all week. If she knew that, she might pass the information along to Tony Pappas, and he, in turn, could pass it along to Stan Muncie. And Muncie was the last person Shep wanted to know. "And as for why I didn't come in, when I heard the reason the meeting was called, to amend the pet policy, I decided it wasn't a matter that required my presence. Sometimes having the bank's attorney present can plant fear or tension in a situation that simply doesn't call for it. I decided last night was one of those situations. Besides," he added apologetically, "I saw no reason to aggravate you, though apparently I managed to do that anyway."

They stood facing each other. Some of the fire had faded from Bailey's eyes. In fact, she suddenly looked awkward, embarrassed. As if she had surprised herself by her own actions in coming to Shep's room.

"May I ask you a question?" Shep ventured.

Bailey did not respond.

"How did you know I was staying here?"

"I went down the hotel listings in the phone book and called each one until I found you," she confessed. Then, in a transparent effort to regain some sense of the indignation that had prompted her visit in the first place, she went back on the attack.

"I want to know how it is that son of a bitch Walcott knows about my being in default."

"Walcott knows that?"

"He certainly does. He made that very clear at last night's meeting. I want to know how he found out."

"Just what did Walcott say at the meeting?"

"He wouldn't come out and say anything. At least at first. He just dropped some not-so-vague references to the fact that I wouldn't be around for long. Then I told the homeowners about the foreclosure. They didn't seem to know about it until then. And they seemed pretty upset about it.

Especially when Walcott said the bank would auction off those units."

"Walcott said *that*?" Shep was stunned. He ran his hand through his hair, which sported several cowlicks from his unusually sound sleep, and shook his head ever so slightly. He was confused as to why Walcott would reveal himself by making such a comment.

"Would you like to sit down?" he asked then, motioning toward the couch and chair.

Bailey appeared to hesitate.

"Please," he said to her, hurriedly clearing several newspapers off the couch. But she refused.

"Why are you doing this to us?" she finally asked.

"Why am *I* doing this to you or why is the *bank* doing this to you? Which do you mean?"

"Same thing, isn't it?"

Shep paused. "You're a law student, aren't you? I think you know the answer to both questions." He looked at her then. "Bailey, you must know how difficult this if for me. It's driving me half crazy. Ever since that night, I . . ."

He caught himself. There was nothing to be gained by proclaiming his feelings for her. Nothing at all. If he really cared for her, he would leave well enough alone. He'd already confused and hurt her enough. Her visit today was proof of that. He could tell she was embarrassed, wondering why she'd come. He knew that in attacking him for being at Edgewater Place during last night's meeting, she was really assailing him for his betrayal. They were talking around all the real issues. And because of his twisted situation—because of his obligation to his client, a client he was keeping only because he wanted to protect Bailey from him—he could do nothing to set her straight.

There was only one way to help her now.

"Don't talk to me about that night."

The sharpness of her words took Shep by surprise.

"I don't know how I could have done what I did. With a man who just wants to destroy everything my brother worked for. Everything he left me. And Clancy."

If she'd wanted to inflict pain upon Shep, she could have found no more effective a means. Stung once more by her words but unable to defend himself, Shep could only maintain his silence. A silence that, to Bailey, signaled indifference.

"I'll be going," Bailey said.

"Wait . . ." Shep reached for her.

She turned. "Wait for *what*?"

"I might be able to help you."

"Help me?" she half snorted in cynical disbelief. "How?"

Shep hesitated.

"You have all of Michael's papers, don't you? His files? Records? Everything having to do with Edgewater Place?"

"Yes. I have everything."

"Would you be willing to let me take a look at them?"

Shep knew the danger of what he was doing. He hadn't planned this—never had he planned to involve Bailey in this. But then, how could he have known she would show up at his door? How could he have known that her simple presence would be enough to override the concerns he'd had about the course he'd embarked upon?

"Why would I do that?" Bailey wanted to know.

"What do you have to lose?"

Bailey laughed. But it wasn't the same laugh that he'd seen light her face with joy. It was a very different laugh, one that made Shep sad.

"You're right," she said. "What more could I possibly lose?"

They agreed to meet back at her place later that morning. While Clancy was down at the pool having her swimming lesson—when Bailey learned her niece did not know how to swim, she'd immediately arranged for someone to come in twice weekly for lessons—Bailey showered and changed from the T-shirt and jeans she'd worn earlier to a sundress. Then, after looking at herself in the full-view bathroom mirror, she removed the sundress and put the T-shirt and jeans back on.

She couldn't believe she was doing this. Allowing him into her home again. Allowing herself to spend more time with him. Was she *trying* to torture herself?

Of course, what greater torture could there be than having just stood in his motel room, seeing him dressed in nothing but a pair of jeans, his hair still wild from sleep? God, that had almost been her undoing. How she'd wanted to reach out to him. To feel the weight of that body on top of her once again, smell the tangy maleness of him. If she'd wanted to torture herself, she had definitely already found the way.

But maybe her acquiescence actually made sense. Shep's surprise at Walcott's actions certainly seemed genuine enough. So did his desire to help her. She so wanted to trust him. Did she dare?

After her search for Michael's plan to save Edgewater Place, she'd stored all of his papers and files in two sturdy boxes and stuck them in a closet in the study. Somehow the intruder—she thought of him in the singular; surely no more than one person could be so twisted—had overlooked them.

The prospect that Shep would be working with her in the small study made Bailey feel more than a little anxious, so before he arrived she moved the boxes into the living room. They'd just unloaded the contents of the boxes onto the floor and coffee table when there was another knock at the door. Before Bailey could answer it, Sam Cummings's voice could be heard.

"Anybody home?"

"In here," Bailey called.

Sam's cheerful face appeared from the hallway moments later, then, when she recognized Shep, went stone-cold.

"Sam, this is Shep Carroll," Bailey said. "The bank's attorney."

Shep had risen and was approaching Sam, his right hand extended.

"You ought to be ashamed of yourself," Sam scolded, approaching Shep aggressively. "Isn't it enough to have this foreclosure thing hanging over her head night and day? How dare you harass Bailey at home?"

Shep stopped in his tracks, his hand still extended.

"No, Sam," Bailey hurried to explain. "You've got it wrong. Shep is here to help." She realized how absurd what she'd just said must sound to Sam.

Sam looked thoroughly confused. Shep was still semi-frozen. Bailey positioned herself between the two of them and placed one hand on Shep's arm, the other hand on Sam's.

"Shep, this is my good friend, Sam Cummings," she said.

Shep tried extending his hand one more time. Sam took it, but none too eagerly.

"It's nice to meet you, Sam," Shep said politely.

"Samantha," Sam corrected him, which made Bailey laugh.

Both looked to Bailey for help with the other.

"Will you please excuse us for a moment?" Bailey said then to Shep. She led Sam into the kitchen, seated her at the table and pulled a chair up close to her.

"I meant it, Sam," she said. "He says he wants to help. He asked to see Michael's files."

Sam looked far from convinced. "And you let him?"

"Well, he just got here, so he hasn't seen anything yet," she answered.

"Good," said Sam, rising from her chair. "Then it's not too late to get him out of here."

Bailey grabbed Sam's arm and pulled her back down into the chair.

"No," she said. "Sam, listen to me. For some twisted reason, I halfway believe him."

"Why would you believe he wants to help you? He works for the bank. I can't believe you'd fall for that."

"Well, for starters, I think he could get disbarred for what he's doing," Bailey said.

"He could?" asked Sam. Then, after thinking about it for a moment, she added, "Yes, I imagine he could." This realization seemed to have an impact on her.

"I don't know if I can trust him, Sam," Bailey said, "but as he pointed out, I really don't have much to lose, do I? The way things are going, this foreclosure is already a sure thing. He's the one with a lot at stake. A client. Maybe even his career. What does it hurt to go along with him?"

Sam thought about that for a moment and then said, "I see what you mean."

"I tell you what," Bailey said. "There's no one whose judgment I value more than yours. Why don't you stay? Then you can tell me what you think."

The idea was very appealing to Sam.

"I'll do it," she said decisively.

They returned to the living room, and together, the three of them started going through Michael's files.

Shep started with the loan documents, most of which he already had in his files at Emerson, Caldwell. There was page after page of documents—the loan application, bids for construction, faxes between Michael Coleman and Muncie. But nothing that would explain the relationship between Muncie and Walcott. After a while, he looked up.

"Find anything?" Bailey asked.

"Not what I'm looking for," he explained. "I hoped to find some connection between Muncie and Anthony Walcott in this file. But there is none."

At his words, Sam and Bailey exchanged a look that Shep could not help but notice.

"Ladies?" he said.

Bailey looked at Sam and said, "Tell him what you overheard that day." It was another leap of faith on Bailey's part, but now that she'd started down this path, she saw no reason to turn back. Sam proceeded to tell Shep about the day she'd hidden behind the bushes and overheard Walcott telling Ryan that the bank was going to foreclose.

"The only way he could have known that information at that time was by having learned it from Muncie," Shep said. And he mustn't forget that he himself had seen the two men together on his last visit. The trouble was, none of it really connected the two of them to any wrongdoing involving

Bailey or Michael Coleman or Edgewater Place. Maybe they were no more than old friends who'd stayed in touch, who confided in each other over business matters like Edgewater Place. But why, then, would Muncie lie about knowing Walcott?

"That's what we figured, too," Sam offered. Bailey could see that her friend was warming to Shep.

"Yet at the time he made that statement, the bank had just agreed to joint control," Bailey added.

Shep shook his head.

"Just doesn't make sense. Let's take a look at the construction file," he said then, reaching for the thickest file. He pored over the documents in it—the contractor's agreement, change orders, blueprints—for the better part of an hour. The task was almost impossible, not knowing what he was even looking for, but he did not want to leave a single paragraph unread.

After a while Bailey and Sam began to feel they were in the way. They excused themselves and went out on the deck. It was another gorgeous early summer morning, sunny but not yet hot. They settled at the patio table. Once out there, Bailey told Sam about finding the note under her door the morning before.

"I wondered why you brought up hiring a building inspector at the meeting last night," Sam said.

"Do you have any idea who this could be from?" Bailey asked, withdrawing the note from her front pocket of her jeans.

Sam took the folded paper and read it carefully, then studied the handwriting. "It's definitely someone older," she said. Bailey had also thought the script, which was a little shaky, belonged to someone older. "It looks like a woman's writing to me, but you can never tell. I wonder . . ."

"What?" asked Bailey.

Sam looked at Bailey. "There's something I never told you. Something I overhead. I didn't tell you because I didn't want to upset you. You had enough to deal with at the time."

"What is it?"

"Remember that day you had lunch with Charlie Eaglequill?" Bailey nodded. "That morning, I overheard another conversation between Walcott and Tom Ryan. Ryan wanted the board to vote on whether to have a building inspection. Walcott was dead set against it. He was adamant. You know how he gets when you push him on something he doesn't want to do. He basically told Ryan he wouldn't even allow the board to consider the matter."

"And Ryan backed down?" Bailey asked.

"Doesn't everyone?" Sam responded. Then she said, "Do you think we should tell Mr. Carroll about this?"

Bailey remained silent for a while.

"No," she said finally. "Let's keep it to ourselves. At least for now." Giving Shep access to Michael's files made her feel vulnerable enough. She wanted to hold something back.

While they were still outside, Clancy returned from her swimming lesson.

"Shep!" she cried happily when she entered the living room. Then she looked around, a fearful expression taking hold. "Does my aunt know you're here?"

Bailey, who'd heard Clancy return, laughed as she entered the living room from the deck. "Yes, I do know," she said. "I invited him."

"Wow!" Clancy said, looking thoroughly confused but happy.

Shep glanced at his watch, saw that it was almost noon and offered to take everyone to lunch. The realization that it was not such a good idea for Bailey and Shep to be seen together in public seemed to register on all of their faces at once.

"Well, maybe I'll just walk down to Hudson's for a burger," he said. "Mind if I take Clancy along?"

Bailey hesitated, but after seeing the look on Clancy's face she finally gave her consent. A happy Clancy gave her a kiss before departing, hand in hand, with Shep.

Sam observed Bailey as she stood in the doorway watching the twosome disappear into the elevator.

"He actually seems like a very nice man," Sam said, studying Bailey's face for her reaction.

"Clancy is quite taken with him."

"So I noticed," Sam said. Then, "And you?"

Bailey's eyes met those of her friend. She still was not ready to tell Sam about the two of them. "What difference does it make what I think of him?" she said with just a touch too much indifference. "The only thing that matters is if he can help us."

Sam smiled at her young friend. "You're right, of course."

Sam left a few minutes later. Bailey found herself checking the wall clock in the kitchen often as she did dishes and waited for Shep and Clancy to return. When they did, Shep returned to the files. By two-thirty, he looked up at Bailey and said, "Zero. Nada. I haven't found a single thing. Is this it? Have I missed anything?"

Bailey noticed that something had slipped underneath the chair in which Shep sat. She grabbed it, then, seeing what it was, said, "Oh, never mind."

"What is it?" Shep wanted to know.

"Oh, just some newspaper article that keeps falling out of that file. It doesn't belong with Michael's business papers. I should just throw it away," she said, crumpling it.

"Wait. Can I see it?"

"Sure," Bailey said. "But it's just an article about a casino that opened on an Indian reservation over near Seattle. I have no idea why Michael cut it out."

Shep took the crumpled paper from her and, running his large hand over it, flattened it against the coffee table. Then he started reading. The Tulalip Tribe, which had been operating a profitable casino on its reservation in western Washington since 1992, had just announced its plan to build a new $50 million resort. Since its opening, the article reported, the casino's prosperity had positively impacted the economic status not only of the once-struggling tribe but of neighboring non–Native American communities as well. The planned resort would include a hotel, theater, museum, movie theaters and restaurants, the financing for which was already in place. The tribe also hoped to include an eighteen-hole golf course in its expansion. Negotiations with a developer by the name of Bayshore, Inc. were currently taking place for development of the golf course.

"What is it?" Bailey asked when, halfway through the article, she saw the change in Shep's expression.

He stared at the wall for a moment, not answering, then said, "Isn't there a reservation near here?"

"Yes. The Coeur d'Alene Reservation."

"Where is it?" he said. Then, "No—let me guess. Is it about twenty miles down the east side of the lake?"

Bailey nodded. "Twenty, maybe twenty-five. Yes."

Shep rose. "May I keep this?" he asked, indicating the crinkled article.

"Sure, but . . ."

He turned and stood face-to-face with Bailey. "Listen, you've been a big help. Thank you."

"But what is it? What did you find? Was there something in that article?"

"Yes."

"And you're not going to tell me what it is?" Her voice was rising with indignation. "You're actually going to come in here and ask for my help like this, then leave me in the dark?"

"I think it's better you not know. At least for now." His eyes met hers. "You have to trust me, Bailey. Please." He reached out and placed his hands on her arms, which she'd crossed in anger across her chest. It was a spontaneous reaction on Shep's part, the first time they'd touched since their night together, and its effect was unsettling on both of them.

Bailey had never before felt such a sea of conflicting emotions. Literally as they spoke, the anger and indignation were building inside her. Had she played right into his hands? Let him use her for some purpose she didn't understand, something that had nothing to do with helping her?

But then he'd said her name. Something as simple as his saying her name. He'd asked her to trust him. After all that had happened between them. He'd reached out and touched her. And in that moment she'd had to fight an overpowering impulse to reach for him, to pull him to her. God, was she going crazy, had she lost her mind?

He was gone before she had the chance to decide which emotion was more real.

The only thing she knew with any certainty was that Shep Carroll was back in her life—in a manner, a role, she'd never anticipated. And nothing that had come before had ever filled her with such fear. Nor such longing.

CHAPTER 12

BAILEY WAS PUZZLED WHEN Estelle Rouchon called her first thing Saturday morning, asking if they could set up a meeting. She knew she and Estelle had hit it off on Thursday night, knew that the woman was grateful for the role Bailey had played in getting her cats back. Bailey wouldn't have been surprised to have been invited to Estelle's for coffee, or even lunch. But the word Estelle had used was definitely *meeting*. They agreed that Bailey would come to Estelle's unit, number 414, at one-thirty that afternoon.

Several hours later, after dropping Clancy off at a friend's house, Bailey found herself standing outside the door marked "414," waiting for a response to her knock. When she got none, she pressed the doorbell. Within seconds she heard Estelle Rouchon's voice on the other side of the door, followed immediately by the sound of the door being unlocked. Many of the building's elderly residents went to the trouble of locking their doors in the middle of the day. After her break-in, Bailey understood. She had more appreciation than ever of the fact that security was a high priority at Edgewater Place. But somehow, the system had failed her the other night. Her first instinct had been to report what had happened at the homeowners meeting; however, the police had asked her not to. They wanted to do their own investigation first.

The door opened to a smiling Estelle Rouchon. She was dressed much as she'd been the night of the meeting, in a knit suit and dainty low-heeled pumps. Bailey felt immediate discomfort at her own attire—blue jeans, white T-shirt and a pair of beat-up hiking boots. But Estelle's greeting had not a trace of disapproval.

"Welcome, dear," she said graciously. "I'm so glad you could make it." Then, leading Bailey by the elbow, she headed down the short hallway toward the living room. Bailey got a quick glimpse of the dining room, off to the right, as they passed it. A large, elegant French provincial table was surrounded by eight ornate, high-backed chairs, the seats of which were covered in a rich embroidered cloth. A multitiered crystal chandelier hung overhead. The effect was elegant.

Just before they reached the living room, a spacious room whose windows framed another breathtaking view of the lake, Bailey heard voices and realized that they were not alone. Still, moments later, as she entered the room, she was surprised to see four faces smiling in greeting.

"Ladies and gentlemen," said Estelle to the three women and one man who were seated on the L-shaped white leather sectional, "I think you all know Bailey Coleman, but let me make the introductions just in case. Bailey," she said, directing her toward a friendly-looking couple in their late sixties who sat side by side on one section of the sofa, "this is Lucy and Al Swanson." Both Lucy and Al stood and shook Bailey's hand.

On the next section sat a rather disheveled, plump and pleasant-looking woman who appeared to be in her mid-fifties. Estelle introduced her as Suzanne Phillips. Bailey seemed to recall Sam's mentioning the fact that Suzanne was a history professor at Gonzaga University in Spokane. Suzanne greeted her with a "Nice to meet you," and smiled warmly, but did not stand to shake hands.

"And of course, you know Sam," Estelle said finally. Sam Cummings smiled affectionately at Bailey from her seat at the end of the sofa. Bailey thought it odd that Sam had not mentioned the fact that she would be there when they had run into each other in the lobby after breakfast.

With her curiosity building, Bailey seated herself in the armchair that Estelle directed her to. Estelle situated herself on the couch between Suzanne and Sam.

"Well, I'm sure you're wondering just what I had in mind when I asked you here today," Estelle started. Bailey smiled and nodded, feeling somewhat uncomfortable at having all their eyes trained on her—friendly though they seemed—without knowing why she was even there. This was definitely not some social get-together. It was, without doubt, a meeting of some sort. But *what* sort? That was the question.

"Many of us were very disturbed to learn that the bank is about to foreclose on all of your brother's units," Estelle said. "Yesterday, a group of us got together to discuss the situation. We came to the conclusion that we want to help out."

Bailey looked pleased but puzzled. "That's awfully nice of you," she said. "But I'm afraid I don't know what you *can* do to help. Michael did everything he could to avoid it coming to this, and as Sam can tell you, since his death I've pretty much exhausted all possible means of saving Michael's interest in Edgewater Place." She paused briefly. "I've never been a negative person, but at this point, short of the bank changing its position, which just isn't going to happen, I don't hold out much hope."

Estelle looked at Al Swanson. "Al," she said, nodding in his direction.

Al Swanson cleared his throat and shifted in his seat. "Well, Ms. Coleman," he said. "We think there is an answer, maybe one you've overlooked. It's really quite simple. The way we see it, you need to sell one point three million dollars' worth of units pretty darn quick. You need to cure your default." He spoke with an authority that hinted at some knowledge of either the real estate or the mortgage business. "And that's what we propose helping you with."

"You mean you want to help me sell units?" Bailey asked. "Are you a real estate agent?"

There were several chuckles, then Estelle spoke up again. "Forgive us, dear, we aren't laughing at you. It's just that you don't seem to understand."

"No," Al Swanson said. "We don't want to help you sell units, we want to buy them."

Bailey's mouth literally fell open. "You mean . . ." Her voice trailed off.

"Yes," Sam said. "We mean we want to buy units in order to help you come up with the one point three million. Five of them, to be exact."

Now it was Suzanne Phillips who spoke. "But there's a catch—the five units that we want to buy, among the five of us, only amount to eight hundred twenty-five thousand dollars. That's still about five hundred thousand dollars shy of what you need. And our offers to purchase must be contingent on your being able to sell enough units—which we're all pledging to help you with, by the way—to come up with the rest of the money in time to prevent the foreclosure. What we don't want is to end up buying these units and still have the building go into foreclosure and auction. We might as well throw our money down the drain if that happens."

"But with all of us helping, we feel it's do-able. We think we can get other homeowners interested and come up with the difference," Estelle added. "Or stir up interest within the community. We're all well connected. I can approach my bridge group. Lucy and Al belong to the country club. Suzanne's a teacher. Sam knows everyone in Couer d'Alene."

"The time frame's the biggest problem," cut in Al Swanson. "The real problem will be getting this all to happen during the thirty days you have to cure. All of us here have our money either in cash or invested in stocks and bonds. It's very liquid. Each of us can close within ten days. But it may be hard to find more buyers in the position to close that quickly. Standard financing is out of the question. Takes too long."

Bailey was still feeling too stunned to speak. "But why?" she managed to say. "Why would . . ."

It was Sam who answered first.

"Because we care what happens to this building. And we care what happens to you and Clancy," she said.

"We've all done a lot of soul-searching since the meeting the other night," Suzanne Phillips offered. "We think we've been guilty of becoming complacent. Of sticking our heads in the proverbial sand, so to speak. There have been things going on around here for some time now that we haven't liked, but until yesterday, when we all got together, none of us realized that there were others who shared the same feelings."

"Your brother was a good man." Bailey turned to see that it was Lucy Swanson speaking for the first time. "We realized yesterday that we all sat by and failed to give him the support he needed to make this building a success. The truth is, we were being selfish, happy to have this lovely building all to ourselves. We weren't anxious for units to sell, and in that respect, we were very shortsighted. Your brother tried to do right by us. Like you, he seemed to care about us as people. We weren't just sales to him. We should have tried to help out earlier."

"The way we see it," Al Swanson said, "we already have a lot of money invested in this place. If all of those units go to auction, our values will drop overnight. If we can prevent that and keep this building the fine one that it is today, buying another unit—or in our case, two units—will prove to be a sound investment."

"I really don't know what to say, how to thank you. But . . ." Bailey hesitated. "But I'm afraid there's another matter."

"What is it?" Lucy Swanson asked.

"I . . ." The words were difficult for her. "I'm thinking of leaving Edgewater Place. Of moving back to Seattle."

Her announcement was met with silence.

"But why, dear?" Estelle asked. "We thought this building meant a lot to you. That you wanted to make it your home."

Tears sprang to Bailey's eyes at Estelle's words.

"It does mean a lot to me," she said. "More than you could possibly know. This was my brother's dream. It's all that I have left of him." She reached out to accept a white handkerchief from Al Swanson. "And now I've come to love it, too."

"Then why would you go?"

It was Sam who answered.

"I think I know the reason," she said. Bailey's gaze met hers, and Sam nodded. "Tell them, dear. I'm sure the police would have no objection to anyone in this room knowing what happened."

"The police!" Estelle cried in horror.

Bailey told them the story then. About receiving an anonymous envelope with the newspaper article, and then about the night she returned from Seattle to find her apartment had been broken into.

"My word," said Lucy. "That's despicable. Absolutely despicable. The mere idea that someone would frighten you like that. That your dear little niece might be in danger."

The story had shocked and frightened every one of them.

"Well, you can't let them do this to you." It was Suzanne Phillips who now spoke. "You can't let them run you out of town."

There were murmurs of agreement.

"That's right," said Al Swanson. "We can't allow something like this to happen. Not in this building. Not in this town."

Small cheers from around the room greeted his words. Sam, who had been quietly observing, now stood.

"They're right, Bailey," she said. "Don't you see? You're

not in this alone. We'll all be here for you. We'll all keep an eye on Clancy. Just let them try some more funny business."

Bailey looked from one of them to another. Concern and anger, deeply felt indignation, were etched across their faces. They had suddenly become an army. An army of refined fifty-, sixty- and seventy-year-old warriors who'd wanted simply to safeguard their homes, their investments, but who were apparently unwilling to stand by, idle, in the face of this other injustice to Bailey and Clancy.

"I don't know what to say," Bailey said softly.

"Say yes," Suzanne responded. "Say you'll stay and let us help you."

"Well, then," said Bailey. Again, her gaze swept the room. "Yes."

At her response, the room erupted in laughter and cheers. Within an hour, the six of them had developed a marketing plan, which included contacting the rest of the homeowners and holding an open house for all local realtors. Al Swanson, who turned out to be a retired mortgage broker, assumed leadership of their committee. It would be Al who would contact the rest of Edgewater Place's owners. Sam and Estelle volunteered to make refreshments for the open house, which would be held within the week. Suzanne would use her office computer to generate the invitations, and Lucy and Bailey would hand-deliver them to the dozen or so top real estate offices in the area. Their goal was to sell either two units on floors seven through ten, most of which were in the low $200,000 range, or one of the remaining penthouses, both of which were listed for more than $500,000.

When Bailey returned home later that afternoon, she was filled with a newfound optimism and something else that she'd desperately needed—renewed faith.

She was not alone. That evening, six of Edgewater Place's residents found themselves in unusually good spirits, unusually at peace with themselves.

While Bailey and Clancy went to see *The Lion King*, Sam Cummings took Gator, via the elevator and front door, for a long stroll along the sidewalks of downtown Coeur d'Alene—all of which, though only blocks away, was new territory for the newly-sprung-from-exile Gator.

Suzanne Phillips invited a colleague over for pizza, beer and one joint, which they smoked in the bathroom, with the fans on, before watching *Casablanca.*

Estelle Rouchon happily shared fresh salmon with her cats.

And, feeling unusually exhilarated and stimulated by the events of the day, Al and Lucy Swanson made love.

The first thing Shep Carroll did on Saturday morning was drive down the east side of Lake Coeur d'Alene. He drove through town, stopping for coffee at Java, Java's then headed south on Highway 95.

The highway skirted the shores of the lake for a while, then fell into a pattern that afforded him only occasional glimpses of its sparkling waters. The country became rolling and wide open. The first ten miles, there were houses scattered on either side of the road and frequent turnoffs that led to the lake. Then farms began to pop up. He passed a Grange Hall that looked like it still saw plenty of activity. He was struck by the rural, agricultural feel of this land, which contrasted sharply with the upscale, resorty atmosphere of Coeur d'Alene, just miles away. The road became a two-laner, with many twists and dips. Soon he was surrounded by wheat fields.

The first sign of the reservation was the town of Halfway—if it could be called a town, as it appeared to consist of one shanty-looking grocery store and one gas pump. The sign advertising the sale of cigarettes and fireworks was at least half as big as the store itself. He pulled off the road and entered the structure, which consisted of one large room and a wide front porch onto which spilled larger merchandise like tires, brooms and buckets. There were several short stepladders leaning against the wall.

He was greeted immediately by an elderly man standing behind the counter and reading a newspaper spread on its surface. "Morning," he said in a soft but friendly voice. Shep would have put his age at sixty. He was a handsome man, an Indian, with a strong, lined face and long black hair streaked with plenty of gray. He wore his hair pulled back into a ponytail.

"What can I do for you?" he asked.

"Got any cigarettes?" Shep joked, smiling. There were cartons of cigarettes everywhere—stacks of them ten inches high along the length of the counter that ran behind the man.

The storekeeper laughed and said, "Nope. Came to the wrong place."

Shep extended his hand and said, "I'm Shep Carroll."

"Joe Curry," the man said, grasping Shep's hand in a strong grip. "You from out of the area?"

"It shows, huh?" asked Shep. "Yep. I'm from Portland."

"It's not that it shows," Joe Curry said. "It's just a guess. Portland's a nice place. My son loves there. And my three grandkids and four great-grandkids."

"Great-grandkids!" Shep said. "How could you have great-grandkids?"

Joe Curry laughed again. "I'm eighty-three years old. That's how."

Shep shook his head in amazement, then asked, "Get to see them often?"

"Not as much as I'd like. I'd always hoped that my kids would decide to stick around. Stay on the reservation. None of them did. All took off for the cities."

"Well, at least your son chose another good place to live. Portland *is* nice."

"You been there long?" Joe Curry asked.

"Nine years."

"It's your home, then," Joe Curry stated.

"Actually, this area feels more like home to me," Shep responded, surprising himself with his own words.

"Sounds like maybe it should be."

Shep paused, thinking about Joe Curry's statement, then he asked. "So why do they call this Halfway?"

" 'Cause we're halfway on reservation land, halfway on

your land. This place sits smack-dab on the reservation line."

Shep was struck by Joe Curry's description of the northern half of the land. "Your" land.

"Can you tell me if there's such a thing as a tribal headquarters around here?"

"Down the road a piece, in Worley. Go left on the main drag for about half a block. Can't miss it. Might not be open today, though."

Shep bought a box of doughnuts and a carton of orange juice, thanked Joe Curry and headed toward the door.

"Come again," he heard Joe Curry say quietly before he reached the door.

Shep stopped and turned. "I'll do that," he said. "You can count on it."

Worley was another eight miles down Highway 95. Joe Curry had been right. The tribal headquarters was easy to find. He was also right that it was closed for the weekend. While Shep stood on the porch of the building reading the sign that posted its hours and trying to peer inside for any other information that might be helpful, he heard a voice from behind him.

"Anything I can help you with?"

He turned to see a young woman standing at the bottom of the stairs leading to the porch. She was striking, with long black hair and exquisite brown skin. She smiled at him.

"I was just hoping to get some information," Shep said.

"Tourist information?" she asked. "Maybe I can help you. I volunteer here at the headquarters part-time."

Shep wasn't exactly sure how to ask for what he wanted.

"Well, I'm not sure you'd call it tourist information," he said. "Actually, I was curious about a golf course that's being planned just a few miles north of here."

At these words, her smile disappeared. It was a while before she said anything. "Maybe you should talk to Charlie Eaglequill," she said, her new businesslike tone contrasting sharply with the friendly voice that had just greeted him.

"Who is Charlie Eaglequill?"

"Our tribal chief."

"And how would I go about finding him?"

The young woman hesitated. It was clear that she didn't know whether or not to answer.

"It's extremely important that I get some information," he added.

"Wait here," she finally said. Digging in the leather bag she carried, she extracted a ring of keys. She walked up the steps, unlocked the door to the tribal building, then shut it behind her as she entered. Shep could hear her turn the lock.

He watched through the paned glass on the upper half of the door as she went to a desk and picked up the phone. Her back was to him, but he could see that she was speaking into the phone. Finally she put it down and returned.

"Charlie will see you," she said. "He wants me to give you directions to his house."

Shep jotted down the woman's instructions and thanked her for her help.

Ten minutes later, he was pulling into the driveway of a pale yellow, wood frame house just off Highway 95. Two small boys played outside on the three-rail fence that enclosed several cattle and horses. Before Shep had his car door open, a man had emerged from the front door. He was of medium height and build, dark, with closely cropped hair. He wore jeans, a long-sleeved denim shirt and well-worn cowboy boots. He approached Shep's car with purpose, a less than welcoming expression on his face.

Shep got out of the car and stood to face him.

"Charlie Eaglequill," the man said, extending his hand.

"Nice to meet you. I'm Shep Carroll."

Shep felt Charlie Eaglequill's eyes keenly. He wondered whether he would be invited inside the house, and in the silence of the next few seconds, he knew he was being assessed.

He must have passed the preliminary test, for Charlie invited him in.

He was taken through a small, tidy living room to the kitchen, where a woman stood washing the dishes. The kitchen was spotless. There was an inviting aroma originating from the oven, reminding Shep of the bread his mother had baked for him when he was a child.

"This is my wife, Susan," Charlie said.

Susan and Shep said hello, then she quickly disappeared through the swinging door to the living room.

"Please, sit down," Charlie Eaglequill said.

Shep and Charlie seated themselves at the kitchen table. There was a full pot of coffee in a coffeemaker on the counter, but Charlie did not offer any.

"What can I do for you, Mr. Carroll?" Charlie Eaglequill said.

"Shep, please."

"Okay, Shep. What is it you're looking for?"

"I'm looking for information on a golf course that's being planned just north of here. About eight miles," Shep said, choosing his words carefully.

"What type of information?" Charlie Eaglequill wanted to know.

"Is the Coeur d'Alene Tribe involved with the course in some way?" asked Shep.

Charlie Eaglequill just looked at him. "Who are you, Mr. Carroll?" he said. "Why don't you tell me something about yourself before you start asking me for information?"

"That's only fair," Shep said. "I'm an attorney, out of Portland."

"And you represent . . ." Charlie asked, his words trailing off.

"I represent the bank that financed Edgewater Place," Shep said. He noticed an immediate reaction in Charlie Eaglequill's eyes.

"What does this golf course you speak of have to do with Edgewater Place?" Eaglequill wanted to know.

Good question, thought Shep. How should he answer?

"It may have nothing to do with it. That's what I'm trying to find out." He could tell he was getting nowhere with Charlie Eaglequill. In desperation, he decided that his best bet would be to be as honest as possible with him. There was, of course, some information he simply could not share, but pulling the article he'd taken from Michael Coleman's files out of his pocket, he offered it to Charlie Eaglequill.

"This is an article that I got from Michael Coleman's sister, Bailey Coleman. It was in Michael's files. It's about a casino over in Washington, on the Tulalip tribal lands. In the article there's mention of a golf course. The developer is a Bayshore, Inc.

"Recently, I learned that the same developer is trying to get planning and zoning commission approval of a golf course just north of here. The fact that it was so close to your tribe's lands made me believe that, like the tribe in western Washington, your tribe might be associated with this golf course. That's why I'm here. To find out if that's true."

Charlie Eaglequill took the article and eyed it for some time, then sat silently.

"How did you get this from Bailey Coleman?" he asked. From the tone of the question Shep suspected that Charlie knew Bailey.

Another tough question for Shep to answer. Again, he decided to go with the truth.

"She gave it to me," was all he said.

"And you're the bank's attorney?"

"Yes."

Charlie grew silent again. Shep knew he'd done nothing to dispel this man's distrust of him.

"What makes you think there could be a connection between Edgewater Place and this golf course?" Charlie Eaglequill referred to the golf course as if he believed it to be a figment of Shep's imagination.

"I have reason to believe the president of the Edgewater Place homeowners association, Anthony Walcott, is involved in Bayshore, the development company." The next statement would be a serious leap of faith for Shep. "And I suspect that the banker I represent, Stan Muncie, may be involved, too."

Charlie Eaglequill's eyes widened at mention of Stan Muncie.

"Stan Muncie? He financed the construction for Michael Coleman?" There was disbelief in Eaglequill's voice.

"Do you know Muncie?"

"Yes, I do," answered Eaglequill. He looked disturbed by what he'd just learned. After another long silence he said, "Listen, would you like a cup of coffee?"

"That'd be nice," said Shep. After a cup for the road earlier in the morning and the carton of orange juice, he really felt that another drink of any liquid was the last thing he needed, but he saw the offer as a good sign and didn't want to do anything to turn the tide.

Charlie was deliberate in his preparation of the coffee. First he went to the refrigerator, took out a carton of half-and-half and placed it in the table. Then he took a sugar bowl from the cupboard and placed it alongside the half-and-half. He set a napkin and spoon in front of Shep and finally poured the coffee into two ceramic cups. Neither man used the sugar or half-and-half.

By the time he'd seated himself again, he'd again donned a deadpan expression.

"I was introduced to Stan Muncie by Anthony Walcott," Charlie said, as if their conversation had never been interrupted. "I had no idea he had any involvement with Edgewater Place."

"Why is it that Walcott introduced you to Muncie?" Shep asked.

It was clear to Shep that, just as Shep had minutes earlier, Eaglequill was now struggling with how much to tell him. He suspected that Eaglequill fully realized Shep had gone out on a limb in disclosing as much as he had, and he hoped that now that fact would encourage candor on Eaglequill's part as well. But what Charlie said next dashed his hopes.

"I have given my word to keep certain information secret. I cannot answer your questions."

"Given your word to whom?" Shep wanted to know.

Charlie Eaglequill studied Shep. "That is a good question."

Nothing he'd promised would prevent him from answering this question. Still, only trust in Shep and Shep's motives could justify an honest answer.

"Let me ask you something. Why is it you are digging around, asking questions about this golf course, when you represent the bank? It seems to me you should be asking Stan Muncie these questions."

"I may have to. But the moment I do, I'll be fired," Shep answered. "And if that happens, there will be no one to stop what I believe may be happening."

"Happening to your client?" asked Eaglequill, confused.

"No."

Charlie Eaglequill was a smart man. If Shep represented the bank in its loan to Michael Coleman, there were only two parties involved. If it wasn't the bank he was concerned about . . .

"Happening to Bailey Coleman?" he asked.

Shep looked Charlie Eaglequill in the eye. "Yes, happening to Bailey Coleman."

"Is that why she gave you this article? Because you are trying to help her?"

"Yes."

"And are you not violating your responsibility to the bank in what you're doing?"

"I hope that I'm not, but you're right, I may well be."

If any man understood the notion of honor, it was Charlie Eaglequill. He also understood, only too well, that there were often conflicting values that caused a man to compromise one matter of honor for another, more important, matter. His instincts told him that Shep Carroll was an honorable man. Still, he'd given his word and that was not something that Charlie took lightly. And his tribe, its future, was at stake. Charlie could not betray his tribe's trust in him. He could not endanger their future.

With an uneasy heart, he told Shep, "I will answer only one question. It was Stan Muncie and Walcott who asked me to keep our dealings confidential. I cannot answer the rest of your questions. But neither will I do anything to prevent you from finding the answers. And you can rest assured," he added, "that nothing you've said to me today will go any farther."

Shep parted minutes later, disappointed in not having found out more, but now convinced beyond doubt that Bayshore, Inc. involved both Walcott *and* Muncie and that the Coeur d'Alene Tribe was also involved somehow in the proposed golf course. He was also firmly convinced that Charlie Eaglequill wanted to help him but that, because of the promise he'd given Walcott and Muncie, he could not.

Several minutes after Shep had gone, Susan Eaglequill found her husband still seated at the kitchen table. He was staring straight ahead—something she'd seen him do many times over the years.

"Well?"

"He wanted to know about the golf course," Charlie explained. "He's the attorney for the bank that financed Edgewater Place. And guess who happens to be the bank's vice president, the one who made the Edgewater Place loan?"

"Who?"

"Stan Muncie."

"Stan Muncie! The Stan Muncie you've been working with?" Suzanne asked, incredulous.

"One and the same," Charlie answered.

"What does it mean? And why is Stan Muncie's attorney interested in the golf course?"

"I'm not sure yet. But it means something," Charlie said. He looked at her then. "Something is wrong here. Something is very wrong. I can feel it."

Suzanne reached out and rested her hand on his shoulder. "What did you tell him?"

"Nothing. I told him nothing." Charlie started to rise. He had work to do. Stalls to muck out. A fence to repair. Weary though he suddenly felt, he had better get at it. Besides, his mind always worked better when he was active.

And Shep Carroll had given him plenty to think about.

* * *

Bailey had not seen Shep since he'd left her condominium so abruptly after finding that article about the Tulalip Tribe. For the past few days, her mind had rarely been free of thoughts of him. She found herself wondering whether he was still in town or whether he'd returned to Portland. Finally, the previous night, after it grew dark, she'd driven by the Motor Inn Express to see if his car was in the parking lot. It was not there.

What had the article meant to him? After reading it, he'd asked her about the Coeur d'Alene Tribe. Did he see some connection between the Coeur d'Alene and Edgewater Place? If there were, it might explain the hunch she'd had after her meeting with Charlie Eaglequill, the feeling that he wasn't telling her everything. It could explain why Michael had met with him in March, why he'd seemed upbeat about the future of Edgewater Place.

But, as important as those questions were, what was *really* on Bailey's mind, what dominated her thoughts, was Shep himself. He had turned her world topsy-turvy. She truly had no idea what to make of him, what to make of her feelings, anymore. Just who was Shep Carroll? One moment she felt such anger at him for what he'd done to her brother's dream and what he was doing now, to Clancy and her, the next she was reliving the time they had spent together and longing for him with such intensity that her insides literally ached.

Had she been a fool to allow him to go through Michael's files?

"This building inspection thing has me worried, Sam." Bailey said over a cup of coffee that Sam had poured for her when she stopped by for a visit. "I'm not sure what to do. Here we are trying to sell units, and at the same time I'm asking for a special meeting of the board to approve a building inspection."

"I've been thinking the same thing," Sam said, arranging fresh yellow flowers in a glass vase. "Maybe you should just sit tight on it for a while."

"And encourage people to buy units when there could be

something wrong with this place?" Bailey asked. "I can't do that, Sam. How can I in good conscience sell more units—sell *you* another unit, of all people—when we know that someone, for some reason, thinks this building needs an inspection?"

Sam was silent for a while. "Maybe we should tell Shep Carroll about this. About the note your received."

"You must be kidding!" Bailey said.

"No, I'm not," Sam answered. "Something tells me that he should know about that note. Maybe he can shed some light on things, help you decide what to do about this building inspection."

"Absolutely not."

"But you were willing to let him see Michael's files."

Sam was right. Bailey's reaction made no sense. Did she trust Shep Carroll or not? The answer one minute was yes; the next, no. Since he'd taken the newspaper article and disappeared on her, it was no.

"I don't need Shep Carroll's help," Bailey proclaimed.

Sam did not push her friend. She was beginning to suspect that there was more to Bailey's relationship with Shep Carroll than Bailey let on. That afternoon he'd been at Bailey's condo, going through Michael's files, Bailey had seemed wound so tight she might implode. And these days the mere mention of his name around Bailey was apt to send Sam or Clancy running for cover. There was no sense in butting heads with her now. Once she'd made up her mind about something, Sam knew, Bailey Coleman was as stubborn as a mule. But Sam was damn sure it would be a good idea to talk to Shep.

Shep had hated leaving Coeur d'Alene on Sunday afternoon. He'd hated turning in the fishing boat he'd rented and stopping by Fins and Feathers one last time to inspect the thirty-two-pound monster cohoe salmon that *he* hadn't caught, the fish that had won the derby. He'd hated leaving the motel room that in just ten days had grown to feel like home to him. But most of all, he'd hated leaving Bailey Coleman.

Going to work on Monday morning had been tantamount to a form of torture. He sat through a two-hour-long staff meeting, one consultation and a meeting with a new client. During each, he'd had to constantly battle to keep his mind focused on the business at hand.

Then it was Wednesday, and things were not getting any better. But then Anna had opened his door to tell him he had a phone call.

"It's a Samantha Cummings," she'd said. "She says you'll know her."

"Please close the door," Shep said, reaching for the phone.

"Hello there," he said into the receiver.

"Hello to you," Sam answered cheerfully. "Have a good trip back?"

He gave a short laugh. "Hard to enjoy a seven-hour drive to a place you'd rather not be going," he answered.

"You don't like Portland?" Sam asked.

Shep knew Sam hadn't called him to shoot the breeze. He was anxious to find out the real reason for her call, but if Bailey Coleman's friend wanted to chat a little first, he was happy to accommodate her.

"Portland's a great place," he answered, "as far as cities go. I'm just not much of a city boy."

"Maybe Coeur d'Alene is more your style," Sam suggested.

"Could be," Shep answered. Then, unable to resist the chance to talk to Sam about them, he added, "Bailey and Clancy certainly seem to like it there."

"Yes, they do. Actually, that's the reason I called. Because they do like it here so much. And because several of us want to help them find a way to stay here."

Sam proceeded to tell Shep what had happened on Saturday at Estelle Rouchon's place. Shep listened without commenting. After explaining the plan the six homeowners had put in place, Sam went on.

"But there's a problem. Bailey is concerned that there could be something wrong with the building. And, if that's true, she doesn't feel right trying to sell more units."

"Why would she think there could be anything wrong with Edgewater Place?"

Sam told Shep about the note Bailey had received before the last homeowners meeting. Then she told him about the day she'd overheard Anthony Walcott and Tom Ryan in the lobby.

Shep asked her to repeat, from memory, what the note had said. When she finished, Shep remained silent.

"What do you think?" she asked.

So Bailey doesn't quite trust me yet, thought Shep at the realization that she had withheld this information from him the day he was at her place, going through Michael's files. *Can't say I blame her.*

"I think that someone knows something very significant and he or she is trying to alert Bailey," he answered. Then he asked, "May I ask, why are you telling me this?"

Sam hesitated, then answered truthfully. "Because all of us want to help Bailey. But she's right. If there's something wrong with the building, she can't be selling units. If Bailey presses the board to hire an inspector, all she'll do is scare buyers off—maybe needlessly so. Yet she can't sell units without knowing that this building is sound. She's stuck between a rock and a hard place."

"And just what did you think I could do about this?"

"If something's wrong with that building, maybe that SOB Muncie knows. And if he knows, I figure you might have a way of finding out, too."

"And you think I'd be willing to do that. To find that information for you?"

"Yes, I do."

"Just why would I do such a thing?"

"For Bailey. And Clancy. I think you'd do it for them."

Shep remained silent for a good long while. Then, finally, he spoke.

"Go ahead with your plan. From what you've told me,

Bailey won't be closing on any units until she gets enough offers to come up with the entire one point three million. She can always offer to let the buyer out if that doesn't happen," Shep continued. "I want you to find some way to overnight me that construction file of Michael Coleman's. The one I went through the other day at Bailey's place. I'm going to go through it again. Give me a few days, during which you and the others should continue to sell your hearts out. And try to keep Bailey from bringing the inspection up with the board again. At least not until you hear from me. Do you think you can do that?"

"Yes, I can," Sam said. "You are a good man, Shep Carroll."

Shep smiled. *I wish Bailey saw it that way.*

"Well, then," he said, "maybe you'd be so kind as to put in a good word for me now and then."

They both laughed.

"I'd be happy to," Sam answered.

That evening, Sam put her plan into action. She arrived at Bailey's door, large grocery sack in hand, at six-forty-five.

"Come in," Bailey said with an affectionate smile. She grabbed the bag from Sam and, with Sam following, took it to the kitchen. As she placed it on the counter, she began to protest.

"Sam, this just isn't necessary. At the very least, I want to stay and help you fix dinner."

"No. Absolutely not," said Sam. "This is my treat. I absolutely insist. While you and Clancy are at the movie, I'll get dinner on. When you get home it will be waiting for you. You promised you'd humor me and go along with this. I never get the chance to cook for anyone anymore."

"But . . ."

"No buts. Now, you and Clancy get out of here. That movie starts in fifteen minutes."

Once they'd left, Sam locked the front door. The adrenaline was coursing so vigorously through her body that as she tiptoed down the hall toward the den, she paused to press her hand to her chest. *Now don't go acting up on me,* she told her wildly beating heart.

But the fact was that Sam Cummings was having the time of her life. How wonderfully exciting all of this was! She was proud of how well her ruse to get Bailey out of the house had worked. She had the place to herself for two hours. Plenty of time to find that file Shep needed, take it down to her condo so that she could overnight it to him in the morning, and return to prepare dinner. It was all working like a charm.

It's just too bad she'd discovered her propensity for this kind of thing a little late in life.

She would have made a heck of a good detective.

CHAPTER 13

SHEP'S PLAN WAS SIMPLE, but he would need help. His experience with construction was all on paper and strictly limited to legalities—who screwed up, who had liability to whom. He needed the real thing. An experienced construction person. He needed Charlie Eaglequill.

He arrived at Charlie's house, unannounced, arms full with the files Samantha Cummings had sent him, first thing Saturday morning. He hadn't known what kind of greeting to expect.

Charlie Eaglequill's face registered no surprise when he answered Shep's knock. He opened the door and invited Shep inside. It was almost as if he'd been expecting him.

Three and a half hours later the two men emerged. Charlie Eaglequill walked Shep to his car, where they shook hands before Shep climbed in.

"Friday night at ten," Shep called out the window as his car started to roll backward.

Charlie Eaglequill's eyes met Shep's calmly.

"Friday at ten."

* * *

Edgewater Place was a popular place to be on the Fourth of July. Residents new to the building were routinely issued the following warning by those with Independence Day experience: Either get out of town or expect everyone you know, even near strangers, to come out of the woodwork in the hope of finagling an invitation to view the fireworks from the lake-facing balconies that afforded virtually every unit in the building an unparalleled view of the goings-on.

Barring nasty weather, which wasn't in the forecast, the spectacular fireworks display put on every year could be expected to draw well over fifty thousand spectators. Many viewed the show from their boats. At dusk, thousands of vessels started streaming toward town from every direction on the lake, their dancing running lights adding another visual dimension to the festive night. By eight P.M., every inch of the beach and the waterfront city park would be carpeted with blankets, bodies, dogs and picnic baskets. Parking became a logistical nightmare.

Residents of Edgewater Place had only to step out onto their balconies to get the best seats in town. For those who liked to entertain, it was the highlight of their social year—a much sought after invitation with a surefire guarantee of a memorable evening. For those who didn't, it was a nightmare, for even if they were curmudgeonly enough to avoid having guests of their own, the influx into the building of outsiders on this night was enough to drive them mad.

Anthony Walcott fell into the latter category. Refusing to extend invitations to view the fireworks from his balcony, he also refused to leave the building and avoid the aggravation this night inevitably caused him. But tonight, instead of sitting in his unit stewing about the whole situation, he was determined to do something about it. He'd made a plan. Even guests had to observe the rules that he'd almost single-handedly succeeded in passing over the years—no liquor in the common areas; no loud, raucous behavior; never more than four persons in the Jacuzzi at once, ten in the swimming pool—and tonight he was going to ensure that, at the very least, his rules were enforced.

Bailey and Clancy had invited a rather eclectic group—Sam, Estelle, Tony Pappas and his wife, and two of Clancy's schoolmates, who would spend the night—over for the occasion. Their company started arriving shortly after seven. Bailey was pleased to have the opportunity to get to know Rhonda Pappas better. There was something very likable about Rhonda. Bailey especially admired the relationship she and Tony seemed to have. Tony was the more flamboyant of the two—the dashing Greek loved attention and got plenty of it. Rhonda seemed to get a kick out of her husband, laughing at his antics and colorful language, but she was also obviously a strong, independent person. One who commanded the respect of her husband, which was demonstrated early on in the evening when Tony began to talk business with Bailey.

"Haven't heard anything from Muncie or Carroll recently," he'd said upon catching Bailey and Rhonda alone in the kitchen. " 'Course, I didn't really expect to. You can be sure we will soon, though, once the thirty days are up."

"Actually," Bailey said, "there's something I've been wanting to tell you. About Shep Carroll—"

Rhonda interrupted Bailey before she could finish her confession.

"Listen, you two," she said. "None of this tonight. This is not the time or place for talking business. Tonight we're here to have fun."

Tony looked at his wife contritely, then turned to Bailey. "Rhonda's right. Sorry about that. Force of habit. Let's just forget about business tonight. Tonight is a night for romance."

With that, he lifted Rhonda's hand and pressed it to his lips dramatically. It touched Bailey to see the humor and affection in Rhonda's dark eyes. They were a good couple, Rhonda and Tony Pappas. Theirs was a good marriage. Bailey left them alone in the kitchen and went looking for her other guests.

In reality, she was relieved to have had Rhonda interrupt them. She was not looking forward to telling Tony that she'd let Shep Carroll go through Michael's files. It sounded ridiculous, even to Bailey. Maybe it was.

She was surprised she hadn't heard from Shep for so long.

Just what was he up to now?

At ten P.M. sharp, two vehicles pulled into the far northwest corner of the parking lot behind Edgewater Place. Moments later, Shep Carroll emerged from the first. Carrying a tube of rolled-up paper, he walked over to the other car, from which Charlie Eaglequill was just emerging. Without speaking, the two men opened the back of Charlie's Jeep and extracted a large tool box and a heavy-duty flashlight.

"Got the plans?" Charlie asked softly as they lowered the Jeep's trunk door back into place.

"Right here," Shep said, raising the tube to the faint light afforded them by the street lamp half a block away.

They walked in silence to the back of the building, then, as Charlie disappeared into the shadows behind the bushes that lined the area under the swimming pool windows, Shep handed him the tube that contained the building's plans and specs, and continued around to the front of the building.

As Shep opened the front door to the vestibule off the lobby, he was relieved to see that the night's guard, sitting just inside Faith Lammerman's office, was the same one who'd let him in on previous occasions. He waved in what he hoped would pass as a friendly, relaxed manner, reached for the phone on the security panel, and pretended to punch in three digits, representing one of the units. On previous occasions he could use a homeowners meeting as the reason for his being there. Tonight he had to appear to be an invited guest. After holding the phone to his ear for several seconds, then pretending to dial again, he replaced the phone in its receptacle, shrugged his shoulders in an exaggerated fashion, then leaned against the wall, appearing to be waiting for his host or hostess to get off the phone so that he could announce his arrival and be buzzed in. His ruse worked. The guard got up, walked over and opened the door.

"Line's busy, huh?" he said. Then, a friendly "Come on in."

"Yep," answered Shep. "Thanks." He entered the lobby, then walked purposefully toward the elevator, calling out "Have a nice evening" before stepping inside.

"You, too," the guard replied. "Enjoy those fireworks. Should be starting any minute now."

Never even asked me where I'm going, thought Shep as the elevator doors slid shut.

He got off on the fourth floor, walked down the hall and opened a door marked EXIT. He used the stairwell to go back down to the ground floor, his sneakered feet taking two and three steps at a time. When he reached the bottom, he stood quietly, listening. When he was confident there was no one near by, he opened the door. Within seconds, Charlie Eaglequill materialized, sliding by him to enter the building. Even with the bulky tool box, flashlight and tube in hand, he moved smoothly and soundlessly.

They had decided to start at the top and work their way down. According to Charlie, the fireworks show lasted approximately forty-five minutes. That was all the time they would have. For at least forty-five minutes they could pretty much count on the fact that all eyes and ears in Edgewater Place, including those of the guard, would be focused on the fireworks taking place over the lake. It wasn't much time, but Charlie thought it might be enough.

With one exception, their mission was simple enough. They were there to conduct their own, unofficial building inspection. After poring over Michael Coleman's construction files and the building plans and specs for hours, Charlie Eaglequill had come up with the approach. They would do a visual inspection of several key areas: the stairwells, the parking garage, the foundation, the mechanical room. They were looking for anything unusual, signs of a problem. In addition, there was one test that they hoped to be able to perform.

Both men had given the note sent to Bailey a great deal of thought. An anonymous note that hinted at a problem with the building. The first thing that came to both Charlie's and Shep's minds was construction fraud. Charlie had described two possible scenarios. Had the general contractor used cheaper, inferior materials in the construction of Edgewater Place? It happened all the time, and it didn't necessarily cause problems down the road. If the substitutions were for fixtures or carpet or even plasterboard, they were usually harmless. But there had been cases where builders substituted inexpensive sand for high-grade gravel in a building's foundation. That could be catastrophic. If that were true, one would expect to find an inordinate number of cracks in the building's floors, in the walls, and in the foundation, especially two or three years after construction. Shep had recounted his conversation about foundation cracks with the jackhammer-wielding workman to Charlie. Charlie had agreed that some cracks were to be expected. "But I can tell by looking at them whether they're superficial or whether they signal something might be seriously wrong with the foundation. There's a big difference."

The other possibility was an unapproved design change. Contractors had been known to increase the spacing between critically important structural beams and supports, then pocket the savings on labor and material. Shep had even read of one case in which a contractor substituted wood beams for the requisite steel. Again, the consequences could be catastrophic. But the only way that Shep and Charlie could test for this type of problem would be risky, at best. And the only night they could possibly get away with it and remain undetected was this night. The Fourth of July.

The two men moved quickly and silently up the stairwell, not stopping until they'd reached the top. Shep placed his ear against the door that said 11TH FLOOR. Hearing nothing, he opened the door a crack, just enough to allow him a view of the corridor. Then, as he stood watch, Charlie turned the flashlight on and trained its beam first on the ceiling. Charlie had explained to Shep that the stairwells were a good testing site. Bare of any camouflage or finishings, they offered perfect samplings of the building's infrastructure itself—nothing but cement and drywall, top to bottom. The light beam swept methodically across the ceiling, back and forth, back and forth. Finding nothing, Charlie moved to the walls, again sweeping the light's arc back and forth in a precise, methodical pattern.

When a loud explosion suddenly shook the building, both men jumped. It was a moment before they realized that what they'd heard was the start of the fireworks show, the initial "big bang." Charlie Eaglequill looked over at his partner. He could see sweat beading on Shep's forehead. Both men were jumpy. But, in reality, the fireworks were welcome. As more explosions could be heard, lesser now but occasionally accompanied by high-pitched whistles, the two men looked at each other.

"Now?" Shep asked.

Charlie Eaglequill nodded.

Shep took one last look down the corridor. There was nothing going on. No sign of anybody. He wondered if Bailey were home, just seventy-five feet away from where he stood. He quietly closed the door, then reached for the rolled-up plans. He held the flashlight to them as Charlie took one last look. Then, using the tape measure he'd extracted from his pocket, Charlie penciled an *x* exactly thirty inches from the right side of the door frame. He reached down into the tool box, extracted a battery-powered drill and a bit. Then, after screwing the bit in, he stood poised—the drill's bit touching the spot marked by the *x*—and waited. It was less than a minute before there was another loud explosion.

"Now," whispered Shep.

At the height of the explosion, Charlie's index finger pressed down on the trigger and the drill came to life, its sharp, lightning-quick bit penetrating the wall easily. Both men were sweating now. Fortunately, the first explosion had been followed by a series of lesser "pops." To Charlie and Shep, the noise of the drill was deafening, but Shep could hear, very faintly, more explosions from across the street. When they stopped, Shep signaled Charlie with a cutting motion across his neck and Charlie let up on the drill's trigger. The bit had penetrated about eight inches.

"Should have hit it by now," Charlie said softly, still holding the tool to the wall.

The two men waited in absolute silence. If someone were to come upon them now, thought Shep, with Charlie standing there, his drill still sticking into the wall, they would be ridiculously, hopelessly beyond redemption. Luckily, the fireworks started up again right away, and when they did, Shep nodded. Charlie resumed drilling. Within seconds the high-pitched whir turned abruptly into a slow moan. The drill stopped dead in the wall. It had hit the steel beam. It was right where the drawings had said it would be.

"That's it!" said Charlie.

Their test completed, the two men quietly and efficiently gathered their tools and papers and, the light sweeping the walls of the stairwell as they went, descended to the tenth floor, where once again, Shep stood guard while Charlie looked for cracks in the floors, walls and ceiling. It was not necessary to repeat the test with the drill. Nor were they anxious to. They had pushed their luck enough already. They moved quickly and without incident, floor by floor, reaching the first floor within twenty minutes. Nowhere did they see evidence of problems—no cracks of any significance, nothing to catch the practiced eye of Charlie Eaglequill.

Their first brush with detection came in the parking garage. They'd just entered the garage from the stairwell door when Shep suddenly grabbed Charlie and pulled him to the ground behind the shelter of a large van. A short, stout male figure moved stealthily across the floor, heading toward the entrance to the lobby, directly opposite where Shep and Charlie cowered. Shep could not get a good look at the man but could tell by his size and clothing that it was not the guard he'd talked to earlier.

They stayed crouched behind the van for a minute or two, then headed for the mechanical room, which was just off the parking garage. By this time, they'd begun to relax a little. Aside from a flashlight examination of the building's exterior foundation and walls, which would be their final act, they were through with all the areas where the risk of their being caught was high. The Fourth of July had been a godsend. The common areas of the building, usually a regular stream of residents coming and going, had been virtually emptied for the event. And the noise outside had masked their first test with the drill. Things could not have gone better. Both Shep and Charlie were feeling relieved not to have found any evidence of a serious problem. Relieved but puzzled. Why was someone determined to have the building inspected?

Entry to the mechanical room presented a bit of a challenge. The door was locked. Charlie used several tools to try to pick the lock to no avail. They needed to get inside. Once inside the shelter of the room, they hoped to conduct another test with the drill. The first had confirmed that the beam was placed where the drawings indicated it should be. It was a good sign, but they needed to do at least one, and, if circumstances permitted, preferably two, more tests. With three random checks to be sure the beam placement conformed to the plans, Charlie and Shep had decided they could feel relatively confident there had been no alterations of structural design. Shep would have some degree of relief in knowing that his client had at least not engaged in a fraud that could endanger lives. Bailey could feel comfortable in selling units. If they could just complete their inspection.

But a simple locked door threatened to cut their plans short. It was Shep who, after Charlie had made several attempts to unlock the door, reached up and ran his hand along the top of the door's frame.

"Bingo!" He grinned, producing the key by which they finally gained entrance.

Once inside, the men went right to work, Charlie measuring and marking while Shep held the plans. The room was filled with equipment, most of which emitted enough noise that Shep and Charlie felt relatively safe in repeating their drill test. At the first *x* Charlie had marked, the drill once again penetrated just over eight inches before hitting steel.

"There she is," Charlie announced. "Right where she's supposed to be."

The second hole he drilled produced similar results. They packed up the drill and quickly eyeballed the ceilings, walls and floors of the mechanical room. In one corner, a neatly organized workbench contained all the normal trappings—paint cans and brushes, a tool box, several saws. Shep noticed something protruding from under the bench. Reaching down, he pulled it out.

"A kayak paddle," he said, turning it over. "Brand-new. What do you suppose it's doing here?"

Charlie, disinterested, shrugged. "Maybe this is where Michael stored his kayak," he said. Then, his eyes surveying the room one more time, he added, "I'll tell you. From what I've seen so far, this place would pass a building inspection with flying colors."

Shep shook his head, puzzled.

"Then why the note?"

Charlie Eaglequill had no answer.

They were almost done with their mission. All that remained was the final inspection of the exterior of the building, which represented little risk of their being caught. Shep put his ear to the door of the mechanical room, then slowly opened the door a crack. Nothing. The coast was clear. With a sense of relief, the two men stepped through the door, back into the garage.

"Hold it right there," a voice commanded. The figure they'd seen earlier stepped out from behind the door. Shep recognized him immediately.

It was Anthony Walcott.

It took Walcott a moment longer to recognize Shep, but when he did, his surprise was considerable.

"Carroll!" he cried. "What are you doing here?" Then, turning to Charlie, he said, "And *you. What the hell's going on?*"

As it turned out, Bailey never got the chance to confess her meeting with Shep to Tony Pappas. He called her on the Monday after her Fourth of July party and, in a strained voice, asked her to come to his office. Immediately.

She was there within fifteen minutes. Her mind raced as she sat in Pappas's waiting room. What was this all about? Why had he sounded like that on the phone—almost angry? Surely he couldn't already know that she'd allowed Shep to go through Michael's files. No one but Sam had been aware of it, and there was no way Sam would have said anything to Tony the other night. No, it must be something else. Maybe he'd heard from the bank.

His office door opened and Pappas emerged.

"Come on in," he said, his face lacking its customary warmth.

Bailey entered, then seated herself in one of the chairs and waited for him to settle back down behind his desk.

"Is something wrong?" she asked, watching as he wiped his glasses with a tissue. He still had not made eye contact with her.

Pappas placed the wire-rimmed spectacles on the bridge of his nose, pushed them in place, and finally raised his gaze to meet hers.

"Shep Carroll has been removed as Chicago Savings and Loan's counsel," he said.

"What?"

"Shep Carroll no longer represents the bank," he repeated, watching Bailey for her reaction. "Actually, he's been placed on administrative leave by his law firm. He's facing possible disbarment."

Bailey let out a gasp.

"Why?" she said softly.

Tony's face registered no emotion. "I think you know at least part of the answer to that question. At least, as it was explained to me by the bank's new attorney, you *should* know."

He then proceeded to tell her what had happened. How Anthony Walcott had come upon Shep and Charlie Eaglequill as they were sneaking out of the mechanical room at Edgewater Place late at night on the Fourth of July.

"Charlie Eaglequill!" Bailey said in amazement. "The Fourth of July. What were they doing?"

"Apparently they were conducting their very own building inspection."

"I don't understand," Bailey said. "Why would they do that?"

"Why don't you ask your friend Samantha Cummings?"

"What do you mean? What does Sam have to do with this?" None of it made any sense to Bailey.

Tony explained Sam's role in the chain of events.

"You mean Sam told Shep about the note?"

"Yes. She went to him and asked for his help. And his little foray with Charlie Eaglequill was his attempt to do just that—to help. To find out just what was going on at Edgewater Place. If their inspection turned up nothing, he was planning to tell Sam it was safe to sell the units you needed to to come up with the money."

As the realization of what had happened finally sunk in, a wave of nausea swept over Bailey.

"Oh my God."

"Now, would you like to tell me what's been going on?" Tony asked. "Can you tell me why the bank feels that Shep Carroll has been trying to help you? Why they've reported him to the state bar for a breach of professional ethics?"

Bailey started at the beginning. She didn't leave anything out. When she got to the part about the note, Tony interrupted.

"Why the hell didn't you tell me about the note?"

"I tried calling, but you were in trial all that week."

"Why didn't you leave a message? I would have called you back. Didn't you think I should know about it?"

Bailey knew her actions were hard to explain. "I was planning to tell you. Then I had that meeting with Shep Carroll and I *knew* I had to tell you about it, tell you everything, but I just kept putting it off. I knew you'd be angry. And I knew you'd tell me not to cooperate with him. But I believed he might be able to help me. I wanted to see if he could. But I never expected this. I never expected this to happen to Shep . . ."

"That poor son of a bitch," said Tony, shaking his head. "He may never practice law again."

"But he thought Muncie was up to something. He suspected some kind of a plot between Muncie and Walcott."

"He said that?"

"More or less," answered Bailey. "I think that's why he was helping me. He thought something was wrong, I could tell. He wouldn't confide in me, but I knew from some of the questions he asked and some of the things he said that he suspected Muncie was some kind of a crook. He had to protect himself, didn't he?" she asked hopefully. "He can't be disbarred for wanting to know what his client was up to, can he? Doesn't he have the right to investigate?"

Tony looked at her.

"You mean there's nothing going on between you and Shep?"

Bailey took a deep breath, then slowly let it out.

"No," she said. Then, "Yes." Then, "There was. At least, something was starting to happen between us. But then the bank foreclosed."

"And he knew it would be a conflict of interest to continue," Tony finished the sentence for her.

"Something like that," Bailey answered. She didn't explain that Shep had offered to quit the case, but that when she deliberately led him to believe he didn't mean anything to her, he hadn't. She couldn't understand her own actions—how could she expect to explain them to Tony?

How could she explain how miserable she had been ever since?

Bailey didn't realize that some explanations were not necessary. They were written all over her face.

"I think an attorney probably does have the right to know, to take it upon himself to *find out*, if necessary, if his client is doing something illegal. That might put this whole situation in another light."

"What do you mean, 'another light'?" Bailey asked. "What light has it *been* in?"

"Well, it appears the bank is suggesting that Shep did what he did out of his feelings for you. That's how they got Emerson, Caldwell to replace Shep with another attorney. And if that were true, he'd have big problems. Big problems. His career could be over."

"That's ridiculous," Bailey cried. "As if he would jeopardize his career for me. I hardly know Shep. They're just trying to cover their own rear ends."

"You could be right," Tony agreed. "Muncie's not going to admit that what Shep was really trying to do was uncover his activities, that's for sure. Especially if he's been breaking the law."

"What will happen now?"

"He'll have a hearing before the Disciplinary Committee of the Oregon State Bar. Soon. They move fast on these things. Until then, he's on leave. And we'll be dealing with a new attorney from now on. He sounded like a real asshole, too. It's too bad," Tony said. "I halfway liked Shep Carroll. Figured he was just doing his job. In fact, if that's what he was doing—trying to find out what Muncie was up to—I have to give him credit. That took guts. He had to know what was at stake." Then, after a moment's silence, he added. "I just wish I knew what it was he suspected."

Both Bailey and Tony Pappas sat quietly, lost in their own thoughts, trying to make sense of all that had happened.

"What is it about that place?" Bailey said finally.

"You mean Edgewater?"

She nodded, then continued, slowly, as if she were

thinking out loud. "The way it's affected so many people, so many lives. It's almost eerie, almost like it has a life, a spirit, of its own."

Tony Pappas was silent for a moment before replying.

"Oh, I've no doubt about that," he said. "I've known that was true for a while now."

CHAPTER 14

WITH ONE EXCEPTION, HE hadn't stepped outside his room at the Motor Inn Express since he'd returned there just before midnight on the Fourth. It wasn't that he'd had no contact with the outside world. No, that wasn't the case at all. He'd had plenty of calls.

The phone had started ringing Monday morning. The first call came in around eleven A.M., from Max Emerson, his law firm's founding partner. Apparently, it had gone something like this: Walcott had called Muncie the night of the Fourth, immediately after confronting Shep and Charlie. First thing Monday morning, Muncie called Max, who called an immediate emergency meeting of the firm's managing partners, and who now had the distasteful job of calling Shep.

Shep had always liked Max. He was the diplomat of the firm, the one who was always delegated to handle "delicate" matters.

"We have no choice," Max said. "In light of what Muncie is alleging, and the complaint they're lodging today with the state bar, we think it best that you take a leave of absence until this whole mess gets resolved. With pay, of course."

Shep had put up no resistance. He'd seen it coming. It was actually good of the firm to continue his pay.

Max's final words to him had helped somewhat. "We believe in you, Shep," he'd said. "I want you to fight this thing. We believe in you."

The next call had been from Charlie Eaglequill.

"You okay?"

"*Me?* Don't worry about me," Shep had said. "I'm just sorry to have dragged you into this mess."

"You didn't drag me," Charlie Eaglequill answered. "I went along willingly. I had to. It was the right thing to do. Don't you forget that."

"Thanks. I needed to hear that," said Shep. "But I'd never forgive myself if this screws things up for you." *Or for Bailey.*

"Walcott's treating me with kid gloves. So don't spend any time worrying about me. It's you I'm concerned about. How serious is this thing with the bar?"

Shep was slow to answer. "Pretty serious," he finally said.

"If I can do anything . . ."

"Thanks," Shep said. "But I'm afraid there's not much anyone can do at this time."

Anna's call came next. She sounded close to hysteria.

"They can't do this to you," she cried.

Shep had comforted her, telling her he was just fine. He'd be back in the office in no time. But even as they left his mouth, Shep knew his words did not ring true.

Luckily, when he'd checked in on Friday night, the same clerk who'd registered him on his last trip was on duty. Once again, despite his lack of reservations, she'd given him a suite with a kitchenette. He'd stocked up on the basics—bread, sandwich meat, fruit, chips and beer—before turning in that first night. It had enabled him to stay sequestered in his room for the past two days. He'd thought briefly about going fishing, but when he walked down to

Fins and Feathers for supplies he'd found a sign that said CLOSED. BE BACK IN 15 MINUTES hanging from the front door. He'd gone back to his room and hadn't left again since.

What he was doing while he sequestered himself in Room 311, basically, was feeling sorry for himself. Wallowing in self-pity and self-degradation. All he could think about was how he'd managed to blow it. All of it. Throw years of work down the drain, take himself out of the loop to where he could probably no longer be of any help to Bailey and Clancy. He'd even put Bailey at the mercy of a new attorney—wouldn't you know it would be Jackson Harrison they replaced him with? Jackson, whose lack of scruples was fodder for a whole collection of lawyer jokes within the firm. All in one night's work.

Way to go, Shep.

And for what? He and Charlie hadn't found a single abnormality. Nothing that could vindicate him for what he'd done. While, on one hand, their failure to discover anything was good news, it did nothing to help him in his current situation.

At least it looked like Charlie would escape any serious repercussions from his involvement. Shep had been greatly relieved that their night of crime—who but Shep would have come up with the idea of a felony building inspection?—would apparently not cause problems for Charlie. At least Charlie would be spared Shep's turmoil.

Turmoil. Never before had he experienced such agitation, such confusion. It wasn't that Shep loved his job at Emerson, Caldwell. It wasn't that at all. But, still, it was all he had. *It was what he was.* For all these years, it had kept him busy, given him a sense of purpose. An escape from whatever it was he'd been running from. After all these years of living alone, without family or truly close friends—the kind you confide in, turn to during the bad times—Emerson, Caldwell had at the very least provided him with a sense of belonging, with people who cared about him.

And while the possibility of losing his job at Emerson,

Caldwell was one thing, disbarment was something entirely different. Disbarment would mean he could never again practice law. The mere possibility of such an outcome threatened to rob Shep, literally, of who he was. For if the truth be known, despite his growing cynicism, somewhere inside him—buried deep now, beneath layer after layer of disenchantment—there was still some remnant of belief in the ideals that had attracted him to the law in the first place: the desire to make a difference, to help those in need, to fight for justice.

It was for all of these reasons that the prospect of disbarment had so shaken Shep Carroll. Certainly not because he held dear his role as Emerson, Caldwell's distressed property specialist. But because Shep Carroll, attorney, partner in the law firm of Emerson, Caldwell, was who he'd become. If they took that away from him, what would be left? He was afraid to find out. And so, two days had passed and still he sat. In a darkened room. Hour after hour. Shades pulled. ESPN his only companion. Contemplating his fate. Feeling utterly alone and disconsolate.

He'd finally drifted off into a desperately needed sleep, still sitting in the armchair beneath the shaded window, when someone rapped impatiently on his door. Awaking, it took him a moment to realize where he was. Coeur d'Alene. The motel. So it hadn't been a bad dream after all. It was all real. Had someone just knocked on his door? He must have dreamed *that* part. No one would be visiting him there.

But then he heard it again. A demanding knock.

He opened the door, shirtless, squinting at the bright corridor lights, to find Bailey standing there, her arms wrapped around herself, trembling as if she were cold.

"May I come in?" she asked, her voice small.

"Sure," he muttered groggily, standing aside to allow her entry. What now? Last time she'd shown up at his door it had been anger that brought her. Was she angry with him again? For botching things, for telling Walcott about the note she'd gotten—the one that had started this whole fiasco?

Undoubtedly, this was what had brought Bailey to his door again. She would tell him just how much he'd screwed things up for her and Clancy, and then she would leave.

But even that was okay, he thought as he clumsily ushered her in. He could take any abuse she dished out. He'd just spent the last two days trying to adjust to the thought of never seeing her again. At least she was there. At least he would get to see her this one last time. For as deep as his anguish had been these past forty-eight hours over the potential loss of his career, it had been the thought of never seeing Bailey again that had threatened to push him over the edge. He knew that he would have to deal with that again. But later. Right now, she was there and he could take her anger, gladly, just to see her one more time.

But when the door had closed and she turned to him, it was not anger that he saw in her eyes. It was sadness. And guilt. It was undisguised caring. She was near tears. She stepped toward him, reaching out to grasp his bare forearms, and in that moment, at her touch, Shep feared he would crumble.

"I just heard," she whispered. "I am so sorry. So very sorry."

She was crying now.

"Shush," he said, reaching out to softly brush away a tear. "You have nothing to apologize for."

And at those words, at his touch, she stepped into his arms.

Oh, sweet Jesus, thought Shep Carroll.

His big hands trembling, he lifted her face to his and, seeing the hunger there, the pain, he knew right then that he would do anything, anything at all, to assuage it.

Bailey lost no time in communicating to him how to accomplish just that—how to ease her torment. Her lips found his with an urgency, then traveled down his unshaven neck. Shep shuddered under their touch.

They'd made love once before. Sweet, passionate love. The love of two people on the brink of something, something so big and powerful and *unknown* that they somehow—on some subconscious level—are wise enough to unleash it slowly, cautiously.

But they both knew this time would be different.

Taking her face again in his hands, he asked her, just once.

"Are you sure?"

"Yes," she whispered. "I'm sure."

She stood motionless in front of him as he slowly unbuttoned her denim shirt, then, as Shep's eyes drank her in—feasted on her—Bailey reached back and unfastened her bra, letting it slip off her shoulders with the shirt, freeing her breasts, their nipples pebble-hard at his audience and aching for his touch. Slowly, reverently, he began to lower himself to his knees in front of her, his hands sliding down her neck, over her shoulders. He cupped her breasts, then gently took one, then the other, into his mouth, playing his tongue lightly over each nipple until a low moan escaped Bailey's throat. His finger traced the line of blond fuzz to her belly and, as she pressed herself against him, aching for more of him, all of him, he kissed her bare stomach and continued undressing her, removing first her jeans and finally her panties.

When he had finished, he drew back and surveyed her. Never had he experienced anything like this, the sheer awe of looking at her, the almost unbearable intensity of the anticipation coursing through him. He stood and gathered her into his arms, carrying her to the bed.

He laid her down gently, and as she watched him, removed his jeans. She reached for him then, and in that instant before he came to her, before his mind lost all capacity to reason, Shep marveled fleetingly that she looked as angelic as she did wanton. And then, lost to further conscious thought, he made love to her. A love equally savage and tender, desperate and soothing.

After each had explored the other—with hands, and lips, and eyes that were alternately frantic, then measured—his mouth found her inner thighs. Kissing them, as Bailey writhed and groaned and clutched at him for release, he brought her just to the brink of agonizing ecstasy before pulling himself up onto her and, finally, entering her.

Then he reached for her hands and, grasping them in his own, on the pillow above both their heads, he rode her, thrusting deeper and deeper, until finally, in a fever of sweet, frenzied anguish, they both cried out.

And it was in that position, hands still clasped, their glistening bodies still pressed tightly together, smiles of awed contentment slowly fading, that Shep Carroll and Bailey Coleman finally drifted off to sleep.

Shep awoke just before midnight.

He lay there, soaking in every detail of the sight of her, naked, lying next to him. When her eyes fluttered open, he reached out and stroked her cheek.

"Do you need to get back to Clancy?" he asked quietly.

"No. She's staying with a friend," Bailey said. Then she added sleepily, and happily. "And I'm staying with *you*."

He pulled her to him. And once again, they made love.

They were almost inseparable after that. The three of them—Shep, Bailey and Clancy—became a familiar sight around Edgewater Place.

"I didn't think this was possible," Shep had said to Bailey just the evening before, after they'd eaten dinner on the balcony of Bailey's condo. They were walking along the beach as the sun dropped into the hills.

"What?" Bailey asked.

"To feel this happy," he answered. "To feel so incredibly good when everything else is so incredibly bad."

He'd just received notice that day of his disciplinary hearing before the state bar. It was scheduled to take place the week after next.

Bailey was worried about him. He refused to talk about it, about what was going on. This was one of the first times he'd even acknowledge it. She still felt such guilt about the part she'd played in what had happened to him. But when she tried to talk to him about it, to apologize, he always stopped her. She knew the thought of the impending hearing, the time away from his work, was getting to him. Yet, as close as they had become these past few days, he did not want to talk about it.

"I know what you mean," she said. Bailey had serious problems of her own, but she was like Shep: their blossoming relationship was a source of such joy to her that it made the situation at Edgewater Place endurable. So far, the committee's efforts had failed to result in more sales. According to Tony, the notice of foreclosure would be filed as soon as the thirty-day cure period expired. Luckily, the actual foreclosure process would take time, during which Bailey would have to make other living arrangements for herself and Clancy. Still, that night, walking hand in hand with Shep while Clancy ran ahead, trying to skip rocks off the water's surface, none of it mattered.

When they'd returned home, Shep had helped tuck Clancy into bed.

"Hey, I've got an idea," he'd said. "There's something I want you two to see. Only problem is I'd have to pick you up about six-thirty in the morning. Are you game?"

"Sure," Clancy answered with her usual zest. "What is it?"

"Can't tell," Shep answered, then, turning to Bailey, he said. "What do you say?"

"Wouldn't miss it for the world."

Six A.M. had come around awfully fast. When the alarm went off, minutes earlier, Bailey stayed in bed, thinking about the evening before. Enjoying her newfound happiness. But then Clancy stuck her head in the door.

"Time to get up," she urged, worrying that Bailey might make them late. Shep had told them it would only "work" if they left by six-thirty sharp. "He'll be here in fifteen minutes."

At six-thirty, when Shep pulled up to the front door, they were waiting for him in the lobby. He had their now customary lattes and hot chocolate in a carry-tray. They took off down the west side of the lake, toward the Coeur d'Alene Reservation.

The sun had climbed high enough to throw some light over the mountains to the east, promising a typical July day of endless blue sky and comfortable, dry heat. Bailey had never seen the country down this side of the lake. She was struck by its raw beauty, its openness. Clancy was appreciative, too. Her little mouth rarely stopped asking questions about any and every thing that popped into her mind. She was especially fascinated when they crossed onto reservation land.

"You mean real Indians live here?" she asked.

"Yep."

"Have you ever seen them?"

Both Bailey and Shep laughed, which promptly embarrassed Clancy into silence.

"We're not laughing *at* you, honey," Bailey said when she saw Clancy's expression. She'd recently realized that sometimes when she laughed at something cute that Clancy said, the little girl took it the wrong way and thought she was being laughed *at*. Bailey was trying to be more aware of her little niece's sensitivity, but judging by Clancy's current expression, she hadn't yet mastered it. "And yes, we've seen some of the Indians who live here on the reservation. In fact, so have you. You've already met their tribal chief."

Just as Bailey expected, there was no way the little girl could maintain her silence.

"I have?"

"Yes. Remember Charlie Eaglequill, that nice man I introduced you to the other day?"

Clancy nodded her head. "He's an Indian? He's their chief?"

"Yes."

"Neat!"

They went another mile or so farther down the highway, then Shep pulled off onto a narrow gravel road. He drove slowly, and after rounding a bend, he pulled over next to a For Sale sign about ten yards from a stand of pine trees that bordered an open, rolling field. Shafts of sunlight were just skimming the top of its crop of golden wheat.

"Shhh," Shep said, holding an index finger to pursed lips as he turned to a still-chattering Clancy in the backseat. Lifting the top of the console that separated his and Bailey's bucket seats, he extracted a pair of binoculars and handed it to the little girl.

"What?" she asked. "What are these for?"

"There," he said, pointing to the middle of the stand, where several dead trees created an intricate web of barren branches extending as high as one hundred feet above where they now sat. About two thirds of the way up, Clancy could see more than a dozen large, dark forms silhouetted against the morning sky.

"What are they?" she asked in amazement.

"Wild turkeys," Shep answered. "Take a look at them through the glasses."

With a little help from Shep, Clancy got the binoculars adjusted.

"They're humongous!" she cried out when she finally got one of the birds in sight with her right eye. Her left eye was squeezed tightly shut, but even a one-eyed view of the creatures was impressive.

"Wait till you see its wingspan," Shep said. "We got here just in time. See how they're starting to move around a little bit, to stretch their wings and their legs? They fly up there at night to sleep where it's safe. Then they come down in the morning and spend the day foraging in the trees and fields. In just a few minutes, they should start dropping down to the ground."

Just as he said it, Bailey gasped. "Look!"

One of the forms, large when it was curled in the tree but now—its wings spread in flight—three times that size, was cascading down to the ground. It landed within yards of the car, took one look in their direction, then, having apparently determined that they presented no danger, started walking slowly, bobbing its way toward the other side of the road. Within a minute, a second form plummeted to the ground.

Then a third. And a fourth. Before long, they'd counted thirteen turkeys in all.

"It's raining turkeys," Bailey whispered in amazement.

Clancy giggled, her face pushed into the glass of the car window as she followed the descent of each bird.

Once all of them were on the ground, the turkeys disappeared, in an orderly line, into the foliage lining the road.

"I've never seen anything like that," Bailey said when they'd gone. "How did you know about them?"

"I hadn't either," said Shep. "Then one morning while I was down this way, trying to find a back road to the lake to do some fishing, I stumbled upon them. Saw them in the tree and couldn't figure out what they could be. I pulled over just like this and watched them, and before long they started dropping to the ground all around me. This is the third time I've seen it and I still get a thrill out of it." His eyes swept the fields surrounding them. "And this country. Have you ever seen anything like it?"

Bailey smiled at him and reached for his hand. "It's beautiful. And so peaceful."

"It would be nice to live here," Clancy's enthusiastic voice declared from the backseat. "You could have all the animals you wanted out here."

Bailey smiled at her niece. For a little girl brought up in Los Angeles, she was fast becoming a country girl. Bailey had seen such a difference in Clancy recently. When she'd first returned from her mother's, she was thin, pale. And anxious—she rarely let Bailey out of sight. But the little girl in the backseat today was a happy, healthy six-year-old, full of life, full of curiosity and enthusiasm. She was fast developing a love for nature and the outdoors, and in Shep she'd found a more than willing teacher. Bailey was pleased to see the attachment forming between the two of them.

Life was good. So good that, at times, the hurt she'd lived with for so long simply disappeared. That's what she wanted for Clancy, too. For the hurt to be gone.

"Aunt Bailey?" Clancy asked, her eyes following the last of the big birds into the long yellow grass.

"Yes?"

"Do we have to have turkey for Thanksgiving this year?"

This time, Bailey knew not to laugh. "No," said Bailey. "We don't. Maybe this year we'll have pasta. How does that sound?"

"I'd like that."

Before heading back to Coeur d'Alene, Shep took Bailey and Clancy into Halfway and introduced them to Joe Curry. Shep and Bailey could tell that Joe, with his long braided hair, beaded belt and well-worn moccasins, seemed more the real thing to Clancy than had Charlie Eaglequill. They sat at the counter eating doughnuts and sipping coffee, and listened as Joe entertained Clancy with tales of life on the reservation when he was a child. He told her about the songs they used to sing, the dances they would do in a circle around a fire. The little girl was mesmerized.

"Did they have wild turkeys on the reservation back then, too?"

Joe looked at Shep. "You folks been out to Winged Food Road?" he asked. When Shep nodded in response, he turned again to Clancy. "We sure *did* have turkeys back then. When I was little there were flocks of them all over this reservation. They were sacred to us, still are. My grandfather used to come and get us sometimes when there was a full moon and take us out to look for them roosting in the trees at night. I'll never forget that. They'd be sitting up there in the top of a tree, with the moon behind them, just sort of framing them in the sky. Grandfather used to call that a Wild Turkey Moon. It's been a while since I've seen one of them, but once you do, you never forget."

When it was time to go, the kindly man, who appeared to have enjoyed their visit every bit as much as Clancy had, reached under the counter and pulled out a burlap sack. Reaching inside, he handed something to Clancy. It was about ten inches in diameter—a branch formed into a crude circle, with feathers and colorful beads woven into the spiderweb of filament in its center.

"What is it?" Clancy said, clearly impressed.

"It's a dream catcher," Joe Curry answered. "My grandmother used to make them. She taught me, just as her grandmother taught her. Our people believed that if you hang one above your bed it will catch all your bad dreams and allow you to sleep in peace."

"What about good dreams? Does it catch them, too?"

"No," Joe said. "It lets the good dreams through. It only catches the bad ones."

Clancy climbed up onto the counter and hugged Joe Curry with all her strength. "Can I come back and see you again?" she asked.

The old man nodded, hugging her back.

"You must tell me if the dream catcher works." He smiled.

When they got back to Edgewater Place later that morning, Clancy ran right into her room to hang her dream catcher over her headboard. That night, before drifting off into a sweet, contented sleep, she told Bailey that it had been the best day of her life.

Bailey merely nodded her agreement—because at that moment, it would have been very difficult to speak.

CHAPTER 15

SHEP HAD FLOWN INTO Portland the night before the hearing. During the cab ride from the airport to his apartment, it struck him that Portland's long-familiar streets and sights no longer felt like home to him. Even his apartment, where he'd lived for nine years, seemed vaguely unfriendly, far less welcoming than his Coeur d'Alene motel room. Was it possible that he had been away only three weeks? It was as though he were walking through a dream or a play. None of it was real to him. The only thing that seemed real was his life back in Coeur d'Alene. Bailey. Clancy. How could he have spent the last nine years in this city, at Emerson, Caldwell, and now feel so detached from it all?

What he did not feel detached about was the business at hand. The day's hearing. The prospect of losing his license to practice law. No, that was not something he could feel indifferent about.

He had not been able to talk to Bailey about it. He did not want her to know how heavily it weighed on his mind. He did not want her to know that he hadn't had one good night's sleep since he'd been caught sneaking around Edgewater Place. That when he allowed himself to think about it, the prospect of losing his license filled him with a black dread. She had enough on her mind. She'd been through enough already. He did not want her to feel responsible.

He did not know how he would have gotten through the past few weeks without her. Having her—the simple pleasure of her company, of looking at her, touching her—had literally saved him.

Bailey had pleaded with him to allow her to accompany him. She wanted to be at his side during the hearing. It was only by telling her that her presence could actually hurt his chances for a favorable outcome that he was able to dissuade her.

He located the administrative offices of the Oregon State Bar, which were on Buck Street. The hearing was at nine A.M. in Room 1204. At exactly 8:58 he stepped off the elevator. "Disciplinary hearing room" the door to 1204 announced to the world.

Shep entered. It was a small room, much like many of the smaller courtrooms he'd tried cases in. There were four people already there. Two men and a woman, clearly the disciplinary committee examiners, all wearing somber expressions and dark suits, were seated at a large table at the far end of the room. A court reporter was setting up in the corner. A smaller table with two chairs, one for the subject of the hearing and the other for his or her attorney, faced the table of examiners. The back of the room was lined with chairs.

Shep was not surprised to see that no one from the firm was in attendance. They were playing it safe. They still represented Chicago Savings and Loan and dared not be too vocal on his behalf. It was the politically correct thing to do, under the circumstances.

He was also not surprised to see that the bank had not sent a representative. Stan Muncie would have been the logical party to attend, but, of course, Stan Muncie was not about to give sworn testimony about anything to do with Edgewater Place. The affidavits he'd filed with the state bar would more than suffice in his quest to get Shep. He needn't be present, despite the pleasure Shep knew it would have given him to watch Shep put through this process.

Shep seated himself at the smaller of the two tables. Just as the man at the center of the examiner's table was asking the court reporter if she was ready to get started, the door opened and in slipped Anna. She gave Shep a smile and a thumbs-up sign before finding a seat at the back of the room. Shep nodded at her. Good old Anna. A true friend to the end.

The examiner cleared his throat and declared, "This hearing of the disciplinary hearing committee of the Oregon State Bar is hereby called to order. Is the subject of this hearing, Mr. Shepherd R. Carroll, present?"

"Present."

"And do you have counsel present, Mr. Carroll?"

"No."

Lawyers representing lawyers. Another absurdity that Shep would have nothing to do with.

"You choose to waive your right to counsel?"

"I do."

"Do you plan to call any witnesses today?"

"No witnesses."

"All right, then, we will proceed. This hearing has been called as a result of a complaint lodged with the Oregon State Bar by a former client of Mr. Carroll's, a Mr. Stan Muncie, of Chicago Savings and Loan. According to the complaint, you, Mr. Carroll, have repeatedly been in direct contact with a Bailey Coleman, who is the lendee on a note upon which Mr. Muncie's bank is about to foreclose, despite the fact that Ms. Coleman has legal counsel, Mr. Anthony Pappas. Mr. Muncie was unaware of your contact with Ms. Coleman. In addition, on the evening of the Fourth of July, you were found to be on the premises of the property that is the subject of the foreclosure action. You had no authority to be present, nor did Mr. Muncie ask or grant you permission to be present on the property. Mr. Muncie alleges that your presence on the property on the night of the Fourth and your contact with Ms. Coleman stem from a relationship with Ms. Coleman that is in conflict with your fiduciary responsibility to the bank. Would you care to respond to these allegations at this time?"

Shep stood to address the committee. "I do not deny the allegations."

Anna let out a gasp at his admission. Wasn't he even going to fight these charges against him?

"Do you wish to explain why you chose to engage in these activities?" the woman examiner asked.

"I believed there to be a strong possibility my client was engaged in fraudulent activity. My contact with Ms. Coleman and my presence on the property on the night of the Fourth were both due to my efforts to discover whether my suspicions were valid."

The moment he'd entered the room, a calm had descended upon Shep. He spoke with assurance, no note of apology or regret.

"And did you find anything to substantiate your suspicions?"

"No, I did not."

"Then the question becomes whether your suspicions were reasonable in the first place. The code of professional ethics provides that no attorney shall be obligated to continue representation of a client who is engaged in fraudulent activity. But before we can address what recourse an attorney has when he suspects his client of illegal conduct, we must ask whether it was reasonable of you to be suspicious in the first place. At this time, would you care to share with us the information that led you to believe your client might be involved in fraudulent activities?"

Shep had given this a great deal of thought. He could try to explain everything to the board of examiners, but he knew that absent any substantiation of fraud on Muncie's part, it would do him no good. All he had against Muncie were suspicions based on instincts and knowledge of his shady past. He had nothing of substance. Nothing that could vindicate him and give the committee a way to justify his actions. He could sit there talking all day about how Muncie "seemed" in too big a rush to foreclose. About his past association with Anthony Walcott. But it was all worthless for these purposes, just as, with no other evidence, it would be worthless in a court of law.

He'd concluded that all he would accomplish by disclosing what he knew, what had motivated him, would be to risk libeling Stan Muncie, further aggravating Muncie's hostility toward Bailey, and further jeopardizing Emerson, Caldwell's relationship with Chicago Savings and Loan. Why bring anyone else down with him?

"With all due respect, I see nothing to be gained by my disclosing that information at this time."

"Very well," said the man seated in the middle. "And are you willing to stipulate to your admission as to the validity of the allegations contained in the complaint?"

"I am," said Shep.

"Is there any further information that you wish to present to this tribunal?"

"No."

"Very well. Based on your statements today and the affidavits on file, this board will issue a recommendation within ten days. As you know, Mr. Carroll, the matter will then be remanded, along with our recommendation, to the Oregon State Supreme Court for action.

"This hearing is hereby adjourned."

Bailey was waiting for him when he disembarked from the plane.

He had never been one for displays of affection in public, but at the sight of her standing just outside the gate, anxiously waiting for him, he felt such a flood of relief, such *gratitude* to feel the cold dread that had inhabited his body since they'd parted suddenly lift, that he couldn't help himself. He half walked, half ran to where she stood and took her in his arms.

They stood there holding each other, oblivious to the rest of the world, while deplaning passengers streamed around either side of them.

"I love you, Bailey Coleman," he whispered hoarsely in her ear. "God, how I love you."

He had never before said those words to a woman.

She lifted her head off his shoulder and turned her face up to him. In her eyes he saw a mirror of what he was feeling—a wonderment, an absolute amazement at the realization of what they had found together.

They headed straight back to Coeur d'Alene, arriving at Edgewater Place shortly after ten o'clock. Clancy was already asleep. Bailey paid the baby-sitter while Shep went in to check on the little girl.

A few minutes later, Shep found Bailey in her bedroom.

"I better get going and let you get some sleep," he said, wrapping his arms around her from behind as she stood brushing her hair at her dresser.

Their eyes met in the mirror.

"Stay with me tonight. Please," she said. "I don't want to spend another night without you."

As she stood facing her reflection, he lifted her hair off the back of her neck and kissed her there. She shuddered in pleasure and anticipation. Still standing behind her, he slowly removed her blouse, then her bra. She watched in the mirror, enraptured with the sight of his hands on her, the feel of his mouth along her neck and shoulders.

"Look at you," he said, pressing himself into her, his hands caressing her breasts. "You're so beautiful."

It seemed the most natural thing in the world to be standing there like that, together, both of them entirely without inhibitions. Ready to give all of themselves to the other, knowing that it was safe to do so.

"I never knew it could be this good," Bailey whispered before he finally turned her around to face him.

And then, just moments later, it got better.

* * *

Their phone calls had now become a daily occurrence.

"Charlie Eaglequill wants to meet with me later in the week," Walcott was reporting to Muncie. "Something's up. I can tell."

"I thought you told him you weren't going to make trouble for him about what happened over there on the Fourth," Muncie said.

"It's not me making trouble for him that I'm worried about. It's him making trouble for us. He's on to us. I can feel it."

Walcott could hear Muncie draw on his cigarette before responding. "The only way he could have anything on us would be if he got it from Shep Carroll. And at yesterday's hearing it was obvious Carroll didn't have a damn thing. He didn't even try to justify what he'd done. I've told you a thousand times, stop being so fucking paranoid. Chief Charlie probably just wants to know how fast you can fund this loan once the governor signs the compact, which, from what I'm hearing from my sources, should be any day now. Every week they delay construction, those Injun friends of yours are losing big money. I read somewhere that a tribe in Minnesota made twenty-two million dollars last year. That's a lot of money. I hope you're charging them up the ass for this loan."

"Two and a half points." Walcott laughed.

Muncie let out a whoop. "And they bought that? I'll be damned."

"Well, I hope you're right," said Walcott. "I just wish I knew who it was that wrote that anonymous note to Bailey Coleman. And why I saw her with Eaglequill that day. I'd sleep a lot easier if I did."

"Yeh, well, I thought you were going to do something about her. How long are you planning to let her run around screwing things up for us?"

"It's not that easy," Walcott answered, angry now. "I've been trying to be subtle about it—the last thing we need is to do something that brings a shitload of heat down on Edgewater Place. Still, I would have thought by now that she'd have packed up and left town. She's either stupider or gutsier than I thought."

"The last thing we need," Muncie corrected him, "is her snooping around. I expect you to stop her."

"I'll do whatever it takes," Walcott said without enthusiasm. Then, "Why is it that I'm stuck out here doing all the dirty work while you sit there giving orders from your hot-shot office two thousand miles away?"

"Because you're the one who gets to breathe all that clean mountain air," Muncie answered sarcastically. Then he grew serious. "And because you know what I can do for you, what I can make you out there."

As the validity of these words hit home, Walcott's whining immediately ceased.

The recommendation of the disciplinary board arrived via Federal Express three days later. It was waiting for Shep at the front desk when he returned to the motel.

He thanked the clerk and took the cardboard letter pouch directly to his room. Once there, he ripped the package open and extracted a two-page document. His eyes skipped to the last line of the second page. "It is the finding of this committee that Shepherd R. Carroll breached his fiduciary responsibility to his client, as set forth in the Oregon State Bar, Code of Professional Ethics. The committee therefore recommends a 30 day suspension of petitioner's license to practice law in the State of Oregon."

There it was then. His fate. A thirty-day suspension. No disbarment.

He didn't know *what* to feel. He settled back on the couch and started reading from the top. The committee acknowledged receipt of several letters of "the highest testimonial to Mr. Carroll's professionalism, character and integrity." It also acknowledged Shep's statement that he believed his client was involved in wrongdoing and that his actions had been prompted by his desire to find out the truth of his suspicions. But the code of professional ethics states that an attorney will avoid "even the appearance of impropriety" and it was ultimately upon this that the committee's decision turned. In working directly with Bailey Coleman, without the knowledge of his client or her attorney, Shep had at the very least taken action that could be construed as improper.

He sat with the document in hand for several minutes. The Supreme Court would issue a ruling the next time it convened. It was certain to go with the committee's recommendation. Thirty more days of unemployment. And then what? Would he still have his job at Emerson, Caldwell?

He felt an acute need to see Bailey again but he knew she had a committee meeting scheduled after lunch. They'd agreed to get together again in the late afternoon. Until then, he was on his own.

On my own. It had been his preferred state for all these years, a status he'd fought to maintain and protect. But since Bailey Coleman had entered his life, that had all changed.

Right then, to Shep Carroll, "on my own" was no longer a desirable state.

The meeting took place at Estelle Rouchon's again. Estelle had laid out an assortment of desserts and a pot of coffee in the dining room, but Al Swanson, eager to get down to business, had shepherded the group into the living room as soon as he arrived.

"I apologize for such short notice," he started as soon as the women were seated. "But we've had some recent developments that created an urgency here."

"What is it, Al?" Sam Cummings asked. She and Bailey had taken a short walk together before the meeting. Neither of them knew what was going on. Al had left a message on their answering machines the night before telling them to meet at Estelle's at one-thirty, but he had not left an explanation.

"Yesterday morning I was down in the social room kitchen. I'd walked down to Java, Java's to get Lucy a latte, and by the time I got back here, it was lukewarm. I remembered our microwave was on the fritz so I decided to put her latte in the microwave in the social room kitchen before I took it up to her.

"Well, I was in there with the door closed—you know how that kitchen is set up, it has those swinging doors that close automatically—when I heard several voices coming from just outside, in the social room. I recognized one of them right away. It was Walcott. They didn't know I was in there—no one uses that kitchen except during parties or homeowners meetings. Anyway, I could hear Walcott talking. He's showing them around, telling them all about the building. Talking about an auction. They stand there, just outside the kitchen, talking, and he's asking them questions, like how long will it take to get the auction scheduled, what the procedure is. Then he asks them, 'So what do you expect the forty-seven unsold units to go for?'

"'No more than fifty cents on the dollar,' some guy answered. 'These lenders just want to recover whatever they can and then get the hell out. Once it goes to auction it's rare for a property to bring more than half what it cost to build the building. They're only worth what they produce in revenue, and obviously, this one hasn't produced enough to even service its debt.' "

The five women listening to him sat in rapt attention.

"Did you ever see who it was he was talking to?" asked Bailey.

"Yes," Al said. "I was afraid Walcott would eventually get around to showing them the kitchen, so after I'd heard enough to know I didn't *like* what I'd heard, I started making a little noise. Running the water in the sink and slamming a cupboard or two. The door popped open immediately. You should have seen Walcott. He couldn't believe I was in there. He looked like he'd been caught with his hand in the till. He stuttered and stammered and finally introduced two men wearing fancy business suits to me."

"Did they tell you who they were? What they were doing there?" Suzanne asked.

"They didn't volunteer it. Walcott just introduced them by name and then tried to hurry them out of there. But I wasn't going to let them out of my sight until I had more information than that. I asked them, point blank, what this was all about, who they worked for." He was clearly pleased with himself about the way he'd handled the situation. "One of them gave me his card. I have it right here." He withdrew a white business card from his shirt pocket and passed it around the room.

"Summersby Auctioneers," it said. "Specializing in distressed property sales."

The room fell silent while the women tried to assess the information Al Swanson had obtained.

"What does this mean, exactly?" Estelle said, voicing the question on all of their minds.

"What it means," said Al, "is that the bank is planning to have the unsold units in this building auctioned off as soon as this foreclosure goes through. And what an auction means is that some company is going to come in here and buy all the available units at half their list price—half of what we paid for them. Then the new owner can do pretty much what he wants with them. He'll have forty-seven votes, which, as we all know from the last meeting, is enough to pass just about anything the owner wants passed. Those units could all end up as time-share condominiums. Or worse. And anyone thinking about selling his or her place here would take a bath that could just about wipe them out. That's what it means."

"Why, that's horrible," cried Estelle. "How can they do that? We have to talk to them."

"We've tried that," Bailey offered. "My brother tried it, Tony Pappas has tried it and I've tried it. The bank is perfectly within its rights to do this. There's really nothing we can do."

"Except come up with the money that's delinquent," Suzanne said.

"Yes," Bailey answered. "Except that."

This was not good news. Despite all of their efforts, they had not even had one serious inquiry regarding the purchase of a unit. Under the circumstances, even the members of the committee would be foolish to purchase more units. The situation was close to hopeless.

"Why would Anthony Walcott be showing these people around?" Sam asked, though of all those present, only she and Bailey already suspected the answer.

"My question exactly," echoed Suzanne.

"And mine," said Al. "I intend to ask him that. I tried to reach him last night but he wasn't home. I left a message but he hasn't returned my call. I want an explanation. But I'm not so sure he'll give me one."

"I just might talk to Alice," Sam muttered to herself, referring to Walcott's wife. Only Bailey, who was seated next to her on the couch, heard her. Bailey had seen a light of anger and determination go on in Sam's eyes as she sat listening to Al Swanson's news.

"Now, don't you go getting yourself in trouble," Bailey whispered to Sam.

Sam looked at her young friend and smiled serenely. "Me? I wouldn't dream of it."

CHAPTER 16

SHEP RETURNED TO EDGEWATER Place about three P.M. Bailey still wasn't home, but she'd left the door unlocked and a note saying she'd be back soon.

Too antsy to sit and wait, Shep decided to go looking for her. He stopped by Faith Lammerman's office first to ask if she'd seen Bailey.

"She left quite a while ago," Faith answered cheerfully. "Headed toward town."

Shep stepped outside and debated about whether to walk toward town in the hope of running into her. At the sound of the clanking of metal on metal, he turned and headed toward the back of the building instead.

The same workman he and Bailey had seen a couple of weeks earlier was now pounding a bolt into a bracket, affixing it to a pad of cement, approximately eight feet square, that was situated just a few yards off the building's back wall. Nearby, on the cement, stood several unassembled parts to what appeared to be a barbecue grill.

"Now what?" Shep asked, half in jest, as he approached.

The man gave the bolt one last blast with the hammer, then straightened.

"Another one of Walcott's doozy ideas," he answered, shaking his head. "He wants a barbecue for the homeowners to be able to use. Like anyone's going to want to cook out back here when they all have decks facing the lake that they can barbecue on."

"Doesn't make a whole lot of sense." Shep agreed. The area, basically a long strip of grass off the garage on the backside of the building, was not particularly aesthetic. Still, Shep had other things on his mind. Besides, he was no longer the bank's counsel. How the president of the homeowners association decided to spend money was no longer his business. He looked at his watch, debating again about heading into town to look for Bailey.

"Maybe it was the full moon," the man said.

"What's that?" Shep asked.

"The full moon. Makes people crazy. Maybe that's what got into Walcott. There was a full moon the night before he had me pour this cement pad. The same night that someone walked across the garage floor I'd just laid. I keep track of the lunar cycle. Sure as I'm standing here, someone's gonna do something goofy then." He laughed. " 'Course, as far as I'm concerned, Walcott's never dealing with a full deck. You gotta really watch out for someone like Walcott when the moon's full."

Shep was not much in the mood for mysticism.

"Yeah, you never know," he said disinterestedly. Again, he looked at his watch. Maybe Bailey was back by this time. He bid his superstitious friend good-bye and returned to her condo, but she was still gone.

While he sat in her kitchen waiting for her, he decided to give Max Emerson a call. He wanted to hear the firm's response to the disciplinary board's findings and recommendations. Did he still have a job waiting for him? He knew he could count on Max to be honest with him.

"Shep," Max said upon picking up the phone. "Good to

hear from you. I thought you'd be out there reeling in trout this time of day."

Shep appreciated Max's attempt at cheerfulness.

"Actually, no. Wish I were, though," Shep said. "Listen, Max, I got the disciplinary board's findings and recommendations today and thought I'd give you a call to discuss how this affects me there."

"We got a copy, too. In fact, several of us had lunch together today and discussed it. We're not happy with what's happened, Shep, but you know you're held in high regard here. Your job will be here when this suspension is over."

Shep let out a sigh of relief that was audible not only to Max Emerson but to Bailey as well. Unbeknownst to Shep, she had just returned home and was standing in the foyer outside the kitchen, about to hang up the rain slicker that she'd grabbed before leaving with Clancy. "That's good to hear, Max. I appreciate you standing by me like this. I'll be in touch with Anna. I'll try to make sure nothing falls through the cracks while I'm gone. Maybe you should put me through to her now so I can give her my number here in Coeur d'Alene."

"You mean you're planning to stay in Coeur d'Alene for the month you're off work?" Max Emerson asked.

"I haven't really formulated my plans yet," Shep answered. "I've just been waiting to learn the results of the hearing. But, yes, I suppose I will spend most of the month here in Coeur d'Alene."

Emerson went quiet for a moment. "Listen, Shep," he said then. "There's one thing that you need to know. Chicago Savings and Loan is still a valued client of this firm. I haven't asked you whether there's any truth to their assertion that you are romantically involved with this Bailey Coleman and I'm not going to ask you now, but—"

Shep cut in before he could finish. "But *what*? What does Bailey have to do with my coming back to work?" he said.

Bailey had just entered the kitchen. Shep was sitting at the table, his back to her. He did not notice her. Upon hearing her name, Bailey instinctively withdrew back into the hall, where she stood listening to Shep's end of the conversation.

"It's the consensus of the partners that your involvement with her while this firm continues to represent Chicago Savings and Loan would compromise this firm's standing with the bank. It could constitute a conflict of interest and it sends the wrong message, not just to Chicago Savings and Loan, but to all prospective clients."

"Are you trying to tell me that I can't have my job back if I'm involved with Bailey Coleman?" asked Shep, incredulous.

"Yes," Emerson answered. "I guess that's what I'm trying to say. If you want to come back to Emerson, Caldwell, you'd best not be seeing her. She's caused this firm enough trouble already."

Shep was silent for what seemed an eternity. Then, in a voice so calm and full of reason as to sound almost mechanical, he responded.

"Well, if that's how the firm feels, I guess I know what I have to do. I'll head back to Portland first thing in the morning. When can we meet?"

Shep was so caught up in his conversation with Max Emerson that he never even became aware of Bailey's presence. He never did hear the almost inaudible gasp that escaped from her lips at what she'd just heard—never did hear Bailey as she silently slipped back out the front door and went running down the hall.

It was Sam who finally showed up. He'd been waiting for more than an hour. What could be keeping Bailey? When he heard someone at the front door, he jumped up.

"I was getting worried about you," he called out as he headed for the foyer. But it was Sam who greeted him there, not Bailey.

Even to Shep, who did not know her well, Sam appeared distraught.

"Has something happened to Bailey?" he asked.

"Of course not," Sam said. "She's fine. I just talked to her." While it might have been a little deceptive, it wasn't actually a lie. The truth was that Bailey was sitting downstairs in Sam's kitchen as they spoke—after overhearing Shep's conversation, she'd shown up at Sam's door. "She asked me to tell you that she's having dinner with a friend. She said you should go on back to your room and she'll call you a little later."

Shep was confused. It was unlike Bailey to do anything like this. When she said she would be somewhere, she was there. Period. But he could hardly put Sam through an interrogation, so, shrugging his shoulders, he walked toward the door.

Just as he started to leave, he thought he heard Sam say, "She's worth fighting for."

Shep turned, his eyebrows scrunched up in puzzlement.

"Bailey?" he asked.

"Yes."

He looked at her then. *What was going on?* He suddenly had a sense of foreboding.

"She's worth more than that," he finally said. "She's worth *everything*."

Then he turned and left.

"Promise me that you didn't tell him anything," Bailey said to Sam when Sam returned to her condo.

"I did just as you told me," Sam answered. Her concern could be heard in her voice. "I told him you were having dinner with a friend, which means, of course, that you will be eating here with me."

"I'm afraid I don't have much of an appetite," Bailey answered.

"I'm telling you," Sam said, ignoring Bailey's response, "that man's madly in love with you. What you two have comes along once in a blue moon. Please, Bailey, think this through carefully before you do anything to jeopardize it."

Bailey looked across the table at this woman who had become so much more than a friend to her. Sam Cummings was now the mother she'd lost as a teen. The closest thing that Clancy would ever have to a grandmother. And a wise, kindhearted confidante and counselor.

But despite the tremendous respect she felt for Sam, Bailey knew that when it came to Shep, she had to follow her own heart, trust her own instincts.

Once in a blue moon. Her mother had used that expression when Bailey was a little girl. She knew what it meant. Sam didn't have to tell her that what she'd found with Shep Carroll came along once in a blue moon. If you were lucky, once in a lifetime. She already knew.

It was because of that—because she, better than anyone, she who had loved and lost so many times already in her short life, knew the value of what they had together—that Bailey had to do it.

"We need to talk," she said to Shep later that evening when he returned. They were sitting side by side on the couch. "I have a confession to make. I was here this afternoon. I walked in when you were on the telephone. I heard you talking to Max Emerson."

Shep's blue eyes narrowed on her.

"I don't understand," he said.

"I heard. I know what he said, that you can't have your job back if you stay with me."

There, she'd said it.

Shep reached for her, but she kept her distance. She could not allow his nearness to compromise her resolve.

"Is that why you had Sam come here and tell me you'd see me later?"

She nodded.

"Look at me," he said then.

When she did, his eyes held hers, refusing to let them go, as surely as if they had been physically locked, one pair to the other.

"Did you honestly think I would do that?" he asked. "That I would choose my job over you. Over us?"

Bailey sighed.

"I didn't know what you would do. I needed some time to

think. That's why I sent Sam here. I'm sorry about that." She took a deep breath. "But I'm not sorry about my reaction. I'm so confused, Shep. I don't want to be the cause of your leaving your job. I don't want us to start out like that, with that hanging over our heads. What kind of a beginning would that be for us?"

When he did not respond, she continued.

"You've worked so hard to become what you are. You can't just walk away from it. And I don't know if I could live with myself, with looking into your eyes day after day and knowing that I had been the cause of your losing something you worked so hard to achieve. That's no way to begin. Is it?"

Shep's face had drained of expression.

"So what are you saying? That I should go back to Portland? Go back to work at Emerson, Caldwell, as if we never happened? Do you really mean that, Bailey? Is that what you really want?"

Her eyes finally broke free of his.

"I don't know," she answered softly. "I don't know if I can live without you. I know I don't want to, that I don't even want to try. But I also know that I would rather walk away now than do anything that would mar what we've had together. If it's a choice between living with the memory of that—these past few weeks—or living with a reality that slowly eats away at us, at our happiness and maybe even at our feelings for each other, I'd choose the memory."

She reached for his hand then.

"Because that—the memory of what we've had up until now—is the most perfect thing I've ever had. I think that alone could keep me going for the rest of my life."

Shep held her slender hand between his and studied her face. After a long silence, he finally spoke.

"You're serious about this, aren't you?"

"Very."

He took a deep breath.

"I tell you what," he said slowly. "I'll go away for a couple of days to give you, give us both, a chance to think."

Bailey felt a panic rise within her.

"Where?" she asked. "Where will you go?"

The mere thought of his leaving was unsettling.

"To Montana. I've been wanting to do some camping, check out a couple of rivers over there. It will give us both a little time. When I come back, we can talk. How does that sound?"

Bailey could not tell from looking at him what he was thinking. But she knew what *she* was thinking. That it sounded terrible. Just awful. Still, she knew it was the right thing to do.

"Good," she said softly. "Thank you."

He stood then and pulled her to him before leaving her.

"I love you," he whispered thickly into her hair.

"I love you, too," she whispered back.

CHAPTER 17

"HELLO, ALICE," SAMANTHA CUMMINGS said with a smile as Alice Walcott invited her inside her seventh-floor condominium. "I'm so glad you had time for a visit today."

"Why, I'm the one who's pleased," Alice Walcott said, "I never get to see enough of you, Sam. How have you been?"

Alice Walcott was a wisp of a woman, frighteningly thin and pale, but with lively eyes and a ready smile. Sam had always liked her. She never could fathom how Alice had ended up married to someone like Anthony Walcott. It took the opposites-attract theory to bizarre extremes. She couldn't help but feel sorry for Alice. Her eagerness to stop and chat whenever she and Sam ran into each other in the lobby made her appear lonely, desperate for friendship. Unfortunately, the prospect of increased contact with her husband was enough to discourage even the friendliest of Edgewater Place's residents from pursuing a relationship with Alice.

Alice never displayed so much as a hint of disloyalty

to her husband, but Sam often suspected that Alice was as aware of his shortcomings as anyone. The two women had once run into each other in the stairwell when Sam was carrying Gator down for an early morning walk. They'd stood talking for a moment at the bottom of the stairs, neither woman mentioning the squirming dachshund, who was eager to get outdoors, but both keenly aware of his unauthorized presence. Alice had apparently kept Sam's secret from her husband, because the repercussions Sam had prepared herself for failed to materialize. She'd felt indebted to Alice ever since, yet she'd never thanked her, knowing that to do so would be an acknowledgment of Alice's betrayal of her husband and his precious rules.

For these reasons, Sam did not feel very good now about the hidden agenda behind her current visit. Her guilt was only amplified by how pleased Alice had sounded when Sam called to suggest they get together. Sam wanted to believe the end would justify the means. Anthony Walcott had successfully avoided Al Swanson for two days, and the committee needed some answers. Sam hoped this visit would provide them.

"I've been just fine," Sam said. "Of course, I've been very concerned about Bailey Coleman. And her niece, little Clancy. I've grown so fond of them. I feel so badly about their losing their home here." They'd settled on the couch, and Alice had arranged a silver tea service on the coffee table in front of them. As she listened to Sam, she poured two cups of Grey's English tea.

"It's a shame, isn't it?" Alice said. Appearing uncomfortable with the subject of Bailey Coleman, she didn't pursue the conversation.

Deciding that the situation called for a more subtle approach, Sam switched gears and asked Alice about her patio garden. Everyone in the building knew that Alice took great pride in the herb and vegetable container garden that she cultivated on the deck each spring and summer.

"Would you like to see it?" Alice asked.

As they talked outside over half a dozen clay pots of

thyme, rosemary, and surprisingly, catnip—which, Alice explained, she was growing for the first time and planning to bestow upon Estelle Rouchon's cats—and several four-foot-long wooden planters that overflowed with fresh tomatoes, green peppers and green beans, Alice grew more relaxed.

"Why don't we sit and drink our tea out here?" Sam suggested.

Alice happily brought the tea tray outside and they settled into the patio chairs. It was a warm, slightly muggy morning, the skies heavy and threatening with the front that had moved in earlier in the week.

As was inevitable whenever two or more Edgewater Place residents got together, their conversation eventually turned to discussion of the latest illnesses and deaths in the building. Like many condominiums, Edgewater Place had a disproportionately high number of retirees and elderly among its residents. Rarely a week went by without someone taking ill. This past week Emmet Wasserman had passed away.

"And how is poor Althea?" Alice wanted to know.

"She's having a hard time, but she's strong. To be honest," said Sam, "I'm more worried about her financial condition than anything else."

"Goodness. Why is that?" Alice wanted to know.

"Well, I suspect if she had the choice she'd move back to the Midwest to be near her children. She and Emmet kept pretty much to themselves. They'd only lived out here a year and a half and they hadn't really made a lot of close friends. With Emmet gone now, I think Althea would like to go back home. But, of course, that's probably impossible now."

"Whatever do you mean?" Alice asked.

"Didn't you know?" Sam feigned surprise. "The units that the bank is foreclosing on are going to be auctioned off. According to Al Swanson—and Al should know, he's been in the business all his life—those units will only sell for about half what the rest of us paid. Althea can't afford to sell her placed once that happens. She told me she'd lose everything. I'm afraid she's stuck here." Sam let out a wry little laugh that, remarkably, lacked any note of bitterness, and added, "We all are."

Alice looked as though Sam had told her she'd just seen someone jump off the top of the building.

"That can't be true," she said. "The foreclosure is not supposed to hurt *anyone*. I've never heard talk of an auction."

This was the hard part, but she had to do it. "Well, maybe you should ask your husband," Sam said. "According to Al Swanson, Anthony was showing the people from the auction house around a few days ago. I just assumed you knew."

Alice appeared embarrassed not to have known about her own husband's involvement in matters that were being discussed openly by other residents of the building. "I bet he told me and it just slipped my mind," she said. "My memory is getting so bad that sometimes I can hardly remember my own name."

She laughed, a silly, empty laugh. Alice Walcott was not a day over sixty, and Sam knew that her mind was as sharp as a tack.

Sam was ashamed of herself. Poor Alice. She looked terribly disturbed. It was clear that she had not known about the auction—and equally clear that the knowledge the building's residents stood to be hurt bothered her deeply. Sam feared that her visit had only succeeded in upsetting the poor woman.

They visited for a while longer, but Sam could see it was taking an effort for Alice to continue playing the role of the happy hostess. Just before Sam left, Alice asked a question that strengthened Sam's conviction that Walcott's wife was as much in the dark as the rest of them, maybe even more so.

"Whatever happened to that young attorney for the bank?"

"Shep Carroll? He's had his license to practice law suspended because the bank found out he'd been investigating what's been going on here without their knowledge. It's a crazy world, isn't it? When your own profession suspends you for trying to do what's right." Sam answered. "He'd been staying here, in town, down at that new Holiday Inn–type motel at the end of Sherman, but I suspect he'll be heading back to Portland soon. There's nothing to keep him here anymore."

A quiet Alice walked Sam to the door.

Before she left, Sam reached out and took Alice's hand in her own. "Listen, kiddo," she said, "I apologize if I've been the bearer of bad news. I'm afraid I upset you and I surely did not want to do that."

Alice took a deep breath, standing tall, and squeezed Sam's hand.

"Don't you worry about me, Sam Cummings," she said. "I'm a lot tougher than I look."

I hope so, thought Sam. *You'd have to be tough to be married to that SOB.*

Still, she did worry about Alice.

And when all was said and done, Sam returned home from her meeting with Alice Walcott wondering what, if anything, she'd accomplished.

The dark, volatile weather that had descended upon North Idaho in defiance of the tourist-perfect predictions of all local forecasts matched Charlie Eaglequill's gloomy mood. This time of year was never like this. From mid-July through the end of September, a single cloud did not so much as darken the fairways of the local golf courses, the sand of the city beach, or the waters of any of the area's many lakes. The Chamber of Commerce would not allow it.

But despite this firmly established dictum, on this early August morning, rain it did. In buckets.

The dash from his car to the rest home's front door had Charlie still shaking water from his cowboy hat and slicker as he entered the activity room where his father sat waiting for his son's regular Wednesday morning visit.

"Who do you expect to mop up after you?" his father asked gruffly, eyeing the small puddle that was accumulating at Charlie's feet.

Charlie looked down. "Sorry," he said. He reached into his pocket, pulled out a blue bandana and, dropping it to the floor, pushed it around with his cowboy boot–clad foot. Then, satisfied with the effect, he retrieved the soaked handkerchief and seated himself in the chair next to his father.

There was silence.

"What is troubling you?" Charlie Eaglequill Sr. said.

"Nothing," said Charlie Junior. "What makes you think something is bothering me?"

"Because you sit where you will not look at me," his father said. He was right. Charlie usually sat directly opposite him.

Charlie got up and crossed to the chair opposite his father.

"How's this?" he said when he was seated facing Charlie Senior. Despite his mood, a half smile tugged at his lips. He never could hide anything from his father.

"Better," the old man grunted.

There was another silence.

"Been playing any bingo?" Charlie asked.

"Some."

"Winning?"

"Some."

The old man was waiting. Charlie knew he could never win at this game his father played so well.

"All right," he said finally. "There *is* something."

"The gambling," his father said. It was a statement, not a question.

"Yes, the gambling. The casino." Charlie answered, shaking his head in frustration. "I don't know what to do. This whole situation seems to be getting out of hand. I'm beginning to have real doubts about the banker who will be lending us the money for the casino."

"What kind of doubts?" Charlie Senior asked.

"I don't know. Nothing that I can really put my finger on, but there's something going on between him and the guy who's developing the golf course for us. Somehow they're both involved in some hanky-panky at Edgewater Place. Some good people are getting hurt by it, but there's no way to stop them. There's nothing anyone can prove."

"Sometimes feelings are proof enough," the older man said.

"This casino is so important to our people," Charlie said, mounting an argument intended as much to convince himself as his father. "Construction is supposed to get under way the minute the governor signs the gaming compact. I can't jeopardize our whole tribe's future, the future of our children, because of some unfounded suspicions, can I? It's just a loan, just money. Money that can make a huge difference."

His father stared straight ahead.

"What's happened at Edgewater Place has nothing to do with us, with the casino. Why would I let that jeopardize our plans? What would I accomplish by backing out of this loan?"

Still no response.

"It's time for our tribe to step into the real world. We've been clinging to tradition for too long. Today's world has nothing to do with ceremonies, and spirits, and tradition. It's a world of business. *This* is strictly business. A business decision, nothing more, nothing less. Building the casino makes good business sense. And it takes money to build a casino."

Charlie Eaglequill Sr. continued to sit—a fisted hand resting on each thigh, his brown, heavily lined face expressionless—silent and stone-still.

Charlie Junior lapsed into his own silence.

Outside, a clap of thunder announced that the skies had no intention of letting up. An orderly wheeled a withered woman into the room, positioned her in front of the portable gas fireplace in the far corner, then tucked a blanket around her legs before lighting a weak blue flame and leaving.

Finally, with a sigh, Charlie Junior said softly, "You're right. You're *always* right. I can't do it. Good business or not, I can't build our people's future on bad money. Tonight at the tribal council meeting, I'll recommend that we back out of the loan from Walcott's bank and drop our association with the golf course."

He looked exhausted but relieved.

"Let's just hope the rest of the council will listen to me."

"They will listen to you," his father declared.

Charlie Junior chuckled.

If the council listened to him tonight as well as his silent father had today, he might not get a word in edgewise.

The next day Charlie paid Anthony Walcott a visit.

When he announced the tribe's decision to forgo the loan, Walcott was livid.

"You must be out of your mind," he stormed. "No one else is going to lend you this kind of money."

Charlie remained calm.

"Other tribes have found a way," he said.

Walcott's neck and face were scarlet.

"Other tribes that have white men leading them, showing the way," he ranted. "You can't do this. We won't let you."

Charlie leaned forward in his chair.

"You won't *let* us?" he said, his face suddenly menacing.

Anthony Walcott, beside himself, stood so suddenly that his chair flew backward. He strode to the door and threw it open.

"You'll regret this," he said. "You, your tribe, the Coleman broad, you'll all regret this."

Charlie stopped even with him before departing.

"What does this have to do with Bailey Coleman?" he said, his eyes piercing Walcott's fury as though it did not exist.

"As if you didn't know," Walcott snorted before slamming the door in Charlie's face.

Before heading home, Charlie made just one more stop. At the Motor Inn Express. When he learned that Shep Carroll was gone for a couple of days but was expected to return to the hotel, he hastily scribbled a note and left it with the perky young woman at the front counter who assured him she knew just who Shep Carroll was.

"Sure," she promised. "I'll make certain Shep gets it."

Then she placed it alongside the package that had been left there for Shep earlier in the day.

After his meeting with Max Emerson and the other senior partners, Shep flew back to Coeur d'Alene. He arranged for the hotel to keep his room available, then took off the next morning for Montana. He would stop for supplies in St. Regis, then cross back over the border a short distance into Idaho, to camp and fish along the waters of the St. Joe River. Later, he might move into the Bitterroot, outside Missoula.

The wet weather did not bother him. In fact, he was grateful for it, for the threatening skies practically guaranteed an empty campground. He was not in the mood for company or conversation. It was time to think.

And think he did.

It was almost funny. The words that had come from Bailey's mouth two nights before might well, at one time, have come from his. *At one time.* At one time, he, too, would have urged caution. Would have balked at the idea of throwing away a career for a relationship. But not now. Now there was nothing to think about. Still, he understood where Bailey was coming from, and he did not want the fact that he had given up his job at Emerson, Caldwell because of her to weigh forever on her mind. He must give her time to make peace with it. For him, it just wasn't an issue, and when he returned to Coeur d'Alene he would convince her that what he wanted, more than anything in the world, was to be with her. At any cost.

But there was another aspect of the situation with Emerson, Caldwell that did trouble him, for which the answer was not so simple. If he were to quit, just what did he have to offer Bailey?

That was another matter entirely. With a disciplinary proceeding on his record, how difficult would it be to get another legal job? Hell, he could pump gas and be happy, just as long as they were together. But Bailey deserved better than that.

The search for a solution, as it always seemed to do, took him right back to Muncie and Walcott, and Shep's suspicions about them. If he could show that Muncie was indeed involved in wrongdoing, he might be able to get a reversal on the disciplinary findings. Finding work in Coeur d'Alene or Spokane would not be difficult then. And he and Bailey could build a future together.

If he could show that Muncie had done something illegal.

But he'd already exhausted every possible lead and had come up with nothing. Nothing that would help save Edgewater Place. Nothing to help him redeem himself as a professional.

He no longer held out much hope about uncovering the truth about Muncie. Still, it occupied his thoughts.

The first day of camping along the shores of the St. Joe gave Shep plenty of time to ponder. He did not see another person, though several times that night he heard the soft crunch of footsteps that signaled he had company of another sort. On his second day, a green van pulled up just as Shep returned to his campsite for lunch. A young, ruggedly good-looking man stepped out and directed a friendly smile his way.

"Hi there," he called out, then, eyeing the fly rod in Shep's hand, he added, "How's it going?"

"Not bad," Shep answered. "Caught a few nice rainbows and one brown this morning. You here to fish?"

"Nope." He nodded toward the river. "I'm pickup man for a couple of friends. They put in upriver earlier this morning. Should be here any time now."

"Canoes?"

"No, kayaks," he answered. No sooner had he said it than a wild battle cry drifted their way from the series of rapids a short distance upstream from the campground.

The man grinned.

"That's them," he said, taking off at a jog for the shoreline.

Shep settled onto a log to eat his sandwich and watched as first one kayak, then another, came into view around the bend. The occupant of the first had no trouble negotiating his craft to shore and climbing nimbly out. But in his attempt to steer into land, the second man ended up turning his boat around 180 degrees. As he drifted, backward, downriver, the pickup man raced ahead along the shoreline. Then, fighting his way into the waist-deep, fast-flowing water, he called out: "David. I'm on your left. Hold your paddle out."

The kayaker, David, complied, and as he surged by, the man in the water lunged for the paddle. Struggling against the current, he succeeded in grasping it, which—since the other end was still held fast by David—caused the kayak to spin sideways. David quickly bailed out, but in the process, with both men focusing their efforts on saving the kayak, the paddle got away from them and soon floated out of sight.

Still, all three of the men were jubilant, exchanging pats on the back and high fives.

"Helluva ride," Shep heard one of them say.

After quickly assessing the situation, the three men decided that the first kayaker would put back in and go in search of the paddle. The other two would drive farther downriver and pick him up at a bridge they were all familiar with.

"Don't come back without it," David yelled brazenly as his blue-helmeted friend drifted out of sight. "That's my only paddle."

"He'll get it," the pickup man said. "It's sure to get caught up somewhere between here and the bridge."

The two men loaded the kayak on top of the van and then, with a wave in Shep's direction, they were gone.

That night, lying in his sleeping bag beneath the star-filled sky, Shep could not get the sight of the two men struggling in the water out of his mind. What must Michael

Coleman have experienced the day he died? He had been kayaking a wilder river, at a time when the water was considerably higher. And he'd had no one to come to his rescue. No one to reach for him as he lost control. No one to retrieve his kayak—or even his paddle.

His paddle.

Shep remembered seeing the kayak paddle beneath the workbench in the mechanical room at Edgewater Place. Unlike David today, Michael must have had two paddles.

Then it hit him.

In preparation for filing a petition to have Michael declared legally dead, Shep had gone over all the sheriff's reports on the incident. Now that he thought of it, he realized that something had been missing from every report he'd read. Nowhere had there been mention of finding Michael's kayak paddle. A helmet had washed ashore downriver, as had Michael's life jacket. And, of course, the kayak itself had been spotted almost immediately.

But just as the body had never been found, there had been no mention whatsoever of a paddle.

How could that be?

Michael had told Tony Pappas that he was anxious to try out his new kayak. So anxious that he was going to go out anyway, despite Tony's backing out on him. The paddle Shep had found in the mechanical room was also brand-new. Most likely Michael had bought it at the same time he bought the kayak. Why wouldn't Michael have wanted to try out his new paddle?

It had never even entered Shep's mind until this moment, had never even occurred to him. The possibility that Michael Coleman's death had been anything other than the tragic accident it was believed to have been. But suddenly the seed had been planted.

Could Michael's drowning have been staged? Is that why the body had never been recovered?

Then, just as suddenly, *Lord, no. What was he thinking?* The strain of the past few weeks must be getting to him, making him paranoid. Or delusional. Yes, that was it. Such thoughts were nonsense. Sheer nonsense.

He had finally succeeded in putting his mind to rest, finally begun to succumb to sleep's elusive grasp, when, suddenly, Shep shot bolt upright.

The moon. There was just a sliver of moon that night, but its sight had been enough to bring back to him words heard earlier. Words spoken by the cement worker, who had commented that two unusual incidents had happened during the full moon in May.

The first was that footprints had been left on newly laid cement in the Edgewater Place garage. Footprints that Anthony Walcott had apparently been quite determined—"frantic," hadn't that been the word used by the workman to describe it?—to have covered up immediately.

The second incident had also involved Anthony Walcott. According to the same workman, on the morning after the full moon, the morning after the footprints had been left, Anthony Walcott ordered him to lay a large slab of cement behind Edgewater Place—just outside the parking garage—for use as a future barbecue pit. A pit that looked out on the back of an eleven-story building and two streets.

Suddenly there was one burning question to which Shep had to have an answer. Had there been a full moon the night before Michael Coleman died?

It took less than fifteen minutes for Shep to pack up his campsite and climb back into his vehicle. The nearest town was St. Regis, almost an hour away.

As he drove, he tried to remember the name on the shirt worn by the cement worker. It had something to do with bodybuilding, didn't it? Or was it a movie star? That's it. *Arnold Schwarzenegger.* That's who he'd thought of that day when he saw the shirt the worker wore. The company name was "Arnie" something, and Shep remembered thinking it funny that the worker and the star shared both the same name and the same body type.

The truck stop in St. Regis was empty. Shep pulled up to

the phone booth, scrambled out of his vehicle and dropped a quarter in before dialing.

"Directory assistance. What city?".

"Coeur d'Alene. Arnie's Construction or Cement or something like that," Shep said impatiently.

There was a pause.

"I have an Arnie's Concrete Services."

"That's it."

He looked at his watch, four A.M., then dialed anyway.

He'd spent enough time in Coeur d'Alene to know that many of the local businesses were one-man operations. He was betting on the fact that Arnie's was, also.

After the second ring, a groggy, and none-too-happy, voice answered.

"What?"

"Is this Arnie?"

"Yeah, who wants to know?"

"Are you the guy who's been doing the work at Edgewater Place?"

Pause.

"Who the fuck is this?"

"This is Shep Carroll. I've talked to you there a couple of times. You told me about the footprints in the garage and the cement patio for the barbecue. Remember?"

"Yeah. I remember you," Arnie said slowly. Then, "You always call your new pals at four in the morning?"

"I'm sorry about that. But this is important. Very important. I have to ask you something."

"Shoot." The hostility in Arnie's voice was slowly giving way to curiosity.

"You said you keep track of the lunar cycles. Can you tell me the date of the full moon in May? The night those footprints were left. The night before Walcott told you to pour the cement pad?"

Arnie snorted. "I don't have the fuckin' calendar memorized, pal." Then, after a pause, "This really that important?"

"Yes, it is."

Shep heard Arnie's condescending sigh.

"Okay, hold on. I'll take a look."

Shep stood there, clutching the phone, waiting for an answer. He knew from the reports that Michael Coleman had disappeared on May 15.

"I'm back. Okay, let me see," Arnie said. "Here we go. It was May fourteenth."

May fourteenth.

"You still there?"

"Yes. I'm here." Shep took a deep breath. "So you found the fresh footprints on the fifteenth? And that was the day Walcott had you lay the cement for the patio?"

"Yeah, that's right. In fact, it says it right here. I write my work schedule on this calendar. 'May fourteenth, west end of parking garage.' I had to do it in sections so's the old farts who live there always had somewhere to park their Caddies."

"Let me ask you another question," Shep said then, compelled to push his theory to its limits. "How many pairs of footprints were there on the garage floor the next morning?"

"That's a good one," Arnie answered. "I spent some time trying to figure that out. 'Cause it wasn't real clear."

"What do you mean?"

"Well, it looked like just one pair of footprints, but they were obliterated sometimes."

"Obliterated?"

"Yeah, you know, wiped out. It was like the guy leaving the footprints was draggin' something, something pretty heavy—it would have to be to leave the impression it did. Like someone dragged a big sack of cement mix or something—you know, I lift those suckers all day long, and they're fuckin' heavy—across the floor. You could just make out his footprints under the path left by whatever it was he was draggin'."

Shep's heart thundered with such intensity that his chest felt like it housed one of Arnie's jackhammers.

"And which direction were the footprints headed?" he asked.

"Well, the footprints were actually pointed toward the other half of the parking garage, the half they were still using for parking. But I figured the guy was heading in the opposite direction, that he was dragging it backwards, out the parking garage door."

"Out toward the new barbecue pit."

"Yeah, actually, that's right." There was a pause then. "Hey, you don't think . . . . Holy shit. Are you thinking what I'm thinking? I mean, it's possible. It's just possible. 'Cause that pit, the area where Walcott told me to lay the cement, it had all been freshly dug up, like . . . Holy shit!"

Shep was intent on retaining his composure.

"Listen," he told Arnie. "This could be nothing. Absolutely nothing. I wouldn't get carried away, start imagining things. I'm sure all of it can be explained. You've got to stay rational."

"Yeah, like this guy I've talked to maybe twice in my life calls me in the middle of the fuckin' night and asks when the full moon is." He snorted. "Then he tells *me* to be rational."

"I see your point," Shep said with forced calm. "All I'm saying is, we can't go jumping to conclusions. I just needed some information. You've given me that, and I appreciate it. Now just go back to sleep. Please."

Arnie was not ready to give up.

"So what are you planning to do with this information?"

"I'm heading back there right now, from Montana. When I get there, I plan to do a little investigating. Then, if I find anything, I'll go to the authorities. They may want to talk to you."

"I don't like talking to authorities," Arnie said.

"Well, then, let's just hope it's not necessary."

His conversation with Arnie escalated his fears to an entirely new level and caused Shep to take advantage of the fact that Montana did not have a posted speed limit. If what he now believed were true, Bailey could be in danger. He had to get back to Edgewater Place immediately.

He had to warn her.

CHAPTER 18

"AUNT BAILEY," CLANCY SAID, her brown eyes heavy-lidded, "where has Shep been?"

Bailey reached out and stroked the little girl's hair back off her forehead. It was bedtime, and as always, Clancy had been delaying the inevitable turning out of the lights with requests to have stories read, and with questions. But this inquiry, Bailey knew, came from the heart—from the simple fact that after two days of his absence, Clancy seemed to miss Shep almost as much as Bailey did.

"I told you, honey," Bailey said. "He went camping. In Montana."

"But why didn't he take us?"

Bailey hesitated. "Well, I'm sure he would have loved our company, but sometimes it's good for people to spend a little time alone. I guess he thought he needed that."

"But he is coming back, isn't he?"

"Yes," Bailey answered, "of course he is."

She kissed Clancy good-night then, and leaving the door slightly ajar, went to check the front door to see that both dead bolts—she'd had an extra once installed after the break-in—had been secured. Then she walked through the apartment, turning out all the lights but one in the study, which she kept on to light the hallway to Clancy's and her rooms.

She, too, sorely missed Shep, but for Bailey the ache from his absence was compounded by the recollection of their last conversation. *What is he thinking now?* she wondered. After putting some distance between them, would he come to the conclusion that he could not, after all, give up his partnership at Emerson, Caldwell? Would Bailey come to regret agreeing to Shep's suggestion that they take some time, think things through?

Thoughts like these had made it difficult for her to sleep the past couple of nights.

Maybe a hot bath would help her relax.

She went to the bathroom adjoining her room, turned the water on, then, while the tub filled, went into the living room for a magazine. A copy of *People* lay on the coffee table. Maybe reading about other people's lives would help take her mind off hers.

Returning with the magazine in hand, she shed her clothes and climbed in. The tub was huge—really meant for two—with a Jacuzzi, which she'd never used. Tonight it might be just what she needed. She pressed the button and settled back as the water came alive with mesmerizing sound and bubbles. Then she reached for her magazine and began leafing through it.

She found herself passing on a story about one man's struggle with AIDS and another about a tragic accident at an amusement park. The title "Animal Heroes" finally caught her eye. Midway through a story about a cat whose mournful cry had alerted a family to a house fire, she thought she heard something. Immediately she hit the button on the Jacuzzi to quiet it.

"Clancy?" Bailey called. She waited, listening, but there was only silence.

Climbing out of the tub, she went to the bathroom door

and opened it, then stood, naked, listening once more. Again, there was nothing. Still, she reached for the robe hanging on the back of the bathroom door and, wrapping it around her, tiptoed down the hallway to Clancy's room. The little girl was sleeping soundly.

Must have imagined it, she thought. Returning to the bathroom, she debated for a moment about whether to just go to bed, but then she looked at the full tub and the half-read magazine. The Jacuzzi *had* been awfully relaxing. And she hated to have all that water go to waste.

Dropping the robe onto the floor, she climbed back in and again pressed the button for the Jacuzzi. As the motor kicked back in, she opened the magazine to finish the cat story.

She was feeling relaxed. She pressed her lower back against the stream of bubbles erupting from one of the tub's vents, and closed her eyes. Yes, this was just what she needed. So soothing.

Tonight she would finally get some sleep. In fact, she might just lie back with her eyes closed for a minute or two now and enjoy the sensation of the hot water massaging her legs and back.

Soon she'd drifted into a light sleep.

It was the silence that woke her. That and the stillness. She opened her eyes to a total void—a complete absence of sound, including that of the Jacuzzi, and complete blackness. All the lights were out. It was immediately clear to her that the power to the entire unit was out. What was not clear was why.

Clancy.

She jumped up and half slipped, half ran across the bathroom floor. Frantically she groped for a towel or the bathrobe she'd dropped onto the floor.

As her hand slid along the wall, she sensed it before she actually felt it—his presence. And before she could let out a scream, before she could call for Clancy—wake her, tell her to run—a hand clamped down on her mouth from behind.

"We tried to warn you," a voice said into her ear. She

could feel his body, his brute strength, pressed against her naked back as she struggled to get free of his grasp. "But you wouldn't listen. Would you?"

Her second-to-last thought, before passing out from the chloroform-soaked cloth he placed over her mouth and nose, was of Clancy.

Her last was of Shep.

Shep pulled up at Edgewater Place about seven A.M. He went to the security phone and dialed Bailey's number to be let in. There was no response. Faith Lammerman would be of no help, since she did not arrive for work until eight. And there was no sign of the security guard, who most likely was making his final round of the building.

His eye scanned the board listing Edgewater Place's occupants and came to rest on "S. Cunningham. Unit 713." He picked up the phone and pressed the digits.

It was several rings before Sam picked up.

"Hello?"

"Sam," he said, "this is Shep Carroll. Listen, I hate to bother you, but do you think you can you buzz me in?"

"Certainly. Is something wrong?"

"Have you heard from Bailey recently?" Shep asked.

"She and Clancy stopped by last night," Sam answered, "on their way home from a movie. Why do you ask?"

"Because she's not answering now."

There was a pause. "Well, I'm sure she's just sleeping. Or maybe she's down in the pool. I'll buzz you in now and you can go check."

"Thanks," Shep said.

"You'll let me know once you've located her, won't you?" Sam asked.

"You bet."

At the sound of the buzz, Shep opened the front door. He took the elevator up to eleven. Ringing the bell, then pounding on Bailey's front door, brought no answer. Panicked, he ran back to the elevator, which had not yet left the floor, and pushed the button for one. He checked the swimming pool and Jacuzzi, but both were empty. Then he walked boldly through the ladies' locker room.

He knew the guard had a master key to all the units in Edgewater Place. Leaving the pool area, he raced down the first-floor corridor looking for him. Having no luck, he climbed the stairs, three at a time, to the second floor and again ran the length of the U-shaped corridor. He repeated this on each floor, and finally, on six, saw a dark uniform just disappearing into the far stairwell.

When he caught up to the guard, he explained his concern about Bailey and asked the guard to let him into her unit.

The guard balked.

Shep stepped into his face then. "Listen, either you give me the key or I'll take it. Got that?"

It would have been an interesting match. The guard, easily six two and obviously in good shape, also had a gun. But Shep was clearly upset, and the guard, though reluctant to cooperate, was not eager to mess with him, either.

At that moment, the elevator's bell announced its arrival on six, and out stepped Sam. She approached the two men and literally stepped between them, pushing them apart with her frail arms.

"Now, what's the problem here?" she asked.

The guard was quick to explain.

Sam grabbed Shep by the arm and said, "Bailey gave me this a while ago." She held up a key chain with a University of Washington logo from which dangled a silver key. "Let's go."

The three of them took the elevator to eleven. Shep took the key from Sam and raced ahead of them. He was already inside before they caught up with him.

There was no sign of either Bailey or Clancy. But neither was there a sign of any foul play. The apartment looked orderly, as always. Both Clancy's and Bailey's beds had been made.

"You say you saw them last night?" Shep said, turning to Sam.

"Yes, about seven o'clock. They'd just seen an early

movie and were going home for dinner. I offered to fix them something, but Bailey said she'd promised Clancy pizza." She was silent for a moment. "Maybe they had an outing planned—you know, a trip to the mountains for a hike and a picnic."

"Wouldn't she have mentioned that to you last night?"

Sam furrowed her brow. "You would think so. But maybe they're just out for coffee or a walk. Clancy loves to ride along with Bailey on her runs. I bet that's it."

"You might be right," Shep said. "Let's go down to the garage and see if the car or bike are there."

They found Clancy's bike in the bike rack. But Bailey's Jeep was missing.

"See?" said Sam. "They went somewhere. I'm sure we'll hear from her soon." Then, studying Shep, she added, "You look exhausted. Why don't you get some rest and I'll have her call you as soon as she gets back?"

Sam was probably right. He was overreacting. Sometimes he wondered if he was going crazy, all these bizarre thoughts running through his mind. Bailey had undoubtedly taken Clancy out for breakfast, or maybe into Spokane. Several times recently she'd mentioned wanting to spend a day shopping for new clothes for Clancy. Maybe they'd started early and stopped for breakfast on the way.

Taking Sam's advice, he decided to head back to the Motor Inn Express. It would at least feel good to shower. Then he could come back and see if Bailey had returned yet.

Mumbling a halfhearted apology to the guard for his behavior, Shep departed.

Not in the mood for their customary give-and-take, he tried to walk past the clerk undetected when he entered the hotel lobby, but at the last moment she looked up from her book and called to him.

"Shep," she said, "there are a couple of things here for you. This has been waiting for you since right after you left town." She held up a brown cardboard tube about two and a half feet in length.

"Thanks," he said, taking the tube from her. It was

addressed to him but had no return address, no postal markings. It had to have been hand-delivered.

"Do you know who brought this here?" Shep asked.

"No. It was here when I came on duty. But I can call Judy and find out if you want me to."

"Don't bother." He smiled in appreciation. "At least not yet. But thanks for offering."

"And a gentleman who was looking for you the same day left this note," she said, handing a folded sheet of paper over to him.

"Thanks."

He opened the note on his walk back to his room.

"Need to talk to you right away," it said. It was signed, "Charlie Eaglequill."

As soon as he got to his room he dialed Charlie's number. The line was busy.

Then he sat on the side of the bed and reached for the tube. Pulling off the cap at the end, he reached in and extracted a long roll of paper. He recognized what it was immediately. Architectural drawings. When he unrolled them he was not surprised to see that they were the plans and specifications for Edgewater Place, which were, by now, extremely familiar to him. In fact, the plans that he and Charlie had used to do their now-infamous building inspection still sat in the corner of the room.

Why would someone hand-deliver these drawings to him? There was no note. Nothing to explain. Maybe there was something in the documents.

He spent the next half hour laboriously going over the drawings, page by page. They appeared to be identical to the drawings he'd already studied for hours before the Fourth of July. After studying the first three pages, one for each floor of Edgewater Place, he pulled out the drawings he and Charlie had used to prepare for their investigation and laid them side by side with the ones that had been hand-delivered to him. They were identical. Who had sent these to him, and why? Finally, feeling extremely frustrated, he got up and went to the mini-refrigerator to find something to eat. He'd had no food since lunch the day before and he was suddenly ravenous. But both the refrigerator and the cupboard had bare shelves.

Charlie's number was still busy. Shep took a quick shower, then, pulling on his jacket, grabbed the fourth page of the plans he'd just received and strolled across the street to the Cove Bowl.

Shep settled into the same booth he'd grown accustomed to using, and when the waitress appeared, he ordered breakfast. Then, unrolling the page of drawings he'd brought with him, he sat drinking his cup of coffee and examining it, inch by inch, top to bottom. By the time the food arrived, he'd still found nothing that he hadn't already seen half a dozen times. It was beginning to look like another dead end.

As she set his plate in front of him, the waitress bumped into his coffee cup, which she had just topped off moments earlier. Coffee splashed out onto the table and across the top of the drawing.

"I'm so sorry! I'm such a klutz today. You sit still. I'll be right back with a rag."

While she hurried off, Shep grabbed a handful of paper napkins and started blotting the coffee from the drawings. There really was no harm done, he observed. The upper right corner was just slightly dampened and stained. The only thing affected was the page number. "Page 4 of 12" had run slightly but was still legible.

The waitress returned and, again apologizing profusely, wiped the table clean.

He was about three bites into his omelette when it hit him. *Page 4 of 12.*

He grabbed the drawing and unrolled it again. Yep. There it was. "Page 4 of 12." Smeared or not, that is definitely what it said. Shep rummaged in his pockets for some cash, then, throwing a ten-dollar bill on the table, he hurried out the door, leaving behind a half-eaten meal.

He dashed across the street to the motel and was back in his room within less than a minute of leaving the restaurant.

He strode over to the desk where the old plans lay next to

the new and grabbed the top page of the old ones, the ones he and Charlie had studied. In the top right corner it read "Page 3 of 11." *Page 3 of 11.*

Grabbing all of the new drawings, he rifled through them. Floor #7, Floor #8, Floor #9, Floor #10, Floor #11 . . . *Floor #12!*

The drawings that had been delivered to him two days earlier were identical in all aspects to those he'd seen earlier, with one glaring exception. They provided for a twelfth floor at Edgewater Place.

Shep picked up the phone and pressed O. The clerk answered.

"Can you call Judy and ask who delivered these papers to me?" he asked, making no attempt to hide the urgency in his voice.

"You bet," she answered cheerfully. "I'll call you right back."

With that, Shep Carroll picked up the phone again. This time Charlie Eaglequill's phone rang through.

Stan Muncie was tempted to ignore the blinking red message light on his phone. He'd just returned from a golf outing with two of Chicago Savings and Loan's biggest accounts. He'd shot a 79, beating the rest of his foursome by a minimum of six strokes, and was feeling good. Soon he'd be leaving this hellhole of a life. He hated Chicago and couldn't wait to start over somewhere where you didn't have to play golf in 95-degree/95 percent humidity conditions.

They'd scheduled the auction for the first of September. Once they owned all forty-seven units at Edgewater Place, he'd quit this stinking job. Still, he had to get by without raising any eyebrows until then, so he'd dutifully stopped by the office on his way home from the golf course. And he dutifully punched in his password to get his voice mail messages. He was pleased to hear there was only one.

But his good mood began to dissipate as soon as he heard

who had called. Anthony Walcott. And even a 79 couldn't buffer the blow of the brief message he'd left.

"We're in big trouble," the voice said. "You better get out here."

Night had almost fallen, but still they sat. They were in Charlie's car, on the side street behind Edgewater Place, where they had a good view not only of the parking garage exit but of the building's entrance as well. They had been there off and on all day and had no intention of going anywhere until they found Bailey and Clancy.

After a brief conversation on the phone, Charlie had driven right up to Shep's hotel. Together they'd pieced together what each knew. With the help of the plans delivered to his room, Shep had uncovered Muncie's plot to skim millions of dollars off the Edgewater Place loan. After seeing the plans that called for a twelfth floor, he'd phoned Chicago Savings and Loan. Apparently not everyone there knew he'd been removed as counsel, because when he'd asked to speak to Linda, a secretary with whom he'd had some dealings in the past, she'd been as friendly and helpful as always.

"Listen, Linda," he'd said. "I'm away from my office. On vacation, and I need the figure on the Edgewater Place loan."

"You know," she replied, "I'm not working on that file anymore. I believe Dottie Engles has it now."

That explained her ignorance about his situation.

"Gee, that's a shame," Shep said. "I've always enjoyed working with you. You know, it's just that one figure I need—for these papers I'm preparing for Stan Muncie. You don't suppose *you* could get it for me, do you? I'd hate to start over with someone new when that's all that's involved."

Linda hesitated.

"Well," she said. "Why don't you hold on and I'll see what I can find."

A few minutes later, she was back.

"Dottie is out today anyway," she giggled. "I've got the file. Now, what is it you need?"

Shep asked for the total loan amount, then tried not to react when she said, "Twenty-four million, two hundred thousand."

That was more than two million over the amount Michael Coleman had actually received, the amount that Shep had on record in his files.

Shep let out a half laugh then. "This next question may sound dumb, especially since I've been there several times, but you know, I just can't remember the answer. Is that an eleven-story building, or is it twelve?"

Linda giggled again. It was clear she was enjoying this conversation. Shep remembered then that on his past visits to Chicago she had always been especially attentive.

"Maybe you've been on vacation a little too long, eh?" she said good-naturedly. "Let's see . . . here it is. Twelve. Edgewater Place has twelve floors."

Twelve floors.

"And Shep," Linda said playfully before hanging up. "I won't tell on you."

Shep startled.

"What's that?"

She giggled again. "I won't tell Stan that you didn't even know how many stories Edgewater Place has."

He forced a laugh.

"Thanks," he said. "That'll be our little secret."

When Shep had told Charlie Eaglequill all this, Charlie had listened, his posture rigid, his face expressionless.

And then Charlie told him about his visit with Anthony Walcott. He told him about Walcott's comment, that he, the tribe and Bailey would be sorry. It was that comment, the implied threat to Bailey, that had caused Charlie to stop by the Motor Inn Express looking for Shep. That was why he'd written the note.

Now the two men were convinced something was wrong. Muncie had apparently skimmed millions of dollars off the Edgewater Place loan. They knew he and Walcott were partners of sorts—Shep had learned through Johnny Barletto that they'd worked together in the past and he had also seen them together, and Walcott had put Charlie in touch with Muncie for the golf course deal. None of it made sense yet, but there was no doubt in either man's mind that they were dealing with two very crooked and, if Shep's suspicions about Michael Coleman's death were true, very dangerous men.

They'd debated about calling the police with Shep's suspicions. But Bailey and Clancy were missing. If their worst fears were valid, and their disappearance had something to do with Walcott and Muncie, having the police swarming all over Edgewater Place might cause the men to harm them. They had to find out first where Bailey and Clancy were. Then they would go to the authorities.

Walcott had not left the building all day. Sam had volunteered to keep an eye on him from inside Edgewater Place. She'd seen him when he went down to pick up the mail. After he'd gone back upstairs, she'd hurried out to Charlie's car and reported that Walcott had mentioned to Tom Ryan having a meeting later that night.

"Did he say where, or what kind of meeting?" Shep wanted to know.

"No, but it's not here in the building. Ryan invited him and his wife over to play bridge and Walcott said he'd be out all night at a meeting."

It was now past eight and still they'd not seen another trace of Walcott. Thunderheads they'd noticed earlier, to the west, had moved in overhead, causing darkness to descend earlier than usual. They sat with their windows down, both men silent, absorbed in their own thoughts, plotting. Waiting.

The car did not have its lights on, which explains why Charlie heard its approach rather than saw it. He tapped Shep's arm, then pointed toward the back of Edgewater Place.

A small, dark sedan pulled up and parked on the other side of the driveway leading from the parking garage. Its occupant did not emerge at first. But after several minutes, a figure—no more than a shadow in the obscurity of nightfall—emerged and went to the trunk. He pulled what looked to be a shovel out and quietly pushed the trunk door back down. Then, moving surreptitiously, he skirted the wall of the backside of the building.

Neither Shep nor Charlie spoke as they watched the figure step tentatively out and away from the building. He was headed directly for the cement barbecue patio.

"Holy shit," Shep whispered as the man thrust his shovel into the ground at the edge of the cement.

With just a look at each other and a nod, instantaneously, both he and Charlie bolted out of the car and raced across the strip of grass separating them from the intruder.

Charlie might have been half a foot shorter and a decade older than Shep, but he was quicker. Ten feet from the man, who had just begun to turn at the sound of their approach, Charlie sprang into the air, and by the time Shep caught up, he had the man on the ground. But the man had amazing strength and agility. Seeing him about to break free from Charlie's grasp, which by now was tenuous and only at the knees, Shep lunged, too, landing on the man's back.

"Motherfucker," the man yelled.

It had been a dozen years since Shep had wrestled with an opponent on a football field, but at that moment he would have sworn this guy was a lot tougher than any he'd run up against back then. Before he knew it, the body had twisted Shep's way, and shortly after, a fist landed squarely on Shep's jaw.

It wasn't until Charlie jumped back in, with both of them wrestling the man's arms to the ground, that Shep actually saw his opponent's face.

"Arnie!"

Immediately the struggle ceased.

"Shep?" Then, "What the fuck are you doing, attacking me like that?"

Shep drew back and waved Charlie off Arnie's other arm. "Me? What are *you* doing here?"

Arnie sat up, brushing a coating of dirt off his shirt, while Shep rubbed his jaw.

"I came to find out what's under there," he said, nodding toward the cement. "I couldn't stop thinking about it after you called. I had to know." He looked then, a less than friendly look, at Charlie and asked, "Who's this?"

Shep introduced Charlie and explained that they, too, were investigating.

"Investigating how?" Arnie wanted to know.

Shep looked at Charlie, who had not uttered a single word throughout the exchange.

"We're keeping an eye on Walcott," Shep answered.

Then he told Arnie about Bailey and Clancy. That they were missing.

"And you think Walcott might have something to do with that?" Arnie asked, his voice rising. "You think he might have done something to them? To that woman who was with you that day, and that cute little girl? The one who rides her bike around the garage all the time?"

Before Shep could answer, the machine that ran the automatic garage door began to hum, signaling it had been activated. The three men jumped up and ran to the building, flattening themselves against it, hidden by its darkness.

Out pulled a green, late-model Cadillac.

"That's him now," Arnie said. "That's Walcott."

Shep and Charlie exchanged looks.

"You're sure?" asked Shep.

"Positive."

"Let's go," Shep said to Charlie. They bounded off for the car. As they jumped in, Arnie opened the door to the backseat.

"Wait a minute," Charlie said. "You're not going with us."

"Yes, I am," Arnie answered, climbing in.

There was no time for debate. Walcott's car was disappearing down the street.

They caught up with it at the traffic light on Appleway. Staying several cars back, they followed Walcott as he headed north on Highway 95. Any other time of year, at that time of night, this stretch of the road would be almost empty. But not in the summer, when the population swelled to three or four times its norm. Even after the highway turned to two lanes there was enough traffic to stay back a car or two and remain undetected.

About five miles south of Sandpoint, however, Walcott's car slowed. Charlie, still several cars back, saw his left turn signal go on. He had to make a split-second decision. When he saw the road Walcott turned onto, he decided to follow. It was still a paved roadway, lined with mailboxes. Hanging back even farther, he hoped that their presence would not attract Walcott's attention.

It did not appear to. Walcott drove with the speed and confidence that comes with knowing the twisted, potholed road, but did not appear to be trying to lose them. They had been climbing for several miles into high country, and the road was getting progressively narrower and bumpier. The cars that passed, heading in the other direction, had also grown progressively fewer.

The chances of detection were increasing with each passing mile, and all three men in the car knew it.

When they saw Walcott's brake lights go on, Charlie slowed, and as the Cadillac turned onto a narrow dirt lane, Charlie picked up speed and drove right by.

When they had gone several hundred yards, and around one sharp bend, Charlie stopped.

"What now?" Shep asked.

"Now we walk," Charlie answered. "No way we can follow him up there in the car."

Arnie had been strangely silent the past few miles. But now he spoke.

"How much do you know about Walcott?" he asked.

Both men turned to the backseat.

"Why?"

"Because I think I know where he's going," Arnie answered. "I think that was Ozzie Randall's place that he turned into."

It was Charlie who spoke next.

"Who is Ozzie Randall?"

Arnie let out a deep breath.

"Ozzie Randall," he said, "is one of those paramilitary types. You know, antigovernment, racist, the whole works."

"What would Walcott have to do with someone like that?" Shep asked.

"You tell me," Arnie replied. "You'd be surprised who all's involved with these groups up here."

"How do you know about Randall?" Again, it was Charlie speaking.

"I grew up in these parts," Arnie answered. "I've know Ozzie all my life. He's tried to recruit me, get me to join up with them. But I don't want any part of it. He and some of his goons beat the shit out of me when I told them as much. That's one of the reasons I moved down to Coeur d'Alene. To get away from these jerks." He paused, then added, almost to himself, "That's when I started pumpin' iron."

All three men sat in silence. It was Shep who broke it.

"Let's go."

They pulled off the road and headed on foot into the blackness of the woods, with Charlie leading. He moved quickly. At first Shep, who'd become more of a city boy these past few years than he realized, had trouble keeping up due to the underbrush and rugged terrain, but then, in an almost surreal transition, he was a boy again. He and his brother were making their way through the Montana woods, hunting with bow and arrow, for deer they would never take aim at.

It came back to him then, the feeling of at-oneness with the night woods, and soon he was striding side by side with his companions. They were an odd trio. One city boy and lawyer, one respected tribal chief, and their newest addition, this bodybuilding man of surprising mettle.

Cutting at a northwesterly diagonal, Charlie's bearings proved faultless when soon, dead ahead, several lights could be seen flickering through the thick pines. Within minutes they reached a clearing. In the center was Ozzie's log cabin.

Three outbuildings could also be seen. In a graveled area next to the house were several cars, one of which was Walcott's Cadillac.

The three men had lowered themselves to the ground, surveying the situation, assessing the best way to proceed. Arnie was quick to note that they were all unarmed.

"And you better believe those guys inside aren't," he said. "In fact, word has it Ozzie's been stockpiling weapons. Word has it that he's connected with big money now and they're starting some kind of military training thing somewhere up here in the woods."

It was Charlie who thought of it first.

"If that's true, maybe he's using one of those buildings to stockpile guns."

As they silently digested Charlie's suggestion, the door nearest them suddenly opened. Out stepped a lanky, unkempt man who stood at the edge of the narrow, lopsided porch and lit a cigarette. All three men froze as they watched him stand there, staring out into the woods in their direction, for what seemed much longer than the few minutes it took for him to smoke the cigarette down to his fingers. Finally finished, he flicked it into the air and, without looking back, reentered the house. As he did so, they got a glimpse of another man, inside, standing against a wall. He appeared to be in heated conversation with someone else in the room, whom they could not see.

Then the door opened wider still, and what they saw in that lightning-quick moment before it slammed shut sent quakes of terror through each and every one of them.

In the center of the room, gagged and bound to a chair, sat Bailey Coleman.

At the sight, Shep jumped up, but he was immediately wrestled back to the ground by both Charlie and Arnie.

"Hold on," Charlie said angrily. "You think you can go in there and rescue her with your bare hands?"

Shep struggled against them for another moment, then grew still. He dropped his head into his hands, trying to get a grip on his emotions. Trying to stay rational.

"You could be right about them having guns in one of the other buildings," he finally said. "Let's find out."

"Problem is, all of those buildings are pretty much out in the open. It's going to be risky approaching them," Charlie said.

"Not if someone creates a diversion," Arnie said.

Both men looked at him.

"What do you mean?" Shep asked.

"I'll go in there, get their attention. Then you can check the other buildings out."

"We can't let you do that," Shep said.

"Yes, you can," Arnie answered. "These guys know me. I'll act like I'm just dropping in. It's the only way." He looked at Shep. "*You* certainly can't go in there. You'd be bear bait before you opened your mouth. I'm the only one who stands a chance."

"But you said they beat the shit out of you."

"They did," Arnie answered. "But I didn't look like this back then. Besides, up here people do that kind of thing, then the next day they act like nothing happened. I'll tell them I'm interested in joining them, that I've had a change of heart. Hopefully, I can distract them long enough for you to surround the place and come in blazing."

He looked first at Charlie, and then at Shep. They all knew the danger Arnie was suggesting he put himself in. Walking into some kind of meeting was one thing. Walking into a kidnapping was quite another.

"And that's what you're gonna have to do," he continued. "Come in blazing. I know these guys. They're not playing games." After what they'd all just seen, they knew that to be true. "Can you do that? If you find weapons, are you prepared to use them?"

It was Shep who answered first, his voice lacking even a trace of ambivalence.

"I can do it."

He hadn't held a gun in his hands since his childhood. Even then, though he and his brother frequently used pop cans for target practice, he hadn't been able to shoot at any living creature. Yet he knew without a grain of doubt that if Bailey's or Clancy's safety depended on it, he could pull the trigger.

Charlie's answer was more reassuring.

"Let's hope it doesn't come to that. But if it does, we'll use them."

They huddled together for a few more minutes, discussing strategy. Then Arnie cut back into the woods. He would approach the house from the driveway, explaining, if questioned, that he had left his car back on the main road.

Several minutes later, Shep and Charlie watched as Arnie emerged from the darkness into the circle of light surrounding the house. His stride was strong and purposeful. Apparently someone inside was, indeed, standing guard, for the door opened when Arnie was still several yards from the porch.

"Stop right there," a voice commanded.

Bailey didn't understand what was going on, but suddenly the room drained of all its occupants save her. She could hear loud voices just outside. She turned and looked in the other direction, toward the room where she'd last seen Clancy, the room where she and Clancy had been kept for the past twenty or so hours. She'd been grateful that when they came for her they'd left the little girl there, where at least she would remain unbound (though locked in) and, Bailey hoped—not being witness to the goings-on in this room for the past hour—less aware of the extent to which their lives hung in the balance.

Any interruption of the argument that had been raging was welcome.

It centered on what to do with her and Clancy. The group of four men had been equally divided on an answer, with two of them opting for freeing her, with instructions that she was to immediately leave the area, never look back, and if she ever talked, she and Clancy would be hunted down and killed; and two others arguing that it was too late to do anything but "get rid" of her. Those two were willing, however, to consider discussion about Clancy's fate.

"After all," the one who'd come to her apartment last night, obviously an ex-military man, had said, "the kid hasn't done anything wrong."

Finally, the four men had decided that "the Colonel," who was due to arrive shortly, would make the final decision.

When she'd first seen him, when he stepped inside the room, she'd actually felt just the briefest flood of relief.

Thank God, someone is here to help me.

But then the four men had snapped to attention and saluted him.

"Good evening, Colonel," the marine said.

And in a voice that Bailey did not even recognize, Anthony Walcott had answered, "Good evening."

And it had been Walcott, the Colonel, who came up with the most horrifying plan of all.

"We'll leave them here and blow this place to smithereens," he'd said matter-of-factly. "They'll never find a trace of them."

At that, one of the men—apparently the owner of the place and one of the two who had earlier voiced his support of "getting rid" of them—had jumped up.

"Not my place, you're not," he'd practically screamed. "Are you out of your fuckin' mind?"

An even more heated argument arose then, so heated that one of the five had stepped outside—presumably for a cigarette, but Bailey sensed he was the most fainthearted of the group. She wondered if he would return, or if perhaps he'd used the cigarette as an excuse to escape. She was actually glad when he stepped back inside. Perhaps he could talk some sense into the rest of them.

And then the man who'd stood the entire time by the window, apparently the guard, had announced the arrival of someone else. Someone, apparently, unexpected.

And at that the room had emptied.

She knew now what they were. That they were members of a militia. A militia led by Anthony Walcott. They called themselves the Panhandle Republic. The title was thrown about frequently, always with great reverence.

"It's for the good of the Panhandle Republic," Walcott had preached. "If she talks, we could all go down. The money will dry up, just like that."

And then, from the cigarette smoker, the opposing view. "The Panhandle Republic stands for something. We are all prepared for war, to fight for our freedom, but do we want to be known as murderers of women and children? Shit, she's scared enough already. Just look at her. Do you honestly think she'll talk after this, that she'll risk running up against us again? I say we let her go. We let both of them go."

When the door opened again, Bailey's eyes widened at the sight of the newest arrival. It was the workman she and Shep had seen at Edgewater Place. So he was one of them, too.

But soon she discovered that that assumption might be wrong. For, with his entry, the mood in the room had changed dramatically. Everyone watched as he stepped inside, watched, in particular, for his reaction to seeing Bailey. But the man merely sneered in her direction.

"Nice work," he'd said.

You bodybuilding prick, thought Bailey.

It was hopeless.

Still, there seemed to be an air of distrust in the room.

"So why did you pick tonight for a visit, Arnie?" the man who owned the place asked.

"I didn't know until now."

"What do you mean by that?" Walcott demanded.

"Well, you see, I believe that everything happens for a reason. When I started up here tonight, I thought it was just to see Ozzie, to tell him I'd had second thoughts. That I was ready to join up, be part of what's happening. I had no idea something like this was going on." He nodded Bailey's way, without even looking at her. "Now I realize that I was sent here 'cause you needed me."

"Need you?" the cigarette smoker said. "How do we need you?"

Arnie laughed.

"I can take care of her," he said. "And the little girl. Before the sun comes up, I can reunite both of them with their long-lost brother and father, Michael Coleman." He turned to the owner. "There's no need to blow Ozzie's place sky-high."

Ozzie clearly liked this idea.

But Anthony Walcott looked more suspicious than ever.

"How do you know about Coleman?" he asked.

Again, Arnie laughed. "Now, come on," he said. "You think I didn't know what was going on that night? When I found the footprints? When you had me lay the cement patio? What do you take me for, a fuckin' idiot?" He watched Walcott's reaction, then continued. "That's why I came up here tonight. All that got me thinking. You guys—what is it you call yourselves, the Panhandle Republic?—are going to be in charge one day. One day soon. I figure I can either be part of it or I can be on your bad side. I don't want to be on your bad side."

That kind of mentality got nods from around the room. Still, Walcott looked unconvinced.

"I say we let him take care of them," Ozzie said to Walcott. "You're not blowin' this place up. I don't care who the hell you think you are. I'll blow your fuckin' brains out if you try."

Another argument ensued. During it, Bailey looked over at Arnie. Had he just nodded at her? It was almost imperceptible, yet she swore he had.

Finally, the argument died down.

"It's actually not a bad idea," Walcott said, then he chuckled. Bailey had never seen his teeth before. They were capped in gold. "Burying them all together. Kind of romantic, don't you think?"

Only Ozzie laughed in appreciation of Walcott's rare display of humor. He, of course, was just happy to have salvaged his cabin.

"Get the little girl," Arnie said casually, "and I'll be gone. You guys can get back to business. Just don't forget that

I'm gonna want a reward for this. Like maybe a title or something."

Ozzie started in the direction of the bedroom where Clancy was being kept.

"You don't think they're leaving here alive," Walcott said to Arnie, his eyes trained on him, still full of distrust, "do you? We'll take care of them here, *then* you can have them."

A look of sheer pleasure suddenly crossed his wooden face.

"In fact," he said, "if you're so ready to become one of us, *you* can do the honors. Right here. Right now."

Bailey had been watching Arnie ever since she'd seen him nod at her. Just before this exchange with Walcott, she'd seen his eyes wandering from one window to the other.

As Ozzie disappeared into the hallway, Arnie called out to him.

"Hey, man," he said, "wait a minute."

Ozzie stopped, turning back.

"Why?"

It was then that Bailey saw Arnie point an index finger to the sky in what looked to be some sort of a signal.

At the same time that he screamed his answer to Ozzie: "Because I'm gonna beat the livin' shit out of you." He lunged, bringing Ozzie crashing to the ground. Instantaneously, the cabin's door exploded open and two bodies literally dove inside the room, landing on the floor with loud thuds, furniture flying and guns spraying the ceiling.

Above the frayed cloth they'd tied over her mouth, Bailey's eyes widened in disbelief.

It was Shep and Charlie Eaglequill!

"Everyone freeze," Charlie called out from his position on the floor as Shep scrambled across the room to Bailey.

But it was too late for that. The marine had already pulled a revolver from inside his jacket. He fired once at Shep, missing, then pushed Walcott toward the door.

"Get out, Colonel," he yelled.

As one of the other men reached for a rifle that he'd left

leaning against the wall, Charlie fired, hitting him in the leg. The man fell to the ground, screaming and holding his blood-soaked pant leg.

In the corner, Arnie pummeled Ozzie with a rage that had simmered too long.

With Walcott safely out of the room, the marine now turned back to Shep, who was struggling to free Bailey from her restraints. As the crew-cut shorn, cammie-clad warrior leveled his revolver at Shep, Charlie's voice came to him from no more than two feet behind him.

"Pull the trigger and you're a dead man."

The marine froze, lowered his arm, and then backed slowly away from Shep.

"Drop it," Charlie ordered.

The marine turned and looked at Charlie. Then, just as his foot shot out, deliberately knocking a kerosene lamp off the makeshift table, he fired. Charlie, hit in the shoulder, dropped to the floor.

It was Shep's bullet that stopped the marine just short of the front door.

Within seconds, almost faster than the time it took any of them to appreciate the danger presented by the overturned lamp, the entire room erupted in flames. The cigarette smoker, who'd taken refuge behind the podium, which was also on fire, lurched toward the door, coughing and wheezing.

"Clancy," Bailey screamed.

"Where is she?" Shep yelled, running back to her, trying again, frantically, to undo the knots tied by the well-trained marine.

"Down the hall," she yelled, "in one of the bedrooms."

By this time, Charlie had struggled to his feet.

"I'll take care of Bailey," he told Shep. "You get Clancy."

Giving Bailey one last soulful look, Shep disappeared down the hallway.

It was difficult to see through the smoke that had filled the entire house, but at the end of the hallway, Shep found a locked door. He stood back and, with one powerful kick, splintered it.

Inside, Clancy sat on a cot. Instinctively, she was holding a pillowcase to her mouth to filter out the smoke, but when she saw who it was, she dropped the pillowcase.

"Shep!" She beamed. "I *knew* you'd find us."

CHAPTER 19

BAILEY WASN'T SURPRISED TO hear from Tony Pappas. The thirty days had been up for a while. They'd been expecting to hear from the bank. Tony had predicted that the bank would approach them to get Bailey to sign a deed in lieu of foreclosure. As Tony explained it, the deed in lieu would save time and money. Tony wanted to propose an exchange—if Bailey went along with the deed, the bank must grant her title, free and clear, to her penthouse unit. Under the circumstances—Muncie was now behind bars—Tony was confident they'd agree. But Bailey had already decided she would refuse. There was no way she would simply hand that building over, make life easier for the bank by signing the deed in lieu, even if to do so meant she and Clancy could stay at Edgewater Place.

No way that she would cease to fight them to the bitter end. For Michael's sake, if not for hers.

She was resigned to losing Edgewater Place. She and Clancy had even started looking at small houses in town. Unfortunately, even the small, older frame houses they'd seen were out of reach. Her savings had dwindled down to almost nothing. In the weeks since finishing finals, she'd gone on several job interviews, two of which looked promising, but nothing had yet materialized. She hoped she'd be working by the time they got kicked out of Edgewater Place. She'd applied for school loans and was in the process of filling out her application to transfer to Gonzaga's law school, in Spokane. She would look for part-time work during the school year, which might mean taking a lighter load at school and a delay in graduation.

"As long as we're together," Clancy had said cheerfully when they'd decided that apartment living would be more suited to their budget. Still, Bailey had been disappointed at everything in their price range. She wanted Clancy to have a yard, some room to play. The little girl had grown accustomed to having the run of Edgewater Place, its swimming pool and rec room, lots of friendly neighbors. If she had to give that up, Bailey at least wanted her niece to have somewhere to play outdoors, maybe even a dog. But all of that might have to wait. Life, as Bailey had long ago learned and just recently been reminded, didn't always turn out as you wanted. It was with a sense of dread that she walked slowly over to Tony Pappas's office.

Tony was standing at his secretary's desk, going through the morning's mail, when she arrived.

"Got my message, huh?" he said. He'd left it on her machine just thirty minutes earlier, asking that she come right over. He looked unusually cheerful, in stark contrast to the last time they'd met, when he'd been waiting for her back at Edgewater Place after her ordeal at Ozzie Randall's cabin. He had been nearly frantic with worry for her and Clancy that night. But today there was a glimmer to his eye that she hadn't seen since before Michael's death.

He laid the stack of mail he'd been rifling through back on his secretary's desk and directed Bailey into his office.

When she'd seated herself opposite him, he just smiled.

"Okay, Tony," Bailey finally said good-naturedly. "Are

you going to tell me what the heck's going on or am I going to have to come over there and shake it out of you?"

"Guess who they picked up this morning in Sun Valley?"

Bailey's face drained of expression.

"Walcott." It was a statement.

Tony's eyes met hers, which had filled with unexpected tears.

"Yes," he said softly. "Walcott."

"That son of a bitch," she whispered.

"You got that right."

He allowed her a moment's silence. A moment to digest the news that the man who had killed her brother, who had staged his death and then buried him right beneath her nose, right at Edgewater Place, had been captured.

"I want to know everything," she said.

For the next half hour, he explained to her how, after weeks on the run, Walcott had finally been captured. After being sheltered by one militia member after another, he'd apparently had enough.

"He liked to talk the talk of the common man," Tony said, his disdain for everything about Walcott apparent, "but when it came down to it—came to the prospect of actually living with them, *like* them—that was another story. This is a man after just two things: power and money. All that ideology crap he espouses, it's just his way to cash in on the undercurrent, the discontent among a certain segment of the population. You know how much he was paying himself as head honcho of the Panhandle Republic? Two hundred grand a year. Know anyone else in North Idaho who makes that kind of money? Not likely.

"Anyway, with his picture plastered all over every newspaper in the entire country and one of the most intense FBI manhunts in history under way, he knew he had to either go underground and stay there—which, of course, would have meant a life without his creature comforts, or . . ."

"Or what?"

"Or change his identity. Become someone new. New name, new face." Pappas snickered. "New body."

Bailey's jaw dropped open.

"Do you mean . . ."

"Plastic surgery," Tony answered. "And lots of it. A whole new face—nose, chin, even the eyes. Jet-black hair. And liposuction." Tony grinned. "No more handles. A flat stomach. Yep, he had a whole new life planned, bigger and better. All at the expense of the Panhandle Republic."

But Walcott's plan, Tony continued, hadn't taken into account a plastic surgeon who would recognize him and call the authorities. He'd been arrested just that morning, as he was being admitted at Sun Valley General. He'd immediately confessed to everything, naming Muncie as the mastermind for everything, in the hope that the prosecutor would go easy on him.

"Could that happen?" Bailey asked.

"No way. The prosecutor made no deals. And he won't. He gave his word on that. With what they've got on him, a murder conviction is a sure thing. And they're working on other charges as well. They'd pretty much pieced it all together already anyway. Walcott's confession just confirmed what they'd already suspected.

"As you know, our friends Walcott and Muncie go way back. This isn't the first time they'd been involved with this kind of thing. But this time there was a difference. This time, instead of going into their own pockets, a good deal of the money was going somewhere else."

"To the Panhandle Republic."

He nodded. "That's how the whole thing started. The excess money, for the twelfth floor that never was, funded by the bank, went directly into the treasury of the national organization, the United Patriot's Republic. It was Walcott's job to lure the local militia groups together and form the Idaho branch—the Panhandle Republic—using the money from the national organization. Guess who serves as its chief financial officer? Our friend, Muncie."

"And Michael somehow got wind of all this?"

"Well, it wasn't that simple. What Michael got wind of

was the fact that gambling was coming to the Coeur d'Alene Reservation."

"What?"

"There will be gambling on the reservation," Pappas announced. "If all goes as expected, the tribe should be opening a casino. I talked to Charlie yesterday, and they not only expect the state to sign off on it soon, they also just got funding. From a Native American–owned tribal gaming company back east."

Bailey could tell by how closely Tony was watching for her reaction that this should mean something to her, but it didn't.

"That's interesting," she said. "But why are you . . ."

Her words drifted off as she stared back at Tony. There was *something*. Something there, in what Tony was telling her. Gambling, the reservation. What was it? *The newspaper article in Michael's files.* The one that had sent Shep flying out the door that day. Still, none of it made sense.

"Michael had an article about some tribe over near Seattle that had opened a casino."

"Michael knew," Pappas stated.

"Knew *what*?"

"About the gambling coming. That's why he was so excited just before he died. He knew what gambling could mean to Edgewater Place. He was planning—"

Bailey interrupted him excitedly. "He had a meeting with Charlie Eaglequill. In March. I met with Charlie and thought he knew something, but he wouldn't tell me what it was."

"He did know something. Problem is, he'd been sworn to secrecy."

"By whom?"

"By Anthony Walcott. And Stan Muncie. It's really a hell of a story," Pappas said. "Let me lay it all out for you."

Michael Coleman was near despair over losing Edgewater Place when Charlie Eaglequill scheduled a meeting with him. Charlie was working on a new project, the scope of which exceeded anything he'd done before. He knew that, in addition to Edgewater Place, Michael had also been involved in a number of shopping centers and movie theaters in his development company in Seattle. Charlie was in the midst of preparing a bid for construction and needed Michael's expertise. But the information was confidential, it hadn't yet received approval, so Michael had agreed not to share what Charlie told him with anyone.

The project was a gambling casino on the Coeur d'Alene Reservation.

Charlie told Tony he'd seen the light go on in Michael's eyes the moment he learned of the project. Gambling brought big money to a region. Big spenders. People who could afford luxury condominiums, strictly for vacation use. Michael told Charlie that with knowledge of the upcoming casino, he was confident he could get new financing for the remaining units at Edgewater Place. As soon as Charlie was able to go public with the announcement of the casino, Michael said he would proceed with obtaining a new loan.

Only problem is that someone else who was involved with Edgewater Place had also recently learned about the gambling.

It was Anthony Walcott, as president of Idaho Fidelity, who had approved the casino loan for the Coeur d'Alene Tribe. But there was a catch. Charlie and the tribe had to swear to continued secrecy over the project. Walcott had explained that his request for absolute secrecy was based on the fact that as soon as word got out, other lenders would be vying for the loan. It was a competitive market. Idaho Fidelity had been the first bank the tribe had approached. It had approved the loan in a matter of days and promised streamlined funding once the tribe succeeded in negotiating a contract with the state gambling commission. Many of the tribes' members had had good relationships with the bank for decades. After a meeting, the council decided to go along with Walcott's request for secrecy. They would repay the faith placed in them by Idaho Fidelity with their loyalty. They would not shop the loan around.

But it turns out that Walcott's explanation of the need for

secrecy was not quite truthful. The truth was that Walcott had gone right to Muncie as soon as he learned of plans for the casino. The two men knew immediately what this could mean to Edgewater Place. The value of the remaining units would skyrocket. *Why should Michael Coleman be the beneficiary?* Sales had been poor; Coleman had already fallen delinquent on payments. With a little help from the association president, it might even be possible to accelerate Coleman's demise. The bank would foreclose. The units would go to auction. And who would be the purchaser? A corporation by the name of Bayshore. A corporation that consisted of Anthony Walcott and Stan Muncie.

"*What?*" Bailey responded, stunned by the revelations. "You mean to tell me, Stan Muncie was going to buy back all the units he was foreclosing on?"

"You got it. Through his corporation, Bayshore. You might have heard that name before. It was mentioned in the article that you found in Michael's files. Bayshore is the developer that was vying for rights to open a golf course in conjunction with the one of the Washington casinos." He saw a light of recognition go on in Bailey's eyes. "Remember?"

"*Yes, I do.*" She could hardly believe what she was hearing. "But what does any of this have to do with that golf course?"

"Plenty. You see, our friends Muncie and Walcott, and their organization, were not just content to skim money off the construction loan for Edgewater Place. Not even content to settle for the profits from the skyrocketing value of Edgewater Place units. They got greedy. Once they got to thinking about this whole thing, they wanted it all. The whole enchilada. They convinced the Coeur d'Alene Tribe that the casino needed to offer more, in order to compete with all the casinos in Washington. Hell, you can drive just thirty miles outside of Spokane and find gambling. The Coeur d'Alene's needed something else, too. They needed a golf course. Bayshore just happened to be in the business of golf course development."

"Did Charlie Eaglequill know any of this?"

"Until he talked to Shep, he had no idea that Stan Muncie, who was his contact for the golf course, was the banker who'd authorized the Edgewater Place loan. He had no reason to think there was a connection between the tribe's plans for a casino and what was going on at Edgewater Place. When you met with him, he wanted to tell you about the casino. To tell you *that* was why Michael had grown optimistic again, but Charlie Eaglequill, as I'm sure you could tell, is a man of his word. And he'd given Walcott his word that he'd keep news of the gambling secret."

"But he told Michael."

"Yes, he told Michael, but that was before he'd gone to Walcott for the loan, while the whole thing was just in the planning stage. The tribe had been keeping its plans very quiet while they waited for the state to reverse its earlier position on gambling, so Walcott never dreamed that Michael already knew."

"Wow."

"Yes, wow. The secrecy issue was big. That's why Muncie was rushing this thing to foreclosure. He knew that word might get out and he wanted those units to go to auction before it did."

"And when Michael learned about all this," Bailey said softly, "they killed him."

"Michael was too close to the truth, about both the gambling and the twelfth floor scam. They had to get him out of the way. That last night after I talked to him, Michael went down to load the kayak onto the truck. He always did that the night before—Michael hated those early mornings. He kept his kayak in the mechanical room. It was Walcott and Ozzie Randall. They followed him in there. That's where they shot him. They left him there until the middle of the night, then, when they were sure no one was around—after Walcott had sent the guard on some bogus mission to get him off the grounds for a couple of hours—they came back and . . ."

"And buried him behind Edgewater Place," Bailey finished.

She took a deep breath. The day after Clancy's and her ordeal at Ozzie Randall's, Michael's body had been exhumed from its secret grave at Edgewater Place. She knew from the coroner's report that Michael had been shot in the head at point-blank range.

Tony nodded in acknowledgment, then continued. "But they made a couple of mistakes. They'd heard Michael say he was planning to kayak the Moyie. What they didn't know was that when I backed out at the last minute, he'd told me he'd be kayaking the Spokane instead. That's why they staged his drowning on the Moyie. And they didn't see the kayak paddle under the bench. That's why it was never found on the river."

Tony studied Bailey. "You okay?"

"Yes," she answered, but, of course, she was not. How could she be when what they were discussing was her brother's murder?

"Muncie, of course, was in on all this. He'll have conspiracy to commit murder charges filed against him, in addition to all the other charges stemming from their little schemes. And the prosecutor feels confident that by the time they're through with their investigation and have brought all the charges they're sure to bring against Ozzie and the rest of his boys, the Panhandle Republic will pretty much be out of business. By the way, the guy who kidnapped you, the one Shep shot, is recovering nicely at Sacred Heart. He'll be able to stand trial with Randall, Walcott, Muncie and the rest of them. Ready to do his time with his buddies."

"Thank God for that," Bailey said. She should be glad to hear this, to know it was over and that at least some good—the elimination of one more hate group—had come of her tragedy. But there was little gladness in her right then. Soon she and Clancy would lose their home, the home Michael had so lovingly and painstakingly created for them, as well as for so many others—others like Sam, and Estelle, and the rest of the committee, all of whom would suffer because of the twisted malignity of people like Stan Muncie and Anthony Walcott.

And there was another reason for her sadness, but she would not allow that into her mind at the moment.

She looked at Tony. How could he be wearing that grin? The same one he'd started the meeting with. Just what was it with him today?

Tony cleared his throat.

"There's just one more thing." He tried to sound nonchalant. "I wanted Shep to be here when I gave this to you, but I haven't been able to track him down."

These words hit home. Shep had been difficult to pin down recently. Right then he was back in Portland. Bailey was all too aware of the fact that he'd been spending more and more time away from her and Clancy.

"Gave what to me?" Bailey said.

"I received something this morning. It's a letter from the bank."

He reached out and picked up a piece of paper from his desk, then, first slipping on his bifocals, he read:

"In light of the discovery that, unbeknownst to Chicago Savings and Loan, one of its officers had engaged in criminal conduct and activities which may have adversely affected your client's ability to meet the terms and conditions of the loan agreement, we are hereby waiving any foreclosure rights on those units at Edgewater Place which are currently in default. Furthermore, we are prepared to enter discussions to enable your client, Bailey Coleman, to restructure her loan so as to continue her efforts to sell the remaining units, thereby ensuring the success of the project that her brother, Michael Coleman, undertook in good faith and to which he devoted his considerable talents, enthusiasm and energies. We look forward to working with you and Ms. Coleman. I remain, Sincerely, Dennis R. Jackson, President."

Tony Pappas looked up from the letter in his hands Bailey Coleman sat staring at him, a heart-wrenching smile transforming her face and tears streaming down her pale cheeks.

"Hey, girl," he said, his voice starting to sound a bit muffled. "Now, don't go getting emotional on me." His voice broke, and reaching for two tissues in his upper desk drawer, he gave Bailey one and kept the other for himself.

Bailey stood and walked over to where he sat, behind his desk. She bent down and wrapped her arms around him. Pappas's big shoulders shook ever so slightly.

"It's been a long haul," he said into her shoulder. "I just wish Michael were here to see it."

She nodded and continued to hold him.

"He sees it," she said. "Don't worry."

"He's here. And he sees it."

Word of the good news spread within the building like wildfire—sparked by Sam, the first person with whom Bailey shared the news, and then eagerly fanned into flames by other jubilant residents of Edgewater Place. By that evening, a computer-generated banner six feet long hung above the mailboxes in the lobby, declaring: NO FORECLOSURE! PARTY, THURSDAY 7 P.M. PLEASE COME AND HELP US CELEBRATE!!

Bailey, who started out in a most celebratory mood, found herself on an emotional roller coaster.

She'd left Tony's office in a state of dazed happiness, the knowledge that Michael's beloved project had been saved literally adding lift to her long strides as she raced back to Edgewater Place to share the news. By the time she'd run up the seven flights of stairs and reached Sam's condominium, where she'd left Clancy on her way to Tony's office, she was gasping for air. She burst into Sam's kitchen, startling Clancy and Sam, who sat at the table reading a letter from Sam's granddaughter.

She stood in front of them at the table, her chest heaving wildly. Several long blond curls, having escaped from the elastic band that held the rest of her hair loosely at the nape of her neck, dangled in her animated face.

"What is it, dear?" Sam asked. Clancy's eyes were also wide with alarm at the sight of her aunt. What had happened at Tony Pappas's office?

"It's over," Bailey huffed. "The bank's not going to foreclose. It's over." She broke into a smile then. A beautiful, no-holds-barred smile that said it all.

Both Clancy and Sam squealed in surprise and delight and jumped to their feet to hug her.

"Does that mean we get to stay?" Clancy wanted to know.

"Yes," Bailey said, swooping her niece into her arms. "We can stay."

When she'd left Sam's condo sometime later, after having shared the details of her meeting with Tony, Bailey's spirits were still high. But by that night, after she'd tucked Clancy in bed, her elation had ebbed, dampened by a realization that had been silently gnawing away at her subconscious all day.

She'd gone to bed knowing she would not sleep but welcoming the chance to lie there in the dark, as she often did, and sort through her feelings.

The skylight overhead glowed with a clear night sky. She'd always loved the sky at night, even as a child; but seldom had Seattle, with its rain and city lights, gifted her with skies like the one above her now. Even within the limited field of vision afforded her by the skylight, there were more stars than she could count—each one distinctive and breathtaking in its clarity. As she'd done for as long as she could remember, she found her eyes instinctively searching for the brightest star, the star that, as a child, she would have wished on. She found it, then asked herself a question that she still indulged in now and then.

What would I wish for tonight?

Her prayer had been answered today. She and Clancy could stay in Coeur d'Alene. In the town that Michael loved, the home that he'd built. Her wish had already been fulfilled. On this night, she should not be wishing for more.

But she could not help herself.

What would I wish for tonight?

She knew, all too well, the answer. Knew what she would wish for if she still believed in wishing on stars. She'd known it earlier today, sitting in Tony Pappas's office, when she'd heard Tony speak his name. That all that really mattered to her anymore—besides Clancy, of course—was a future with Shep. And at the moment, that possibility—of a future together—seemed about as likely as the other unreachable dreams she'd wished for as a child.

In the days immediately following Shep's, Charlie's and Arnie's courageous rescue of Clancy and her, Shep had rarely left her side. Even through the trauma of learning the truth about Michael's death, during his short, private burial, with Shep there with her, Bailey had been filled with such love for him and for Clancy, with such relief at their safe passage through such a horrendous experience, that she'd actually felt more joy than pain.

They had never had that conversation they'd planned to have. The one discussing their future. At first she'd believed Shep was holding back, giving her time to grieve, to recover from her ordeal.

But it had been several weeks, and Shep had made no mention of the future, no mention of his plans. Though she was too proud to discuss it with him, for fear that he'd think she was pushing him, she'd overheard Clancy telling Shep about apartments she and Bailey had looked at. And he had never, not once, brought the topic up with Bailey. She'd heard what he'd said to Clancy that day, when she described the last apartment they'd looked at.

"So, did you like it?"

And Clancy had answered, truthfully as always. "It was okay. It's not as nice as where we live now."

If Shep had any intention of their having a future together, wouldn't he have interceded at that point? Wouldn't he have become involved in their plans?

But he hadn't. Instead, it seemed that he was spending more and more time away from them these days.

She knew he cared about her. That he cared deeply. Knew

it from when they made love. That had not changed at all. It was as sweet and wild and intense as ever.

But he had apparently decided that he could not give up a career he had worked so many years to establish. And apparently he did not want her to join him in Portland.

And so, as great as her joy was at the latest turn of events, there was a sadness in her that dulled everything else. A sadness that she did not expect to go away. Just as her grief over Michael would never leave her.

She'd finally drifted off into a light, restless sleep when bright light, shining directly into her eyes, woke her. Startled, she sat up. She expected to see Clancy standing at the door, her hand on the light switch. Perhaps she'd been frightened by another bad dream and wanted to climb into bed with Bailey.

But the room was still dark. She got up and went to the door. She looked down the hall toward Clancy's room. Nothing. What had that been? It wasn't until her eyes swept her darkened room again that she saw it. The square of light on her pillow. A square so bright as to look artificial, like some shrunken, illuminated movie screen, waiting for the film to start. Her eyes followed its beams up to the skylight.

She climbed back in bed, laid her head back on her pillow and looked up. Shining down on her, so large it almost filled the frame of the skylight, was the most glorious moon she'd ever seen. It reminded Bailey of an ivory cameo—milky white, bearing a finely carved image—her parents had given her when she turned thirteen. The moon was not quite full. She lay there in its glow, transfixed, and found herself wondering whether Shep might be looking at the same moon. Feeling its magic. Maybe he was thinking of her just as she lay thinking of him.

And with that comforting thought, the thought of their spirits connecting somewhere in the heavens, Bailey Coleman finally drifted off to sleep.

The No Foreclosure party the next night was a huge success. Excitement in Edgewater Place had been building ever since the word got out, and by the time Bailey arrived at seven-fifteen that evening, the gathering in the social room was unequivocal evidence of the residents' reaction to the news that the bank had agreed to halt the foreclosure proceedings.

As Bailey and Clancy walked through the door into a nearly full room, it started. At first Bailey wasn't sure what it was, but as it grew, and as more and more heads turned toward them, each face uniform in the smile it wore, she realized what that sound was. It was clapping. Applause. One by one, as they realized she'd arrived, the residents of Edgewater Place were stopping in mid-conversation and turning to greet Clancy and Bailey with applause.

Clancy beamed and took her aunt's hand.

"They're clapping for us," she said, looking up at Bailey proudly.

For Bailey, it was almost too much. She tried to say something, to thank all the kind faces around her, to tell them what their support meant to her, but words could not get past the lump in her throat. Luckily, Sam Cummings stepped forward and rescued her. Her diminutive friend reached up and wrapped her arms around Bailey. The rest of the committee followed in Sam's wake—Al and Lucy Swanson, Suzanne Phillips, Estelle Rouchon—each of whom hugged her gaily as the room once again filled with the sounds of a festive social gathering. It was from within Estelle's embrace, over the shoulder of her pink knit suit, that Bailey saw Alice Walcott standing quietly, waiting for her turn with Bailey.

At the sight of Alice, her meeting with Tony came back to her.

"They've finally figured out the identity of the person who left the architectural drawings at Shep's hotel," he'd said. "The one who'd been writing anonymous notes urging a building inspection."

"Who was it?"

"You won't believe this," Tony said. "This person knew what was going on all along and wanted to blow the whistle on these guys. But she didn't dare come right out, she wanted someone else to discover it."

"She?"

"This is the real clincher. It was Alice Walcott. Anthony Walcott's wife. See, she knew what was going on. Seems old Anthony spoke fairly freely around her, figured she was too mindless and weak to cause problems. It was Anthony who had the same Coeur d'Alene architectural firm who drew the plans for Michael draw plans for a twelfth floor, too. Alice got her hands on them, then started writing notes. Turns out she sent the twelfth floor plans to Michael just before he died. Anonymously, of course. Then one day she leaves them on Shep Carroll's doorstep, hoping he'll figure it all out."

And he had. Thanks to Alice.

"Alice," Bailey said after accepting Alice's congratulations. She extended her hand to grasp that of the other woman. "I don't know how to thank you."

Alice Walcott shook her head. "No, there's no need to thank me. I should have done something to stop them long ago. I hope you'll accept my apology for all the grief my husband has put you through, for my not stopping them sooner."

Bailey could see how important it was for Alice to have her say.

"Of course, I do." She pulled Alice to her and hugged her. "You mustn't blame yourself." She could feel the frail shoulders quiver under her touch.

Sam appeared then.

"Did Alice tell you that she and I have agreed to be roommates for a while?" she asked.

Bailey had been concerned for Alice, hoping she had someone to turn to after having exposed her husband. Leave it to Sam to take care of her. She felt great admiration for Alice. Her frailty obviously belied a great strength. It took courage to do what she had done. And courage to now face Bailey and the rest of Edgewater Place's residents. But somehow she suspected Alice felt a sense of relief. Her eyes lit up with pleasure at Sam's announcement that they were roommates. Perhaps now she would find the friendship she'd so desperately wanted.

Though it was well past eleven, the party was still going strong when Bailey went looking for Clancy to take her home. As grateful as she felt for the reception given her tonight, as happy as she felt about the recent turn of events, as the evening progressed her heart grew increasingly oblivious to the occasion. Wherever she turned, whichever cluster of homeowners she found herself surrounded by, talk inevitably turned to Shep Carroll. He'd become something of a folk hero among the building's residents. The bank's maverick attorney who'd stuck his neck out for them. And each time she heard his name, it hurt just a little more than the time before. Until finally she'd had enough. Was this how it would always be?

She finally found Clancy in the kitchen, licking chocolate frosting from the knife that had been used to cut the huge sheet cake that bore a replica of Edgewater Place, while Sam, Estelle and Alice Walcott cheerfully wiped countertops, tossed dirty plates and napkins into the garbage and loaded dishes into the dishwasher.

"Hey, you." She rested her hand on the top of Clancy's head. "It's way past bedtime. We'd better head home."

Clancy looked at Sam.

"Listen, kiddo," Sam said, turning to Bailey, "I've invited Clancy to spend the night with me. I hope that's okay."

"Oh," said Bailey, somewhat surprised that Sam would have done so without first asking her permission. "It's getting so late. Maybe another night would be better."

Again, Clancy's eyes turned to Sam.

"But this is such a special night," Sam said. "Just this once. Please?"

"Please, Aunt Bailey. Please?" Clancy's voice echoed.

Feeling less than happy with the idea of going home alone, and somewhat hurt at being left out on this night, of all nights, she still could not help but relent.

"Okay," she said good-naturedly. "I'll come by in the morning. You two have fun."

She pecked Clancy on the cheek before turning to leave.

"I love you," Clancy said.

"Love you, too, sweetie." She thought she might cry. Here she was, a grown woman, upset about going home alone.

"Have a nice night," Sam called out after her as she left.

Fat chance, thought Bailey, but all she said was "Thanks. You, too."

CHAPTER 20

BAILEY COULDN'T DECIDE WHAT to do when she got back to her condo after the party. Though it was past her regular bedtime, sleep was out of the question. She settled on the couch and picked up the book she'd bought the day before, then put it back down. Not in the mood for reading.

What *was* she in the mood for? She felt ridiculously out of sorts and restless. Lonely.

Why did I agree to let Clancy spend the night at Sam's?

Finally, for lack of anything better to do, she turned on the television. David Letterman. Usually he made her laugh. Not tonight.

During the first commercial break she got up to pour herself a glass of wine. It was rare for her to drink alone, but that didn't matter. She opened a bottle she'd been saving for a special occasion.

She was just returning to the living room, carrying her wine and a giant chocolate chip cookie, when the shrill ring of the house phone startled her. Maybe Clancy had changed her mind and wanted to come home.

"Hello?"

After a slight pause his familiar voice said, "Hi. It's me."

Shep.

"Hi. I thought you were in Portland. Want me to ring you in?"

"Just got back," he said. "Actually, no. I know it's awfully late, but I wondered if you and Clancy would consider going for a little ride with me. There's something I want to show you."

When Bailey hesitated, he continued, "I know it sounds crazy, but I think you'll understand once you see it."

"Clancy's spending the night at Sam's."

"Oh." Then, "Well, how about you?"

She paused. What she really wanted was for him to come upstairs and hold her. At one time that's exactly what she would have told him, but now, now she didn't know how she was supposed to act with him.

"Sure," she said. "I'm still wide awake. I'll be right down."

She hung the phone back up, grabbed her jean jacket and headed out the door.

When she opened the stairwell door, she saw him, through the glass door, in the vestibule. Standing there in well-worn jeans and a long-sleeved denim shirt, he looked tanned, fit, more handsome than ever. Their hello—a kiss that was just too quick—was almost awkward.

His car was parked at the curb. He'd left it running. It felt good to climb into its warm interior.

"How was the party?" Shep asked as he turned south onto Highway 95.

"Nice. It's too bad you didn't make it back in time. You were a main topic of conversation."

She caught his smile in the headlights of an oncoming car. He looked happy.

When he reached for her hand, pretending not to notice, she kept it on her lap. She was hurt. Hurt that he hadn't bothered to come back to town in time for the party.

hurt that he seemed so content with this new distance between them.

Why was he heading toward the reservation?

They rode mostly in silence. When they'd gone about fifteen miles, Shep turned onto a narrow gravel road. It looked vaguely familiar to Bailey, but she could not read the road sign.

It wasn't until she saw the stand of trees that she realized where he was taking her. And realized *why*.

The turkeys.

High above, silhouetted against a fabulously full moon—the same moon that had soothed her to sleep the night before, only full now, and, if possible, even more glorious—they sat. At least a dozen large, still forms, magnificent in their size and almost prehistoric appearance. Bailey's breath caught at the sight.

Shep had gotten out of the car and come around to open her door. Quietly, she climbed down from the seat and pushed the door shut. He led her to a spot on the road several feet from the base of the trees and there, standing side by side, they witnessed what Joe Curry had described seeing on the reservation as a child.

"My God," Bailey whispered. There was a mythical quality to the moment. No wonder it had stayed with Joe Curry all these years. "Clancy has to see this."

"Oh, she will."

Bailey turned to him then and realized that he had been staring at her.

"What do you mean?" she asked.

Shep's mouth drew up in a smile. "Can I show you something?"

She nodded, and before she knew it, Shep was leading her by the hand through the tall growth bordering the road.

"This way." They encountered a barbed-wire fence almost immediately. Shep placed his boot on the second strand and pulled up the third, creating enough space for Bailey to step through.

"Is it okay for us to be doing this?" Bailey asked.

"Yes," Shep said, offering no explanation.

They started up a short, steep embankment through waist-high wheat. Bailey thought of protesting. If they were trespassing, someone might just take a shot at them. She'd had enough of that kind of excitement to last a lifetime.

They reached the crest. Before them, sitting in the center of a vast, open field, awash with moonlight, was an odd-looking structure—short and square. As they neared, Bailey recognized what it was. The beginnings of a log cabin. The walls were less than three feet tall. Nearby stood several stacks of logs, a saw and a wide assortment of other tools.

She turned to Shep.

"I don't understand," she said. "What is this?"

Without taking his eyes from her, Shep responded. "It's mine."

"Yours? Do you mean you bought it, the land?" She remembered the day he'd brought Clancy and her out there. The For Sale sign. She remembered how he'd stared so longingly at the golden field. Suddenly she realized she had not seen the sign tonight.

"Why?" she asked, the significance still not registering.

"So no one else would buy it and force the wild turkeys away. So that Clancy could always come out here and see them, anytime she wanted," he answered. Then his voice grew softer. "So that I would always have a reminder of the second-best day of my life."

"The second-best day of your life?" Bailey echoed.

"The day the three of us came out here to see the turkeys."

Bailey felt her breath leave her. *Ask him,* she told herself. *Go ahead and ask him.*

"What about the *best* day of your life?" she half whispered, her eyes searching his for an answer.

"The best day of my life," said Shep, returning her gaze with equal intensity, "will be the day I marry you."

The moment was so surreal, with the magical moon filling half the sky and a flock of wild, roosting birds framed in its light, that Bailey feared she might be dreaming.

"Will you?" he asked her softly, his eyes alive with hope and love. "Will you be my wife?"

With a sharp cry of joy, half sob, half laugh, she stepped into him and wrapped her arms around his broad shoulders. Pressing her face against his chest, she said, "Yes, of course. Yes, I'll marry you."

He lifted her face to his.

"I am going to make you the happiest woman on earth," he said.

He kissed her then, a kiss full of promise. A kiss that said anything was possible.

Suddenly, Bailey pulled back. "What about your job?" she said. "What about Emerson, Caldwell?"

"I don't work at Emerson, Caldwell anymore," Shep answered. "I haven't since that day I left for Montana."

"You mean, you haven't been working back in Portland? But you've been gone so much. Isn't that where you've been?"

"No." Shep explained, studying her face for its reaction. "I have been back there, closing out my files and arranging to sublease my apartment. But I quit my job the day after you heard me on the phone with Max. I told him that if I had to choose between you and my job, the decision would be easy. I wouldn't be coming back to Emerson, Caldwell when my thirty-day suspension was up."

"But I never even knew. Why wouldn't you . . ."

"Why wouldn't I tell you?" he asked, a half smile sneaking over his lips. "Because I needed a little time to work some things out. And I thought you needed some time to grieve for Michael, to come to terms with everything that's happened. I couldn't come to you when I didn't even have a job. I had to be able to offer you more than that." Bailey could see by the sudden seriousness of his expression how important this was to him. "And I didn't want you to feel responsible for my leaving Emerson, Caldwell. It was a choice I made freely—and, to be honest, quite happily."

He smiled again.

"You see, once you'd wormed your kindhearted, noble way into my heart, once you'd helped me see things through your eyes, my leaving Emerson, Caldwell became inevitable. I'd known for a long time that my work wasn't making me happy. I just didn't realize why that was until I met you. Until you helped me realize something."

Bailey stared into his starkly handsome face.

"What did I help you realize?"

"That even when the law is on your side, there's nothing noble or fulfilling about kicking people when they're down. That we only have one lifetime, one chance to use whatever God-given gifts we have, to make a difference. And that I'd wasted enough time already. I couldn't ask you to share my life until I had a future I could be proud of. One that, hopefully, you would be proud of, too."

"And do you?" Bailey asked. "Do you have that now?"

"Yes, I believe I do."

"In Portland?"

"No, right down the road. I'm going to work for the Coeur d'Alene Tribe," Shep said proudly. "Once the casino opens, they'll need full-time legal counsel. It will never make us rich, but somehow I didn't think you would mind."

"Is this what you really want?" Bailey asked, in a state of disbelief.

Shep pulled her over to one of the half-constructed walls and sat her down on top of it.

He pulled a book of matches from his shirt pocket Lighting one match, he held it up to the log she was sitting on.

"See this?" he said, pointing.

It was freshly carved into the wood. "Bailey and Shep," i said. The line underneath read, "1997."

"All my life, I've wanted to do that," Shep said with a grin. "Carve a girl's name into the trunk of a tree."

"You never did it?" Bailey asked softly.

Shep shook his head. "Nope, but my best friend, Cono Clayborne, did. It was when we were in junior high. I Montana, that kind of thing doesn't go over very wel

Conor took no end of grief for it, for getting soft. The guys harassed him for months afterwards. But it never bothered him. He was proud as punch of his girl and of what he'd done. I remember thinking, I hope that someday I'll feel that way. That I'll care that much about a girl." He looked at her, the grin now gone. "But I never did. Until now."

He blew out the match, and lowering his large frame to one knee in order to bring himself eye level with her, he took her hand in his.

"I have never, ever, in my entire life been so sure of anything, never wanted anything as much as I want this. To build a life with you. And Clancy. Bit by bit, one piece at a time, just like I'm building this cabin. And I can tell you now, one hundred years from now, this cabin will still be standing here, solid and strong.

"And when I'm an old, weathered man, my love for you will be just as solid, just as strong as this cabin." He pressed her hand to his lips. "That I promise."

With her free hand, Bailey reached out and stroked his face. A single tear's trail glistened down her cheek.

"Can we get married out here?" she asked. "A big wedding. With everyone from Edgewater Place. And Charlie. And Arnie." She laughed then at the sheer joy of it all. "And Clancy as a flower girl?"

Before Shep could answer, the night filled with a hauntingly beautiful sound. Bailey and Shep both looked up to the sky, where it had originated. There in the trees, one of the turkeys stood tall, stretched from its resting position to its full height, its face turned to the moon, coyotelike. Again, the turkey cried out. A lovely sound that belied the big bird's comical appearance.

Turkeys, both Shep and Bailey knew, did not make sounds of such extraordinary beauty.

But tonight was a magical night. A Wild Turkey Moon.

Tonight, anything was possible.

Available by mail from 

CHICAGO BLUES • Hugh Holton
Police Commander Larry Cole returns in his most dangerous case to date when he investigates the murders of two assassins that bear the same M.O. as long-ago, savage, vigilante cases.

KILLER.APP • Barbara D'Amato
"Dazzling in its complexity and chilling in its exposure of how little privacy anyone has...totally mesmerizing."—*Cleveland Plain Dealer*

CAT IN A DIAMOND DAZZLE • Carole Nelson Douglas
The fifth title in Carole Nelson Douglas's Midnight Louie series—"All ailurphiles addicted to Lilian Jackson Braun's "The Cat Who..." mysteries...can latch onto a new *purr*ivate eye: Midnight Louie—slinking and sleuthing on his own, a la Mike Hammer."—*Fort Worth Star Telegram*

STRONG AS DEATH • Sharan Newman
The fourth title in Sharan Newman's critically acclaimed Catherine LeVendeur mystery series pits Catherine and her husband in a bizarre game of chance—which may end in Catherine's death.

PLAY IT AGAIN • Stephen Humphrey Bogart
In the classic style of a Bogart and Bacall movie, Stephen Humphrey Bogart deliver a gripping, fast-paced mystery."—*Baltimore Sun*

BLACKENING SONG • Aimée and David Thurlo
The first novel in the Ella Clah series involving ex-FBI agent, Ella Clah, investigating murders on a Navajo Reservation.

Call toll-free 1-800-288-2131 to use your major credit card or clip and mail this form below to order by mail

---

Send to: Publishers Book and Audio Mailing Service
PO Box 120159, Staten Island, NY 10312-0004

❑ 54464-1	**Chicago Blues**	$5.99/$7.99	❑ 53935-4	**Strong as Death**	$5.99/$7.
❑ 55391-8	**Killer.App**	$5.99/$7.99	❑ 55162-1	**Play It Again**	$5.99/$6.
❑ 55506-6	**Cat in a Diamond Dazzle**	$6.99/$8.99	❑ 56756-0	**Blackening Song**	$5.99/$7.

Please send me the following books checked above. I am enclosing $_______. (Please add $1.50 for the first bo and 50¢ for each additional book to cover postage and handling. Send check or money order only—no CODs).

Name ______________________________

Address ____________________ **City** ______________ **State** _____ **Zip** _____